UNICORN HIGHWAY

"Reminiscent of WINDMASTER'S BANE:
interesting, warm and understanding ...
This is surely the way to tame a unicorn"
Piers Anthony

"A different kind of unicorn story:
refreshing, charming, and with a
delightful sense of humor"
A.C. Crispin, author of *THE STARBRIDGE CHRONICLES*

"David Lee Jones's Kansas is a magical place,
and UNICORN HIGHWAY is a magical book.
I'm sorry that this is his first novel;
I'm going to have to wait for his next one
instead of running out and grabbing it"
Joel Rosenberg, author of *THE ROAD TO EHVENOR*

"Mr. Jones can make a believer out of the reader—
which is the highest form of achievement"
Andre Norton, author of *WITCH WORLD*

*Worlds of Fantasy
from Avon Books*

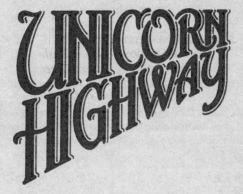

UNICORN HIGHWAY

DAVID LEE JONES

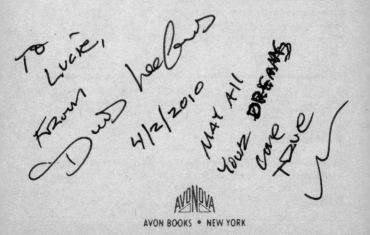

To Luck,
From David lee Jones
4/2/2010
May All your DREAMS Come True

AVONOVA

AVON BOOKS • NEW YORK

UNICORN HIGHWAY is an original publication of Avon Books. This work has never before appeared in book form. This work is a novel. Any similarity to actual persons or events is purely coincidental.

AVON BOOKS
A division of
The Hearst Corporation
1350 Avenue of the Americas
New York, New York 10019

Copyright © 1992 by David Lee Jones
Cover illustration by Kevin Johnson
Published by arrangement with the author
Library of Congress Catalog Card Number: 91-93034
ISBN: 0-380-76506-3

First AvoNova Printing: April 1992

AVONOVA TRADEMARK REG. U.S. PAT. OFF. AND IN OTHER COUNTRIES, MARCA REGISTRADA, HECHO EN U.S.A.

Printed in the U.S.A.

RA 10 9 8 7 6 5 4 3 2 1

For my daughter Rosemary, my mother,
and all of the Tompkins family

A first novel is usually the most difficult to produce. For this reason and many others, I have many people to thank for their priceless contributions to this book.

To my wife, Paula, for her many suggestions, comments, and patience while I wrote and rewrote the manuscript.

To Carla Berkowitz for doing a fine first edit, to Sylvia Berkowitz for believing in unicorns, to Sheri Prior for reading my early work and still believing. To Dr. Pat Kubis for encouraging me in the beginning, Connie Andersen for reading, suggesting, and cheering me on, and Melody Ghandchi for showing me how to write a synopsis.

To my agents, Michael Larsen and Elizabeth Pomada, for seeing an oak tree in an acorn, and showing me how to water it, and Antonia for her help and faith in it.

To anyone I have left out due to space constraints, I offer sincere apologies.

And finally, to Avon Books and my editor, Chris Miller. Avon Books for being there when the book needed a good publisher, and Chris for shaping the book with a keen eye and sensitive hand, for choosing the title and cover, for promoting it tirelessly, and for believing in a storyteller's dream.

*"Now I will believe
that there are unicorns."*

WILLIAM SHAKESPEARE,
The Tempest iii, 3

1

Paradise Remembered

It was a long time ago when the unicorn came to Kansas.
You can imagine the impression it made on an eleven-year-
old boy. Even now, forty years later, I still ask myself
sometimes if it actually happened, though it was as real as
any experience on earth.

It reminds me of one of those articles you read in the
newspaper about a whole town seeing a space ship. The
photographs and eyewitness reports can't quite convince you
that it really happened. You just can't believe it unless you
were there, but I was there, and it did happen. At least
that's what all of us believed in the summer of '47.

I remember standing in the barn with my sister. I'll never
forget the way she looked in her pink and white checkered
dress, her long blond hair resisting the curling iron from
the night before. She was a slender girl with long legs that
she liked to hide beneath her calf-length dresses, or inside
a pair of jeans. Her eyes were as blue as cornflowers in
bloom, and the freckles splashed on her cheeks looked like
amber suns in a pink sky.

I always accused her of giving me a case of the freckles, as if they were contagious, but she swore we got them from our mother. She looked the most like Mom—just add a few pounds, a few inches in height, and one or two small lines on the forehead, and you have the image of our mother.

Folks always said the same thing. She looked like Mom, and I looked like Dad. Kind of corny, I thought, but somewhat hard to deny. I did have my father's bushy hair, which had the color and thickness of an old thatched roof. I had his walnut-brown eyes, too, and his slightly darker tint to my skin, but what about that straight nose of mine? My mother's, I guess. And the freckles—well, you already know where I got those.

The real mystery, though, was the big front teeth. I almost looked like a critter, and some kids called me Chip behind my back. I guess with the bushy hair, small hands and feet, and the teeth, maybe I did look like a chipmunk.

I grew into my teeth eventually, and the freckles have all but disappeared. The bushy hair is now thinner and grey. Funny how time changes things, especially memories. The bad ones grow fainter, and the good ones sweeter, but when I was eleven, it was not a time to spend remembering. It was a time for making memories, and all of the necessary ingredients were there.

2

Daydream Believer

It was just after World War II, and the troops were home from overseas. There was Ed Dirkson's boy back to help raise cattle, and Sally Penhurst, who had been an Army nurse, was home helping Doc Yeager with the stork's newest deliveries. There was Bob Greison, our local baseball standout, except he wasn't going to be throwing baseballs anymore since he caught something from the front lines in his pitching arm.

Still, he was happy to be home in Kansas. My sister loved him just the same, despite his souvenir, and we all expected a wedding announcement before the summer was out. My sister loved me, too, but that didn't change the look on her face when I told her that a unicorn had come to Kansas.

"There aren't any unicorns in Kansas, silly," she said on that warm June morning, "they only exist in fairy tales. Everyone knows that, Thaddeus. The idea of such a beast actually living is just the product of someone's overactive imagination." She shook her head at me in polite dismay.

We were feeding the animals, so I looked at our horse,

3

Petula, for sympathy in the matter. But she just rolled her big brown eyes and took some hay from my hand.

"And don't go spreadin' stories around," Cathy warned me, knocking my straw hat off my head with a playful swing of her hand, "or you'll have everyone in Flint Hills thinking you're crazy."

It was just like her to say that, since she had a mind more suited to worldly matters than flights of fancy. I always thought it was because she was the first born, and Dad had taught her about machines and farm equipment when I was still in diapers.

She wasn't trying to scold me for storytelling as much as protect me from the rest of the folks in Flint Hills, who had mostly decided I was crazy to believe in Mr. Tucker's daydreams. Sure, they knew I was just a kid, but most of them had already decided I would be a dreamer like my dad, who persisted in growing wheat in cattle country.

I reached down for my hat, but it was too late. Petula had already grabbed it with her teeth, and wouldn't let go.

"No, Petula," I said as I pulled with all my strength, "you can't eat that, you stupid old horse. Here you've got the best darned hay in Kansas—why, probably in the whole world—and you want to eat my hat. Ain't you got no smarts, you dumb animal? Aw, I guess not," I added with a sigh, "you're just an overgrown critter. No offense, Petula," I said as I patted her head to coax the hat from her grinding teeth, "but you sure ain't no unicorn."

I turned to my sister, not giving up on the hat, but still wanting to convince her I was right.

"But Cathy," I began, "Mr. Tucker *said* there were unicorns around here. He even saw one right on his own property. And he ain't never been wrong before, except about the rain and taxes once in awhile. But everybody's wrong about them things. Dad says even *we* got tax troubles; we're two years behind, or something."

"Thaddeus," she said, shaking her head at me in disapproval, "you believe everything people tell you. And what would an eleven-year-old know about taxes, anyway?"

Petula loosened her grip on my hat, and I fell backwards on the ground with it. "That ain't so," I argued, trying to dust the dirt off my overalls. "Just because you're sixteen, you think you know everything. Well, I've got news for you. No one in the world knows what I know. 'Cause I know what Mr. Tucker told me. And he said . . ."

"Mr. Tucker is not well, Thaddeus," she replied, trying not to hurt me, "and I'm afraid he may have made up a story just to keep the state from selling his land. You know how much he loves that farm. I'm not saying that he's lying, but . . ." She placed her hands on my shoulders. "What would you say if the government was trying to take your farm away?"

I put my hat on my head and pulled it down over my ears. Then I walked out from under her hands. "It ain't fair," I mumbled to the ground as I walked away, "it just ain't fair. Nobody believes anything kids say. They think we make up stories." I turned around with my hands thrust deep into my overalls. "Kids and old people don't get any respect in the world. Everybody thinks we're liars."

"No, Thaddeus," she apologized, "I didn't mean *that* exactly. It's just . . ."

"Aw, forget it," I said quickly, and pulled my hands out of my pockets. "Boy, if I could make these hands into magic wands, I'd make the whole world disappear. Better yet, I'd make everyone believe, just like me and Mr. Tucker. He says you just have to believe hard enough, and the unicorns'll come."

I looked up into my sister's face. "He says that's the trouble with people nowadays. They just don't believe anymore, and so they'll never see a miracle. Not with a closed mind, they won't. That was exactly how he put it. 'Not with a closed mind,' he said."

I turned and walked away. Behind me I could hear my sister say, "What are we going to do with you, Thaddeus? So smart for your age, but so gullible. Whatever would Mom and Dad say? Can you imagine the expressions on their faces? Unicorns in Kansas? Even if it was true, who on earth would believe such a story? You'd better keep this

one under your hat, what you've got left of it.'' She giggled.
I could barely hear her voice by then, since I was almost
to the house. "You and your wild stories,'' she said faintly
in the distance, but I wasn't really paying much attention.
I was thinking about critters again.

Sometimes I thought about real-world critters, like Elmer,
our black and white pig, or Becky our Guernsey milk cow.
Sometimes, though, I thought about storybook animals, like
fire-breathing dragons, or funny horses with horns on their
foreheads.

Sure, I knew there was a world out there beyond my
thoughts, and I knew that I had to live in it most of the
time, but I didn't want to live in it all of the time.

I wanted to travel to distant lands and faraway places,
and since I couldn't do that with my body, I liked to travel
in dreams. It's just that sometimes the night dreams forgot
it was light out, and did some sleepwalking around my head
during the day. When that happens to you, people call you
a daydreamer, and I got called that lots of times. That
summer was no exception.

3

Headin' West

My dad first laid eyes on Kansas in '30. He started from New York and just kept headin' west, at least that's the way he tells it.

The name on his driver's license was Aristotle, but his friends called him Ari. Some of the ranchers called him "Ari Throttle" because he went almost as slowly driving the car as he did on the tractor.

"The road's in no hurry," he always said, "and it still gets where it's goin'. What's the rush to get somewhere quick? You just have to slow down your heart when you get there anyway."

He talked that way even before the heart attack. Besides, the 'attack of the heart' as my dad put it, was on account of the weak ticker he inherited.

His parents had been Welsh immigrants, his dad a steam engine designer, and his mother the prettiest woman in upstate New York. My dad, at eighteen, had been working on those newfangled gas engines at the tractor factory when

7

his dad died of a heart attack. His mother went the next winter of consumption.

He sold everything they owned and bought his own automobile, an almost new, shiny, black Model A. Folks thought he was just plain crazy, since it was 1930 and the Great Depression was picking America apart like a buzzard stooping over a carcass.

He claims he got the car cheap, from the widow of a banker who tried to fly from a fourth floor window during the crash of '29.

My dad always was a dreamer, and he figured rather than stand around in the city in some breadline, he'd find a way to make his own bread. So he stuffed what little he had left into the Model A and headed west, into the late afternoon sun.

The Model A overheated just west of Missouri at a place called Flint Hills, Kansas. He took it as a sign to sink his feet into the soil and stay awhile, but decided that he'd better get his radiator leak fixed just the same. He hitched into Wichita with the radiator. They told him they'd have to send to St. Louis for a new one, since it was beyond repair, and it would take three days to arrive.

Well, he decided to wait on the porch of that radiator shop all weekend, since they wouldn't let him take it into the hotel room with him, and he sure wasn't going to let go of it until he had the replacement in hand.

He spent the night and the next day waiting on the dealer's porch, and then got a little bored. So he followed the sound of fiddles playing in the distance to the barn dance they had every Saturday night.

You can just about guess who he saw through the window. It was the prettiest woman he'd seen since his mother, only this one had straight blond hair.

They wouldn't let him take the radiator inside, so he set it down by the door where he could keep an eye on it, and went on in—except he couldn't keep an eye on it. Both of his were glued to Elizabeth Tompkins of Wichita, Kansas.

He and the radiator spent that night at her mother's house, where the radiator had to sleep on the porch while he slept on the sofa. He and Elizabeth spent Sunday together. When the new radiator arrived on Monday, she drove him back to the Model A in her mother's Chevrolet, and the romance began in earnest.

On the way back he got a real good look at the wheat fields, and a real good look at his heart. That was when he discovered his real profession in life, and also chose his wife.

His dad had always been a thinking man, and the story goes that when he took one look at his son's deep-set brown eyes, he thought he saw a look of contemplation, and named my dad Aristotle, after the great Greek philosopher.

It turned out to be an accurate assessment. Though he had a pretty good mechanical bent, engines could never really hold his full attention for long. He was always wondering about the purpose of engines, which led to the purpose of work, which led to the purpose of life.

When he first set eyes on those Kansas wheat fields, he got an idea to combine all three: mechanics, thinking, and the beauty of making your own bread straight from growing wheat.

It wasn't until he saw my mom's farm, though, that he put the idea into action. Our farm had been her father's, but he had been killed in World War I. His widow couldn't manage it alone with three small children, and had tried to sell it. There had been no takers, so she kept it in the family for the kids when they grew up. But once they got a taste of town life, the kids never wanted to go back to that three hundred forty acre farm in a town with a hundred people; all except for one—Elizabeth.

When she met Dad she knew he wasn't an ordinary drifter looking for a new radiator, but a man looking to put down roots.

For the next three weeks their heads spun faster than a Texas twister, and they finally set down on that deserted farm in Flint Hills. It was enough time to let them know they had each found someone for life. So they were married, and honeymooned, of all places, on the broken-down farm.

Love is like a twister, Dad told me. It picks you up

wherever you're standing, spins you around in circles and sets you down just about where it sees fit. Our old farm was fit enough to start a life, he said, and a family.

They couldn't afford a tractor right off, so Dad traded the Model A, new radiator and all, for a big young filly named Petula. Well, you just about know the rest. Later on, when times were good, he bought a Chevy pickup for trips to town.

That Model A sure picked a fine spot to overheat, and I probably owe my life to a blown radiator. Sure seems like a funny thing to be indebted to for your existence, but I'm grateful just the same.

4

Kansas Wheat

I left the barn on that warm spring morning in '47 to chase daydreams, went to my room and sat on the bed. Petula had taken a pretty good-sized chunk out of my straw hat, and this made me angry. It was the third hat that year, and I was determined to tell her a thing or two about the proper eating habits for a critter.

In order to do that I'd have to hide out from the school bus as usual. I found my regular hiding place in the well house, lowered myself down gently into the water tank, and waited until the bus came. Fortunately, the water level was low enough so I wouldn't get wet, since the wind had stopped for awhile.

Of course, there was the usual shouting of my name by Mom and Dad, which ended the same old way. Dad was telling Mom that you can lead a boy to learnin', but you can't make him think, and Mom was saying I had no shortage of thinking, since I'd dreamed up a pretty good hiding place. Sooner or later though, she said, I was going to have to start thinking about real life, and stop frittering away my time with daydreams and fishing.

The bus pulled off down the road towards the schoolhouse, and left me hanging high and dry in the well. I couldn't see where school mattered much, especially when there was only a week left before summer vacation. Besides, kids in other parts of the state were being let out to help harvest the winter wheat.

Everyone in Flint Hills country was a cattle rancher except my dad and Mr. Tucker, who both had the same peculiarity: they both insisted on being wheat farmers in a part of the state where, because of the flint and limestone in the soil, only short grasses grew. Dad also grew a couple of acres of grass for hay, but that was only enough to feed the animals.

Every year I tried to get myself let out of school for the wheat harvest. Everyone always laughed, while Miss Garcia just said no. I could tell she was thinking that my dad was a square peg in a round world, and didn't fit very well into cattle country. So I took to playing hooky in the spring, when a young man's fancy turns to courting laziness.

I slowly pulled myself out of the water tank and closed the door to the well house. It was at a perfect angle from the kitchen window so that the big oak tree between the house and the barn blocked me from view. This protected me from being discovered and subjected to excessive learning.

I snuck on my stomach across the dirt to the barn. My dad had already looked for me there and wouldn't search it for the rest of the day. My mother would stay in or near the house, since she never went in the barn, while my dad would be on the tractor most of the time, harvesting a different section of wheat each day until July. He always said that in our part of Kansas we needed an extra week or two to let the summer sun awaken the lazy kernels that slept through June, and that accounted for the late harvest.

I climbed up and lay in the loft, staring at a patch of blue sky through the hay bale hole. I thought about the heavenly choices of being able to sit in the barn and daydream, go fishing when I got tired of that, or join my dad in the fields when it was too late to be sent off to school.

I didn't really hate learning; I just didn't like having to sit at a desk to do it. Besides, Sheriff Johnson's boy, Billy, was there, and he seemed to get a certain satisfaction out of picking on me. He was only fourteen, but he was pretty darned big for his age, and about as wide around as his dad, who had about the same shape as our hog. And Elmer was two hundred and fifty pounds.

I always thought that Elmer was pretty smart, since he knew how to dig his way out of his pen whenever he wanted, but the Johnsons couldn't dig their way out of a dirt pile with a shovel, near as I could tell. They could, however, dig into my life and cause trouble when they had a mind to.

Billy figured he could just about say or do anything he wanted after his dad practically inherited the tin star from his brother, the previous town sheriff.

I did my best to avoid Billy, but at school there was no place to hide. It wasn't really the learning so much as the company of certain human animals that made me want to play hooky on a regular basis.

As I lay in the loft, I could hear the sound of the tractor in the field behind our house, and I just couldn't resist running out to meet my dad. He pretended to be mad at me for a minute, but then he took me up in his lap and we moved across the acres of ripe wheat. We rode along in silence for awhile, and then we played a game that we always played. I'd ask if there was a heaven for people when they died, and he'd say the same thing. "This *is* heaven, Thaddy. The sky ain't any bluer up beyond the stars, and the air ain't any fresher, either. And . . ."

He'd pause for me to answer, and I'd say, "The wheat ain't any more golden in summer, is it, Dad?"

"Not like here, son," he always answered back, "the wheat ain't any better anywhere."

"Except on Mr. Tucker's farm, huh, Dad?"

He would look at me and nod his head approvingly, and then I'd ask, "Why is the wheat so gold on Tucker's land?

I mean, it's not dusty-looking like ours. It's shiny, like pure gold.''

"Some say it's the soil. And some say he's got some special formula for growin' wheat. But I think it's just a place on earth more special than the rest.''

Usually, I didn't say anything, but on that particular morning I asked, "Is he going to have to sell his land?''

"I don't know, Son.''

"Are you sure we can't buy it?'' I asked, grabbing his knee. "I mean, we could keep it up. I know we could.''

"I wish it were so, Thaddy,'' he said, looking me straight in the eye, "I really wish it were. But we can barely afford the land we got right here. Some people've got to be satisfied with a smaller chunk of earth than others. But we're proud of it just the same.'' He pushed my hat down on my head. "Ain't we, son?''

"You bet, Dad. You bet we are.'' After a bit I asked, "You know what, Dad?''

"What's that?'' he answered, slowly turning the tractor around to trim another row. The sun bounced off the blades of the windmill, and hit me in the eyes, blinding me for a second. Then I was able to absorb it, and I could see again.

"When I get older I'm going to buy it for us,'' I said, placing my hand on my father's arm to get his undivided attention. "I'm going to buy Mr. Tucker's land. And then we'll have the goldenest wheat in all of Kansas, probably the whole world.''

"Sure, son,'' he answered, but his voice was far away. I could see he was lost in the steady chugging of the engine as we moved slowly over the wheat.

How he loved to ride on that green and yellow John Deere tractor! Whether it was planting time or harvest time, he could be found sitting in that seat and rolling across the land. It was almost like he was in church, and that tractor seat was his pew. It was where he watched the ground turn over fresh in the fall, and where he sowed his seeds. It was where he watered those thirsty seeds, and where he fed them food. It was where he cut the ripe wheat, and where he plowed it new. And in the end, when time finally took him into eternity, I swear they should have buried him right there in that tractor seat—him and John Deere, together forever in the soil. That would've been the way he wanted it.

After another long silence I asked, "How come us and Mr. Tucker got the only wheat farms left in Flint Hills?"

He looked at me with a keen eye, knowing that I already knew the answer. But I loved to hear his explanations anyway.

"Well," he began with a grin, "nobody's had much luck growin' wheat in this part of Kansas, what with the flint beds bein' so close to the surface and all. And the funny thing is . . . ." He wiped beads of sweat from the deep lines on his forehead with the sleeve of his plaid work shirt. "His is the best darned crop in the whole state, and he don't even harvest it. Just lets it grow wild on its own. And you know what else?" It was more like a statement than a question, and by the tone of his voice, anyone could tell this was one of his favorite subjects. "Nobody can figger it out," he said, and shook his head slowly.

He reached up with his rough hand and scratched his long, crooked nose. "Scientists from the university have been over there several times," he began again, "takin' soil samples and all. But they don't understand it none."

"Why not?" I asked, though I had heard the reason many times before.

He tipped his sweat-stained straw hat back. Then he stopped the tractor and we got off. He reached down like he always did and picked a few strands of ripe wheat, putting one in his mouth and handing me the other.

"See this wheat?" he asked at last. I nodded, holding the wheat carefully in my hands, as if it were a fresh-cut rose. "That's pretty good wheat for Flint Hills country, but you know what? I have a pretty hard time, even with the fertilizers and all, and I got a piece of land the Lord forgot to fill with flint rock. But Tucker's place is almost solid stone, just a foot below the dirt, and his wheat is better than any in Kansas, perhaps the world."

"Why's that?"

We climbed aboard and chewed our wheat straws. They had a sweetness in them that comes from tilling your own soil, Dad told me, from hard work, sweat, and the feeling of making something grow. And when you chew that kind of wheat, he said, you chew long and slow, savoring the taste as long as you can.

He put the tractor in gear and slowly let out the hand clutch. We eased forward and rolled off down the field. "Some things ain't meant to be understood, Thaddy," he answered at last, "they just is."

"But you must have an idea about his special wheat?" I insisted.

"You're not playin' with me, are you, son? You know I don't think nearly as sharp these days."

"No, sir," I said and shook my head to prove it. Besides, it was his heart that had the attack five years back, not his mind. That seemed to be working just fine.

"Well," he said, looking out across the field, "even if you are, it don't matter none. I just got old a little early in life. But you know somethin'?" he added, and patted me on the shoulder, "a fella has to do with what resources he has, and not think about the past."

"The wheat, Dad. Tell me about Tucker's wheat," I pleaded, grabbing his sleeve.

"You're a mighty inquisitive boy, for a kid that don't like school."

I didn't reply, so he stopped the tractor and took it out of gear. "Well, son," he began, "back some years ago, the wind took most of this land. Only the flint remains. Now, we're downwind from Tucker, just got the trees between us. But out on Tucker's place, the wind changes directions. Nobody knows why. 'Cause nobody tells the wind which way to blow. But it sure is funny."

"How come?"

"His land's right out there in the open, with just the back of it buttin' up against the foothills—and yet, the wind don't ever blow strong on it. Always just a gentle breeze. It's like somebody put up an invisible window, and Tucker opens it a little whenever he wants. It's the darnest thing how the twisters always jump right over his place. Even that big one back in '40 that took the courthouse jumped clean over him like he wasn't even there."

"You're still the smartest person in the world to me," I said, looking out over the wheat field.

"Why don't you run along to school and make your mother happy?" he replied, pushing my straw hat down on my head.

He had me where he wanted. "Yes, sir," came my reply, "but I guess I'll have to take Petula."

"All right, son," he answered with a grin, and put the tractor in gear.

I turned and ran off towards the barn, stopping to pick up my hat a couple of times when it blew off my head. When I was almost to the barn he yelled at me. His voice was barely audible by then, but it sounded like, "Don't let Petula eat your hat again, Thaddy." But I couldn't say for sure. I was excited about being able to ride Petula to school, and lost in the hope of discovering whether there really were unicorns in Kansas, and whether they could be caught.

A warm, gentle breeze blew against my face, and the summer sun beat down from the cloudless blue sky above. The only sounds were the steady chugging of the tractor in the distance, and the whir of the mower as it sliced the ripe wheat. I ran along, kicking up clouds of dust, and thinking about what my dad had said. He must have been right. This *was* heaven, or at least a small corner of it, and there was no better life anywhere, as near as I could tell.

5

Tucker's Grove

Petula was startled when I made my way inside the old wooden barn. I suppose I really didn't scare her much, since she was a pretty good-sized horse. She stood almost seventeen hands high, and had pulled a pretty mean plow in her younger days. Dad even won a pulling contest with her some years back at the county fair. That was before John Deere took her place in the fields.

She was a big, strong, old mare, with a coat the color of straw. Her long, thick mane and tail were just a shade lighter. When she galloped, they waved in the wind like wheat blowing in a dust storm. But despite her great size and strength, she was as gentle as a ladybug walking on your arm.

I fully intended to scold her about the hat. But when I saw her chewing hay and looking at me with her soft brown eyes, I lost my purpose, and started up another conversation instead.

"He told me they were in the pasture by the trees. You know, Petula, the wheat field over at Tucker's place. That's where he saw them, or at least one, anyway. It was night and the moon was out, 'bigger than an old pumpkin,' he said, and the stars were blinking overhead.''

Petula gave me a funny look, so I answered her. "Oh, no. He ain't blind like people says. He can still see a little, even if it's only out of one eye.

"So anyway," I continued, stroking her mane, "a mist came over the meadow like it always does in the summer, and everything got real still and anxious, as Mr. Tucker tells it. 'Pretty as you please,' he said, 'pure white stallion appeared from outta the mist.'

"And it had a horn right here," I said, reaching up and touching her where it would've been. "Right here on the forehead. And it was shaped . . . You do believe me, don't you, Petula?" I asked, looking at her intently. "Good. It was shaped like a spiral, and made out of the purest ivory.''

I hugged her head, and she cleared her nostrils. She tried to free herself from my firm embrace, but I didn't care. I knew there were unicorns, right here in Kansas. Mr. Tucker said so, and I believed him, even if nobody else did.

I took my time saddling up Petula, and then headed off at a slow trot down the dirt road to the edge of town. The schoolhouse used to be downtown with the city garage, bank, and the general store, but a few years back, Mr. Tucker had donated a sizable chunk of his land for the purpose of educating the children.

A town meeting had been held in the old schoolhouse, and everyone voted to accept his land offer. Folks were wondering how they were going to be able to afford a schoolhouse, since we were just a small town of ranchers and farmers. That was when Mr. Tucker walked into the town meeting and held up a strong, black, calloused hand.

"Don't no one worry 'bout it," he said, stroking his thick grey whiskers, " 'cause I already took care of the lumber situation. And if I can get a couple of dozen volunteers out to my place on Saturday, we can commence with buildin' the new school."

He pushed his worn-out straw hat back, exposing a forehead black as a raven's wing, furrowed deep by time, wisdom, and a bit of mystery.

His vision was better then, but he still had to squint to fight the glare of the bare light bulb. It hung from the ceiling fan and swayed gently overhead, casting strange, shifting shadows on the walls.

He scratched his round nose like he was peeling a ripe plum, and then he scratched his oval ears. He had whiskers in them too, growing straight out like porcupine needles. He sat down on the floor in his high military boots and waited for an answer.

I always thought he looked like an old miner who had lost his mule, especially with the sweat-stained lumberjack shirt. He wore a belt and suspenders to hold up his canvas pants. It reminded me of a suspension bridge across a blue river. I never thought of him as being overweight, though he had a bulge around his waist like he was hiding a thick, coiled snake under his shirt.

The real mystery was the faraway look in his eyes. Some said his sight was going, some said his mind; but others, more kind in their opinion, said he was just far away in thought.

The downtown school became our courthouse the following winter, after the new school was built. Everyone got quite a shock when we showed up at Tucker's to commence with the building. We knew that he liked to surprise us kids with stories, but what he did was beyond storytelling.

Tucker's Grove had always been a place of wonder to all of us in Flint Hills. And now we were equally mystified, since it was no longer a grove of trees. You can imagine the looks on our faces and the lumps in our throats when we gazed upon what had been forty acres of walnut trees. Now all that remained were fallen branches and sawed-off stumps that looked like stepping stones. Only a dozen acres at the back were left standing. That was where the Flint Hills began and civilization ended.

No one ever figured out how Mr. Tucker got those walnut trees to grow on that shallow rocky soil in the first place. But for twenty years, there they stood. The grove was a monument of struggle and strength to all of us, and now all that was gone, right before our eyes.

He had planted them himself on that unfertile rectangle snuggled up against the foothills of eastern Kansas. My father said everyone thought he had lost his reasoning, spending his whole life savings on walnut trees, since no one had ever grown anything of the sort on that rocky ground.

No one really expected those little trees to survive in that soil. That must have been why he got the land so cheap; nobody wanted that worthless parcel on the outskirts of town. But the trees survived and grew, and produced bushel after bushel of some of the best walnuts we'd ever tasted.

Folks came from two counties away just to taste the sweet, rich meat inside those shells. It was the darndest thing, how Mr. Tucker could grow world-class walnuts on that rocky soil. Nobody could figure it out. Several people figured he must have struck some kind of special underground spring, and the roots of the trees fed themselves to contentment on it.

The only ground water was a well that he had somehow dug himself. It was a marvel to behold, drilled through fifty feet of layered flint. There was a foot of dirt, six inches of rock, and another foot or two of dirt, all the way down to the bottom.

The school didn't need the walnut trees left over after the building was completed, so we sold the wood and paid Tucker's taxes. Everything just about came out even—until, that is, some county clerk reevaluated the situation and figured Tucker still owed more money to the state. That ended up being the cause of his tax condition in '47.

When the stumps were burned out, he planted wheat. Mr. Tucker says that it wasn't ordinary wheat, though, but a special blend he'd been working on for a long time. The walnut grove was all a part of his original plan, and he was just making the dirt ready for his wheat crop.

Folks didn't have much time to wonder about it, though, since the very first year the grandest crop of golden wheat came up out of that field. The funny thing was that Mr.

Tucker didn't even harvest it, just let it go to seed for no
reason at all. At least that was what it looked like to everyone.

So four years later, he's broke and has no income. He
won't harvest the wheat, or sell the twelve acres of walnuts
he has left. Says they're for a special purpose. I'd known
this for some time, but when I passed his field on the way
to school that June morning, it occurred to me there must
be some connection with the unicorn.

He'd told me about the coming of the creature the week
before. Of course, it was a big deal to me, being a curious
eleven-year-old, and never having seen any such critters
except in story books. But what did it mean to him?

He sure didn't care about selling tickets to see one, I
reckoned, and history making wasn't his thing. There must
be some other reason.

That was why I turned into his place, instead of going
right to school that day. I had intended to obey my father
and ride Petula to school, but when the dirt road got near
Tucker's place, Petula seemed excited and uneasy, like no
other time I could recall, except when a pack of wolves had
run across the foothills one day. Something inside her
wanted to bolt, and it took all I had to hold her back.

I could have made her stay on the road this time, too,
but all I needed was a little excuse to turn off into Tucker's
place. I didn't fight her as hard as I could have. I let her
take me down the drive and up to the front porch. She still
seemed nervous when I tied her up to the rail out front. I
wondered if Mr. Tucker had bought a horse or something,
but I didn't see one around.

I approached the porch cautiously, not knowing whether
he would send me on to school, or take me in like last time.
One thing I did know: my heart began to pound in my chest,
and I could swear it was thumping loud enough to rattle the
walls of the cabin he called home.

As I climbed the steps to the porch, the sign on the
overhang that said TUCKER'S GROVE was swaying on its
squeaky hinges, though I couldn't detect a breeze coming
from anywhere.

6

Sir Lancelot

Mr. Tucker had come to Flint Hills in '22, after thirty years in the army. He was fifty when he finally called it quits. He'd been a private in the Spanish American War, and a combat sergeant in World War I. The funny part was that he said he never did like fighting, but sometimes that's the way it works out.

He'd joined the Army to have a better life than his parents, who had been born slaves and were set free after the Civil War. He'd planned on being in the Army Corps of Engineers, but when the fighting broke out with Spain, it changed the course of his life. They told him they didn't need any more engineers, just soldiers, and that was how he ended up fighting instead of building bridges and things.

When World War I broke out, his experience had been in fighting, and so that was where he ended up again. He didn't talk too much about war, but he did talk about faraway lands, the kind you find in fairy tale books. He was always a fine storyteller. I think he started doing it during the wars to escape the fighting, and it seemed to be his real talent.

He was always telling stories, especially to us kids. Maybe that's why folks didn't believe the unicorn story. He'd told us so many stories about dragons, witches and warlocks that everyone thought it was just another fairy tale.

When most of the kids were little, we used to gather on Mr. Tucker's back porch and listen to him tell his tales. Dragons and demons came to life on that porch, and we always sat motionless and silent, eyes fixed on his face. The air was always alive with excitement, and I think he enjoyed watching the looks on our faces as much as we loved watching the stories twirl off of his tongue and tickle our ears.

Even the sheriff's little boy loved to sit and listen; but I noticed that as he got older, he began to get mad because he knew the stories weren't real. I think that was part of the reason he got so mean later on: he felt that he was being cheated, since he could never live in those tales. He had to live in the real world, and it could never have the magic found in stories.

Eventually, as everyone grew up, I was the only one who came back to listen, and try as I might, I couldn't stop believing in the magic of those stories. I believed them all, especially the new one about the unicorn. Besides, this story didn't take place in some faraway land in a distant time. Mr. Tucker swore the beast was in his pasture, and it was here in the present.

He'd never said that before, and it was enough for me to believe him—until I stood on his front porch that day.

Suddenly, I felt silly and stupid. I knew I was alone in my notion of accepting his stories as truth, and my faith began to shake. Perhaps everyone was right, and it was only me who held on hopelessly to fairy tales. I'd never doubted him before, but alone on that porch, and alone in my belief, I was unsure.

I got the urge to turn tail and run. Run as fast and far away from there as possible. I wanted to forget all of my silly notions about unicorns and hightail it out of there forever.

I turned and stepped off of the porch. I'd planned to sneak

away real quiet-like and forget the whole crazy idea, when I heard this voice behind me.

"Thaddy," Mr. Tucker said loud and clear, "is that you, son?"

I didn't answer, just ran to Petula and grabbed the saddle horn, not even noticing my hat was gone. I jumped up on her, but I was in such a hurry I missed the stirrup and landed flat on my back. I looked up and saw a big piece of blue sky. Then a black face and grey whiskers blocked my view.

"If yer plannin' on ridin' that old mare to school," he said with a laugh, "then you'd better get up and get goin', or you'll be late even by yer standards."

He reached down and held out his hand. I grabbed hold of it, and almost pulled him on top of me. He gave out a deep groan, and with great difficulty pulled me to my feet. He heaved a big sigh and began to cough.

I couldn't say a word. He held the reins and I climbed aboard. I took them from his hand and turned Petula away, patting the dust off my pants. Just when I was about to trot off, he stopped coughing.

"Come back when yer ready," he said and smiled.

I whirled around in the saddle and looked at him. He was walking slowly toward the cabin, catching his breath from the coughing fit. It wasn't the sweat-stained lumberjack shirt that caught me funny, and it wasn't the stretched-out suspenders or the blue canvas pants, and it wasn't the long underwear he wore underneath, even in summer. It was those old military boots. They weren't like the sheriff's; they were higher up on the legs, and he had his pants tucked inside them. Those boots must have been in battle, because they sure looked like they had seen action.

"Ready for what, Mr. Tucker?" I called.

"Well," he said with a grin, "unless I'm mistaken, one of us came ridin' in here lookin' fer a way to capture a creature with a horn in the middle of its head."

I felt a burning sensation in my ears. I was sure they were turning as red and hot as stewed tomatoes on the fire. "Well, I . . . No, sir," I said, and tried to look away. "I was just on my way to school, and Petula here picked up a stone. Right outside your place,'' I added, gaining confidence in my story, "and I figured I'd better pull over and take a look at her shoes.''

"That's the thing to do,'' he said. "Which hoof you reckon's got the stone in it?''

"Oh,'' I said, surprised that he was interested, "it's the front one there.'' I pointed at her right leg.

He picked up Petula's hoof and looked at the shoe closely.

"But I already got it out,'' I added in a hurry.

"So I see,'' he said, like he didn't want to press the issue, "and you did a mighty fine job of it, too. Why, you can't even see the impression the rock made.''

I looked down at him, embarrassed by my story. What made matters worse was that I'd just told my sister about nobody believing kids and old people. "They think we're liars,'' I'd said, and now I'd proved they were right, about me at least. I wanted to go and hide somewhere.

I looked at Mr. Tucker standing there in his baggy pants and combat boots. His hands were sliding the length of his suspenders like he was playing a slow tune on a bass fiddle. He had his straw hat cocked over his left eye—the bad one—and was sucking on a wheat straw he had pulled from his front pocket. He didn't say a word, but I could tell he was feeling sorry for me as I tried to hide behind my story.

"I reckon you'll be needin' yer hat,'' he said, trying to break the silence gently. Just then his dog came out from behind him like a rabbit out of a hat. She was a short-haired black Labrador, and was carrying lots of pups inside her, which made her stick out way beyond her sides. She was holding my hat in her mouth. I was amazed at how gently she held it in her teeth, not biting down or anything. She sat down at Mr. Tucker's feet.

"Hi, Cindy,'' I said, "how's my number one girlfriend?'' I turned to Petula. "Except for you, old girl,'' I assured her.

"Give Thaddy his hat, Cindy,'' Mr. Tucker said, and motioned for her to bring it to me. She waddled over and stood up on her hind legs, bracing her front paws on the saddle. I reached down and took it from her mouth, patting her on the head in the process. She smiled, and her long pink tongue fell out of her mouth. She started to pant from the heat, and let out a friendly whine.

"Yeah," I said, bending down to stroke her ears, "it must be pretty hot for you in your bloated condition."

She licked my face, and almost knocked my hat off with her tongue. "Cindy," I said, wiping my face with my sleeve, "how did you ever get so wide?"

"Got lots of pups inside that belly," Mr. Tucker said, "and if you don't take one home after she drops the litter, she's goin' to be mighty upset with you."

"Yeah," I said, placing my hat on the saddle horn, "I could use another critter. Especially since Sir Lancelot got hit by that big old truck last year. Sure do miss him something fierce."

"Well," Mr. Tucker said, pointing at Cindy's belly, "there's a lonely pup in there just lookin' fer a good home." He got a thinking look on his face for a second. Then he asked, "Did I ever tell you the lonely pup story?"

"Yeah," I said, "lots of times. But you can tell it again if you like."

"Naw," he said, and waved his hand at me, "just take one of them pups when they arrive. Least I can do fer you puttin' up with an ol' man and his stories."

"Thanks, Mr. Tucker. You're not so crazy as . . ." I caught myself in mid-sentence. "As I am," I said, and flushed red a little.

I heard crunching sounds, and turned around. Petula had grabbed my hat off the saddle horn when I wasn't looking, and I had to fight her for it. I ended up sliding off the saddle and lying on my back in the dirt again, staring up at the sky. My hat spun off in the dirt.

Petula almost stole it again, but Cindy beat her to it, and laid it on my stomach, away from Petula's reach. The hole was a little bigger from Petula's chewing, but otherwise, it was okay. I looked up and shook my head. Mr. Tucker just grinned.

I stood up, dusted myself off with my hat, and tried to

change the subject. "Well," I said, getting a firm grip on my hat, "you got yourself a deal." I was pleased by the thought of a dog being added to my animal collection. Right then I only had Petula, Becky our milk cow, Elmer the wayward hog, and the old hoot owl that hung around the barn at night. I sure had room enough in my life for at least one more critter, especially a dog to replace old Sir Lancelot.

"No trouble," Mr. Tucker said about me taking a pup, "no trouble at all." He reached down and patted Cinderella on the head. She panted and stuck out her long pink tongue. "Best darned dogs in North America," he said with pride.

I placed my hat carefully on my head, with Petula's bite facing forward. "Must've come off in the wind when I rode in," I said, looking out across his field of shiny golden wheat.

"I don't reckon so," he grinned, turning to walk back to the cabin, "Don't get much wind out here. Seems to change directions out by the schoolhouse. Wind hasn't blown hard enough to scatter a dandylion in Lord knows when."

"Well," I said, surprised by his comment, "I must've been riding too fast again."

"I don't reckon that, neither," he answered, turning partly toward me. He slipped his hands over his suspenders and began to play his silent tune, sliding his hands slowly up and down. "I would've heard hoofbeats movin' faster than yers when you rode up," he added.

I didn't answer, but looked out across the wheat field instead. "Be glad to help you with the harvest," I finally said. "Sure would be a shame to let all that good wheat go to waste."

"Yep," he said, smiling, "it would go to waste, if there weren't a critter eatin' on it."

There was a long silence. Then he turned his back and started shuffling off towards his cabin. "Come back," he said about ten steps down the path, "when you reckon yer ready."

He coughed and began to wheeze. It sounded so terrible that I almost got off Petula to see if I could help, but he raised his hand and said in a broken voice, "Just don't make it too long. 'Cause I want to be around when you catch it." He turned and walked away. Then he stopped suddenly. "But never you mind"—he looked over his shoulder— "you come when yer ready, and not before, understand? Because nothin' . . ." He coughed again. Cinderella whined and snuggled close to his leg.

"Nothin' can happen 'til yer ready," he said, looking at me with a squint. " 'Til you want it so bad you can't sleep at night. Can't go on another day without it. 'Til that day comes, a man's only playin' with his feelin's."

"But," I said, "I don't even know if I believe."

He chuckled. "Oh, you believe, all right. Else you wouldn't be tryin' so hard to resist. Go on now, and when you can't sleep no more on it, I'll be here. But be careful," he added, suddenly turning serious, "there's trouble on the road fer the one that seeks the unicorn. The demons will try to scare you off, but you must look 'em square in the face. When you can do that, and not run, yer ready to catch a unicorn, and not before." He headed for the porch.

I turned Petula around and rode away, feeling a struggle deep inside. Here I was going along in life minding my own business, feeling that what I knew about life was enough to get by on; but Mr. Tucker had set off something in me that wouldn't keep quiet. My heart had picked a fight with my mind, and they were going to battle it out to the finish, whether I liked it or not.

One part of me was sorry that I had ever cut across Tucker's grove the week before and had seen him standing in his field, talking to the wheat—about unicorns, of all things. Now, here's a guy who used to be a combat sergeant, and he's talking to wheat. It didn't really bother me much, since I talked to my animals. But it wasn't too often that you saw a grown man talking to plants about fairy tales. I'd asked him who he was talking to, and he'd said he was asking for some help to catch a dream, and just then I'd come along.

Of all the daydreams in the whole world, I had to barge

in on his. And then, like it or not, it had become mine, since I could never resist a good one.

It was already starting to consume me as I rode off down the road towards the schoolhouse. My mind almost stopped it, but my heart got wings somewhere along the way, and I imagined that Petula was painted white, with a spiral piece of ivory coming right out of her forehead. And as I rode that fantasy, my mind made friends with my heart.

I became lost in a mist of feelings, and for a moment I thought Petula was starting to fly. Fly as far and as high as my imagination could go—to a far-off land where school never mattered, and no one ever grew old or got sick. It was a grand fantasy, but just the same, it was the greatest feeling on earth.

I knew for the first time that Mr. Tucker was right: I could never go back to the world I had known, or sleep easy. I had already crossed the line between myth and reality. And I liked fantasy better.

He had said there was going to be trouble on the road, but I didn't understand what he meant, and I didn't care. I figured nothing could be that bad.

I would, of course, go back to the world. But I knew I couldn't rest until I'd captured that magic creature and ridden it to the stars. And I would find a way, if there *was* a way, to make it happen, no matter what.

You can imagine how strange it felt to arrive at school with dust on my clothes, dreams in my head, and a hole in my hat. There were many, I'm sure, who believed the hole extended into my head as well.

7

That Johnson Boy

The door squeaked, and everyone turned around and stared. Everyone always did when I arrived late.

Miss Garcia looked at me briefly and then told the class that the lesson was up front on the blackboard and not in the back of the room—unless they wanted to learn about the fundamentals of being late.

All fifteen kids turned back around. I sat in the back row by myself as usual, but I really wanted to sit up front so I could get a closer look at Miss Garcia. She was the prettiest woman I'd ever seen. Long, thick black hair fell softly on her shoulders, and flowed down her back to her waist. She had big, deep brown eyes that were just a shade darker than her rich brown skin. She wore a simple, pale yellow country dress.

Miss Garcia had a habit of always drawing things on the board to show us examples of what she was talking about. Word had it that she secretly wanted to be an art teacher, but took the job in Flint Hills until something better came along. She stayed on longer than the six months she had

agreed to in the first place, even though she had to deal
with a certain hooky player with a big straw-colored horse.

On that particular morning, I was planning to sit in the
back and mind my own business until noon, then maybe
sneak away and go fishing down by the creek. But Miss
Garcia interrupted my scheme of silence by asking me a
question.

"In your opinion," she began, as soon as I had settled
at my walnut desk, "is it possible to have a perfect memory?" She looked past everyone and focused her piercing
brown eyes directly on me. "Yes, Thaddeus," she added,
"I mean *you.*"

"Well, ma'am, I . . . I reckon you might want to ask
someone else. I mean, I don't want to take away someone's
chance to answer."

"I see," she replied, picking up an eraser from the blackboard and smiling. "Well, that is very considerate of you,
but I don't recall your answering any questions yet this
morning. Do you?"

"No, ma'am, I said softly, "I've been real quiet today.
Just didn't want to disturb no one, that's all. I can leave
right now if you want me to. I got my horse parked right
outside."

Everyone laughed, but she didn't lose her composure.
"No, Mr. Williams," she said right back, looking as though
she wanted to chuckle, "we need you here in class. In fact,
I need you after class as well, because my blackboard is
getting too dirty to write on, and the erasers are a disgrace."

She held up an eraser to show me. It was filled to overflowing with chalk dust. "But you haven't given us the
benefit of a reply as yet, have you? At least, I don't recall
hearing one."

"No, ma'am," I answered, feeling my face and ears grow
hot and flush red.

"No, ma'am what?" she asked patiently.

"No, ma'am, I don't think anyone has a perfect memory."

Billy Johnson began to wave his arms wildly to get her

attention. "Okay, Billy," Miss Garcia said, "you can answer if you like."

"Well, ma'am, my Pa says there is cases where the mind can take a pitcher of somethin', and 'member it whole. He called it photogenic memory."

"Photographic memory, Billy, not photogenic," Miss Garcia said, shaking her head in dismay.

"Yes, ma'am," he said, scratching his big head, "that's what I meant."

"So tell the class, Thaddeus," she said, looking back at me, "do you have one of these photographic memories?" She looked around at the class.

"Oh, 'course not. I have to write things down." I smiled, pleased by my response.

"Then I suggest you find a friend from whom you can borrow a pencil and paper, young man."

This time the class laughed really loud, especially since it was obvious that I didn't bring anything with me, including my memory.

"Oh, and Thaddeus," she said, straight-faced, "do stay after class and clean the erasers."

My sister lent me a pencil and paper, and I took notes violently until lunch. Then I went out to talk to a certain four-legged critter tied up at the post.

"Well, Petula, looks like I've done it again," I said. "How come kids have to go to school, when they'd just as soon be doing something else?

"*You* know," I answered, as if she had asked a question, "like chasing some fish around the stream, or chasing dragons across the hills. Wouldn't that be something, Petula? If you were a big white stallion, and I was Sir Lancelot?"

I looked up into her innocent brown eyes. "No, not my old dog. He got run over, remember? I mean Sir Lancelot the knight. Yeah, we could charge across those hills and look for a castle to capture. And I would be . . ."

"Hey, Chipmunk!" I heard from behind, and recognized the voice. It was Billy Johnson, the local bully and bigmouth. He grabbed my hat off my head when I wasn't looking.

"Hey," I said, "give me back the hat. It wouldn't fit on a big head like yours, anyway!"

"Oh, yeah," he said, trying it on his large head. "Well, I guess it's made fer a peabrain." He tried to push it down on his head, but it was several sizes too small. "Hey, what's this?" he asked, noticing the bite out of the brim. "I didn't know chipmunks ate straw. I thought they only ate nuts."

Some of the other kids were starting to gather around by then, waiting to see what was going to happen. Billy took my hat off his head, dropped it in the dust, and raised his big boot over it. I made a run for the hat before his foot came down, and kicked it away. But he hooked my leg with his boot and I went down. Then he jumped on top of me.

Now, even though I was a foot shorter and about a hundred pounds lighter, I've always been good at wiggling out of tight spots. So he had more trouble with me than a greased pig at the county fair. We tangled around for awhile, with the other kids yelling and screaming and carrying on like it was a state wrestling championship. The bad news was that he finally managed to get on top of me again, and I just couldn't budge him. He sat on me so I couldn't move. Then he looked around for my hat and started laughing.

"What are you laughing at?" I asked from underneath him.

He didn't say anything, just kept laughing. Then he got up and grabbed his stomach, doubling over with laughter. Pretty soon everyone was laughing and pointing at me.

I got up and saw my hat. It was lying where I had been, and was squashed out pretty flat. I reached down and picked it up. It didn't hurt so much that the hat was all but ruined; what hurt was the kids standing there laughing.

My sister and Miss Garcia came out of the school just then and walked up to us.

"Okay, what's going on here?" Miss Garcia asked.

"Aw, nothin'," Billy said, "Chipmunk here just sat on his hat."

"Is this true, Thaddeus?" she asked.

I didn't say anything at first. I just kept looking at Billy Johnson grinning at me, his small straight teeth in neat little rows in his mouth. It grew real quiet and tense. Everyone was waiting for me to say something.

"Yes, ma'am," I finally said, staring at Billy, "I reckon it is."

"Okay, then," Miss Garcia said, "that's enough for today. All of you go home and study your lessons. Except for you, Thaddeus." She was trying not to laugh at the flattened hat in my hands, but she wasn't doing very well.

Cathy looked at me, and then glared at Billy Johnson. "Why don't you pick on someone your own size?" she said, her hands on her hips. I thought she was going to duke it out with him right there. She probably would have won; she had pretty firm muscles from turning wrenches. I didn't think anyone could go ten rounds with her, except maybe her boyfriend.

I didn't give anyone a chance to find out, though. I just pointed at Billy and said, "The only one's his size is my hog Elmer."

I stomped off to the classroom. The crowd broke up and everyone went home, but Billy Johnson couldn't resist turning around to take one last shot at me.

"Hey, Chipmunk!" he yelled. "Don't go eatin' too much chalk dust. I hear it makes the front teeth grow." In the distance, I could hear the other kids laughing. "And the ears grow, too," he added, "so you can listen to Mr. Tucker's stupid ol' stories."

"Oh, yeah?" I said. "Well, why don't you just take your photogenic memory and go home?" I stomped off towards the classroom. When I got inside, Miss Garcia came in and got her things. She didn't say anything, but I could hear her trying to keep from laughing. Just before she left she said, "Please lock the door before you leave."

I knew she had figured to have a talk with me, but I guess the sight of my squashed hat sitting on her desk somehow hit her funnybone in just the right place. She knew she couldn't have a serious talk with me as long as that hat was in the room. And *I* wasn't going to toss it out, since it looked like maybe I could still straighten it.

8

My Sister the Engineer

My sister Cathy was an oddity in '47. She wasn't inclined towards sewing and cooking, but was more interested in how the sewing machine and stove worked. This made lots of folks think she was mighty peculiar, if not downright unladylike. The fact that she had long legs, a slim figure, and blond hair made her even more of a wonder in our little town.

Girls were supposed to be studying husband hunting and home economics in school, or maybe English and nursing, but Cathy was always taking things apart to see how they worked. She studied math and engines instead of muffins and hemlines.

One of my first memories was watching her get a doll that cried. She had it apart before the day was out, and when I went to her room to look at it, she showed me the little mechanism that made it cry. She explained it a couple of times, but I never quite understood the workings of it. "It's so simple," she'd said, "a child could make it."

Well, it didn't look that simple to me—a bunch of little gears and parts I could never figure out.

Needless to say, that was her last doll. After that she got tools so she could take things apart and put them back together, and she never had parts left over like I always did. Dad didn't say too much about it, but I could tell he was proud to have her help with repairs around the house.

That didn't satisfy her, though, and she soon started fixing tractors and transmissions. When she first stuck her head under the hood of a car, it was all but over. She fell in love—with carburetors, fuel pumps and regulators. There was so much to take apart and put back together. Under the hood of a car she truly found herself.

It was fun to see the excitement on her face, not to mention the grease, when she raced in from the barn to tell us something new she had discovered—dirt in a fuel line, a clogged carburetor jet, a faulty voltage regulator. Whatever she found was like buried treasure, and though me and Mom couldn't understand the details, we still shared in the excitement.

So when I set to my chore of banging erasers with my arms stuck out the window, I was not completely surprised to see her waiting for me in the schoolyard. I was grateful for the company. It was her way of telling me thanks for listening, even if I didn't really care about points and plugs.

She always found little ways to let me know that she appreciated borrowing and bending my ears a little. Besides, I did the same to her ears with the stories I passed on from Mr. Tucker. So it was a mutual toleration society.

As I was cleaning the blackboard, I just couldn't resist drawing a knight aboard a unicorn engaged in battle with a dragon. I was erasing it when I heard some rustling behind me.

I turned around and saw Cathy working on restoring my hat. She had managed to get it back to its original un-squashed condition—well, almost.

"Still drawin' up dreams," she said, looking at the blackboard. "Well," she added, thinking it over for a bit, "I guess the world needs *some* dreamers."

"Yeah," I agreed, "there's got to be a place for dreamers somewhere in this world, doesn't there?"

"Sure," she answered, nodding, "or else there wouldn't be any fairy tales. You go right on being yourself, and if that Billy Johnson messes with you again, I'll sock him square in the nose."

"Why the sudden change of heart?" I asked. "I thought you didn't like it when I daydream."

"I guess I changed my mind."

"What made you do that?"

"When I saw you and Billy Johnson, I thought about how nature has all sizes and shapes of things. And if nature is big enough to include you, I figured I might as well include you too, daydreams and all. It's not that I'm against Mr. Tucker's stories, but there comes a time when you have to stop believing in fairy tales. When you have to accept life for what it is."

"Yeah," I agreed, "I see what you mean." But I was far away in thought. "Cath," I began, like I hadn't heard a word she had said, "you ever wonder what it would be like to ride a unicorn?"

She lifted her head and looked out the window. I followed her gaze across the school yard to the neatly spaced walnut trees beyond.

"Now you're dreaming again, Thaddeus," she said, scolding me a little. "And just when I thought we were making progress."

"But if I believe in them . . ."

"Just because you believe in something doesn't make it real," she protested.

"But . . . we believe in things all the time that nobody has ever seen." She didn't say anything, so I went on, "Like . . . like time, and . . . and heaven . . . and . . ."

"Well," she finally said, glancing down at my hat, "I suppose you can believe if you want to, at least until somebody proves absolutely that unicorns don't exist. It would help, though," she said after a pause, "if you had actually seen one."

"I'm working on it," I answered. "Mr. Tucker's got one on his place, remember? But he says it has to be caught first."

"Okay," she said. "Let's suppose that he actually has one on his land. Would you know how to catch it?"

"No," I admitted, shaking my head, "guess I don't."

"Well," she said, "legend says that you need a virgin girl."

"A what?"

"A vir . . . A really pure woman," she said carefully. When I didn't say anything, she added, "Like a nun."

"Really? What for?"

"Because that's what the legend says, and if you're going to believe in unicorns, you have to accept the legend."

"Anything else? I mean, what else do I need?"

"Well," she said, "the school has a book on mythology, and it explains all that stuff."

"Yeah?" I asked. "Where?"

"Come on, I'll show you."

We got up and went outside to the rear of the schoolhouse, and opened the storm door. We were soon inside the cellar. She found a kerosene lamp and some matches to light it. We cleared away the cobwebs and chased away the mice. Then we began looking through the piles of blankets and stacks of books, kept there in case a twister snuck up on the school and we couldn't get home in time. The idea was that we could bundle up and read until it blew over.

As I searched, a mouse ran up my pant leg. I yelled and jumped backwards. There was a loud crash, and the mouse scurried off.

"Thaddeus!" Cathy screamed, more surprised by my shout than by the mouse. "Are you all right?" She picked up the lamp and moved it towards me. I was lying under a pile of books, with only my hands and feet sticking out. I must have looked like some kind of book monster trying to come to life.

"Yeah," I said through the books, and began to push

them off me. She set the lamp down and helped me unload them, reading the titles as she went.

We went through every pile twice, but couldn't find the book on mythology. It just wasn't there, and no amount of hoping and believing was going to find it. We couldn't say a word. The looks of disappointment on our faces told how we felt. Cathy reached over and put her hand on my shoulder. I blew out the lamp and put it down, as we started up the stairs.

When we got to the top, she put her hands to her face. I thought she was going to cry, but she sneezed instead. Dust exploded from her hair.

"Bless you," I said.

She sneezed again and noticed that her hands were covered with book dust.

"We'd better get going," I said, "Petula's probably wondering what happened to me."

"Yes," she said, "it's getting late."

We were halfway home when I realized how much I should appreciate my sister. She had done a very important thing for me that summer: she had encouraged my dream. And what wonderful things dreams are—unless, of course, you wake up. But I wasn't about to wake up from mine, not without a good fight.

9

Vampires in the Loft

Bob Greison's arm wasn't really that bad. True, he had caught a piece of shrapnel in it from the war, but they had dug it out. It left a little hole inside that never quite filled up with muscle, but you sure couldn't tell by looking. Except for the little scar on his bicep, his bad arm looked just as big and strong as his right one. "Besides," he once said, "it only hurts when I pitch."

Now that might not sound like a tragedy, except pitching was the one thing he did better than anything else in life, and the war had taken that away from him. He still had his studies to look forward to in college, but he didn't seem to like the agriculture business as much as baseball. The Kansas City Athletics were our closest team, and he had dreamed of pitching for them someday. Now that dream had to be changed, whether he liked it or not, and I knew he didn't like it. He did, however, like my sister.

They had practically grown up together, since his Dad's dairy was just down the road. They hadn't really noticed each other, though, until after he came back from the war.

He had left as a shy, skinny sixteen-year-old, and came back a strong young man of nineteen.

He had seen some action, and had been wounded at Normandy during the D-day invasion in '44. One of his buddies stepped on a mine right in front of him, and Bob had caught a piece of flying metal in his pitching arm. It was just a small hole, but it had shattered a big dream.

When he came back, we gave him and Sally Penhurst a hero's welcome. She was the general store owner's daughter who had been an army nurse. Everyone thought they would hit it off, having both been in the war and all, but that's not what happened.

He rested up and moped around the dairy farm for a while, and then his parents decided it was time for him to get a college degree in agribusiness, so he could improve the dairy.

It was in the winter of '46 when he and my sister began to see each other. They had been doing a lot of seeing each other when June '47 rolled around. They always seemed to be up in the loft, and I couldn't figure out why they spent so much time up there.

They always said they were studying for their college placement tests or something, but sometimes they forgot to bring books up to the loft. I spent months trying to figure out what they were up to, until it finally occurred to me exactly what was going on. It was on the day of my fight with Billy Johnson, and it came to me when Cathy and I rode Petula back to the farm, but I had to wait for the right moment to spring it on the world.

It was late in the afternoon when we arrived home. According to my stomach, it was not far off from dinnertime. Petula was breathing pretty hard after the fast ride home, so I dropped Cathy off at the barn door and stopped by the well to share a bucket of water with a thirsty horse.

After we emptied the bucket, I led Petula into the barn and unsaddled her. I could hear papers shuffling in the hayloft overhead, so I figured Cathy had started working on one of her school projects. She liked to sit up in the loft and study where no one would bother her. But this time I could hear more than papers moving. It sounded like rats chasing each other, or people wrestling.

Cathy giggled, and then a familiar voice said, "You don't get away that easy."

I climbed the ladder to see what was going on, and when I reached the top, there they were, Bob Greison and my sister.

At first I thought it was a wrestling match, because he had her pinned, though she didn't look like she was trying too hard to get loose. Besides, he was trying to bite her neck, so I finally figured out what they were doing. They were playing Dracula, and it was time to let them know I'd figured it out.

"Hey, guys," I said, "I got some neat teeth you can borrow." They scrambled to get up. I guess they didn't want me to know about their vampire game.

"Thaddeus!" Cathy said, heaving a deep sigh and putting her hand over her heart, "what are you doing here?" She straightened her pink checkered dress and pulled up her white socks.

"Well," I began, "I was putting Petula away, and I heard you guys playing Dracula."

"Yeah," Bob said with relief. He ran his big hands through his red hair, and then buttoned up his cowboy shirt. "That's what it was, all right," he agreed, "I guess you found us out." He looked at Cathy nervously. "You see . . ." He stopped and scratched his head. "I . . . I was the vampire and . . . Wait a minute. Why am I tellin' you this?"

"Because you don't want me telling Mom that you're not studying."

"That's right, Thaddy," Cathy said. I knew she was trying to make friends. Otherwise, she'd have used my whole first name. "Mom thinks we're studying engines, not folk legends. So be a sport and don't give us away, okay?"

"Well, 'bye, guys," I said, starting down the ladder,

"see you in Transylvania." When I was halfway down I said, "You owe me one. And what did you say you were studying?"

After a long pause she said, "Internal combustion."

10

The National Freckles
Championships

Grandpa—my mom's dad—got killed in World War I. Afterwards, Grandma took the kids and moved to Wichita to stay with relatives. It was in Wichita that my mom showed an interest in art and Indian pottery. She showed such promise in crafts at school that she won an art scholarship to Kansas State University. After graduation she went to work for a well-to-do widow who owned the Indian Arts Museum in Wichita.

In all likelihood she would have kept working there, except one Saturday night she got dragged to a barn dance by her girlfriend. There she met a handsome young drifter with a broken radiator. Well, I reckon you know the rest.

If Dad was the dreamer in the family—besides me, of course—then Mom was the practical one. She knew that with the price of wheat being so low, Dad could barely make enough to pay the back taxes on her parents' farm, which had lain fallow all those years since her dad's death.

He sure didn't make enough to get us through the winter, so we needed extra income until the wheat woke up in the spring. Besides, in our part of the state, the kernels slept an extra month, so by the time we got our wheat harvested, dried, and ready for market, the farmers to the west had already sold most of theirs. The markets didn't really need a whole lot more.

We had to take a lower price to sell it off, but my dad loved farming wheat just the same, and Mom loved him. So, along about October, she would load up the Chevy and our horse trailer, and head off to Wichita.

Truck and trailer were stacked to overflowing with her pottery, but she always sold it all. Some of the better pieces were bought by the museum gift shop, and sold as American farm works of art. The general store bought the rest. She made enough to buy cloth for clothes, household supplies, Christmas presents, and enough clay to make another year's worth of pottery. That was how we got through the winters, and we could find no reason to complain, because it kept us on the farm.

Unfortunately, Dad's heart attack meant he wasn't going to be spending near as much time farming the land, so the squeeze was on. We all knew that the summer of '47 might be our last summer on the farm. I just hoped that a miracle would happen and we could stay in Flint Hills forever, but forever seemed to be only true in fairy tales.

I left Cathy and Bob in the barn. Halfway to the house, I could smell a pot roast cooking in the oven. When I opened the screen door, Mom was standing at the stove, salting boiling water, and getting ready to cook potato dumplings. I let go of the screen door and it banged against the doorway. I knew I was in trouble for that.

"Call your sister," she said without looking up from the stove. "We eat in five minutes. And stop slamming that screen door," she added, shaking a wooden spoon at me. "We can't afford another one."

I turned around and opened the door again, stuck my head out, and yelled, "Cath! Dinner!" I closed the door carefully and started to walk down the hallway towards the stairs to my room.

"I could have done that," Mom said, looking at the screen door and rolling her eyes. "And wash those hands," she added as my boots hit the stairs.

I spun around and stepped towards the bathroom like a soldier with marching orders, arms swinging stiffly, head back. When I passed the mirror in the hall, I checked my profile and noticed my hat was gone. "Darn," I said aloud, "I must have left it at school."

I tried to walk quietly down the hall to the back door, but Mom caught me as she was setting the table. "And where do you think you're going?" she asked. "That doesn't look like the bathroom to me."

"I left my hat at school," I explained, opening the screen door.

"Oh, no you don't, mister," she said, stacking the dishes at the end of the table. "No more lost hat stories from you. Now, get those hands cleaned up and help me set the table, like a good boy."

I let go of the door, and then caught it just before it slammed. "Oh, all right," I said, disappointed. I knew she wasn't going to let me out of the house again that day, so I decided to please her with something I knew she wanted. "But," I said with my chin on my chest, "can I have a hug first?"

She put her hands on her hips and looked at me with those blue eyes, her long blond hair curled slightly at the ends. She was tanned and a little burned from working in the vegetable garden. Her color really stood out against her pale yellow house dress. Cathy in twenty years, I thought, except for the career.

Mom always took good care of us first and foremost. But when she had a spare moment, which wasn't often enough, she could be found spinning bowls and things on the wheel she kept on the back porch.

My dad was interested only in thinking and wheat farming, as near as I could tell, and he especially liked it when Mom painted wheat designs on the bowls and plates. She even painted a special one of him on John Deere, and it hangs over the fireplace to this day. I preferred the pottery with the Indian symbols of suns, harvest, and the happy hunting grounds beyond.

Mom wiped her hands on her apron, although they were already clean, and held them out to me for a hug.

"Okay," she said, her expression softening, "come on."

I ran and threw my arms around her, and we hugged pretty hard for awhile. Then she pushed the hair back from my forehead and kissed me there. As usual, I pretended not to like it, and that I was doing her a big favor. She held me at arm's length to look at me.

"Little man," she said, taking my hands in hers, "I'll bet these are still dirty."

"Yes, ma'am," I admitted, shying away.

I pulled myself free from her embrace, and ran off towards the bathroom. Before I got there I heard her say, "And leave some dirt in the sink, Thaddy, and not all of it on the towel."

When I finished washing my hands and leaving most of the dirt on the towel, I went to the kitchen and found the room full of people. Dad was there with Mom and Cathy and her boyfriend.

We had a pretty quiet meal, except for the usual "Glad to see the both of you going to college," from my mom, and "Startin' to look like twister weather," from my dad.

"Why don't you kids invent a machine to divert all twisters around Kansas?" Dad said after dinner, lighting his corncob pipe.

Everyone laughed pretty good at that one, but they laughed even harder when I said, "Cathy and Bob are studying infernal combustion for their college entrance exams."

"Internal, Thaddeus," Cathy corrected, "*internal* combustion."

"Yeah, I know," I answered, "like the Chevy."

"Thaddy's right," Mom laughed. "That truck is not internal. It's *infernal*."

"I thought Cath and I had it all fixed up," Dad said through his pipe smoke.

"It's that darn transmission," Mom said, shaking her head.

"Cathy can fix it," Bob said, grinning and put his arm around her. "Fixed the one on my pickup last weekend."

"That explains it," Mom said, cutting into the thick crust of a peach pie.

There was a nervous silence, and then Dad asked, "Explains what?"

"The dirt under her nails," Mom said.

Cathy and her boyfriend laughed—and sighed with relief at not having been discovered wrestling in the loft. Cathy hid her hands under the table.

"That's all right," Mom finally said. "If you can fix that transmission, I don't care if you've got grease up to your elbows. Anything's better than listening to that old food grinder."

"Well," Dad said, "transmissions don't last forever."

"I'll look at it tomorrow," Cathy volunteered. "Bob can help me. Besides, he might learn something about gear ratios."

"He seems to be shiftin' 'em pretty fast with you," Dad said. Judging from his expression, it must have slipped out of his mouth.

Bob took his arm off Cathy's chair, but Dad had already started to leave the table. "Reckon I had too much pie," he said, standing up. "All that sugar loosened my tongue a little."

Mom tried to act like nothing had happened. "Don't pay any attention to him," she said as Dad walked out. "He's just jealous because he hasn't got any freckles."

Everyone laughed, and then I took a good look at Bob for the first time. I hadn't really paid him much attention before, but now that my mom mentioned freckles, I could see he was a candidate for the national freckles championships.

He was big and muscular, with hair like red flames, and

freckles all over—about a hundred times more than Cathy and me. Heck, we only had a few cheeks full. He even had freckles on his arms, all the way up to his muscles. He didn't have freckles on his teeth, though. He had peach pie on those.

11

The Night of the Wolf

After dinner I escaped doing the dishes. Bob, being the polite guest, volunteered to help. I went out on the porch to watch the sunset with my parents. My mom brought her crocheting and sat down on the porch swing, upwind from my dad's pipe smoke.

Watching the sun go down was our entertainment. No one really felt the need to say anything, except my dad, who said it seemed like twister weather—but he was always saying that in the summer.

The sun sank slowly into the plains, painting the sky in shades of amber. When it disappeared along the horizon, I went upstairs to watch the stars from my bedroom window, and think about things.

All of those stars and planets, and we lived on this one, spinning like a bowl on my mom's pottery wheel. Wouldn't it be something, I thought, watching a star shoot across the deep purple sky, to fly across the galaxy. Not just to far-off planets and strange worlds, but to where the world came from, to where the universe began.

When I was eight my dad had told me about astronomy, and how some scientists thought the universe was created. The story says that the universe was born out of a big explosion from its center, and the planets and stars are still moving away from their birthplace. I couldn't appreciate the purely scientific explanation, so he interpreted it for me. He said that if the universe was born with a big bang, then the earth would go out from the center as far as it could, but someday it would return to its origin. I said it sounded like a ball on a rubber band, but he had a better explanation.

He said that when the Earth was born, it was thrown in the air like a child tossed by its mother. The child went up high, but not out of arm's reach. It looked around and got a glimpse of things. It got excited and a little scared, and then fell back into its mother's arms.

I felt this strong attraction to venture out into the stars overhead, even though I wasn't ready to fall back to the origin of the universe just yet. But I wanted to have the feeling of falling, so I'd know what it was like when I was through looking around, and ready to slide back into the arms of the universe.

As I got ready for bed, I remembered my hat was still at school. I figured I should go back and get it before it turned up lost again.

There was a cool breeze that night, so when I snuck downstairs I took my boots in one hand and my leather bomber jacket in the other. Bob Greison had brought it back from the war, and had given it to me to stop me from spying on him and Cathy. The jacket was 'way too big, and a little worn in spots, but I loved it anyway. It smelled of smoke and airplane fuel, though the scent was starting to fade. When I wore it I dreamed of flying.

Mom and Dad were still on the front porch and Cathy and Bob were in the living room as I saddled up Petula and walked her out behind the barn. When I was far enough away so I wouldn't be seen, I climbed up and we trotted off down the dirt road. The house seemed small and distant from out there, but I could see pretty good, since the moon was almost half full. The farm seemed strange to me that night, like a planet I had just explored, and was leaving to return to the stars.

Soon I passed Mr. Tucker's place. As I rode by the mist was just beginning to come over the meadow. I could see the faint glow of his cabin lantern, filtering its way through the mist like a lighthouse beacon.

When I reached the school, the lights were off, and Miss Garcia, who sometimes came back and worked late, had gone home for the night. I managed to pry open the side window with my pocket knife, and looked around for my hat.

The moonlight shining through the window lit up the whole room, and it was clear that my hat wasn't there.

It must have been down in the storm cellar, which was always unlocked in case someone got caught near the school by a tornado. An owl hooted nearby as I made my way outside and around to the back. I looked up at the school bell tower, but there was nothing there except the bell.

Opening the cellar doors, I walked down the steps. The moonlight was bright enough for me to find where the lantern sat on the table. I lit it and poked around in the piles of books and blankets.

Sure enough my hat lay beneath some books. It was all crushed, but still in one piece, except for the chewed part. Just when I got it reshaped, Petula whinnied kind of nervous-like outside.

Suddenly, a hot wind blew down the cellar steps like a dragon's breath, and almost put out the lantern. I put my hat over it, and was just able to keep it lit.

Books flew open and pages rustled like leaves in a swirling wind. A wolf howled in the distance. It startled me, and fear crept up my throat. I was just about to blow out the lantern and leave, when I noticed the book sitting under the lamp. In big letters it said: THOLO. I reached down and rubbed the cover with my sleeve. THOLO became MYTHOLO. I rubbed harder and it became MYTHOLOGY.

I smiled and opened the cover, but a second hot wind raced down the steps and this one blew out the lamp. Petula gave another nervous whinny; I could hear her raise up and pull against the reins.

The wolf howled again, this time much closer. Book under one arm, hat in the other, I bounded up the stairs, slammed the cellar door, and raced toward Petula. She pulled so violently at the reins that I thought they were going to break.

"Hoo! Hoo!" the owl cried, and my heart began to pound. I fumbled with the reins, but Petula had pulled them so tight that I couldn't loosen the knot. When I finally looked up, her eyes were wild and scared. Then I felt something watching me from behind. I turned around and saw the barn owl that usually hung out at our house perched atop the bell tower. "Hoo! Hoo!" he cried again, and the sound seemed like a terrible warning.

Another wild howl pierced the air, closer than the last. The wind picked up so fierce that it rang the bell, and the owl flew off.

Petula began to buck and pull hard at the reins. I struggled with the knot, but I still couldn't get it loose.

A menacing growl ripped the cold night air, and sent more shivers down my spine. I looked up at the moon. Clouds swirled across its face, blotting it out. The moon seemed to be struggling to free itself from the clouds, but they were moving much faster, and wouldn't let it get away.

Then I saw something moving like a dark shadow on the flint hills. It was coming this way fast.

I shot my hands into my pants and fished for my pocket knife, but it was down too deep inside, and I couldn't straighten out my pockets all the way.

A black shadow came swiftly off the hills and bounded towards the school. I thrust my hands back into both pockets again, never taking my eyes off the streak of blackness barrelling across the field towards me.

When he got a hundred yards away, I could make out his features. His eyes burned like wild prairie fires. His long pointed snout was covered with white foam. He was a hundred pounds of powerful muscle and sleek black fur. He was a hungry, lone wolf, and I was his prey.

Petula saw him racing straight at us and screamed with fear. My right hand hit the bottom of the pocket, and this time pushed the fold out straight. I felt something cold and smooth in my fingertips.

I pulled out the pocket knife and unfolded it just as he shot across the school yard. He was fifty yards away. I knew I didn't have time to cut the reins and ride away. I'd have to face him down. I thought he would jump me right away, but he slowed and stopped, looking me over with a fierce glint in his eyes.

I waved the blade out in front of me, and slipped out of my jacket, passing the blade to my other hand. He looked me over, sizing up his prey. He growled as I wrapped my jacket around my arm, but he didn't attack. He was waiting for the right moment.

I made circles in front of me with the four-inch blade, trying to scare him off. My hands felt sweaty on the knife, and my throat was as dry as a dirt road. Petula had suddenly grown calm behind me. An eerie silence filled the air for a long, slow second, and then the moment came.

The moon broke free from the clouds for an instant, flashing a beam of light on the shiny steel blade in my hand. It bounced off the blade and lit up the eyes of the wolf like white embers.

We began to circle each other, not ten feet apart. He bared his teeth and growled. I shuddered when I saw them— long, sharp, and gleaming white.

I waved the blade, slashing the air in front of me as we circled. I stared straight into his burning eyes, red with blood and fire. White foam dripped from his jaws into the dirt. He didn't look like an animal. He looked like a demon.

I waved the knife again. Suddenly, it slipped out of my hand and landed in the dirt at my feet. He saw his opening. He let out a deafening growl and lunged at me. I dove for the knife.

He misjudged his leap and went clear over me. I went to the ground and came up with the knife. I didn't have time to get up. If he came at me again, I would have to plunge the knife into him as he dove on top of me.

He turned quickly and got ready to lunge again. Then, without warning, the cry of a stallion shattered the air. The wolf stopped in his tracks. His ears shot up.

Heavy hoofbeats pounded the ground behind the schoolhouse, and they were coming this way. The wolf gave me a look that said he would be back for me later, and ran off towards the hills. The hoofbeats disappeared in the distance.

I was dazed for a second, and couldn't get up off my knees. After a moment I pulled myself together and stood up, knife frozen in my right hand. I unwrapped my jacket from my arm and put it on, then walked over to Petula and cut the reins. She was excited and ready to ride. I picked up my hat and stuffed the book in the back of my pants.

I jumped aboard and rode away, galloping as fast as I could toward home. Just before I got to Mr. Tucker's place, I saw Petula's ears shoot straight up. There was vicious growling behind us. I couldn't believe it.

I turned and saw the sleek, black form behind me. The wolf had circled back and taken up the chase. It was gaining ground, and I was too scared to look back again. I whirled forward in the saddle and kicked Petula in the sides.

"Faster, Petula! Faster, old girl!" I yelled, trying not to lose the book stuffed in my pants. I clenched my hat in my left hand so hard that my knuckles turned white. The growling was getting closer.

We reached Tucker's meadow in full stride, but the beast was right on our tail. I knew it was going to leap soon, and judging from the power in that piercing growl, it could go right up Petula's back. It was at our heels when I heard another set of galloping hooves, much faster than ours, coming up from behind.

We passed into a fog bank at Mr. Tucker's turnoff. The hooves were almost upon us, right behind the wolf. I heard the wolf leap with all of its strength and speed, and felt its crushing weight on Petula's back.

Petula screamed, and slowed for a second. Then she lunged forward as fast as she could go, trying to run out from under the wolf.

There was a snapping sound behind me. The wolf sprang

forward and sank its teeth into my jacket. I couldn't reach in to grab the knife. It looked like we were done for.

Suddenly, the wolf howled and fell to the ground, taking a piece of my jacket with it, and whimpering when it hit the dirt road.

Heavy hoofbeats moved off towards Tucker's grove. I whirled around in the saddle, but there was only the faint outline of a white horse, the biggest I had ever seen, disappearing into the mist.

I didn't go back, just rode straight home and put Petula in the barn. She had some scratches on her back behind the saddle, but it wasn't too serious. I had a pretty good-sized piece missing from my jacket, though, and that was going to take some explaining. I stashed the jacket behind some hay bales until something could be figured out.

Sneaking into the house, I made it to my room, took the book out of my pants and stared at it. It was gouged with two sharp lines. They went clear through the cover, and halfway into the pages.

I lay on my bed to recover, and soon heard my mom coming up the stairs so I hid the book under the bed. There wasn't enough time to change into my pajamas, but I pulled the covers up and pretended to be asleep.

Moonlight shone through the open window, so Mom didn't have to turn on the light. She noticed that my feet seemed awful big under the covers, so she lifted the blankets at the foot of the bed and pulled off my cowboy boots. She tucked the covers in at my feet and closed the window halfway.

I could feel her looking at me from the window, probably wondering what she was going to do with a boy like me. She walked over and kissed my forehead. Then she went to the door and held it open. She said in a whisper, "Wash up and get into your pajamas, Thaddy. You're hot and sweaty from the ride home."

I didn't open my eyes until she closed the door, but it was clear what had to be done. Walking to the bathroom, I washed up, this time leaving most of the dirt in the sink. It did feel better to be all cleaned up, especially since she had put clean sheets on the bed that day. I lay awake, staring at the sky outside my window.

A thought suddenly flashed across my mind: Mr. Tucker had told me there would be trouble on the road, but I never expected it to be like this. Maybe it was just a wolf come down off the hills, but it didn't look that way to me; it looked like the face of death. And now there was no backing out. I had trespassed into a fairy tale, and I was trapped inside it.

Around midnight the owl hooted out at the barn. His tone was much gentler now, like a lullaby for Petula and me.

Heavy hoofbeats echoed in the distance. I ran to the window, looking over towards Tucker's place. I couldn't see anything, but there had been hoofbeats out there.

I took the mythology book out from under the bed and was just about to open it when footsteps creaked on the stairs again. I shoved the book under my pillow and jumped into bed, pulled the covers up to my chin, and closed my eyes.

Mom came in and kissed my forehead again. "Thanks," she said, "for not leaving all the dirt on the towel."

I soon fell asleep. Somewhere in the night I began to dream. Petula was my unicorn, and we rode like the wind across Tucker's meadow. We approached the hills, and the world slowly began to disappear. There were stars below where the earth had been, and I had the strangest sensation, like I'd been away on a long journey, and had wanted to return home for some time, but didn't know the way. But now, aboard my unicorn, I could at last go home.

Then I fell into a deep, dreamless sleep, and didn't wake again until morning light replaced the darkness.

12

Once Upon a Unicorn

The next morning I could hardly wait to check on Petula. I went to the barn to have another look at her right after breakfast. She didn't seem to be hurt too bad, just a couple of marks where the wolf had dug his claws into her back, but not too deep.

I stopped by to milk Becky, and we talked about the events from the night before. I think you know who did most of the talking, and who did most of the listening and flyswatting with her long black tail.

"Becky," I began, looking up at her from the milking stool, "to tell you the truth, I'm a little scared. Last night was too close for comfort, if you know what I mean."

I squeezed warm milk from her big udder into the pail at my feet, and she let out a low moo. "You like that, don't you, old girl?" I asked, and leaned my head against her side. "Sometimes I feel the same way. Why, my head is so full of things that they've just got to come out. That's what I like about Mr. Tucker, I guess. He takes the ideas out of my head nice and gentle. But then he puts a whole

59

bunch of them back in again, and my head's more full than when I started.

"You know what I mean, Becky? Well, anyway..." The pail was full, so I stood up and walked around to her front end. "I know he said that there would be trouble on the road, but he didn't say nothing about a wolf."

I looked straight into her big brown eyes. She mooed and chewed on her cud. "Just between you and me," I said, "I want you to know that I was shaking scared. I thought me and Petula were dead ducks for sure. Why, if that big old stallion hadn't come along when he did, I'd be buried down at the cemetery with my grandparents."

I thought for a moment and added, "I wonder if they'd bury me along with Petula if I asked them to. Me and Petula, together forever in the good old Kansas dirt. Our bones could keep each other company while we went back to the origin of the universe. Oh, and you too, Becky. That's if you want to join us.

"That's what Dad says, Becky. That when we die we go back to where the universe began. Some folks call it heaven, and some call it becoming a part of the universe again, and some folks don't believe it at all. They think that we just dissolve into the dirt and became worm food. Well, anyway you look at it, we return to the universe, don't we?"

Becky swatted a fly on her rump and mooed at me.

"Oh," I said, "you want to know what *I* believe. Well, I'll tell you, since you asked. I got a feeling there's a big farm and barnyard up there in the sky, and we can all be together after we're gone. It'll be me and my folks, and Elmer and Petula, and you, of course. There'll be Mr. Tucker and Cathy. Yeah, she can bring her boyfriend if she wants. And there won't be any Billy Johnson. Just the people we like."

I patted her on the forehead. "And there'll be unicorns of every size and color, and no wolves, either." She reached over and licked my face with her rough tongue. "Sure, Becky, we'll get you a boyfriend too. A sweet girl like you deserves the best bull we can find."

I could hear the tractor in the field behind the house, and realized that I'd better get going. There was still Elmer to feed and some eggs to gather from the hen house.

"Gosh, Becky, I gotta go," I said, reaching over to give her a pretty good hug. Then I hurried out of the barn toward the house. Dropping off the milk in the kitchen, I raced over to Elmer's pen. It took some time to find him, since he had dug his way out again.

He had put his nose to work sniffing up something extra to eat. By the time I found him, he was halfway to Tucker's, and had a snout full of dirt. I hosed him down and put him back in his pen. Then I shoveled in the hole.

Now, Elmer was a darned big Hampshire hog, at least two hundred and fifty pounds, and was big enough to ride. I tried a bunch of times, but he wiggled around so much that I kept slipping off and landing in the mud.

There's just nothing to grab onto when you're on the back of a pig, except maybe his ears, and if you grab hold of those, you're asking for an early trip to boot hill.

Oh, I tried to saddle him once, but he absolutely refused to hold still long enough to let me get the saddle on his back. You can guess who ended up in the pig food holding the saddle.

Now, pigs aren't stupid animals, despite what people think, and Elmer was a pretty smart guy. I think he suspected something about the ultimate fate of a fattened hog, especially from the way my dad looked at him when he had a knife in his hand.

"No, Dad," I always said in Elmer's defense, "he's not quite big enough yet. You've got to wait until he gets full grown before you start thinking about ham sandwiches."

"Now, Thaddy," Dad would say with that knife in his hand, "I wasn't thinkin' nothin' of the sort. We can wait." And then he'd wink at me and say, "But not too much longer."

It didn't bother me all the time about Elmer's future on the kitchen table, but it did bother me some. It also bothered me that my dad and Mr. Tucker got to drop the "g" off the ends of words like "working" and "sleeping," but

Mom never let me do it. From the very first time I learned that some words ended in "ing", she made me always finish my words with the "g" intact.

It was a pet peeve of hers. I didn't complain too much about it, since she overlooked most of my language-slaughtering altogether. Some things in life just have to be endured, including a little education.

Now, an education is one thing for a human and quite another for a farm animal. Elmer was always putting his mind to work on great escapes of twentieth century farm animals, but Becky, our milk cow, put just about all of her thinking into making moo juice.

She was not a great thinker or a natural leader, but she was good at following Elmer's escapes, and like most animals, was a darned good listener.

After I finished up my morning chores, I was going to saddle up Petula and ride off to look for that horse I saw disappear into the fog. But I decided that first I'd take the mythology book up to the hayloft and look at it. It was hard to open, since the teeth marks had almost sealed it shut. They were nearly halfway through it, and it was at least an inch thick.

When I managed to pry it open, I saw witches, wizards, and dragons everywhere on the pages. Towards the back there was a chapter titled "The Legend of the Unicorn."

I learned that they came in all sizes and colors, just as I'd hoped. They had been in fairy tales for hundreds of years. The legend said that they could only be captured with the help of a virgin—or pure person, as Cathy had put it.

Their horns were said to have magical powers. A horn could purify water and heal the sick. There were also stories about princesses and knights riding them to faraway places. Unicorns were even used as mounts in battle. That excited me the most. I wanted to ride, to experience for myself that magic feeling aboard the wild beast. At the very end of the chapter was a poem, and it went like this:

ONCE UPON A UNICORN

Once upon a Unicorn
A lovely girl came riding.
The sun and stars
Played in her hair,
And softly she brought tidings
Of grace and peace
And sweet good cheer
And something more upon her hair:
A new-found hope
That all is well,
Love endlessly abiding,
For once upon a unicorn
A lovely girl came riding.

That poem made me want more than ever to catch one and ride aboard its back. I went to the house and stashed the book under my bed. Then I saddled up Petula and rode forth like a knight in search of a magical beast.

13

The Two-Legged Wolf

It was true that Sheriff Johnson had inherited the job. His brother, who was the sheriff in '36, had gone off to Tennessee to attend a friend's funeral.

Well, he never came back, so they made Jake Johnson the official sheriff. It turned out that his brother had found himself a wife whose father was the mayor of the town. You can guess who became the new sheriff of Smokey Mountain, Tennessee.

By that time, Jake had been sheriff six months already. Nobody really minded all that much, except folks said that he didn't have the smarts of his brother, or of a mule, for that matter. What bothered me was that folks with no common smarts often ended up in positions of authority. But at least he wasn't downright mean like his son, though he was just as big.

There was another thing that bothered me. How can un-mean parents have mean kids? The sheriff just didn't have smarts enough to set a good example, I figured, or run herd on his oversized son. Billy walked around like a bull in a china shop, not really breaking anything, but scaring every-one and getting in the way.

The man who *was* mean, or at least so it seemed to me, was the government man who came to our town that sum-mer. He had something in him that smelled of sinister, and from the moment I laid eyes on him, I could tell he was up to no good.

He had that sly, tricky look about him that you just couldn't trust. He was one of those people who poke around where they're not invited and don't belong.

When I reached Tucker's turnoff, the sheriff was there, standing over the wolf. There was another car nearby with government license plates.

"Trampled to death," the sheriff said to the man with the government car, "and by a darn big horse at that. Crushed his back. Musta got a bite outa somebody, though. Still had leather in his mouth."

I got off Petula and walked up to get a good look. The sheriff glanced at me and tipped his cowboy hat back. Then he asked, "You know anythin' 'bout this, Thaddy?"

"No, sir," I said quickly, and leaned over to get a closer look at the dead wolf lying in the dirt. He was asphalt black, and speckled with grey, like a highway on which ashes had rained. He looked asleep, lying on his side that way, except for the crooked back. He was a big one, all right; he must have been over four feet long, and looked sleek and strong.

Petula whinnied nervously behind us, so I stood directly between her and the wolf to shield her from the view. I didn't want her giving away any secrets about last night, especially with an empty seat in the sheriff's pickup truck just waiting for a passenger.

"Rabies, I figger," the sheriff said, wiping his forehead with the sleeve of his uniform. "That's what made this here wolf come off the hills. He was prob'ly chasin' somethin', judgin' by the hoofprints on the road."

Even with short sleeves and no undershirt, Sheriff John-son was sweating like someone who wasn't used to the ninety-degree heat. He was one of those people without much difference between his chest and his waist size. Both were about a yard and a half around. I wondered how he kept his holster from sliding off, but I could see his thick black belt was set a notch tighter than it should have been, creating an artificial waist to secure his Colt .45.

He took off his sweat-stained hat. His round head had lost most of its hair, except for a few silver strands across the top. His forehead, forearms, and large nose were more red than brown. He wore black boots that were soiled with dirt, and sank deep into the dust.

He looked odd standing next to the government man, who was tall, slim, and pale. He wore a plain khaki suit, an army shirt with a couple of medals pinned to it, and a brown tie to match the shirt. Standing together, they looked like Laurel and Hardy, except the government man wasn't making me laugh.

"Yep, rabies, I reckon," the sheriff said again, as if to confirm it. The government man wrote it down, then walked over and stared me in the face.

"You ever on this road at night, son?" he asked. He had a cold air about him that made it sound like an accusation, so I acted like I didn't understand. He chewed slow and easy on a big wad of tobacco, not taking his eyes off me for a second.

"Tell Captain Wingate," the sheriff said with authority. "You ever on this road at night? We're tryin' to solve a crime here, and you'd best be tellin' us, else you'd be in big trouble."

I hung my head a little, so that my hat covered my face. "No, sir," I said through the hole in the straw, "not too often." I wasn't about to tell him I liked to ride along the road at night, especially in the summer.

"How about last night?" the stranger asked, tipping my hat up with his thin pale hand. He looked away and spit a big wad of brown tobacco juice in the dirt.

"No . . . No, sir," I answered, shaking my head, "I . . . I was home last night."

He chewed the tobacco carefully, as if he was grinding my answer with his teeth. "All night?" he asked, looking quickly back at me. I thought he was going to stab me with his long pointed nose, so I backed away. I was startled by his insistence, and didn't answer, so he added, "The sheriff here tells me the school was broken into last night. Seems somebody pried open a window. Made a pretty good mess out of the cellar too."

"Yep," the sheriff said, scratching his belly, "somebody pried open a window, and got in the cellar too. Mighty 'spicious lookin' to me."

"They don't lock the cellar," I said, more to myself than to him.

"Don't lock it, eh?" Wingate asked, looking at Petula. He handed his notebook and pencil to the sheriff. Then he walked slowly towards Petula. His street shoes sank into the dusty road.

"No, sir," I said, taking my hat off and walking after him, "in case of twisters."

He heard me say it, but he didn't seem interested. He was making straight for Petula. She whinnied nervously and pawed the dirt. When he reached her, her eyes got big and she backed away. He grabbed the reins with one hand and the saddle horn with the other. I could tell she didn't like him.

"Pretty big horse you got here, son," he said, suddenly trying to act friendly. He looked her over real close.

"Yes, sir," I said proudly, standing beside her. "She's still a strong old girl."

"I'll *bet* she is," he sneered, and began inspecting her legs and hoofs. Then the scratch on her back caught his eye. He reached up and touched her near the wound. She backed away and snorted in disapproval. "Looks like she got hurt," he said, looking suspiciously at me over his shoulder.

"That . . . that was my fault," I replied, trying to think, "I . . . I dropped a hay hook on her in the barn."

"I guess you'd better be more careful, son," he said, turning to face me. He looked down at me, his hands on his hips. "Or somebody could really get hurt," he added. I was running my hands up and down my bib overalls like Mr. Tucker did with his suspenders. I was nervous about

the line of questioning. When I didn't answer he asked,
"How strong you reckon this old mare is?" He patted her
on the neck.

"Strong enough to win a plowing contest," I said with
pride.

"That was some years back," the sheriff said behind me.
"She ain't won nuthin' lately." I'd almost forgotten he was
there, and his voice startled me for a second.

"Yeah," I finally admitted, "but she ain't lost much."
I reached up and grabbed her head with both hands. "Have
you, Petula?"

"Nope," the government man said, turning to look at
the wolf, "I bet she ain't. In fact," he said, spinning around
and looking me straight in the eye, "I'll bet she's strong
enough to crush a wild animal."

"Yep," the sheriff repeated, "a wild animal." Before I
could object, Wingate turned around and walked towards
his beige sedan, got in and drove up to us, kicking up dust
with his tires. There were dark brown tobacco stains streaked
over the emblem on the door, but I could still read most of
it.

U.S. GOVERNMENT

ARMY CORPS OF ENGINEERS

He rolled his window down and looked towards Tucker's
cabin. "Sheriff," he said, "you got that piece of leather?
I can't seem to find it anywhere."

The sheriff searched his pockets, but he couldn't find it.
"Well, I'll be," he said, "it was just here a minute ago.
Don't you worry none though, Captain," he added, "I'll
find it. It couldn't just walk off."

Wingate nodded. "Good," he said. "We may need it
for evidence. Tell old man Tucker he's got three weeks."
He spun his tires and drove off down the road in a cloud
of dust.

"Or a man!" I yelled at the dust cloud. "She's strong
enough to crush a man!" I was thinking that just when one

mean creature was gone, here came another one to take its place, only it was the two-legged kind.

"Now, Thaddy," Sheriff Johnson said, putting his arm around me, "he's just doin' his job like everyone else." The sedan had disappeared behind the cloud of dust, but the cloud was taking its time settling, since there was no wind.

"But why does he care about a dead wolf on the road?" I wanted to know. "And what does he mean, Tucker's got three weeks?"

He didn't answer right away, so I followed him back over to the wolf. He pulled his pickup closer and lowered the tailgate. We looked around for the leather patch the wolf had taken out of my jacket, though I hoped the sheriff didn't know it was mine. We couldn't find it, so we gave up. Of course, if I would've found it, I'd have stuffed it in my pants without telling anyone. I didn't need any more trouble.

"Here," he said at last, throwing me a set of gloves from the bed of the truck. "Put these on in case a' rabies. Don't want no rabies germs to get us. Then we're done fer."

I put the oversized gloves on my hands while he put a pair on his. I doubted I could catch rabies from touching a dead animal that way. I always thought you had to get bit.

"I'll get the front," he said when we were ready, "and you get the back." I grabbed the hind feet and lifted as best I could. The flies that had started to gather buzzed away and back again. The sheriff threw the front end up onto the bed, and then helped me with the rear.

"Hold out yer hands," he said. When I did, he pulled my gloves off and tossed them on top of the wolf. Then he shook his gloves off on top of mine. He put a grey blanket over the wolf and turned to me. "It ain't the wolf that bothers Captain Wingate," he explained, "it's the 'citement it might create."

"What do you mean?" I asked.

"You see," he said, holding out his hands to stop any more questions, "he wants things nice and quiet when they come in to take Tucker's land."

"Take his land?"

"State wants his land fer some special study, so I hear. They figger out here on the edge of nowhere, nobody's goin' to bother 'em." He wiped the sweat from his forehead with his sleeve. "Didn't yer folks tell you anythin' about this?"

"No, sir," I replied, shaking my head in disbelief.

"Why, I'm afraid they want yer folks' place, too. They don't want no neighbors snoopin' around these parts. Plan to use yer farm as headquarters, I hear."

I couldn't believe my ears. "Three weeks?" I asked.

"Naw," he said taking a swipe at me with his hat. "That's just when they take Tucker's place. 'Lessen he comes up with back taxes, that is." He put his hat on his head. "Yer place ain't goin' 'til September."

"September!"

"Thaddy," he said, looking me straight in the eye. "Don't go gettin' me in trouble with yer folks, now. They'll never speak to me again. I thought you already knowed."

"No wonder Mom's talking about moving to Wichita," I said, as if suddenly discovering a secret. I walked over to Petula, took the reins, and led her off down Tucker's road toward the cabin.

"And Thaddy," the sheriff yelled from the truck, "be shore and wash yer hands soon as you can. Rabies is not a clean thing." I didn't answer, so he added, "And have ol' Doc Yeager look at Petula. If that scratch gets infected, she'll prob'ly have to be shot."

"Yes, sir," I said quietly, not really paying much attention. I couldn't believe what he said about Tucker's place, and having to move. I thought about it for awhile and got mad. I didn't like pulling up roots, because sometimes when you try to reroot things, they die.

"Come on, Petula," I said with conviction, "we've got work to do."

14

The Trunk of Dreams

I grabbed Petula by the reins, and we walked down Tucker's road. I forgot about the scratch on her back and the chance of rabies. It was one of those times in a person's life when he's so preoccupied with something else that he forgets to do the right thing.

I was worried about Mr. Tucker getting thrown off his land, because if he did, it just might be the last of any unicorns in Kansas. And after what Sheriff Johnson had said, I realized that I didn't have much time.

When I arrived at Tucker's, a funny sensation came over me. I felt like I wasn't visiting anymore, but walking up the drive to my own house. It's funny how you can visit a place lots of times and feel like a stranger and then, as if somebody flipped a switch in your head, a light comes on and you're at home.

That's how I felt that morning as I tied Petula up to the rail. She seemed pretty calm, too. I think she sensed something in the air. It felt like somebody was about to unfold a map to some kind of buried treasure.

I found Mr. Tucker sitting on the back porch, surveying the wheat. That and the walnuts were all he had left standing between him and closing his farm unless something little short of a miracle happened. He really didn't have to say a thing. We both knew why I'd come, and it wasn't to save his farm.

Mr. Tucker said that the world was on loan to us anyway, since we had to turn it in like a library book in the end. That way our children could check it out and pass it on as we had done. We never planned or dreamed of keeping it. We just wanted to borrow it for awhile.

Mr. Tucker wore red long johns for a shirt, baggy blue jeans, and those military boots. He raised an arm to his mouth and coughed into his sleeve, then leaned forward in his wooden rocking chair and stared at the field.

"We both know why yer here, son," he said in a weak voice, "so I'm not goin' to waste yer time talkin' about the weather. If yer goin' to catch that critter, yer goin' to need this wheat." He motioned with one arm and coughed into the sleeve of the other. He seemed pale for a moment, his skin no longer rich and dark, but grayish. He rocked backwards and stopped, planting his feet on the porch.

I was sitting on a wooden crate a few feet away. I reached for him, but my arms weren't long enough. "Mr. Tucker, are you okay?" I asked.

He waved me away and suddenly looked better, as if what he had to say was more important, and it was silencing his sickness so he could speak without interruption. "Yer goin' to need this wheat," he repeated, leaning forward, "and some walnuts."

"What about water?" I asked.

"He drinks from the river out on the hills," he said. "Heck, he don't need wheat and walnuts neither, but he'll come if they're here."

He turned and looked at me, squinting against the morning sun. Then he looked at his dog. She was walking up the porch steps, slowly wagging her tail and panting from the heat. Her tongue looked almost as long as her tail, only it was pink and wider.

"Yer also goin' to need a pure woman," he added, reaching out to pet Cinderella. "And yer goin' to need patience, as much patience as that unicorn. He's waited years fer us to plant the right crop. Now we must wait fer him to appear." He pushed his straw hat back and scratched his forehead, wiping off beads of sweat with his sleeve. He leaned over and scratched under Cinderella's chin, and she sat down at his feet. "And he'll appear," he assured me, "but the conditions must be right. The ground must be ready or the seed won't sprout. The soil must be watered or the sprout won't grow." I looked at him curiously, waiting for an explanation.

"Yer heart," he said, looking at me suddenly, "is the ground. Belief is the seed. Stories are the water. Yer heart is ready 'cause it's open, as open as a piece of ground turned over with a plow. Belief's taken root in you like a seed in the soil. The stories I told only watered the seed, now it's fer you to harvest the crop."

He looked again at the field. A slight warm breeze came up and rustled the wheat like a hand smoothing a blanket. "I came to you, Thaddeus—" he said, and began to cough again. This time it went on for what seemed forever, but was really only a minute. When it stopped, he continued as if he had never coughed at all.

"I came to you 'cause I'm old," he said. "My time's short, and the world is runnin' low on believers. Everyone has dreams locked inside 'em, like memories stuffed in a trunk. That's what makes folks special, 'cause inside 'em are the secrets of all they want to be, if they only had the chance. But they don't always get the chance, or they give up 'cause the road is too rocky and filled with chuck holes, and they don't want to bust an axle tryin' to get there.

"The great secret of the unicorn is that he holds the key to yer trunk, and when you ride him, the lock's opened and the dreams fly out. While you ride him you become all them things you always wanted. It's a great feelin'."

There was a long silence, and then I asked, "But what about when the ride is over?"

"You must remember the feelin'. You must take it with

you and keep it inside, so that whenever you want to, you can be whatever you want.'' He began to cough again, much deeper this time. Cinderella started to whine. I think she knew.

Finally, after much coughing and wheezing, he stopped and said, ''Find a virgin girl and come to the field when the moon's bright. The unicorn'll appear.''

''Does the moon have to be full?'' I asked.

He coughed and began to laugh. ''No, 'course not,'' he said. ''That's only fer yer benefit, so you can see and not trip on the stumps or step in a hole. The unicorn'll have no difficulty with the meadow. He's surefooted and fast, and never loses his balance.''

''Oh, good,'' I sighed. ''I was worried that he wouldn't come.''

''To tell you the truth,'' he said, ''he's always out there in them hills, but since we don't believe, we don't see 'im. Don't worry none about it though. He's always ready to come if we want 'im bad enough.''

''It's a *he* then?''

''Oh,'' he said with a twinkle in his eye, ''not necessarily. It's whatever we want it to be. Male or female, black, brown, or white isn't important. What's important is that it holds the key to our trunk. Whatever's in our trunk of dreams, that's what we'll experience when we ride.''

''But . . . I want to go to where all of the stars come from, where the universe was born.''

He smiled broader than I'd ever seen him smile, and then he looked at me and said, ''It may take awhile aboard the beast to reach yer destination, but that's okay. Once you start the journey, you'll get there; it's only a matter of time. But don't disappoint yer folks,'' he said suddenly, ''finish yer schoolin' first. How long you got now?''

''Only a week.''

''Well,'' he said with a nod, ''the unicorn's waited this long, it'll wait another week.''

''But . . . my trunk's so full, it just might split at the seams.''

''Nope, it'll only seem like it. Come back in a week,

when the time's right. Oh, and one more thing."

"What's that?"

"See Doc Yeager about yer horse."

"Then you know about the wolf?" He just smiled, so I asked, "What about the government? Are they really coming in three weeks to take your land?"

"Not if we catch us a unicorn," he said, shaking his head. "I reckon we can get this land declared a national preserve, only place in the world where unicorns live. Sort of like the buffalo, only a lot more endangered."

"Yeah," I said, "and we could be the caretakers."

"That we could," he said chuckling, "that we could."

I walked away with my head in a daze. I saddled up Petula and rode off as fast as I could towards Doc Yeager's, but before I got halfway down the drive, I could hear Mr. Tucker yelling at me.

"Once you climb aboard," he shouted, "you'd better be ready, fer it ain't no pony ride at the fair. This is the stuff dreams are made of."

I circled back and asked, "You won't start without me, will you?"

"Yer the future," he answered, standing by the front porch. "What good's it if an ol' man rides before passin' on? You must carry the secret forward into the future I'll never know. Then my dream'll be fulfilled."

"Okay," I said at last, "I'll do it for the future—and myself, of course. But . . ."

"But what?"

"You're . . . you're not going to pass on before next week, are you?"

He laughed very hard at this and slapped his knee. "No, Thaddy," he answered, "I wouldn't miss this fer the world. Now don't you go worryin' about me. I'll be all right, at least fer one more week."

I turned and rode like a comet towards Doc Yeager's place. I was excited to be charged with the task of carrying the secret into the future, and I think Petula knew it, for she never seemed to ride so smooth, galloping swiftly down the road towards town.

15

Believing Is Seeing

Doc Yeager had been in World War I, except he spent his time patching people up instead of creating places that needed patching on people. He tended to critters, too, since the nearest vet was all the way to Wichita, and would be sent for only when major critter problems arose. But for emergencies, ordinary calf deliveries and such, Doc worked out just fine. Our town was sure glad to have him back after the war. It meant that folks no longer had to travel all the way to Wichita to see a doctor, and emergencies were a lot easier to take.

He was older in '47, but just as important to us. Sally Penhurst was helping him out in the downtown office with deliveries and stuff. It made his job a little easier, especially since he never took a wife. Never had the time for it, he said.

He had been our doctor for forty years, and had brought most of Flint Hills into the world—some of us crying with joy, and others crying because they didn't want to come, even if it was America in the twentieth century.

Cathy came out practically swinging fists at the world; she was up to the challenge. There was plenty for her to sink her mind into, what with engines, airplanes, and the like.

I was one of those who didn't want to come out, and from what I hear, it took several shots of penicillin, some prayers, and lots of mother's milk to get me up for the main event of living. Like it or not, though, I had come out into the world, and was determined to make the best of it.

When I got to Doc Yeager's that day, he was in the barn looking at his cow. Daisy was so pregnant it looked like she was going to have twins, but only the Doc and Daisy knew for sure.

Doc was one of those people that never gained any weight, not even around the waist. He was a tall, lean, muscular man, with only a wisp of grey in his sideburns, despite his sixty years. He was otherwise clean-shaven, and washed his hands and face more than anyone I ever saw, on account of being a doctor, I guess.

That was how I found him the day of the dead wolf, standing beside Daisy and wiping his hands on a towel. He saw me out of the corner of his eye. "It's going to be twins, Thaddy," he said. "Think your Dad could use another cow?" He turned his head and looked at me, and as always came right to the point. "But I guess you won't be needing one in the city," he said, like a goodbye.

All of a sudden, I knew beyond all doubt that we were moving. Not that I hadn't believed the sheriff, but Doc never stretched the truth. He'd been the one to tell my dad straight out there would be no more plowing for him, at least not walking behind Petula. That was after the heart attack in '42. I don't have to tell you that it shattered my dad. He took to sitting on the front porch most of the time, and got awful quiet.

Then one day about six months later, Doc was delivering a calf down at Greison's dairy, owned by Bob's dad. He went behind their barn to toss out some warm water, and he saw something big and made of steel. It was covered with dust.

He talked to Mr. Greison, and the next thing you know Bob came driving something rusty down our driveway. He had got John Deere running good enough to make the trip. Dad and Cathy spent a month in the barn overhauling the engine and transmission, but the carburetor still had problems.

Mom whispered something to Mrs. Jones at church, and the next thing you know, Jones Hardware was minus some paint, and John Deere was bright yellow and green again.

Dad had been moping on the back porch for nearly a month after giving up on the carburetor. But when Cathy drove that steel horse out of the barn and into the field, he came to life like a drowning man who had suddenly found a way to the surface. He's been riding that tractor ever since, but he still spent too much energy harvesting and threshing wheat, and Doc said he had to rest more.

In those days there only seemed to be two ways to approach life: hard work or no work, and my dad had the darndest time with the second one. But after the close call with his ticker, he agreed to do only those chores that he could do riding the tractor.

The threshing was supposed to be farmed out to anyone needing work, but it turned out there was no extra help available that summer except for me, Cathy and Mom. Bob Greison had to help out on his parents' dairy farm, the ranchers were too busy raising cattle, and there weren't any drifters passing through. So work was more plentiful than people in Flint Hills in the summer of '47.

Threshing went slow when it went at all, and I finally figured out that my mom didn't much care, since the farm was being sold. I learned that the government told Mom they would buy the wheat in the field anyway, threshed or not. So it didn't matter much to her if it got done, especially if it might save Dad's life.

Dad had reluctantly agreed to relax on the porch until summer was over, only needing to ride John Deere and pull the cutter about six hours a day to harvest almost three hundred forty acres. He saved a dozen acres for corn, alfalfa, oats and the like, but in late June, we were only cutting wheat.

He took up the only other thing he knew how to do—front porch philosophy. Back porch philosophy was when you looked out over your land and talked about the past and crops. Front porch philosophy was when you looked out over the road in front of the house, and thought about where it led. That small dirt road going by our house led to town, and into Wichita and the future.

My dad wasn't a man to look back and cry about his condition. He would move on if he had to, and make do with what he had. He was stubborn, but not to the point of stupidity.

"No, sir," I answered to Doc Yeager's question about needing another cow. "Besides, Becky and Elmer are going to need homes pretty soon."

"Yes," he said with sympathy, "I guess they will." He looked at me and then back at Daisy. "You know," he said, "this old cow could use a little rest after springing the twins. She and Becky might have a lot to talk about."

"Really?" I asked, excited by the offer.

"Sure," he answered, "and old Elmer. Why, he ends up here so often, he thinks this is his second home."

"You mean it, Doc?"

"Sure," he said, messing up my hair. "And what about Petula? Looks like she's going to need a home too." He pointed to my hat in my hands. "And maybe a fresh supply of straw hats to eat."

"Petula?" I asked in disbelief. "I never even thought. Why, I can't give *her* up. I'd just die! Oh, no. I can't. I've got to talk to Mom right away. Moving to the city is one thing, but giving up Petula is something else. They must allow horses in Wichita, don't they? What am I going to do, Doc?"

"Yeah"—he nodded—"they still allow horses in Wichita. Heck, it isn't St. Louis, you know. But I suggest you have me check her over before she goes with you." I was still pretty stunned, so he went on. "Just to be sure, you understand."

"Oh," I finally said. "Yeah, that's why I came over in the first place. Seems . . . seems that she got scratched in the barn when I dropped a hay hook on her."

"Well, then," he said seriously, "we'd better have a look." He walked outside and greeted her with a pat on the forehead. "Well, old girl," he said, "remember me? When I brought you into the world, you were so big I thought you were going to bust your mother's belly. They don't come much bigger than you." He stroked her neck, and she nodded her approval. "And they don't come any sweeter. Now, where does it hurt?"

"Behind the saddle there," I said, pointing towards the spot. He reached up and felt around through her hair. He stood on his toes and looked at the place where she had been scratched. "Well," he finally said, "whatever wound was inflicted is healing up rather nicely. Just took off a little hair, that's all. When did it happen?"

"Last night."

"Hay hook?" he asked. "Funny, looks more like claw marks to me."

"Doc, could I tell you something, if you promise not to tell a soul?"

"You have my word on it," he promised, looking down at me. "A doctor never talks about his patients . . . or their owners. Now, tell me all about it."

"She got attacked by a wolf last night out on . . ."

"Tucker's Grove," he said. "Tucker called me this morning. Said he had a dead wolf out there. He also told me you'd be coming by with Petula, and to check her out just in case." He scratched his head and wrinkled his brow. "He told me I wouldn't find anything wrong with her, though, since she was saved by a wild stallion. He insisted the scratches would be gone in a day or so, though I don't know why he would say such a thing." He shook his head in disbelief.

"And you know what?" he added. "If she was clawed, I sure can't see it. It looks like she just lost a little hair, is all. I was joshing you about the claw marks. I only knew about it from Tucker's phone call."

"But they were there," I insisted. "I saw them myself. Let me take a look."

I put one foot in the stirrup and hoisted myself up. There were the last traces of a healing wound. I brushed her hide back and forth looking for claw marks, but they were very faint. "But, Doc," I said jumping down, "I wouldn't lie to you twice in one day."

"Well, she's okay now," he said. "Just like Tucker told it. Just the same, keep an eye on her for a couple of days. If she starts acting funny, you'd better bring her in."

"But how?" I asked. "How can it be?"

"He said she was in the presence of a special stallion," Doc said, real serious.

"And you believe him?" I asked, a little excited.

He sat down on the steps of his back porch. "I've seen birth and death," he began, "and just about everything in between. And there are still some things in life that nobody can explain." He paused for a moment and added, "Some things may never be explained."

"Like unicorns?"

"Unicorns?" He smiled. "Well, they say they don't exist. But think of it this way. Sometimes the things we have a need for, and create in our minds, are so powerful that they take shape in the world. Take miracles, for instance."

"Like what?"

"Like people who heal themselves simply by thinking the right thoughts," he explained.

"Hmmm," I said. "Then the saying 'Seeing is believing' works both ways."

"Now you've got me," he said, and wrinkled his forehead.

"Well," I began, "not only is it true that seeing is believing, but it's also true that believing is seeing. In other words, if I believe in something hard enough and long enough, I will see it, just like the people who make themselves well. Hey," I added with excitement, "maybe my dad could do that, make himself well."

"I don't think so, Thaddy," he said seriously. "His condition is inherited."

"But," I said, "if he believes hard enough, maybe . . ."

"Sometimes you have to be realistic," Doc said. "You're getting to be a young man now, Thaddeus. So I'm going to tell you the truth, so you don't push him too hard." He placed his hands on my shoulders, and looked straight at me. "His heart can't be repaired. He has to learn to live with his condition."

"Sure it could," I said, a little frustrated, "if he just believed hard enough."

He didn't answer. He just took his hands off my shoulders and shook his head, knowing I wasn't ready for the truth yet.

"Hey, Doc," I said, jumping up at last. "I'd better get on home."

"Sure, Thaddy," he said, but he was lost in thought. I walked over and climbed aboard Petula.

As far as I was concerned, if Dad could ride that unicorn on Tucker's place, his heart could be fixed. Maybe the mythical beast *was* conjured up by me and Mr. Tucker, but that didn't make it less real, especially after what had happened to Petula.

I was certain that it hadn't been a wild stallion protecting us last night. It was nothing less than my belief come to life, and I would do anything to ride it. I just had to capture it first.

16

Turkey in the Straw

I arrived home in the early afternoon, still excited about Doc Yeager's announcement that Petula was fine. But just to be sure, I decided to check her again. I unsaddled her and led her into the corral.

She drank some water out of the old bathtub we used as a trough. Then she ate some hay from my hand. I stood on the edge of the old porcelain tub and checked her hide. I checked again. It wasn't there. There wasn't a scratch or a hair missing, not even a clue that there had been anything wrong.

"Something mighty funny's going on around here," I said half-aloud. The vision of the wild stallion that killed the wolf raced across my mind. It had been big and strong, and looked ghostlike in the mist, kind of a pale, phantom white color. I thought of something I hadn't remembered before. There was a light glowing out in front of it as it rode away, cutting through the fog like a lighthouse lantern at midnight. But what was a horse doing with a fog light on its forehead?

"Well, old girl," I said, "fog light or no fog light, things don't look too good for us saving the farm." She sniffed like she didn't believe me, so I said, "There *was* a light, Petula." I reached over to hold her head. "I swear there was a light."

She made a grab for my hat, but I was quicker this time. Unfortunately, I fell back into the tub, so me and my hat went for a little swim. I got up and waved it at her. "Got you this time," I said. She gave me a funny look, so I glanced down at myself, dripping wet. Then I looked up into her innocent brown eyes. "What with Dad's heart condition and all, I guess I'm going to be a city slicker whether I like it or not. And then these clothes will have to go, I suppose."

She didn't say anything, so I reached up and threw my arms around her neck as best I could. "Don't worry," I said as she tried to pull away. "I'm not going without you. If they won't let you go, then we'll just ride off together into the Flint Hills where they'll never find us. Why, we'll ride all the way to Missouri if we have to, but they ain't taking you away from me.

"Yeah," I said, looking down at myself dripping into the bathtub. "Farm clothes are much more comfortable than city clothes. When they ain't wet, that is."

I suddenly lost my footing, and before I could do anything about it, fell face down in the water. By the time I figured out what had happened, you-know-who had my hat in her teeth.

"Oh, no you don't," I said, standing up in the tub and grabbing my hat out of her mouth. "You already had your dinner."

I climbed out and dripped my way toward the house, stopping once to yell at Petula. "One more week of school!" I shouted. "Why, I can do that standing on my head. Heck," I said, turning towards the house again, "I once waited longer than that for a tractor ride."

It had come about from a front porch philosophy session with my dad. Cathy and I had just come back from a Flash

Gordon movie in Wichita, and I had asked about the possibility of alien life forms.

"Thaddy," Dad had said, "the number of stars in the Kansas sky is more than you can count in a lifetime." He stopped and blew pipe smoke into the warm summer air. "Heck," he added, "one of them could have life on it, and since nearly half of them are older than earth, they could easily be more advanced. And maybe, just maybe, the beings on them could travel across the stars. Who knows, they might just land on our little planet. Besides, we send out signals."

"What kind of signals?"

"Radio signals. More than that, actually. Haven't you ever noticed how people send signals way across a crowded room? That's how me and your mom met."

He stopped the rocker that had been going steadily all the while, and leaned forward, staring across the road as if seeing the past. "We were sendin' out signals so strong that everything else disappeared."

He laughed and shook his head, took a deep puff on his corncob pipe, and started rocking again. The sweet odor of his special blend of tobacco filled the air. It reminded me of corn syrup, though he never let anyone close enough to his tobacco curing shed to get the ingredients. It was one of those secrets people got to have in life.

It seemed like his thoughts were in the tobacco, and when he lit up, they danced in the smoke in front of him. He picked the ones he wanted to talk about the way people pick out radio programs.

It was his private world. No one had the right to intrude, and so we didn't; we just let him pick the programs in his mind that he'd talk about in the evenings. I'd happened to pick one he liked that night, and so he kept on talking.

"When we got on that dance floor," he said with fond remembrance, "steppin' to 'Turkey in the Straw,' why, there was no turnin' back. Your mother always said that I'm just like that song. I'm a turkey got out of the pen and ended up in the straw. Don't belong there, but haven't found a way back to the pen yet."

"When I grow up, Dad," I said with pride, "I want to be just like you."

"Ah, no you don't," he said, and waved his hand at me. "You don't need to be like no one. When you grow up, I want you to be just like yourself. Anyway," he went on, "the whole world is sendin' out signals."

"And what do they say?" I asked.

"Well, son, judgin' from that war we just had, I reckon they're sayin' 'Save us. Save us before we do ourselves in for good.'"

"Aw," I said, joking, "maybe we should just end the world and let it start over."

As soon as it slipped out I knew it was wrong, and I knew that I couldn't take it back. Dad didn't say anything but compared to the possibility of living in the city, maybe the end of the world didn't seem so bad at the time. I was sure leaving the farm would put an end to my world anyway, if not everyone else's.

As I dripped and sloshed my way to the house, I knew I couldn't keep silent. I had to know exactly why my dad had finally gone belly-up on his dream, and was willing to give up his tractor rides forever. I couldn't picture him rocking himself to sleep on the porch every night, watching stars shoot by and wondering if one of those streaking white lights was a spaceship come to save us from ourselves.

17

Hog Heaven

My mother was a strong, practical woman. She seemed more like a father than my dad, since she was the one who wanted me to make something out of myself, while my dad was willing to just let me be.

I needed both of them, and like team horses that didn't really need to speak much to get the job done, they pulled me and Cathy along like a pair of shiny new plows.

My dad had the kind of love that lets you do almost anything you want, and given that alone I probably wouldn't have done enough to even graduate from high school. That's where my mom came in. She kept enough pressure on me so that I wouldn't daydream my entire life away. Not that she was against daydreaming, but her view was that it was a pleasure you were entitled to only after plenty of time had been given to work and study.

After dinner, I was reminded that it was my turn to dry and put away the dishes. Mom was cleaning up the kitchen, and stuck around to direct the Flint Hills Dish Symphony.

Cathy was on the washrag and pump faucet, and I was on the towels.

I liked drying the best, since you could hand the dishes and silverware that didn't quite get clean back to the washer, and you could stall around and let them drip dry until a quick swipe with the towel fixed them right up. The bad part about drying was not being tall enough to put some of the weird dishes, like the two-piece gravy boat, on the top shelf where it belonged. But I still preferred it to washing.

Dad was already sending smoke signals into the sky from the front porch, so that gave us all a chance to talk about him. I started off the dish talk, as usual, with my own view of things. "Dad seems better to me, Mom," I began. "In fact, I'll bet he's strong enough to bale hay again."

"No he's not, Thaddeus," she said, wiping the stove. "Doc says if he doesn't stop farming, he might not make it through the summer."

Cathy dropped a dish in the soapy water, and almost broke it. "Is it really that bad?" she asked in a worried voice.

"I'm afraid so," Mom said, and carried the stove grates to the sink.

"But do we really have to move?" I asked. "I like it here."

There was a long, nervous silence. Mom gave Cathy an anxious glance, and then went back to the stove. "What makes you think we're moving?" Mom asked, like she didn't understand.

"Aw, come on," I answered, placing a dried dish on the kitchen table. "A little bird told me." It was an expression I had heard many times from her.

"Well," Cathy said, "that's not very reliable."

"And Doc Yeager," I added, grabbing a handful of spoons and running them through the towel.

"Oh, he did, did he?" Mom asked. She walked back to the sink, rinsing her washrag in the hot soapy water.

"And he doesn't tell lies," I said boldly. "Only old folks and kids do that." I looked at Cathy and placed a dish back in the soapy water. She splashed some rinse water on the plates I was drip-drying.

"Hey!" I said, kind of loud, "I'm drying these."

"They looked a little soapy to me," she said.

I made a whip out of my towel and flung it at her backside. "Oh, yeah?" I said. "Well, take that!"

"Thaddeus Williams!" Mom said. "Over here to the table! You too, Cathy."

"But, Mom," I protested.

Mom looked at us intently. "I have something to say," she announced. "You'd both better sit down."

We sat down and waited for our punishment like bad kids waiting to get the belt across our bottoms.

"Your father is not going to be able to farm anymore," she said, looking straight at me. "Not ever."

"But . . ."

"Be quiet and listen first, Thaddeus," she said. "Then you can talk."

I shut up and she went on, drying her hands on my dish towel. "Besides that, I've been offered a job as curator of the Indian Arts Museum in Wichita."

"That's great!" Cathy said, but I knew she had other motives besides just being happy for Mom.

"And your sister," Mom continued, looking at me, "has been accepted at the University in the Engineering department."

"But . . ."

"Hold on, Thaddeus," Cathy said, "until Mom's finished."

"The truth is," Mom went on, "we can't afford to stay here on what little we make on this run-down farm."

"Run-down!" I protested, putting my hands on my hips.

"Yes," she said calmly. "That barn needs paint. The roof on the house needs repairs, and the fence is practically falling down. We just don't make enough on your father's wheat and my pottery to afford anything. Besides, we can't even pay our taxes. The government's fixing to auction off the farm if they don't get their money."

"Auction?" I protested.

"Either that, or we sell the place."

"How long have we got?"

"Until the end of summer," she said, and I could see she was serious about the whole thing.

I said just one thing as I got up to leave. "Heck, I don't want to move. I like it here." When I got to the hallway I stopped. I'd thought of something. "Mom," I asked, "can I take Petula?"

"Thaddeus," Cathy blurted, "they've got much better horses in town than . . ."

Mom grabbed her arm. "I'll think about it," she said.

"Well," I remarked, walking out the door, "I ain't going without her."

I went to the barn to apologize to Becky and Elmer, wanting to tell them the bad news about moving. Once inside, I put a rope around Becky's neck. I knew if I tried to put a rope around Elmer, he just might drag me halfway to Doc Yeager's when he got the news about being left behind.

I don't know if Elmer really cared much about being left, but if he knew he was ending up at Doc's, he'd probably just as soon start on their garbage now as later. Doc always had the world's best garbage, and good garbage was hog heaven. Folks always brought Doc pies and cakes, on account of him being single, I guess. Doc didn't want to insult his patients by refusing the gifts, so naturally some things got thrown out. Don't ask me how Elmer figured all that out, but I suspect he discovered it on one of his many food gathering expeditions.

He was a rooting Hampshire hog, and had the dirty nose to prove it. One day while digging in his pen, he discovered that he could dig clean under the fence, which is how he got his nickname "The Wayward Hog."

I dreamed once that Elmer had died, and when he got to heaven, the gatekeeper told him he had been bad to run away and therefore couldn't enter. But when the gatekeeper turned to someone else, Elmer snuck around to the side of the fence—and sure enough, dug his way into hog heaven.

I got Elmer and Becky together for the sad occasion, away from Petula, since I had decided she was going to Wichita with me. Then I broke the news.

"Well, guys," I said with my head down. "You both like Doc Yeager, right?"

Becky didn't say too much, but Elmer snorted a little. "Yeah," I said to him. "I figured you'd like the idea just fine, but aren't you going to miss me just a little? I know Becky is, aren't you, girl?"

Becky mooed real low and nudged against me. "Yeah, I know. But Doc's got Daisy, and two calves coming to keep you company. I know you'll be happy there."

She licked my face with her big, rough tongue. "Yeah," I finally said. "I know, but you'll be okay." She mooed again. "Sure," I answered, "I'll miss you too. But I'll come back and visit, okay? Just keep an eye on old Elmer. But with all of Doc's garbage, he'll think he died and went to heaven. So he probably won't be running away like he does here."

I turned my head. "Right, Elmer?" But he was halfway under the fence. I ran over and sat on his rear end so he couldn't get away. He wiggled and twisted, but he was stuck under the fence, and with me sitting on him, he couldn't dig his way out.

"Serves you right," I said. "Now are you going to stay home this time?" He stopped wiggling and started squealing. He didn't like being stuck and sat on at the same time.

"Okay," I said at last. "I'm going to let you up. But you're going back in the pen, understand?" He oinked a few times, so I think he knew what I meant. I got up and he wiggled back into his pen. He stuck his nose in some mud and started digging around like he had found something, so I went over to see what he was doing. When I got over to him, he lifted his head real fast and threw mud all over me with his nose. He oinked and grunted a few times, but I swear he was laughing at me.

"Elmer," I said, "you ain't seen the last of this." I wiped mud off my face and walked Becky back to her stall. "I'll get you for this!" I yelled over my shoulder. "You just wait and see!"

I don't think he was paying attention, though, because

he was rooting around in his mud hole and grunting with great satisfaction.

"That's the trouble with hogs nowadays," I told Becky as I left her stall. "They just don't appreciate their own backyard. Well," I said, shaking my head, "I guess the garbage is always sweeter on the other side of the fence."

18

A Prayer for Petula

I figured the best time to confront my dad about why he dropped his dream was after dinner. So I waited until Mom was crocheting by the lamp in the living room and Cathy was "studying" with her boyfriend.

It was a perfect time for philosophizing. I just hoped he was of a mind to talk about it. Because I knew if he wasn't, I'd have an easier time making gold out of flint than prying thoughts out of him.

Lucky for me, it was a night for making gold out of words. When I got to the front porch, smoke had filled the warm night air like mist on a meadow. I walked up and sat down on the rail, facing my dad. I was all set to start in about how he should put his foot down and prevent the move, but when I looked at him, I saw something I had never seen before.

I didn't see the strong, unbreakable man I had believed in for so many years. I saw a tired man with a sunburned face and a forehead furrowed deep by time and hard work. My father was human, with limited power and strength, a man who would not live forever, no matter how much I wanted him to. I knew that people got old in life, but I didn't want it to happen to my family, at least not yet.

So when I looked at my dad, all I could say was, "I . . . I hear we're moving."

"End of summer," he answered. There was a long awkward silence, and then he read my thoughts. "Thaddy, sometimes a man's got to do things for the sake of others, even though he'd rather just live for himself. Especially if he has a family he's got to provide for. He has to do what's best for them."

"Even if it means giving up his dream?" I asked.

He took a long puff on his pipe. "Do you know what my dream is, Thaddy?" he asked.

"I think so, Dad. Farming wheat."

"Almost," he said, and rocked forward. He placed his feet on the floorboards and stopped the slow, steady rocking he had been doing the whole time. It reminded me of an oil pump out on the prairie that had suddenly got to the bottom of the well, and come to a standstill.

"Ridin'," he said.

"John Deere," I confirmed.

"You bet, son. Me and that steel horse understand each other. You see, that tractor ain't happy unless it's put in gear and rollin' across the land. And me . . ." He sat back and began to rock again, slow and deliberate. "Well, I ain't happy unless I'm ridin', and you know what? If a fella closes his eyes and leans back, why, sittin' in this rocker is just like ridin' that tractor. I guess we're both just a couple of riders, hey, Thaddy? We just got different mounts, that's all."

"Yeah, Dad. Mom says I might get to take Petula with me. I won't go without her," I insisted. "I just won't."

"Good," he said, leaning back with his eyes closed, " 'cause I'm takin' my tractor."

"Really?" I asked excitely.

He opened his eyes and leaned forward. "Ain't I goin' to be a sight," he said with a grin, "ridin' down the streets of Wichita on old John Deere."

"Sounds good to me, Dad. Hey, know what I'm going to ride next?"

"No, you tell me, son."

"A unicorn."

"A *unicorn?*"

"Yeah. You know, with a horn in the middle of the forehead and all."

"Well," he said, leaning back again, "won't Petula get jealous?"

"Naw," I answered. "She ain't the jealous type. Besides, I think she wants to meet *this* unicorn. It saved her life. How about you, Dad? You want to ride him?" He didn't say anything, so I asked, "You do believe in them, don't you?"

He started rocking again, slow and easy. "Well, Thaddy, to tell you the truth, I can't say one way or the other. I guess I believe in what they stand for—the idea and all."

"What idea?"

He stopped the rocker and thought, wrinkling his brow. "They were dreamed up a long time ago," he said. "to fill in what's missin' sometimes in life. And what's missin' nowadays is wonder."

"Then you don't think they're real?"

"Oh, they're real all right," he answered, looking me straight in the eye. "Same as courage and kindness. What unicorns are, Thaddy, is the feelin' of wonder come to life, in us once again. Workin' and eatin' and sleepin' is just existin'. But to see the wonder and dream our dreams: That makes life more complete."

"I mean a real live unicorn," I insisted. "Big as a twenty-hand horse and white as a snowstorm, like the one Mr. Tucker has on his land. Don't you believe they can actually exist as critters?"

"Sure," he said, thinking it over carefully. "The mind can make anythin' real. It can make anythin' come to life."

"Then they *are* real," I said with relief. "Well, when I catch him, do you want to ride him? 'Cause that's where the magic is supposed to be, in the riding."

"Well," he said, nodding, "I certainly appreciate the invitation, but I already got my mount."

"Yeah," I said, "guess you're right. Everybody's got to ride their own mount."

We didn't say anything more that night, but sat in a warm, friendly silence. I felt much better knowing he was taking John Deere to Wichita with him. What a sight we would make riding down the streets—him on John Deere, and me on my unicorn. I wondered if they had ever seen a tractor in the big city before, and I was quite sure they had never seen a unicorn.

Despite the visit with my dad, I went to sleep that night with some trouble on my mind, waking up once to the sound of hoofbeats outside. Getting up I went to the window, but there wasn't anything there except the old barn owl hooting away.

Then I remembered what was bothering me, and looked out towards the barn. I got dressed and snuck downstairs.

"Don't worry, Petula," I said once inside her stall. "I ain't dumping you for no unicorn. We're gonna be together no matter what."

Throwing my arms around her neck, I hugged her long and hard. She groaned a little and licked me on the ear with her big, rough tongue. I lay down in the hay next to her and prayed. "If there's Somebody up there, please listen, okay? I know that I ain't nobody to be asking for anything, but when my unicorn gets here, could You please make it a boy? Oh, it's not for me, you understand. It's for Petula."

I went back to bed and drifted off, feeling much better about almost everything. We might have had to move, but since Petula was going with me and maybe bringing a boyfriend, It wouldn't be so bad.

19

Windmill on the Prairie

The following week was the slowest one of my life, but school finally ended on Friday and I graduated from the sixth grade. I had studied extra hard to avoid summer school. This made my parents very happy, and allowed me to goof off for what figured to be my last summer on the farm.

My mom did some checking up on me that last week of school, just to be sure I wasn't drawing pictures of dragons and unicorns in my room. Unfortunately, when she came up the stairs one day after sundown, I was just putting the finishing touches on a big old horse with a horn on his head.

"That doesn't look like schoolwork to me, young man," she said, shaking her head. "Now look, you've got just this week to go, so let's try to concentrate for once. You're a bright kid, Thaddy, but you need to apply yourself. Why not put that brain to work on history and math, instead of drawing these . . . these . . ." She picked up the drawing. "Well, just what *is* this supposed to be anyway?"

"Come on, Mom," I said. "It's a horse with a horn on its head. They call them . . ."

"I know," she answered. "Well, one thing's for certain, you inherited your father's imagination."

"Don't you think it's any good?" I wanted to know.

She walked over to the window and looked out towards Tucker's Grove. "I think it's too early to tell if you're going to be a major art talent, but I know there's a brain in that head that can do math and history."

"But they're not any fun," I answered, throwing my hands up.

"You've got to study, Thaddy, so that you can get yourself a real job someday."

"But, Mom . . ."

"Thaddy," she said seriously, "you're old enough to understand, even if you play dumb sometimes. That's why I'm telling you this."

"Telling me what?"

She turned and looked at me. "It's not that farming and philosophy aren't important," she said with a sigh, "but the world is changing. Little farms like ours will soon be a thing of the past. Wheat farming will most likely be done by big corporations. Little guys like us will become just about extinct, like cowboys and Indians."

"Well," I said, "if those are the facts, I'm not sure I want to grow up at all. Let alone make it to the seventh grade."

"It's kind of sad," she said, picking up one of the flint arrowheads I kept on the window sill. "The plains Indians were once a great race, and they really took care of the land, because they loved it. Now, all that's left are some people on reservations and a few pieces of flint and clay."

She squeezed the arrowhead in her hand and looked out the window again. She turned her head, and I could see that she was looking up at the top of the windmill. "The cowboys and Indians are all but gone," she began, "and small farmers will someday belong to the past. There won't be anything left of us but a bunch of broken-down windmills, standing as reminders that we were here."

"Sort of like the pyramids," I said.

"The winds of change could blow harder than the winds

that took our topsoil,'' she said. ''The winds in '33 blew us off the land for awhile, but someday the winds will pick up lives and blow them a thousand miles away. Anybody who's got any dreams left about farming around here, had better pack them up and plant them somewhere else. Because the winds are picking up fast. Well,'' she said, laughing ''that's your history lesson for tonight.''

''Mom,'' I said, walking over to her. ''You want to stay, don't you?''

She put her arms around me. ''Just to see the smile on your father's face when he rode that tractor was enough reason for me. But now it's time to move on. We've got to let go and say goodbye. We can't hold on forever.''

''Yeah,'' I admitted. ''I guess you're right. But can we stay at least until the summer is over?''

''Sure,'' she said. ''I like long goodbyes.''

We held each other for a second, and I felt much better knowing she really didn't want to leave. She was just better at facing reality than me and Dad. I'd need her to pull me through the move, because I sure couldn't have said goodbye by myself. It was just too hard.

She held me at arm's length and looked at me. When she spoke again, her voice became brighter. ''Why,'' she said, ''just about all your friends have moved to the city anyway.''

''Aw, Mom,'' I protested. ''I don't need no friends. I got my animals.''

''Would it make you feel any better,'' she asked, ''if I let you keep Petula?''

''Hey,'' I said, suddenly getting excited. ''You mean it?''

''Sure,'' she answered. ''I called Wichita this morning. Seems they got a place for Petula to board at the junior high school.''

''You mean I don't have to run away?''

She laughed and looked out of the window again. The warm evening breeze blew her hair like wheat in a meadow. ''Funny thing, though,'' she said with a curious grin. ''The school doesn't take any boys that are not at least in the seventh grade, and you can't board your horse if you're not a student there.''

"Okay," I said, "I get the picture. Now, get out of my room, will you please? I'm trying to study." I picked up my math book and opened it. "And take the picture of that funny-looking horse with you," I added. "I've got work to do."

She took the drawing of the unicorn in her hand and walked to the door. Just before she closed it I said, "Mom, do you believe in . . ." She looked at me funny, and I just knew that she could never believe in something she hadn't seen. "Aw, never mind," I said.

I didn't love her any less for not believing, especially since she gave me the green light for taking Petula to Wichita. It sure sounded a lot better than my original plan of running away.

Studying that week was the hardest thing I ever did. Not because the subjects were so difficult—just that I had a regular case of spring fever, and a real bad case of wanting to catch a wild stallion with an ivory horn.

I wondered if I would ever see him again, for I was certain that the unicorn had killed the wolf and then galloped off.

To this day I will never know what brought him to me, but I always believed it was my heart that called him into existence. In all the world there was no one who wanted to see him more than I did, and so he rode into my life that summer and changed it forever.

20

A Unicorn in the Hills

On the following Saturday morning I did my chores, including trying to round up Elmer, who had wiggled his way under the fence. He was halfway to Tucker's Grove when I found him rooting around in the dirt beside the road, looking for buried treasure.

"Elmer," I said as I got off Petula, "what's the matter with you? Can't you stay in your pen and eat hog food like other pigs, instead of digging around in the dirt way out here?"

He just looked at me and snorted. Then he put his nose, all covered with dirt, back to work in a pile of garbage someone had left by the side of the road.

"You, mister," I said, shaking my finger at him, "you are two hundred and fifty pounds of big trouble. Yeah, you! Look at me when I'm talking to you. I'm not one of your pig friends, you know. And you know what else?" I put my hands on my hips to emphasize the point. "Dad says if you keep running away, then somebody's going to make

ham out of you, and you'll be giving up that pigskin, and
Dad says nobody should go until they're good and ready.''

I pushed my straw hat back on my forehead. "That is,
if they have a choice in the matter. But you do have a
choice, Elmer Pigskin. You can turn yourself in and go back
to your pen, or we can make ham sandwiches out of you
right now!''

Elmer didn't stick around to find out if I was serious. He
took off running toward Tucker's place. I yelled at him to
stop, but he wouldn't listen. I got back on Petula and rode
after him. You'd be surprised how hard it is to catch a pig
on the run, even when you're on horseback.

Old Elmer just kept turning and twisting and weaving his
way towards Tucker's. I tried to lasso him a bunch of times,
but he kept his head down when he had to and managed to
duck under the rope every time.

By the time I finally caught up to him, he was five miles
from home and already on Tucker's property, disappearing
behind the cabin. I got off Petula and ran out back. There
was Mr. Tucker sitting on the porch, his straw hat pulled
down over his eyes.

"You seen Elmer around here, Mr. Tucker?'' I asked,
looking through the hole in my hat.

"Yep,'' he said.

"Where'd he head off to?'' I asked, almost out of breath.

"Thataway,'' he replied, but he didn't lift his hat or point
with his hands.

"Which way is that?'' I asked, a little frustrated.

"Whichever way you ain't,'' came the reply. When I
couldn't think of anything to say he added, "Well, if I was
a pig runnin' away from home, I'd go where the rootin' is
new, or the garbage is good. And since there ain't any good
garbage 'cept down the road at Doc's, I'd head fer the hills.
If I was a pig, that is.''

"Yeah,'' I said, "I suppose you're right.'' I pushed my
hat down firmly on my head. It made my hair stick out like
crabgrass growing under a fence. "Well,'' I added, "I ain't
letting no pig get the best of me. I'm going after him.''

Mr. Tucker sat motionless in his walnut chair on the

porch, and talked through the tiny holes in his straw hat. "Gonna have a heck of a time findin' a pig out there," he said, "with all them hills to hide behind. But I don't suppose I could stop you, could I?"

"Nope," I said, turning to leave. "I think we both know the answer to that one. A man's got to do what a man's got to do," I added, remembering one of my dad's sayings.

Mr. Tucker and I both knew that none of us kids were allowed out on the Flint Hills since Johnny Hobson was lost out there in '44 looking for wild stallions. They sent out a search party the next day, but they didn't find any sign of him or his horse for a week. When they finally found him, there wasn't a whole lot to see. The wolves had gotten to him first.

They never found the horse. Some said he ran all the way to Missouri, and some said the wolves got him too. But my dad, who was trying to put a lighter note on it, said that Johnny went to heaven because he was searching for his dream in good faith, and the horse probably got picked up by a twister and dropped in the Mississippi. He said that sometimes, when people and things disappeared forever.

After the funeral, they told us kids we were not allowed out on the hills without an adult, and never at night.

Mr. Tucker knew that I wouldn't take no for an answer when it came to catching Elmer, so he didn't try and stop me. "Thaddy," he said, "be real careful out there. I don't wanna be the one to tell yer parents yer lost out in them hills."

"Don't you worry none," I said. "Petula will protect me."

"I reckon," he said, "but be careful just the same."

I climbed aboard Petula and rode through the back of Tucker's Grove, past the walnut trees and the schoolhouse, and out onto the Flint Hills.

It looked like a door had opened into another world, a world that was big, strange, and green. Wave after wave of gentle, rolling hills stretched out in front of me as far as I could see. I heard they went all the way to Missouri, and that was a hundred miles away.

I rode along calling for Elmer and holding onto my hat, because the wind always blew out there. I looked back and noticed that the school and Tucker's place had disappeared behind the hills. Everywhere, green grass stood waving in the wind.

The only things anyone had ever seen out here were wolves and wild horses. So the sheriff didn't advise anyone to venture out too far into the hills, or they'd be like a ship lost at sea. And if they got turned around and rode in the wrong direction, they might ride for a hundred miles just trying to get out of the hills.

I rode to the top of the biggest hill I could find, and saw the schoolhouse way off in the distance. It was small and far away.

The wind was warm that day, but then it began to blow cold. That meant only one thing: a twister was on the way—and, judging from the strength of the sudden burst of wind, it could be a big one.

The sky began to darken down south, and I saw black clouds coming my way in a hurry. From what I could tell though, they were still pretty far off.

The wind died down for a second, and I heard hoofbeats over the next rise. I galloped toward them as fast as Petula could go, but they were over the rise before I could catch them, so I raced to the top of the next hill. Suddenly there he was, standing on top of a ridge, not fifty feet away.

He was big and strong, just as I remembered, and as white as a cloud; yet he looked ghostlike, like he could vanish at any moment.

He had a long, full mane and tail, both as white as a dove's wing. There was a slight wisp of hair under his chin, about as long as my hand. He pawed the ground, lifting his front legs, revealing hair shaped like feathers growing over his hooves, covering them completely. A spiral horn shot out of his forehead, as long and wide as my arm. It looked like pure ivory, and came to a sharp point at the end.

He looked at me, and in his eyes I saw everything. Strength and wildness were in them, yet there was gentleness too. They seemed to change with my feelings, until I realized that whatever was in my heart was in his eyes, like a mirror into my soul. I saw all my hopes and dreams and all of my deepest fears. Whatever crossed my mind was reflected in those deep brown eyes.

They suddenly became like a silver screen, playing my life before me. I remembered being very young, and catching my first glimpse of the stars blinking in the summer sky. Ever since, I've been fascinated by them. My mother would set my cradle out on the front porch at night while she crocheted and listened to my dad spin his homegrown philosophy. She would bundle me up so I wouldn't catch a chill when it got windy, and I would lie there and stare for hours at the stars flickering overhead. She told me that I used to try to climb out of my cradle and reach up to grab them.

I saw myself grow older and become an adult. I was standing on the front porch with my parents, now real old and grey-haired, and I was reaching out beyond my dad into the night sky. I wanted to touch the stars blinking overhead.

One of them suddenly streaked across the black sky, and stopped in front of the house, hovering by the windmill overhead. It set down on the road. Bright light flooded everything. Then the light came together into one beam and shined on our porch. My dad walked into the light pouring from the star. He entered the light, and I could see his silhouette waving to me.

He climbed aboard the star, and it began to pull away. As it turned to leave, I could see it was not a star at all, but a unicorn, and the light was pouring from its horn like a beacon. My dad was aboard his back, waving goodbye. I wanted to go with him, but my mom held me back, saying it was not my time to go.

He flew away, racing across the face of the moon, and then he was gone. I felt a sense of tremendous loss, as if something had been torn out of me, leaving a deep hole.

The next thing I knew I was back on the Flint Hills, being

blinded by the sun as it came out from behind a cloud. The unicorn was gone.

It took a second for me to recover from what had happened. When I did, I galloped over hill after hill, but he had disappeared. I hardly noticed that the wind had changed direction, and later I heard the twister had turned east and touched down over Missouri.

blackened by the sun, as it swung out from behind a cloud. The unicorn was green.

It took a second for me to focus. Suddenly there had been

21

A Cloud on the Wind

I rode back to Mr. Tucker's place in a daze. When I passed by the porch, he lifted his hat and motioned me over.

I climbed down and walked slowly over to him. For the longest time I sat on the rail and didn't say anything. Then I was finally able to speak.

"I . . . I saw him," I said, hanging my head.

"Yep." He nodded. "I know."

"I . . . I've got to go back and look for him," I said in a rush. "I had some kind of daydream or something. He took my dad, and they rode off into the sky. It was really strange."

He leaned forward in his rocking chair. "Thaddy," he said, "I have tell you somethin'. Now listen real careful." I looked up and he began. "You must not go out on them hills again."

"But . . . but why? I've got to find out where he took my dad."

" 'Cause you can't enter the unicorn's world, at least,

107

not yet. He lives on the other side, where folks can't go, at least while they're livin'.''

"But . . . I . . . have to see him," I argued. "And what about my dad? Why did he come for him?"

He looked past me into the field of wheat behind his cabin. "I reckon he'll come back," he said, "but you must wait, and you must be patient. What you saw was a vision. A vision of the future, and you can't live there yet."

"No," I said, standing up, "I can't wait. I'll ride out there tomorrow and find him. I will."

"Then I suspect you'll never see him again."

"I don't get it," I said, frustrated and confused.

He reached over and patted Cinderella, who had curled up at his feet. "Yer a little more than lucky, Thaddy," he said with a squint. "You got more than most folks ever get. You looked into his eyes and got a glimpse of the future. He has the power to let you see the past, present, and beyond. He did you a favor, I figger, sort of a reward fer believin', I guess."

"What do you mean?"

"When a person dies, either the wolf comes fer 'em, or the unicorn. If the wolf comes, then it ain't good news. He takes you to his den, and the wolves feast on yer bones." My eyes widened, and I listened more closely. "But if the unicorn comes," he continued, "then you ride off to the other place."

"But in church they say . . ."

"I ain't tellin' you no different," he said with a wave of his hand, "but the part they don't tell you is who comes to deliver you to yer destination. The unicorn and the wolf are the messengers."

"Then," I said, swallowing hard, "the unicorn only comes for you if you're . . ."

"Naw," he said with assurance, "he can come anytime he wants. In fact, if yer faith is strong enough, he'll come while yer still alive. And when you can talk him into comin' early, he has the power to grant whatever's in yer heart. That's his special brand of magic. If you catch him and hitch a ride aboard his back, yer dreams come true, at least while yer ridin'."

"And when you stop riding, then what?"

He leaned back and started rocking, slow and easy. He chuckled a little and looked me square in the eyes. "Well," he said, "I reckon you got two choices. You can either take that feelin' and make yer own dreams come true, or just forget all about it, and let it be a dream. The choice is yers, but one thing's fer sure: once you've ridden 'im, you'll never be the same again. Yer changed forever."

"Wait a minute," I said, "let me get this straight. He's the messenger that takes you after you die, depending on your destination, and he also makes your dreams come true. What's the connection?"

"Ain't goin' to the place of yer dreams after you die the grandest dream of all? I reckon there can't be a grander dream than that. And if he has the power to fulfill that dream, the little ones are easy."

"Are you sure about all this?" I asked, surprised by my own doubt.

"Only way to tell is to ride 'im." He stopped rocking and looked out at the wheat. "Heck, I don't think you've got much choice, now that you've seen 'im."

"But how does he make your dreams come true?" I wanted to know. "How does he know . . ."

"The dreams are already inside you. He just brings 'em out when you ride. Nobody knows how he does it; he just does. That's what makes 'im special."

"But how can you tell if he's come to take you away forever, or just to bring your everyday dreams out?"

"Well, if you ain't dyin', you got nothin' to worry about, 'cause he ain't come to take you away. And if you are dyin'," he added, "just be thankful it ain't the wolf come fer you."

"But the wolf came after me the other night."

"That weren't the wolf of death," he assured me.

"How can you tell?"

"The death wolf vanishes into thin air after he's been

killed by the unicorn. The unicorn killed that earth wolf just
to do you a favor. It was not yer time to die.''

"Good," I said with a sigh, " 'cause I ain't quite ready
yet. I've got things to do. But why didn't you tell me all
this before? I mean, all you told me was that there was a
magical beast come to feed on your wheat, and about there
being trouble on the road.''

"Didn't want to scare you off, I reckon, with all of the
death talk and all. But now that he's come fer you, and you
ain't dyin', he'll come again. You shouldn't be scared.''

"Yeah, I guess not.''

"But don't go into them hills. The unicorn has to meet
you in yer world. And yer world ends where the hills begin.
Folks have been lost out in them hills. Even with the best
of scouts, a person is hard to find out there. If you get
yerself lost out there lookin' fer him, then the wolf of death
might come fer you. It's fer you to wait and fer the unicorn
to come. And he *will* come.''

"When? I sure don't want to die to find out.''

"Naw, you don't have to. Tonight is a good night. The
moon is near full, so you'll be able to see. Tonight, when
the sky's full of stars and the moon has lit up the night,
come to the meadow and wait. He'll come to feed on the
wheat and walnuts.''

"But why *your* wheat, Mr. Tucker?'' I asked and
scratched my head. "Why is it so special?''

"Oh, it ain't the wheat that attracts 'im. It's what's in
the wheat.''

"Like what?''

He placed his hands gently on my shoulders, and looked
me straight in the eyes. "I grew it just fer him,'' he said,
"and he knows it. So he can't stay away, not from someone
who planted it special.''

"And the walnuts?''

"Why,'' he said, "everyone likes dessert.''

We both laughed, and then it was time for me to go. I
climbed aboard Petula, and then remembered something
else. "Oh,'' I asked, "should I bring anything?''

"Well," he said, and thought about it a little. "The legend says you need a virgin girl."

"I'll talk to my sister. Maybe she can help. Anything else?"

"Just yerself."

I rode home on a cloud of hope, knowing I would be back. I just hoped I could get my sister to come with me. If I couldn't convince her, then I figured the heck with it. After all, legends were meant to be broken, weren't they? Well, maybe not. But part of the reason unicorns were special was because they *were* . . . you know . . . legendary. I still had to give it a try, though, with or without my sister.

I knew that I had to go back to the meadow. The unicorn and Mr. Tucker had opened my eyes, and once your eyes are opened, they can't be closed without seeing the truth written on the insides of your eyelids. For every time I shut my eyes, there he was, galloping across my mind, as big and white as a cloud blowing across the Kansas sky. I just didn't know if I'd be able to catch a cloud and ride the wind.

22

Wheat with the Chaff

When I got back to the farm, Elmer was in his pen. I could only scratch my head and wonder how he beat me home.

I found Cathy and Bob in the hayloft. I knew I couldn't tell them about the unicorn coming for you at death, or the wolf. They would really think I was crazy. I had to keep that part to myself, but I still needed my sister.

When I got to the top of the ladder to the loft, I asked, "Hey, Sis, you a virgin?" She and Bob looked at me kind of funny, so I explained, "You know, a pure person."

They both seemed to like my explanation, because they heaved sighs of relief. They looked at each other and laughed so hard I thought they'd fall out of the loft. I couldn't see what was so darned funny.

Cathy finally caught her breath, and asked, "Why do you want to know?"

" 'Cause I need one to catch a critter."

"What kind of critter can you catch with a virgin?" Bob asked with a puzzled look on his face.

Cathy kicked him playfully in the leg. "A mythical one," she said.

"What?" he wanted to know.

"A . . . a unicorn," I said.

"Aw, go on, kid," he said, and waved his hat at me. "Go bother somebody else."

"I would, except . . ."

"Except what?" he asked, getting kind of annoyed.

"Except you're supposed to play the legend by the rules. Besides, I saw him today."

"Who?" Cathy asked.

"My unicorn. He was out on the Flint Hills."

"Thaddeus Williams," she scolded, "you know you're not supposed to go out there. You could get lost, and then the wolves . . ."

"Yeah, but I was chasing Elmer."

"Well," she said, rolling her eyes, "you didn't do a very good job of it. He came back by himself about a half hour ago, so I let him in his pen. If he gets out again . . ."

"Yeah, I know," I answered, and hung my head.

"Well, kid," Bob said, "it's been nice talkin' to you, but me and Cath . . ."

"Okay, I get the message," I said, looking at him, then I started down the ladder. When I reached the barn door, I said, "It sure would be a shame if Mom found out about the vampires in the loft."

"What's that supposed to mean?" Bob asked, sticking his head over the edge.

I turned around and threw up my hands. "It's just with all the neck-biting," I replied, "somebody could get hurt."

"All right, wise guy," Cathy said. Her face appeared alongside Bob's. "We'll go with you, just this once. But if we don't see your unicorn, then you can forget it. We're not going on any wild goose chases. Either we see it or we don't, and that's it."

"Cath!" Bob protested.

"Aw, give him a chance," she whispered.

"There aren't any such things as, as uni-corns," he said, wrinkling his brow.

"Then you have nothing to lose," she said. "We go once, and that's it." She elbowed him. "Besides," she added, "the fog is neat out at Tucker's place. It hangs pretty deep in that meadow."

"Okay, kid," Bob finally agreed. "You got yourself a deal. But unicorn or no unicorn, we go once and that's it. Got it?" He pointed his finger at me.

"Deal," I said, thrusting out my hand. "Meet me here tonight after dinner, when you first see the smoke from my dad's pipe on the porch."

That night at dinner Mom said something funny. She said she was glad that Cathy was saving herself for marriage, and she said it right in front of Bob.

"I'm . . . well . . . glad for you both," Mom said, looking at them and scooping mashed potatoes at the same time. It was her way of saying they were spending too much time in the loft.

"Yeah," Dad agreed. "Why, Jenny Parks and Bill Haskim are gettin' hitched next week, and I hear that Jenny's dad is dustin' off his shotgun just in case the Haskim boy changes his mind."

I was a little surprised at Mom and dad. They had never really brought up the subject of marriage before, at least not directly, and I didn't know how serious the subject really was with them. Of course, Mom always was a person to follow the rules, but in her own creative way, like when she convinced me to study so I wouldn't lose Petula; and Dad seemed lost in his own world of wheat farming. But when it came to some things, like love and marriage, they both were not to be messed with. They wanted a proposal if a young man was seriously necking with their daughter.

Bob choked on his roast beef. My dad had to slap him on the back a couple of times.

"Honestly!" Cathy said. "I can't believe you two."

"No," Mom insisted, with a wink at my dad. "We mean it. Don't we, Ari? We're glad you're not going to have a shotgun wedding. Besides, your dad's a pretty good shot with a . . .''

"Mom! Please."

"Well," Dad asked, "you *are* gettin' hitched, aren't you?"

"I'm so embarrassed!" Cathy said, and put her face in her hands for a moment. "How could you ask such a thing? You know we want to start college first."

"Ye . . . Yes, sir," Bob finally said, all red in the face. "We're plannin' on gettin' hitched, soon as we can afford it."

"Okay," Mom said, raising her hand. "We'll say no more about it, especially since you're . . ." She looked at Cathy.

"A virgin?" I asked.

"Thaddeus!" Cathy screamed.

Dad began to laugh, and Bob gave me a dirty look.

"Thaddeus," Mom whispered, "don't go sticking your ears in where they don't belong." She buttered a piece of bread. "This isn't something for you to be talking about."

"All I know," I said, putting down my fork, "is that Cathy said a virgin was a pure person, like a nun. From what I can figure out, purity goes away when you get married, and sometimes before, especially if you have children."

"Well, son," my dad said before anyone else could speak, "I reckon that's as good an explanation as I've heard. And besides"—he winked, pointing his fork at Mom—"I believe we've talked just about enough for one night. Now, let's take a fork to some of that apple pie before it gets too cold to eat."

Well, that just about put an end to dinner conversation that night, and none too soon, I reckon, because I was just getting ready to ask about the details of having children. That could wait awhile, but what couldn't wait was my eagerness to get back to unicorn hunting. Since I'd seen the mythical beast, I wouldn't give up until I rode him.

I knew that once aboard his back, you'd want to ride forever. At least that's what Mr. Tucker said, and I wanted to find out for myself. I didn't mind taking Cathy with me if that was the only way to catch him, but I wasn't too hot on Bob.

Sometimes you have to take the wheat with the chaff, and separate them later. I figured after I caught my mythical critter, I could separate myself from Bob and Cathy. I never even thought they might take a serious interest in the unicorn, let alone want to ride him.

What bothered me the most was that if the government came and sold off Mr. Tucker's wheat field, the magic might go with it, and the unicorn with the magic. And if he went away he might not ever come back, at least while I was still alive, and I sure didn't want to die to find out.

After dinner I went to my room and read something out of the mythology book. It seemed to sum up my situation, and went like this: "The heart of the believer flies on wings of hope, and sets down on the golden meadow to await the white steed with the single horn. The meadow becomes purified by the presence of the virgin. The steed appears and feasts on the wheat, and is enchanted by the virgin. He is drawn to her and is captured by her spell. She mounts the steed and rides into a dream that lies buried in her heart. And she is fulfilled.

"And once she has ridden, all who believe can ride, and their dreams become real. And once they have ridden, the dream does not cease, unless they stop believing. But do not let the steed be caught by those who cannot believe, for it will surely die, and the dream will cease forever, for nonbelievers are the killers of dreams."

23

How the Unicorn Lost Its Horn

That night, when the moon was bright and the smoke from my dad's pipe rose high on the porch, we met in the barn. Cathy and I rode double on Petula while Bob followed on Chester, his brown quarterhorse with a black mane and tail. I don't think Petula liked Chester much, though, especially since she'd got a good look at the unicorn.

When we reached Tucker's Grove, a lamp was on in the cabin. Mr. Tucker came out on the porch, stretching his suspenders with his hands. "Well, what do we have here?" he asked with a squint.

"This is Cathy, you remember her. She's my vir . . ."

"Thaddeus!" she said.

"My sister," I corrected.

"Hi," Cathy said, "we're out here to help catch . . ."

"I know," Mr. Tucker said. "Girl, you sure have grown some since I saw you last. Why, yer almost a woman."

"Not quite," I said. Cathy gave me a dirty look, and then introduced Bob.

"Bob is our protection," she said, "just in case a wolf or a wild horse comes out of the hills."

Bob didn't say anything, but tipped his cowboy hat instead. Cinderella came out of the front door. "Boy," Bob said at last. "That's a mighty pregnant dog you got there."

"She's been actin' funny lately," Mr. Tucker said. "I think she hears somethin' out there. I suggest you tie up yer horses and come out back."

While we went around to the back porch, Mr. Tucker turned off the lamp inside his cabin. The moon was almost full, so we could see pretty good, except when clouds wandered in front of it and blocked the light.

"We'll wait right here on the porch," Mr. Tucker said. "But when he comes, only Cathy is allowed to go out in the meadow and greet 'im."

"But . . ." Bob protested.

"Them are the rules," Mr. Tucker said sternly. "Either we hunt by the rules, or we don't hunt at all."

"Okay," Bob said sarcastically, and muttered to himself, "you old coot."

Mr. Tucker pretended not to hear. "Well, as long as we're waitin'," he said, "I'll tell you the story about how the unicorn lost its horn."

"Yeah," I said excitedly. "Tell us!"

Bob smirked, but Cathy thought it was a good idea. It was her look of encouragement, I thought, that really started Mr. Tucker on the story.

"It was a long time ago," he began, "in a land not far from here. It was known as the golden age. Folks lived a long time then, and there were unicorns on every continent. They were wild and free, and were said to have magical powers."

"Like what?" Cathy asked.

"Don't interrupt," I said, so she kept quiet for the rest of the story.

"The unicorn could take his horn," Mr. Tucker continued, "and dip it in a pool of bad water to purify it. Later, folks discovered that unicorns could be captured in the presence of pure young maidens. And once caught, they could be ridden. It's said that once aboard the back of this magnificent creature, the rider could see wonderful sights. The tip of the horn cast a brilliant light at night, and it would guide the way through dark places.

"Some said that the tip of the horn was like a sword and could cut through the veil of this world. And behind that veil lies another galaxy. They said that the unicorn could take you on a magic journey, to wherever yer heart wanted to travel, to the stars and beyond.

"Folks figgered that the horn was the source of all the unicorn's powers. So they began to capture 'em and take their horns, like elephant hunters takin' ivory tusks. By the time it was discovered that the horn by itself was nothin' without the unicorn, it was too late—all the unicorns had been destroyed.

"The critters that were left were called horses. But legend says there was some unicorns that were never captured, and they escaped to other parts of the universe. And once in awhile, if the desire is great enough, one returns to earth. It's our desire that brings 'em back. And if we capture one, we can ride again as in the golden age. They say at night when you look up, it's not shootin' stars that you see blazin' across the sky, but the light shinin' from the tip of a unicorn's horn as he travels across the universe."

It was silent for a very long time, and then Cinderella perked up her ears. Petula and Chester stirred a little at the hitching post.

"Here he is now," Mr. Tucker whispered. "I can feel 'im comin'. He's not far off."

We all sat motionless, listening intently for any sound in the meadow over the crickets. Mist had crept in from the hills, forming deep pockets of white fog over the wheat like low-lying clouds on a golden forest. The bright silver moon threw beams at the meadow, bursting through where the mist was thin. It looked like spotlights from the sky searching the meadow. Fireflies danced in patches of mist, like stardust scattered in a silver cloud.

Our eyes joined the moon in its search across the meadow, but the mist was growing thicker, and coming all the way to the back porch. The light from the moon grew fainter as mist engulfed the cabin. The silence was long and deep, like waiting for a rock to hit the bottom of a well.

Then we heard it. Faintly and far away at first, but then louder and closer—hoofbeats on the meadow.

Suddenly, from out of the mist, a mighty stallion raced across the meadow. Heavy hoofs pounded the ground, his huge body parting the wheat as he galloped by. We could only catch fleeting glimpses of him through the mist, and nobody was sure whether he had a horn.

He stopped on the far side of the meadow, and the crickets stopped singing. It was so silent that we could hear him breathing and pawing the ground. Then we heard the wheat rustle.

"He's eatin'," Mr. Tucker whispered.

Cathy slipped out from Bob's arms, and started for the meadow.

"Wait," Bob said, grabbing her arm. "If it's a wild stallion, he could be dangerous."

"And if you both go," Mr. Tucker said, "he'll surely run. Faith," he added half-aloud, "it's faith that conquers fear. Let her go alone."

"I have to know," Cathy said, turning to Bob, "whether this is for real. I have to see for myself. No matter how wild and incredible it sounds, I'll only know if I go out there."

My sister really surprised me that time. I didn't figure she was much interested, but I should have known her natural curiosity would make her go out on that meadow and prove it to herself.

Bob still didn't like the idea, but he finally let go of her arm. "Be careful, Cath," he said. "If anythin' happens I'm comin' out there. Understand?"

"Okay," she said, nodding. "Now wait here." She slipped off the porch and walked slowly into the mist.

"Infinity," I said before she disappeared. "I named him Infinity." Mr. Tucker and Bob looked at me funny. I couldn't explain why I had called him that; the name just came out.

"Infinity?" Bob asked, wrinkling his brow.

"I don't know," I shrugged, "it just seems to fit."

Cathy wasn't fifty feet away when she vanished completely into the mist. It seemed like an eternity passed, and then, suddenly, she screamed.

Bob and I bounded off the porch and raced out on the meadow. The stallion snorted and let out an ear-piercing cry. He began to circle the meadow, his hooves pounding the ground like rolling thunder. He stopped and reared up full length, his front legs pawing the air. I tried to get a look at his head, but it was bathed in mist. All I could tell was that he was huge and white, like the unicorn I had seen on the hills. I was sure it was him. He bounded across the meadow and disappeared into the hills.

By the time we got to Cathy, my heart was pounding with fear. She was lying on the ground near a stump that had been sliced off at ground level, and she was rubbing her ankle.

"I slipped on this wet stump," she said, looking up at us. "I guess I scared him off." She had a look of disappointment on her face.

"Was it . . . ?" I asked.

"I . . . I don't know," she answered. "I couldn't tell. He was standing in a patch of fog. I was walking up to him and I saw a light surrounding him, or maybe it was just the moon. It blinded me, and I slipped on this stump. I think I twisted my ankle."

"Well," I said, "we'll come back tomorrow."

"Did anyone see a horn?" she wanted to know. Me and Bob both shrugged.

"No," I replied, "but he was big and white, just like the one on the hills. I know he'll be back." I turned to Mr. Tucker, who had just caught up to us. "I know it was him," I said. "If Cathy hadn't slipped, we would've had him. We'll just have to come back tomorrow night, that's all, and . . ."

"That's what *you* think, Chipmunk," Bob said sarcastically. "Come on, Cath." He reached out his hand and pulled her up. "Are you all right?"

"Yeah," she said, favoring her right foot, "I just twisted it a little."

She didn't seem to be able to put weight on it, so Bob put his arm around her waist and she put her arm over his shoulder. "Now look what you've done with your stupid story," Bob said to Mr. Tucker. "Well, I've had enough of this unicorn stuff. We're goin' home. And we're not comin' back, you hear?" He looked over his shoulder at us. "Not tomorrow, not ever," he said. "It's just too dangerous."

"But, Cath," I pleaded, but she didn't answer. She was too busy trying to walk off her sprain. Bob finally picked her up and carried her the rest of the way to the horses. She managed to get aboard Chester, and sat behind Bob. Then she looked back at me.

"I just can't be sure," she said, shaking her head, "and I was so close."

"Well, Thaddy," Mr. Tucker said with his arm on my shoulder, "I think the boy could be right. I should've never let her come out here at night. Why, who knows what could've happened? I must be losin' my senses. I must be gettin' senile or somethin'."

"No, you ain't," I argued, "and I'm not letting you get off that easy. Not after what you've put me through, making me want him so bad and all. So none of this feeling sorry for yourself stuff. I'm coming back, even if I have to find another virgin." I threw my arm around his waist as best I could. "He was here," I said, "wasn't he?"

"Yep," he answered, "I reckon he was. And we just about had him too, didn't we?" He shook his head. "Without yer sister, though, we ain't got much of a chance of catchin' 'im."

"That's okay," I said, "I'll get someone else."

"Nope," he said, "can't chance it. Too dangerous."

We reached the back porch of his broken-down cabin. I looked at it like I was seeing it for the first time. It never really occurred to me before, but the roof was sagging, and it had some shingles missing. You could see moonlight pouring through the holes where the shingles had been.

The porch was sagging too, and the boards on it were buckled and brittle. He could have used some of the good walnut wood he gave to the school to rebuild his cabin, but the only thing that was walnut was his rocker. I figured it meant more to him to watch the kids playing ball in the playground next to his meadow than to have a fancy cabin.

"Well," I finally said as I turned to leave, "I'll think of something."

I mounted Petula and rode slowly away, shaking my head and muttering to myself all the while. I could hear Mr. Tucker begin to cough in the distance, and I swear he sounded worse than ever.

"Something," I said to myself. "I'll think of something."

24

East of Wichita

The next day I did chores in the morning, went to church, and went fishing in the afternoon. The stream ran just the other side of the road from the school, heading away from Tucker's Grove and my parents' farm. By the time it got to our place it was a couple of miles away. Then it circled back and just about went through town, skirting it on one side.

That was why the town was built out in east Kansas. The stream was a clean source of water for those who lived near its banks. Flint was as far as you could go before bumping into the hills, and the good land lay mostly to the west, but it was all most of us had.

As you might expect, the homesteaders who settled near the foothills got on the prairie wagon a little late, and had to settle what was left—the land butting up against the Flint Hills. The early arrivals took one look at the flint lying beneath the topsoil and kept moving west. That left the rest to the late arrivals, like my mom's folks. It was home just the same to a lot of sod-busting dirt farmers—that is, until the big winds came. The funny part about the wind was that it turned the windmills that supplied the prairie with water, but then it got to blowing too strong in the '30s, and blew away the reason the farmers came here in the first place: the good rich dirt. Some people's dreams blew away with it.

Our small town got hit pretty hard by the dust storms in '33. I hear that dust as thick as smoke was blowing clear to New York. It wiped a lot of folks out. Most of them packed everything they owned into overloaded and over-heated cars and headed west.

Only a few of us farmers stayed. The wind somehow forgot our addresses, so it didn't pick up all our dirt and send it east. It blew almost clean around Tucker's, and missed our farm, too. We only caught the tail end of the big winds, though others were completely destroyed.

By the time I got to the river, the sun was getting high in the cloudless blue sky, and that meant another ninety-degree day. The sun looked down on me and the Flint River like a giant egg yolk crackling in a cast iron skillet. The burning yellow light bounced off the slow-moving river like the sun off a mirror and almost blinded me a couple of times, so I decided to give my eyes a rest and cool off at the same time.

I slipped out of my clothes, hung my straw hat out of Petula's reach on a big oak tree branch, and dove in for a swim. I had my fishing pole resting over a low-lying limb with the line in the water, just in case I hadn't scared all the catfish away, but I knew I had when I jumped in.

I swam around for awhile and then I saw something on the bottom. It had drifted into my favorite fishing spot, and it caught my curiosity. It was too square to be an old tire, and too flat to be an engine.

Petula whinnied when I stuck my head underwater for a look-see, so I came back up and reassured her. "Don't worry, I ain't going nowhere. Just diving for sunken trea-sure."

I dove and tried to look around, but the water was too muddy to see anything. I groped around where I had seen

the dark object, and was finally able to get my hands on it.
I realized by the feel that it was an old radiator, maybe like
the one that blew up on my dad when he first came to
Kansas. It was all filled with water, so I couldn't manage
to lift it, but I found a small object lying next to it, and
brought it to the surface.

When I stuck my head out of the water, Petula was making
quite a stir, neighing real loud, and pulling hard on her
reins. "Easy, girl," I said, gasping for air, "I'm right
here."

Then I heard the laugh of my least favorite person. Billy
Johnson had gathered up my clothes and was sitting on his
old farm horse, a few feet from Petula.

"Guess you won't be needin' these," he said, waving
my clothes in the air. "Chipmunks don't need clothes. They
live in their nat'ral skin."

He turned and galloped away before I could say anything
except, "Hey, you Hampshire hog, come back here with
my clothes!" He didn't even turn around; he just kept riding,
laughing, and hollering all the way to the road.

I climbed out of the water, still holding the rusty object
in my hand. I wiped it off as best I could, and saw what I
had been looking for written on it: *Ford Motor Company*.

Luckily, Billy had been in such an all-fired hurry that he
forgot to steal my hat, so I rode back home wearing my
straw hat, holding the fishing pole in one hand and the
radiator cap in the other. I hadn't bothered to put a saddle
on Petula that day, and now I was glad for it, since I was
able to use her long bushy mane to cover up the parts of
me that usually didn't see the light of day.

When I passed the dairy, old man Greison gave me a
mighty funny look. I heard him say something to himself
about Lady Godiva but I couldn't quite make it out.

I raced into the barn and put Petula in her stall. My jacket
was behind the hay bales where I had stashed it the night
of the wolf, and now I put it on. The torn-out piece of
leather had been sewn back in. It didn't surprise me that
my mom had sewn it back together. It was her way of telling

me she knew what was going on without informing the whole world. But she never went into the barn, and where did she get the patch? Maybe Doc had found it inside the wolf and returned it. I would have to call him and find out.

The jacket, being a few sizes too big and all, covered all the necessary places. I stuffed the radiator cap in one of the pockets and went to the house.

Mom was on the side porch spinning her pottery wheel. Seeing me through the open window at the end of the hall, she stopped the wheel and stuck her head in the window. "The rest of your clothes were in the mail box," she said matter-of-factly. "Seems the postman couldn't get any letters in the box with all of your clothes stuffed in there. Said he saw that Johnson boy riding away pretty fast, grinning from ear to ear."

"He stole my clothes at the river," I said, standing there in my leather jacket.

"So I see," she said, pointing at me with a clay-filled hand. "Well, you'd better get cleaned up. Your dad could use some help bundling up that wheat he cut today."

"Oh," I said, turning towards the stairs, "thanks for patching up my jacket. But how'd it get out of the barn? You never go in there."

"I sent your father in after it," she replied, shaking her head. "Doc brought the missing piece over." She kneaded the clay in her hands. "Seems the sheriff dropped the wolf off," she went on, "so Doc could check it for rabies, and he found the piece of leather lying where the wolf had been."

"*Had* been?"

"That's the funny part," she said, shaking her head. "It seems the wolf just disappeared."

"Disappeared?" I asked in disbelief.

"Somebody must have run off with the carcass, I guess. Stole it right out of the lab. Heaven knows why. Somebody wanted the claws and teeth, I suppose, though Doc claims all of the windows and doors were locked from the inside, and only he and the bank have keys. He says it just vanished into thin air. I suspect he accidentally left a window open and forgot about it. Things don't just vanish into thin air.''

"Yeah," I agreed, thinking about what Mr. Tucker had said about the wolf of death disappearing. I didn't like it none. That may have been the wolf of death, and he might have been coming for me.

I turned and went to the stairs. When I got an arm on the rail, my mom said, "Thaddy, be careful when you go out riding at night. You could have been killed."

"But Mom, I . . ."

"And stay off those hills. Sheriff Johnson said at church this morning that Billy saw you riding out past the school the other day. He says you went out on the hills."

"You gonna believe a thief?" I asked, trying to defend myself.

"Don't make me ask Mr. Tucker," she said, staring at me down the hall, "because I know he'll tell me the truth."

"Then you believe him?" I asked excitedly. "About the unicorns and all?"

"I believe he saw what he could, but with his vision, it was probably a wild horse standing under a tree branch."

"Well," I said, "if I capture one, *then* will you believe?"

"I suppose," she said, smiling at last, "that seeing is believing. But don't go out on the hills anymore, okay?"

"Okay, I'll wait 'til he comes back to the meadow."

"And that's another thing," she said, shaking her head. "Your sister twisted her ankle out there, and . . ."

She never finished her sentence. Not wanting to hear any more, I had left.

When I got upstairs, I pulled the catch of the day from my jacket pocket. It was all rusty and pitted from the river, but you could still read *Ford Motor Company* on it pretty clear. I rubbed it off with a bath towel, and knew I'd be in trouble for that, but a lot of the rust came off, enough for me to use it for a Sunday night show-and-tell with my dad.

My plan was to present it to him. Maybe he'd remember how he and Mom had taken this broken-down farm east of Wichita and turned it into home. Maybe it would make him remember how hard we had fought the wind and time and progress to keep the farm. Maybe it would make him take one last stand, even if it turned out to be Little Big Horn.

I decided I was big enough to take some of the load off his heart now, just to keep the farm. I would work the land for him. I would bale the hay and separate the wheat from the chaff and somehow get it all loaded into the silo to dry out. Then we could stay a little longer, and maybe, just maybe, we could save the farm. It was worth one last try.

I thought about the unicorn I had named Infinity, and Cathy's sprained ankle. I figured even if I couldn't capture a unicorn, I could at least get another look at one. Maybe he'd even set the part of the legend about needing a virgin aside for once, considering the circumstances. Besides, I was too shy to ask any girl except Cathy if she met the qualifications needed to catch one. I figured she might think it was some kind of joke. And Mr. Tucker had said it was too dangerous. Anyhow, I first had a Dad to convince about staying right where we were.

25

Holding on to Paradise

Our old farm was almost as broken down as Mr. Tucker's cabin. I really didn't mind the leaks in our roof, since we still had enough pots and pans to catch all the rain, but my mom didn't like it one bit. She didn't like the warped boards on the front porch, or the missing slats in the picket fence much either. But it was home.

A couple of years back we had whitewashed the house and fence and painted the old wooden barn red, but those cold white Kansas winters worked like a potato peeler on the paint.

In '44, our grain silo had collapsed from old age. We had just about filled it up when it split its belly like an overripe watermelon, making such a racket you could hear it all the way from school. When I raced home on Petula, the old silo was sitting there with its sides all busted out and grain scattered all over the yard. It looked like it had snowed grain a foot deep between the house and the barn. My dad just stood there staring at the wheat spilled all over the yard. It took just about all our savings to rebuild it.

That event sort of marked the beginning of the end. The fact that the summer of '47 was to be our last summer on the farm had really started with the busted silo of '44. It just took the end awhile to catch up to us.

My dad sold the grain at a loss to the government. That was the first time we got wind of their taking our land, and taking Mr. Tucker's place if they could get it. I can still hear the government man's voice over the trucks they sent to haul away the grain. "Too bad!" he'd yelled over the engine noise. "This place'll probably have to be auctioned off."

So when Captain Wingate showed up at our place in '47, he was the third government man in three years to stop by the farm. This time, though, they knew we were finally on the ropes. We had held out about as long as we could, but with my dad's heart condition and the price of grain in the cellar, we wouldn't make enough to pay the taxes and buy more seed.

They were not going to let us wait any more on paying taxes. They told my dad they shouldn't have let Mr. Tucker get so far behind on his taxes, and they weren't going to let us go for another year. When they came to talk to Mr. Tucker that Sunday afternoon about having only two more weeks, it was just five miles down the road to our farm.

I was proud that Mom had not called them, that she had waited for them to come to us. I knew she had wanted to call. It was a tough decision for her, worrying all the time both about our going broke, and Dad's heart. But she was strong enough to bear up under the strain, stronger than that old silo had been, anyway.

She bore it all, mostly in silence, and waited for my dad to accept our fate. Sometimes dreams could come true with a lot of wishing and hoping, and sometimes they had to be changed. That was the biggest lesson of my life at eleven, that not all dreams could come true just by believing, no matter how hard you tried.

The one thing I'll never forget is the look on Wingate's face when he first arrived at our farm. He looked like a beast that had found his prey and was closing in for the kill.

It was on that same day I went fishing for the radiator cap. I had no idea that would be one of the longest days of my life, and one of the most painful.

I saw Wingate's car pull up, and snuck downstairs to watch him up close. When he started walking out to the field to meet my dad, I crawled over and hid under the steps, so I could listen to the conversation.

He stood out by the back fence, with his hands thrust deep in his khaki pants pockets, medals swinging on his chest in the warm afternoon breeze. My dad made him wait until he finished mowing a row, and then he shut off John Deere and walked slowly over to the fence.

"Afternoon, Mr. Williams," Wingate said politely.

My dad just nodded, as if to say, well what do you want, though we all knew why he had come.

"This used to be homestead land, I hear," Wingate said, trying to sound friendly, but anyone could see he was working on a point he was about to present. Dad still didn't say anything, so Wingate went on. "So you'll be returning it to the government with the forclosure."

"I worked this land pretty hard, Captain," my dad said at last, turning to look at the wheat field. "And if that darned silo hadn't broke in '44, I'd still be here, bum ticker or no bum ticker. Just you remember that, G-man. I didn't go without a fight. You tell them that in Washington. Unless you're fixin' to give us an extension on the taxes until we get that new silo filled up."

"My orders are to collect on the property, Mr. Williams," Wingate said, chewing on a wad of tobacco. He turned and spat in the dirt. "You got two weeks," he added, his voice suddenly turning cold, "same as Tucker. Then we'll have to take possession of this land."

"Two weeks!" my dad said in disbelief. "You said on the phone that we had 'til summer was out. And what's the army doing here anyway? Why'd they send *you* collecting on this land? Didn't want to get their three-piece suits dirty?"

"The brass in Washington changed their minds," he said with a sneer, "when they saw they could make one trip for the both of you. Saves time and money, since the corps is out here to convert old man Tucker's place.''

''Convert? To what?''

Wingate didn't answer at first. He turned, spat, and ignored the question. ''I have orders to take both these farms first of July,'' he finally said. ''I'll be back tonight with the papers. Just be ready to sign. 'Course if you don't believe me, we can get Washington on the phone.''

My dad was doubling up his fist and getting pretty red in the face. ''First you tell me end of summer!'' he shouted, ''then you say two weeks. Then you say you're coming back tonight. Well, make up your mind. Which is it?''

Wingate looked down at my dad's doubled-up fist and spat on the ground again. ''Papers got to be signed tonight,'' he said. ''I told you that on the phone. That is, unless you're planning to come up with the taxes in two weeks. They're already two years overdue, and we can't let you go on any longer. Even if you get stubborn like Tucker, and don't sign, we're gonna take this land anyway. Ain't nothing you can do to stop it. Signing the papers is just a formality. But if that's the way you want it . . .'' He turned and walked back toward his car.

''That's all it is to you wolves,'' my dad said to his back, ''one more thing to devour. You wait 'til a guy's bleedin' before you move in for the kill. Just like pickin' the weak ones out of the herd. I oughta stay right here and fight you anyway!'' Dad yelled, but Wingate just kept walking away. Dad turned and went back to his field.

When Wingate passed the porch I couldn't stop myself. I reached out and grabbed his leg. He dragged me along for a couple of feet, and then he broke free. He whirled around and kicked me square in the stomach with the toe of his shoe.

I doubled up in a ball, grabbing my belly. It felt like it was on fire. I couldn't breathe; he had knocked the wind out of me. I tried to call to my dad, but he never looked back at Wingate, so he hadn't seen any of it. I realized that Wingate had waited until my dad wasn't looking before he kicked me. I struggled on the ground, trying to catch my breath.

"Some mighty pesky horseflies around here," he said, looking down at me with a mean squint. "Sometimes you have to kick real hard to shake 'em off your shoes. If I was you, though, I'd do something about that horse of yours. I wouldn't stand behind her so close. She's liable to kick you so hard we'll have to take her away for being mean.

"I'll tell you, though," he went on, all the while chewing on his wad of tobacco, "if she kicked me that hard, I'd have her put away right now. She'd better not get loose, because I'd hate to see her picked up. A big old horse like that sure'd make a heap of glue."

He leaned over and spat on the ground next to my face. Then he turned and walked away. When he got to his car, he reached in and picked up the radio speaker. He must have known I was out of earshot, and I was at first, but then the wind picked up his voice and sent it straight to my ears.

"When the 'dozers come for Tucker," he said, "have them level the Williams farm too. Make it look like an accident. Like they got the wrong address by mistake."

He got in the car and sped off, leaving a cloud of dust that just about engulfed the house. I ran out and told my dad, but I don't think he believed me. He thought I just made up the story to keep the farm, and he didn't want to talk about it when he was riding John Deere; to him that was like talking in church—not allowed unless you were talking about the sermon.

I ran and told Mom, but you can just about figure what she said. "Thaddy, you've got to stop making up stories. You must have heard him wrong. They're coming tonight with the papers, that's all. Nobody's going to bulldoze anything."

I showed her my stomach, and Mom said I shouldn't stand behind Petula when she was eating. She probably hadn't seen me and went to kick at a horsefly, like she did sometimes when she couldn't swat them with her tail. I finally gave up on my story, and went to my room to think.

Mom looked at my stomach real good though, before she let me go, just to be sure I wasn't hurt too bad. I was just a little red around my belly button, so she let me go up to my room.

I lay on my bed and tried to think, but the same thing kept popping up in my mind. I had to stop Wingate. If he found a way to steal Petula and ship her off to the glue factory, I would never forgive myself.

I pulled the radiator cap out from my pocket, and began to rub the last of the rust off with a bathroom towel. I looked at the cap real hard. I had something to say to my dad before he came in from the field. I just hoped it would be enough.

In my mind I ran over the conversation between Wingate and my dad. Until that moment I'd had no idea we were in such immediate danger of losing the farm. I was almost ready to offer to sell Elmer, Becky and Petula, but I knew that wouldn't get us enough money to save the farm, so I didn't have to think about it too seriously. I hadn't even prepared myself to move come September—let alone July first. Heck, we wouldn't even get to stay for Independence Day, not that there was going to be much of a celebration.

It hit me even harder when I realized that if Dad signed the papers that night, we were all but gone. And if he didn't sign the papers, we'd still have to come up with the taxes in two weeks. But there was another way: if we sold the grain in the silo, and got the rest of the field harvested, we would probably have enough to pay the taxes. Dad always said that silo had enough grain in it to pay Uncle Sam, and give us just enough left over to last until Mom sold some pottery in October.

Maybe, just maybe, I could talk Dad into staying one more year; and then, who could tell? He'd always said we took it one season at a time. And one more season could mean a lot when you're trying to hold onto paradise. It was worth a try.

26

Long Goodbyes

I couldn't wait any longer to talk to my dad about staying on the farm. I decided not to bring up Wingate again, knowing it was a sore subject, but I could still reveal my plan. Maybe I should have waited until I saw pipe smoke rising from the porch to try to sell my story, but with the farm on the line, there just wasn't time.

I walked slowly out to the field, so it wouldn't look like I was too excited, and caught him about twenty rows deep in the wheat. He saw me coming and stopped the tractor so I could climb up on his lap.

He pushed my hat down on my head and put John Deere in gear. We rolled off slowly, moving through the waist-high wheat, the mower cutting the stalks and laying them down behind us.

After mowing, we would stack it in bundles all over the field. We couldn't afford a threshing machine, so we did that by hand when we got the bundles to the barn. We had an old wooden wagon that we hitched to the tractor for moving the bundles. Then we'd make bales out of the straw and load the silo from the side of the loft, using a bunch of pulleys to lift the grain, and slide it down a chute into the silo, since we didn't have an air blower for the grain in those days. We were a little behind in our techniques, but that was only because we were too poor to afford any modern machinery.

Well, Dad had the field about half mowed, and the silo was about half full of fresh grain. It had to dry out real good before we called the trucks to take it to market, so we could get a better price.

"Dad," I said, pulling the radiator cap from my overalls, "look what I found in the river."

I handed it to him, and he turned it over with his rough fingers. "Looks like an old radiator cap to me," he said with a puzzled expression. "Suppose I could use an extra for the pickup, though your Mom says it needs a transmission. You didn't find one of *those* in the river, did you?"

"Naw," I answered, "just this rusty old cap." I paused and asked, "Remember when you and Mom first came to Flint Hills, and your radiator blew up?"

"Yeah," he chuckled, "I reckon I do. Why, if that radiator hadn't blown, I might never have met your mother. Reckon I owe Henry Ford a favor."

I grabbed his sleeve, all stained with dirt and sweat. He had big sweat stains on his back too, since he never put an umbrella on the tractor. He preferred his straw hat for shade. "Do you remember," I asked, "telling me this was the promised land, and that once you find paradise you'd fight till your last breath to keep it?"

"You got one heck of a memory for a kid that don't like school," he said smiling.

"Well, the way I figure it, I'm ready to take over the running of the farm. I mean, you can tell me what to do, and I'll do it. No more fishing and goofing off. I can do the plowing, harvesting, and threshing, along with my other chores. Why, I'm almost eleven and a half."

He stopped the tractor and took it out of gear. He stared at the radiator cap and then motioned for me to get down. When I did, he got off and picked a couple of wheat straws, sticking one in his mouth and handing me the other. It still tasted as sweet as ever.

He just stood there gazing at the wheat field. I could see the look in his eyes; I knew the wheels in his head were turning sure as the windmill was spinning over the well. He looked back at the house, standing like an outpost on the edge of the world—but it was our world, and I figured we had a right to fight for it.

"Get up there in that tractor seat," he said at last, turning around, "and mow to the end of the row. See if you can get John Deere turned around without makin' too big a mess."

I jumped up in the tractor seat and fooled around with the gear shift. I couldn't quite work the clutch, but I finally got it in gear, and the tractor jerked forward, pulling me across the field. When I got to the end of the row, I made a turn so wide I could have circled St. Louis before coming back, but I got the tractor lined up and mowed down the next row. When I got to my dad, I couldn't get it out of gear, and I had to do another row. Well, three rows later I managed to pop it out of gear.

Dad walked up slowly. He had about the biggest grin you ever saw on his face. "Givin' up already?" he asked.

"Well," I said, "I thought we should get washed up for dinner."

"Yeah," he agreed, "I reckon we should."

I got down and began to rub my stomach where Wingate had kicked me. "Pull a muscle shifting gears?" he asked.

"Yeah," I replied, "but I'll be okay. It only hurts a little."

He shut off the tractor and we walked back to the house. The sun was getting pretty low in the sky, and it bathed the house in yellow. Great beams of light reflected off the windows, making the house look like it was filled to overflowing with sunshine, and was sending out sunbeams to the world.

The windmill caught a breeze and spun in our direction. The sun caught the blades, and a powerful circle of spinning light showered the field, blinding us for a second. The windmill looked as if the sun had perched atop a platform, like someone had made a spot for it to rest awhile, before it went on home.

The wind changed directions again, and the windmill spun away from us, taking its sunbeams with it. This time it poured sunshine over the house like a spotlight.

"Mind if I keep this for awhile?" my dad asked, showing me the rusty radiator cap in his hand. "I want to do some thinkin'."

"Thanks, Dad," I said, "for thinking it over."

"Least I can do for a man that don't drop the 'g' off of words," he said. "How do you manage it? I never could."

"Mom said she'd take Petula away if I didn't work on my English," I said. "She wants me to go to college someday."

"You do as she says," he agreed. "She's livin' in the future, while I'm still tryin' to hold onto the past."

"Does that mean we're not . . ."

"Didn't say that," he answered. "Sometimes you need a short farewell, and sometimes, when you're leavin' for good, you need a long goodbye. We can't keep the farm forever. But maybe we can drag it out a little before we say goodbye. It makes the memories sweeter."

We got to the house and I went to my room. I could smell my mom's cooking creeping up the stairs. Fried chicken, mashed potatoes and gravy, baked bread and canned peas. But there was another smell coming directly up the outside of the house into my window. I knew it was hot peach cobbler cooling on the windowsill from the peaches she had canned last year.

The big peach tree in the front yard supplied us with plenty of fruit, but Dad always said that Mom picked them too early, and the peaches should have stayed on the tree another week or so. Mom defended herself by saying that she would be darned if she would let the birds beat her to them. She sweetened them up with honey I gathered from the old beehive by the river, and I couldn't taste the difference, even if my dad could.

But I agreed with Dad about staying on the farm, even if it was only a week or two longer. It might make the goodbye sweeter.

27

Figuring Out Infinity

We didn't talk about Wingate and the papers at dinner, but I could tell that my dad wanted to talk to my mom alone, so I saddled up Petula and rode off to Tucker's place. Cathy was eating dinner at the Greisons', and my parents hoped there would be an engagement announcement to go with it. They must have had an early dinner, though, 'cause when I saddled up Petula I couldn't help hearing the sound of laughter in the loft.

On my way to Mr. Tucker's I got to thinking. If only I could get me a ride on that unicorn, then maybe my most urgent dream of saving the farm would come true. I put the idea of traveling to where the universe was born out of my mind for the time being; somehow, it seemed a lot less important than trying to borrow a little time. Survival seemed more important than traveling to the far reaches of the universe. That's the way it must have been for Mom and Dad most of the time, and it made me understand why they didn't have much time for daydreaming. It took about all they had just to keep us from going down for the third time.

The first time was Dad's heart attack, the second the busted silo, and now the third: Wingate had come to finish us off, and Mr. Tucker as well.

I passed a set of headlights on the way, but when I looked back I couldn't quite make out the plates. The car sure had a strange resemblance to the army car I had seen the day of the wolf. I was sure it was him.

I waited up with Mr. Tucker for the longest time, and asked him if he had a plan to hold off the 'dozers. He told me that the world had to do what it had to do, and that he was too busy helping me catch a myth to worry about it. "You catch that critter," he said with a glint in his eye, "and you won't care what happens. But if savin' the farm is what's in yer heart, then that's what the unicorn'll do."

I sure hoped he was right, because we stayed up a long time waiting for the unicorn to come. I told him about what had happened with Wingate, and he said that some people were just plain mean, and that the best revenge would be to make my dream come true. To tell the truth, I would have liked something more direct, like smashing his car or something.

"Whatever you do," Mr. Tucker said at one point, "don't let Wingate get ahold of that unicorn. He could make mighty big trouble if he did. His people would prob'ly think Infinity was some newfangled military weapon, like the Trojan Horse or somethin'. That is, if they didn't think he was a space alien. But you can be sure they'd try to take 'im apart to see what's inside. Even if they didn't, he'd die in captivity. He ain't meant to live in a cage. He has to be free, so he can come and go from this world to the next."

"He wouldn't let himself get caught," I insisted. "He's too strong and fast for that."

"Trouble is," Mr. Tucker said with a stone-cold expression, "once he's been caught by a virgin, then he's vulnerable. He'll only leave when he knows that whoever called him up is safe. So be careful."

"Don't worry," I assured him, "I ain't letting that Wingate near him. You can be sure of that."

"You figger out yet why you named 'im Infinity?"

"I know this sounds stupid," I answered, "but the name just came out of me, like a fish jumping out of a stream, and then it swam to the bottom and I haven't seen it since. It must have jumped too fast for me to get a good look at the reason."

"Don't worry none about it," he reassured me, "that fish'll jump again. Most likely when you ain't lookin'."

I told him about the poem I'd found in the mythology book and he said he knew about it, and that what I had read was only the first verse. He recited the next one, and it went like this:

VERSE 2

Once upon a unicorn
Your heart flies like the wind,
And if you let your feelings go
Your soul will soon begin
To soar and sing,
To laugh and shout,
And in a moment feel
That life was surely meant for this—
And only this is real

I asked him to recite another verse, but he started to cough, and said I would have to come back another time.

"One verse is enough to think about fer one night," he said through his coughing and wheezing. He sounded so bad that I didn't argue, especially since I wanted to hear all the verses, no matter how many there were.

"Maybe you should see Doc Yeager about that cough," I suggested.

"Nope," he said, "I don't reckon he can do much fer it. Seems whatever is livin' inside me is fixin' to use me fer its last meal. If these diseases had more sense, they'd try to make me last long as possible, so they wouldn't have to look fer another body to sponge off of. Don't worry yerself none, though. It ain't infectious, and I don't talk about it much. Town folks got enough to gossip about without addin' a dyin' old man to the list."

"But," I protested, "you said you were going to live a long time yet."

"I'll live long as I can," he explained, "but sometimes we get called home a little earlier than we planned."

"But . . . you have to ride the unicorn." I insisted. "With his magical powers, I bet he could heal you."

"Well, that's what they say. But I figger if I don't ride 'im in life, then I'll ride 'im on the other side. I want you to promise me somethin', though, if I don't make it."

"No," I said, "don't talk like that."

"If I don't make it, I want you to ride him fer me. Will you do that fer me, Thaddy? If you do that, then I'll have my dream fulfilled."

"I . . . I don't want you to die."

"Hey, now, even if I do go a little early, I promise I won't leave without sayin' goodbye."

I put my arms around him. I knew that people didn't live forever, even people we wanted to, but it hurt having to face it.

It was getting late and I had to leave. I pulled myself away from him, and said, "Guess he's not showing tonight."

"Oh, he'll be here," he said. "He just might be waitin' fer us to go to bed. He ain't used to the place yet, and he wants to be sure we really want 'im. That's why he's makin' us wait. But it won't be much longer, 'cause he knows we're runnin' outa time. He's just testin' us a little and seein' if we're really serious about catchin' 'im. But we are, aren't we, Thaddy?"

"You bet," I said with enthusiasm, "you bet we are! Hey," I went on, getting an idea, "can I sleep here on the porch?"

"Not without yer folks' consent," he answered. "They already think I'm an ol' crank, I expect, and I sure don't need any more enemies. Now you'd better get on home before it gets too late.''

"Yeah," I said, disappointed, "I suppose you're right."

I said my goodbyes, noticing that Cinderella couldn't get much more pregnant, and rode off down to the main road. I turned towards the school, where the commotion in the pasture had taken place the night before. Petula seemed to like the idea, so I tied her to the split rail fence and made my way through the mist toward the wheat in Tucker's pasture.

I lay down and looked up at the stars. So many stars and so many worlds, I thought. It sure seemed funny how it took a billion years to make an earth, and people only got a handful of years to contemplate the whole thing. Then something my dad had once said occurred to me. I had asked him why we have trouble thinking about forever and infinity, and all of those kinds of things.

"The human mind," he'd answered, drawing on his pipe, "has its limits. It can't stretch big enough to figger out infinity. It's baffled by things without fences around them. The heart, though, doesn't have fences. It can stretch big as the sky, if we don't let the old mind get too much in the way. Love is the heart's way of figurin' out infinity."

It was then that I knew why I had named the unicorn Infinity. The fish had jumped, and I got a good look at him. The name was painted right on his side.

Suddenly, a star shot across the night sky and disappeared over the Flint Hills. A few minutes later Petula stirred behind me, and it startled me out of my thoughts. I could hear heavy hoofbeats on the meadow, and then I saw a flash of white with a great horn on its forehead. It was him.

He raced across the meadow through the mist, then lowered his head and began to feed. I knew I couldn't come near him, not without a virgin girl.

"Now, wait right here," I said, standing up. "Don't move till I get back. Okay?"

I backed slowly away. When I was about halfway to Petula, I turned and ran. I stood on the fence, jumped up on her, and rode off as fast as I could toward home.

When I got there, I jumped down and ran into the barn. I climbed up the ladder just in time to stop Count Dracula in the middle of a big bite on the neck.

"Wait!" I yelled. "I need her pure, and with no teeth marks!" I was hoping Bob hadn't broke through Cathy's skin during previous attacks. I figured that if he had bitten into her, it would be all over. She would no longer be eligible to catch me a creature. My virgin would be lost forever.

"What are you talkin' about?" Bob said, unhappy to be interrupted.

"You've been trying to keep it from me," I said, "but I figured it out."

"Figured out what?" Cathy asked.

"How a girl loses her virginity."

They both looked at me kind of peculiar, and a little nervous-like.

"It's the bite on the neck, isn't it?" I accused them. "If he bites you on the neck and leaves teeth marks, then you're no longer a virgin. That's it, isn't it? That's what makes people different from animals. I mean, I know what horses and hogs do, but Mom said it was different with people, that there was something else that made it special. She said it was love, and when I asked her about those red marks Dad gave her on the neck, she said they were love bites.

"So that's it, I reckon," I said with satisfaction. "I put the love and the bites together and figured out why humans are different. Animals don't leave red marks on each other's necks." I beamed with pride, having discovered one of life's greatest secrets.

"Well, Thaddy," Cathy said with a laugh, "I guess you've figured it out, all right."

"Yeah, kid," Bob said, winking at my sister. "Now that you've finally got that figured out, you can get lost, okay?"

"But I need her as is, no marks."

"Get lost, kid. L–O–S–T. Lost!" Bob was getting mad.

"Okay," I said, "I'll go ride him myself." I started down the ladder. When I got to the bottom, Cathy hung her head over the edge.

"Wait, Thaddy!" she shouted. "You saw him?"

"Aw, what do you care?" I said. "All you care about is getting bit on the neck so you can become a woman. Well, the heck with you. I saw him first, so I'll just ride him myself."

I walked out of the barn without looking back, hoping my plan to roust them out had worked. As I climbed up on Petula, I heard Bob behind me.

"This better be good," he said, "or you're goin' to have a hole in more than your *hat*, Chipmunk."

I rode ahead on Petula. Cathy and Bob followed on Chester. When we got to Tucker's, we tied the horses to the fence and waited by the edge of the meadow.

It must have been an hour later when Bob finally said, "That's it. You had your chance."

"But he was here," I said, my hat in my hands. "I saw him."

"And I saw the man in the moon," Bob said. "Come on, Cath. Let's go."

Cathy didn't say a word; she just limped off on her sore ankle. When she got to Chester, she turned to me and said, "I'm sorry, Thaddy. But seeing is believing."

"No," I argued, "believing is seeing too! Sometimes you can't see until you believe."

I wanted to give her a big speech about how believing is seeing, but I was all choked up. I was pretty disappointed, and a little mad at my unicorn for not showing up. I took one last look at the meadow and stomped off. "Thanks a lot," I said. "Here I go all the way back home and bring you a virgin, and you don't even wait for me. Some kind of dream you are."

When I got home again, I noticed there was a car in the driveway, and I didn't like the look of the license plates.

28

Seein' Space Ships

Wingate was sitting at the kitchen table talking to my parents. Now I *really* didn't like the look of things. It was just a little too friendly for me. Dad must have cooled off too much from their talk earlier that afternoon. He had probably discussed it with Mom when I went to Tucker's. My mom wasn't the kind to take a wild gamble, but if Dad thought we could make it, with me helping out a lot more in the fields, she just might let him. It was my only chance.

Cathy could go off to college anyway, and stay with my mom's relatives in Wichita whether we stayed on the farm or not. My mom had made that clear long before the papers arrived, and my dad would never purposely stop Cathy from going to college.

I hoped that Mom had decided to let us stay. Seeing Wingate at the kitchen table, though, made me wonder. If he'd been in the living room, I would have felt better. That would have meant my folks were just being polite. All guests made it as far as the living room, except peddlers whom my dad headed off at the front door, but this guy had made

147

it to the kitchen. From my point of view, that was just like letting a wolf in the hen house. Mom had even served him a piece of her homemade peach cobbler. That wasn't a good sign, either.

The kitchen was, after all, a sacred place. Food belonged there. Sometimes life seemed to pass from room to room. Meals always belonged to the kitchen, work to the back porch, since it faced the wheat field, and philosophy to the front porch.

It was where time stood still and cares floated away with my dad's pipe smoke, and mom crocheted her feelings into an afghan or sweater. Her serious art was on the side of the house in the pottery shack. The front porch was not for being serious in the worldly sense; discussing daily problems was done in the living room.

Arguments were not allowed at the kitchen table, because they ruined the meal. So when I saw Captain Wingate in the kitchen that night, it sent out a signal that a deal was in the works, and it was on friendly terms.

When I walked through the side door, Mom said: "Thaddeus, you are a *very* late young man. Where have you been?"

I glared at Wingate. "Oh, just riding around," I said.

"Well," Mom said, "your sister came in an hour ago. She said you were out at Tucker's."

Wingate looked up quickly at this, and then went back to the plans laid out on the round oak table.

"Yeah," I replied, "I was looking for a wild . . . horse."

Wingate didn't look at me, but talked to my parents instead. "I heard from folks in town," he said, "that Mr. Tucker thinks he's got some kind of special animal out on his farm."

"Not really," I answered. "Folks are always exaggerating."

"And from what I hear," he continued, as if he hadn't heard me, "it's supposed to have a horn in the middle of its head." He raised his hand to his face to show me where the horn went. I didn't like the serious look on his face. Those thin lips and narrow nose spelled wickedness, especially with the BBs he had for eyes, and the way the brim of his hat hung over his face.

"Well," I said, a little steamed at his snooping around, "that's just a dumb old fairy tale. You don't believe in that stuff, do you?"

"But, Thaddy," Mom said, looking up from the papers, "I thought you said . . ."

"Naw," I said, waving my hand, "I just made that up so I could go out riding on the . . ."

"On the what?" she asked, her eyes suddenly getting big.

"Oh, the road by the school," I managed to reply. "And as for that critter with the horn, why, that's just an old story Mr. Tucker made up to get us kids to come back and visit. Everyone knows there ain't no such things as unicorns."

My mom gave me a funny look, while my dad never looked up from the papers that wanted his autograph. I knew Mom was shocked by my sudden change of belief, but I was trying to head off Wingate before he got too hot on the trail of my mythical beast.

"I wasn't thinking of unicorns," Wingate said, turning halfway around in his chair, and boring a hole in me with his bottomless eyes. "But if there's something alien out on those hills, then the folks back in Washington need to investigate."

My dad just shook his head. "Them folks in Washington are pretty clever," he said. "First, they send us a big shot who tries to act like a country boy with his down-home talk and chewin' tobacco, and now you think we got spaceships." He laughed and scratched his head. "I suppose now the government will have to take our land away so they can use it to trap Martians. What will they think of next?"

When Wingate didn't answer, I took the opportunity to put in my two cents' worth. "Yeah," I said, "why don't you just go away and leave us alone? We don't need you around here. We were doing just fine before you came, and we're doing just fine now. So why don't you take your chewing tobacco and go back to Washington where you belong?"

"Thaddeus Williams," Mom said, "apologize to the man." I didn't say anything. I didn't care if I got grounded for a month; I wasn't going to say I was sorry. I stomped off to the stairs.

"Thad . . ." Mom started to say, but Dad grabbed her arm.

"Seems the boy's a little upset," he interrupted, "about the move and all. That's what we're here discussin', I thought, so let's get down to business."

I could tell he was talking to Wingate, and it was serious enough to be discussed in the living room, but the coffee table in there wouldn't have been big enough to hold the plans.

My mom looked at me down the hallway, so I started up the stairs. When I got to the top, I walked to my room. Then I snuck back so I could lean my head over the rail and listen.

"Well," my dad said, "now, let me get this straight. If we sign, the farm's gone, and if we don't, we have to come up with the taxes in two weeks. Otherwise . . ."

"The farm's ours anyway," Wingate said smugly.

"Captain," my dad said after a long silence, "we're poor people here. Even the cattle ranchers are barely breakin' even. Someday we'll all be gone. We may not have modern equipment, but it's been our way of life."

I could hear him stand up and walk to the back door. "You see that land out there?" he asked. "It's not the best farmland, and it's filled with flint, most of it, but it's all most of us got in life. To you it's just a piece of real estate to be bought and sold. But you can't buy the feelin' that comes from farmin' a piece of land.

"Have you ever seen a piece of earth turned over with a plow, Captain, when it's fresh and damp and brown? It smells richer than a hot cup of coffee. You toss a bunch of seeds in there and cover them up with a blanket of dirt, and then nature covers them up with snow and they sleep all winter.

"In the spring, with a little sun and a little luck, the seeds come reachin' out of that soil like babes stretchin' their arms in the mornin'. And then they're baked until May, maybe June. Then you fire up the old tractor, hook up the harvester behind, and slice it off. You bundle it up like a pile of gold and separate the wheat from the chaff. And that's just what your people are doin' these days, separatin' the wheat from the chaff. Only you're takin' the chaff and leavin' the wheat. I hate to disappoint you, Captain, but I aim to stay right here and keep plowin' that soil.''

There was a long uneasy silence, and then Captain Wingate spoke. "I'm sorry, Mr. Williams. But unless someone comes up with the taxes in two weeks . . .''

"Well," Dad said, "maybe we're just like that old mare of Thaddy's. We may have outlived our usefulness in the fields, but there's still a place for us in this world. You tell them bureaucrats in Washington that farmers planted the seed for the American dream. That's all I got to say. Now, there's the door. Don't let it hit you on the way out.''

There was a long silence, and then my dad raised his voice. "Go on," he said, "get out of my house before I kick you in the stomach like you did my son! And if I ever hear about you layin' so much as a finger on him again, I'll kick you so hard you won't come down till you get to Washington!''

I heard Wingate gather his papers and walk to the door. "I don't know what that storytelling kid of yours said, Mr. Williams," he said menacingly, "but if I catch that horse of his out on the road, she's going to be made into glue. She can kick that kid of yours all she wants, but if she takes a kick at me, I'll have her shot. And in case that kid of yours forgets, those hills are government property. I don't want to catch him out there. That land's strictly off limits from now on, until I get an investigation team out here to see what's on those hills. You got that?''

"I oughta break your . . .'' my dad said angrily.

"Ari," Mom interrupted, raising her voice, "let him go.''

Wingate was outside by then, and I heard him say before he walked off, "Two weeks. You got two weeks and then you're gone!''

My dad went back and sat down. "Thaddy!" he shouted. "Come down here!" When I got to the kitchen, he motioned for me to sit down. "I ain't gonna repeat everythin'," he said straight out, " 'cause I know you've been listening on the stairs. But you stay off them hills, you hear? And if that G-man lays a boot or a hand on you again, you come and tell me, okay?"

"You mean, you believe me after all?" I asked, surprised.

"Can't say I do," he said, looking at my mom. "Can't say I don't. But we got two weeks to get that wheat harvested and that silo filled up. I reckon if I can prove we got some grain in that silo, we can stay one more year. I'll pay the taxes all right, and make him count it grain by grain."

"Can we do that?" I asked. "I mean, pay with grain?"

"Don't know, Thaddy," he said, looking me straight in the eye, "but it's worth a try, and right now it's about the only chance we got. Besides, if worst comes to worst, we'll have the trucks come and take it to market. Even if the grain ain't dried out, we'll get somethin' for it, enough to pay the taxes, I hope. But it'll be close. Now, get some sleep, and you and Cathy be in that field at sunrise tomorrow. We got work to do."

He looked around. "Where is that sister of yours, anyway? Flattenin' out the hay in the loft again? Well, never mind. You be in the field first thing tomorrow. Now get some sleep. We got a big day comin' up."

I slugged him playfully in the arm. "You got it," I said with an ear-to-ear smile. "We'll show 'em." I turned to my mom. "Thanks," I said, "for whatever you said."

"Just stay off those hills," she answered, shaking her head.

"He won't have much time for ridin' by the time we get through in the fields," Dad said.

I walked off to my room, but before my feet hit the stairs, I turned around and came back. "Dad," I asked, "are they really hunting space ships from Mars?"

"I heard on the radio the other day," he answered, "that Washington's got some new department for investigatin' such things. Must be lookin' for another way to spend tax-payers' money, I guess.''

I walked quietly off to my room, got undressed and climbed under the covers. Then I leaned over and pulled the mythology book out from under the bed. The drawing of the unicorn paled in comparison to Infinity.

I closed the book and held it over my chest, wondering how I was going to be able to work all day in the fields and have enough energy to chase a unicorn at night. But when you're eleven, energy is no obstacle. Besides, since I had seen Infinity, wild horses couldn't drag me away from him, though I knew that I'd better not chase him out on the hills again. I would have to draw him in. I'd done it once; I just hoped I could do it again. Because I wouldn't give up until I had captured him.

I fell asleep with my arms around the book, counting funny critters with horns jumping over a fence.

29

The Far Side of Forever

I awoke to the sound of hoofbeats in the field between Tucker's place and our barn, went to the window, and looked out. The old owl hooted from the oak tree. The visibility wasn't very good, with dark clouds covering the moon, but I knew those hoofbeats.

I started to get dressed, but after putting on one boot, I stopped myself, walked back to the window and looked out across the field.

"No," I said. "I'm not coming out tonight. I'm tired of your stupid game. This time you'll have to wait for *me*. Besides, I've got a farm to save. So you can just go away."

Still half dressed, I took off the boot and got back into bed, pulling up the covers. I had to get up early the next day, and couldn't go chasing after some beast that wasn't supposed to exist—but he did exist, and the more I tried to push the vision of him out of my mind, the stronger it became.

The owl hooted again, calling me to the window. I put the pillow over my head to muffle his cry. He stopped, but the pillow stayed over my head just in case. He hooted again, only much louder. I looked out from under the pillow. The owl had perched in my open window, and was hooting up a storm. Pulling the pillow off, I looked at him.

"All right," I complained, "I'll go. I'll go, but stop that racket or you'll wake up my parents."

He gave me one last look and one last hoot, and flew off toward the barn. I went to the window and watched him disappear into the night. Not much could be seen out by Tucker's except the faint glow of lights in the distance. There weren't any other houses in that direction. It could have been one of the big trucks on the highway five miles away, but I couldn't be sure.

Suddenly a distant beam searched the sky, as if looking for something in the heavens. It was coming from the field towards Tucker's.

Putting the rest of my clothes back on, I lowered myself down the rope tied to the eaves outside my room. I had tied it there in case that strange critter appeared and I wanted to leave in a hurry. The hoofbeats were getting farther away. I ran toward the fence between our farm and Tucker's trying to catch up before they disappeared completely.

I ran past the barn to the field. But the hoofbeats were gone, so I stood on top of the fence. There, outlined faintly against the midnight-blue sky, I saw the silhouette of a beast with a horn, standing on top of the highest hill.

The clouds had parted for a second, and the bright moonbeams poured directly on him. He reared up on his hind legs and pawed the air, giving a powerful cry like a wild stallion.

The moon disappeared again behind dark clouds. I started to turn away, knowing I could never catch him on foot. All of a sudden a brilliant flash of white light beamed out of the tip of his horn and pierced the sky, tearing it open like a bolt of lightning in a thunderstorm.

There was another sky beyond, as if our universe lay on top of us like a blanket, and on top of it lay another universe, with its own set of stars, suns and planets.

I could see three suns, giving off amber, green and blue

light. There were a dozen colors of planets visible in a dark
sky, like shining crystal spheres against black velvet, and
there were stars flashing beyond the spheres like diamonds
sewn into a royal robe. Light danced everywhere in the sky,
shooting rainbow-colored beams between the planets.
Faintly in the distance I could hear a faraway sound, as if
a country band was playing, but I couldn't make out the
tune.

It was altogether unbelievable, as if another universe was
lying just beyond ours, only we could never see it because
we couldn't penetrate the blanket over our own universe.
Yet Infinity seemed to tear right through it. He brought the
blinding white light from the tip of his horn into a single
powerful beam and started to scan the sky. He focused on
a distant star and the beam began to vibrate, shaking the
ground at my feet like an earthquake. His beam remained
fixed on that star; a star so far away that it seemed on the
far side of forever.

He turned and shined his beam directly on me. The light
was brilliant, and I had to hold my hands over my eyes to
keep from being blinded by the flash. I stood there, shaking
a little with fear, bathed in the light, but unable to take my
hands away from my eyes for fear of going blind.

A strange sensation came over me, as if all my cares
were dissolving and floating away, like mist lifting from a
meadow. I felt very light, as if I could just about float away
if I wanted to. I only felt it for a moment, while the light
was on me, but I wanted it to last forever.

And then, as suddenly as it had come, the light stopped.
I took my hands off my face and slowly opened my eyes.
Infinity was gone. I stood in a daze, not knowing exactly
what to do. The clouds had returned, covering the moon
completely. The sky, once split wide at the seams, was
mended together again, as though it had never been torn in
the first place.

I shook my head, trying to figure out if what I'd seen
had really happened, or if I'd just imagined the whole thing.
I couldn't decide, so I went back to the house, still spinning

from the experience. When I got there, my mom and sister were leaning out of my window.

"Thaddy," my sister said, "what was that great flash of light?"

"Oh," I said, looking at my mom, "I don't know. I went out to see, and there was nothing there. Must have been some big truck on the road."

"Funny," she replied, "we sure didn't see one pass by the house."

"Must have turned around," I answered.

"Yeah," Cathy said, "must have turned around." I could see that she didn't believe me for a minute. She knew that something was up, because I couldn't wipe the grin off my face. It had crept up when I wasn't looking, and had taken over my whole face. I don't even know for sure what caused it, except that the light pouring out of Infinity's horn had wiped the troubles out of my mind, just like a clean eraser on a chalk-filled blackboard.

I just couldn't find a way to wipe that dumb happy look off my face, though I really didn't try too hard. My mom knew that it wasn't moonshine. That would come six years later and give me a headache that felt like wolves biting on my brain.

"Thaddy," she said at last, leaning out of my bedroom window, "you've been smoking one of your father's corn-cob pipes again."

"Naw," I said with a wave and a laugh, "that stuff makes me sick."

"Well," she said sternly, "you'd better get some sleep. You and your sister have got a big day tomorrow, and I don't want you falling asleep on that tractor seat, you hear?"

"Yeah," I said, losing my smile a little, but getting it back when I thought about riding John Deere all by myself. "I hear you, all right. I'm coming right up."

"And use the door, Tarzan," she said, pulling my rope back up to the window.

On the way upstairs I was able to get some thoughts tied around the reasons for the grin. I had seen Cathy in the window on my way back to the house, and figured I didn't need her anymore, since my unicorn had come. Cathy's presence in the window had been enough, I reckoned, to catch a unicorn, and I knew I could get him to come now.

I'd go to that meadow tomorrow night and wait, and this time I wouldn't run away. I'd wait until the Kansas dust turned to smoke if I had to, but I wouldn't leave until I'd caught and ridden him. There wasn't going to be any turning back next time—I'd sit by the side of that meadow until dawn if necessary. There was no power on earth that could keep me from him.

I passed Cathy on the way to my room, and she grabbed my arm in the hallway. "Okay," she whispered, "what's the big secret?"

I turned and smiled. "I already told you," I teased. "Some big truck got turned around on the highway."

"Come on," she pleaded. "I won't tell a soul. Was it him? Was it Infinity?"

"You don't believe in that stuff, do you?" I asked, wrinkling my brow.

"Look, Thaddy," she said, folding her arms across her chest, "maybe I was wrong. Maybe there really is something out on those hills with a horn on its head. I did see some kind of horse at Tucker's, but that darned fog was so thick I couldn't tell if he had a horn. But he could have had one, I guess."

"You mean you'd believe even if there weren't some scientific explanation for it?" I asked, walking into my room.

"Science doesn't know all the answers," she admitted, following me inside. "There are still some things that can't be explained."

"There may be some hope for you yet," I replied, hitting her gently on the arm.

"Just tell me," she coaxed, looking out of my window towards Tucker's Grove. "Was it him?" When I didn't answer she added, "You know, I did see some kind of light just before I tripped, and . . . Who knows, maybe that Captain Wingate is right. It could be a space ship or something."

"Wingate don't know nothing," I said with anger. "He's just trying to get us off this farm."

"Well," she replied, turning away from the window, "If you still need a virgin . . ." She walked over and stood in the doorway. "I'm still available."

"Thanks," I said, "but I don't think I need one anymore. I'll keep you in mind, though, just in case."

"Good night," she said, closing the door.

"I'll let you know," I said to the closed door. "I'll let you know."

As I lay in bed, my heart was on the back of that great white beast, my feet on the edge of the planet Earth, and my head in the silver clouds.

"Infinity," I said, "I'll ride you through that hole in the sky, to where that far-off star is. That's where I want to go. And you'll take me there."

I fell asleep repeating his name, and didn't wake again until a bright warm beam poured into my window, and bathed my bed in sunlight.

30

Crazy With Happiness

It was very hot the next day, without a breeze to cool things off or a cloud in the sky to block the sun. When it got that way, the old tractor sometimes got a little overheated, on account of its nose sticking out to the world, and a small leak in its radiator. So our big plans to spend the whole day harvesting were spoiled, and we knocked off about noon to let John Deere cool off. We decided to harvest again in the late afternoon.

It was a good thing we stopped, Mom said, because we could get sunstroke in that hundred-degree heat. Even though I loved riding on that tractor seat almost as much as Dad did, in this case I had to agree. I was beginning to feel a little faint behind the wheel, and I was soaked with sweat, even though I wasn't wearing anything but my cut-offs.

There was plenty of work to do in the barn, though, once we hauled some cut wheat in there. Dad and I threshed for a while, and then piled the grain on one side and the straw on the other. Usually, Dad would take a length of wire and bale straw, but we needed to get that silo filled up, so we concentrated our efforts on hoisting the grain up to the loft and sliding it down the chute into the silo.

Cathy got a reprieve, since Mom wanted her to take a look at the radiator on John Deere. Dad got a little mad at that, saying if we didn't get the grain loaded, there wouldn't be any use for the tractor except using it to move to Wichita. I think he suspected Mom and Cathy were in cahoots, and really wanted to move right away, instead of holding on for one more year. What he didn't know was that they had made some secret plans involving the tractor, which Cathy had taken over to the Greisons', since they still had some spare parts behind their barn.

They came back after lunch, Cathy on the tractor and Mom and Bob in the pickup. When Cathy came driving into the barn, with grease up to her elbows and more smeared on her cheeks, Dad got a funny look on his face. I think it must have been on account of that big pulley hooked up to the front of the tractor.

"About time you got here," Dad said, a little perturbed. "And what have you done to John Deere?" He pointed his pitchfork at the pulley.

Cathy just grinned real wide. "This is our new labor-saving device," she said, swelling with pride. Bob climbed out of the pickup. Mom had already gone to the house.

"Why, Mr. Williams," Bob said, wiping his forehead with his shirt sleeve, "she's gone and hooked up a grain loader for you."

"How's that?" Dad asked, a little skeptical, and still pointing the sharp end of the pitchfork at the pulley.

"Quit pointing that thing," Cathy said, "before you stab somebody." She wiped her hands on her blue jeans. "Now, listen for once, will you, and see what we've got here."

"Yeah, Dad," I agreed, "let's see how it works."

"Well . . ." Dad finally consented, and put down his pitchfork. "All right, but this better be good. Even if Bob here helps us, we're barely goin' to get that field harvested before time runs out on us."

Cathy smiled at me. We both knew this was Dad's way

of asking for help, since he would never come right out and ask directly; it was beneath his dignity to ask outsiders for charity. He was a farmer, and farmers like to pay for what they get. Handouts were for people who couldn't work, and as long as someone could put one leg in front of the other, he could still work.

Cathy took a wide rubber fan belt from behind some hay bales. She had made it from tractor tire inner tubes. She and Bob spent about ten minutes hooking up the old hand-cranked system to the front pulley on the tractor. She got behind the steering wheel and waited for Bob to make the final hookup at the top and attach the grain buckets to the system. He gave an arm signal from the loft and she fired up John Deere.

The pulley didn't move.

"Well," Dad said, picking up his pitchfork, "nice try, but I've got to get back to work. So if you'll just shut off that contraption and . . ."

Cathy pulled a lever and put the machine in first gear. The pulley began to turn. Dad got quiet in a hurry. Cathy had it rigged up so that when she pulled the lever she had added and put the tractor in gear, the pulley rotated and moved the grain buckets up to the hole in the loft, but the tractor stayed where it was.

It was the darndest thing you ever saw. The buckets came down and passed into the wooden box we had filled with grain, and came out the other side filled up, with just a little helping hand. The buckets lifted up, and when they got to the loft, Bob dumped them into the silo chute, sending the empty buckets back down to the grain box for a refill.

The look on my dad's face was just about enough to stop the wind from blowing. The industrial revolution had come to our farm when John Deere first arrived, but this was something else. The diesel-powered grain elevator had arrived, and it was pretty hard to resist, even for my dad.

"Well, don't just stand there gawkin'," Dad said to me with a stern look, "start shovelin'." But his expression couldn't hide his happiness and surprise. For the first time in a long time, a genuine smile came over his face. It made all of us happy to see it.

That afternoon was abuzz with excitement. Working together, we just about got the whole barn cleared of cut wheat. The tractor didn't overheat anymore, since Cathy had patched the radiator at the Greisons', but that didn't stop it from running out of fuel. We all had a good laugh when it sputtered to a stop, and called it quits for the day.

We went back to the house pretty hot and tired, but with the good feeling that only hard work can bring. Cathy put her arm around Dad. "I'm just using the tractor until I get the pulleys hooked up to the windmill," she said. "That will be a lot more efficient. We'll let the wind do the work next week. I just wanted to try it out first on John Deere."

My dad slipped his arm around Cathy's waist, and slapped Bob on the back with his other hand. "If that don't beat all," he said. "Who would have ever thought—except for you, that is—that progress would help us stay on the farm? He nodded to Cathy. "Now, come September, you go off to college and find some more ways to help us keep this place."

"She ain't through yet, Ari," Bob said. "I . . . I mean, Mr. Williams. She's fixin' to make you a threshin' machine like the big farms got, only on a smaller scale. But in the meantime, we're fixin' to hook up a headlight to that old tractor so you can harvest at night. Be a lot cooler then, you know."

"At night?" Dad asked with disbelief.

"Yeah, Dad," Cathy said, pushing her hair out of her face. "Bob gave me the idea. He says all the big farms out west are doing it."

"Is that right?" Dad asked, stopping by the well for a drink.

"Yes sir, Mr. Williams," Bob assured him. "All them big farms do it. And like I said, it's a heck of a lot cooler at night, so you won't overheat and get sunstroke."

"Well, I'll be," Dad said, shaking his head. He took off his straw hat and dipped it in the cool well water. Then he poured it over his head. "What will they think of next?"

"My folks said I could help you get your field harvested," Bob added. "That is, if you'll let me, Mr. Williams."

"Son," Dad said, dipping his hat in the water again, "I reckon you can call me Ari if you want to. Heck, you can call me Ari Throttle if you want; everybody else in this town does. Just be here tomorrow to help with the harvest. I won't even ask no more nosy questions about your intentions with my daughter. How's that?"

"Dad!" Cathy protested.

"Deal," Bob said, and reached for my Dad's hand.

Dad looked at his hat filled with water and did something I've seen him do only a couple of times: he got crazy with fun. He looked at the water spilling slowly through his straw hat, and then threw the water at Bob, splashing him square in the face.

All of a sudden, an epidemic of happiness and fun broke out all over. Every darned one of us was scooping water and throwing it on whoever he could catch. Mom even came out of the house and joined in the celebration, cooking apron and all.

Elmer got so excited watching us that he didn't even bother to burrow out of his pen, he just found a loose board and broke right on through the fence. By the time he joined us, the dirt around the well had turned into a mud hole.

We got even crazier trying to catch Elmer, chasing him around the yard and grabbing hold wherever we could, but catching a muddy pig is about as easy as catching a Texas twister.

Well, after about an hour of wallowing in the mud and laughing till our sides nearly split, we pulled ourselves together and headed for the horse trough to get cleaned up for supper.

I finally caught Elmer by offering him a green peach that I pulled off the tree. I put him away and fixed the fence.

We laughed and joked all through dinner, and were just about as happy as folks could be. Afterwards, Mom and Dad took to the porch to relax, Bob and Cathy ran off in his pickup to count stars somewhere, and I got an itch to go unicorn hunting. I figured that with all of Cathy's new inventions, we could get the silo loaded and stay on a little longer. That meant I could go chase a funny horse across the meadow without anything bothering me.

I told Becky and Petula that we had saved the farm, and everything was fine again. I didn't bother to tell Elmer; I figured he already knew. I looked at the doghouse beside the barn I had never torn down and thought about Cinderella.

"I want me a big old black Lab pup," I told Becky, "with a white spot on his chest. We can go fishing together, just like we used to before Lancelot got killed; and all of us can live happily ever after, just like in fairy tales."

I knew that sometimes fairy tales and life collide. I just hoped my life zigged when the bad news zagged. I knew life didn't stay perfect forever, and it made me want to hold onto it that much harder for as long as I could. I just hoped it would be long enough.

31

Cowgirl Princess

As I galloped down the road that night, there was a slight chill in the air, and a cold wind began to blow off the hills. On the way to the meadow, I passed Cathy and Bob parked on the side of the road. They were in Bob's pickup truck. I couldn't tell what they were doing in the front seat, but the windshield was sure steamed up.

I really didn't want to, but I decided to give Cathy one last chance, so I turned around and rode back. I got off Petula and left her to graze, then walked to the passenger-side door. I tapped on the window, and there was a lot of scuffling inside.

My sister rolled down her window a little.

"Okay," she asked, "what is it?"

"I'm giving you one last chance," I answered, "while you're still available."

She laughed and said, "The way you tell it, you'd think I was the last virgin in Kansas."

I looked at her neck as best I could and as far as I could tell, she didn't have any teeth marks on her. "If you're still interested,'' I said, "you know where I'll be.'' I tipped my hat like I was saying goodbye to a stranger. She didn't answer, but slowly rolled the window back up until it was shut.

I walked around to the back of the truck and broke up the beginning of a love affair between Petula and some wild grazing grass.

As I rode to the meadow, I didn't see a light in Mr. Tucker's cabin, so I decided not to disturb him. I waited as before, certain that I'd have a visit from my dream horse.

I didn't have long to wait. Pretty soon, fast, heavy hoofbeats echoed across the meadow. A flash of white raced through the mist and stopped.

He bent his large head down to feed on the wheat, and I couldn't wait any longer. I stood and walked slowly towards him. When I got some twenty yards away, he raised his head and looked at me. Those piercing brown eyes went right through me. I stepped closer.

He stirred and backed slowly away. I ran for him, but he turned and disappeared into the mist. His hoofbeats stopped nearby, and he began to graze.

I stalked him, but just when I got close, he moved away again. I did this over and over, but I couldn't get close enough to do anything.

Then I lost my patience. I stomped back towards the road. When I was almost there, I turned with my hands on my hips and shouted: "Look, I came here and waited for you and you didn't even give me a chance! Well, I've got news for you. I'm a virgin too. See!'' I opened the collar of my shirt to show my skin. "Never been bit on the neck in my life! Well, if I'm not pure enough, then the heck with you! I don't need you if you're going to act this way. I can live without you, you hear? So go away. Just go away. I don't need you!''

I turned and stomped off. When I got to the fence, Petula stirred and pulled on her reins. I heard hoofbeats behind me, and they were getting closer.

I whirled around and there he was, ten feet away. I tried to talk, but couldn't say a word. I took a step toward him, and he backed up a little. He looked over my shoulder at something behind me. I turned my head around and there Cathy was, and from what I could tell, there was not a single tooth mark on her.

"Thaddeus," she said, brushing a strand of hair from her face, "you know the legend. I must approach him first."

"Yeah," I finally said, "I suppose you're right. But where's . . ."

"I made him wait back at the truck," she said with a grin. "Some things need to be experienced alone."

She walked past me, still limping slightly. Somehow, she looked different, and I saw her as never before. Her features were the same, but that night in her cowboy shirt, blue jeans, and boots, she looked like someone else. I'd never really noticed it, but she was beautiful.

Her long blond hair streamed from under her cowboy hat, and her face glowed with excitement. I could tell Infinity had made a big impression on her. The legend said the presence of a virgin would tame the wild beast, that he would be drawn to her purity and unable to escape. But she seemed just as entranced by the sight of him, by his snowy white coat and ivory horn, so that they were captured by each other. It was like a maiden meeting her handsome prince for the first time, and with her slender figure and long legs, she looked like a cowgirl princess in a western fairy tale. She was not just my sister anymore. She was a woman, and from that moment on, I'd never look at her the same way again.

When she reached Infinity, she held out her hand as if to have it kissed. He lifted his head and brushed her hand with his nose. Then he stirred a little and shied away, pawing the ground and gently neighing. Just when it looked like Cathy was going to stroke his head, he seemed to get anxious and pull away. Then he'd come back and get close to her again. This happened a couple of times, and then she reached up to touch his horn.

Suddenly, a car started not more than a hundred feet away. Headlights flashed on, and Infinity bolted for the trees. He was gone in an instant, disappearing into the mist without a trace.

Cathy and I ran back to the road, but the car was pulling off past the school. I couldn't make out what the license plate said, but those tail lights sure looked familiar.

"Wingate," I said nervously. "Do you think he saw anything?"

"I hope not," she replied. "We're having enough trouble catching Infinity as it is. If anyone else shows up, I don't know. I just don't think he'll stay." She looked me squarely in the eyes. "I was *this* close," she said, holding her hands a few inches apart in front of her face. "I almost had him. I could feel his whiskers brushing my hand. And those eyes . . ."

"Did you see that horn?" I asked. "It must have been two feet long."

"It was ivory," she said. "I'm sure of it. He's a big one, Thaddy. Why, he's even bigger than Petula."

I looked over at Petula. "Just a little," I said. "Just a little bigger, old girl." I reached over and hugged Petula's head. She whinnied in a friendly way, and licked me on the neck. "That was too close for comfort," I said. "We've got to ride him before anyone else finds out."

"Finds out what?" a voice behind me said.

Cathy and I were both startled; then we figured it out. "Where'd you come from?" Cathy asked, turning around. "I thought I left you back at the truck."

"When the government car passed me and shut off his headlights," Bob replied, "I knew somethin' was up." He put his big hand on my shoulder. "Hey, Thad," he said, "I . . . well . . . I'm sorry." He pushed his cowboy hat back on his head. "I was wrong."

"You mean you . . ."

"Sure did," he answered, "I don't believe it, but I saw it, horn and all. And seein' is believin'. I snuck out here by the fence and saw Cathy tryin' to pet the unicorn. But"— he scratched his head—"answer me somethin'."

"What?" I asked.

He turned around and got me in a headlock. "How the

heck can you scare somethin' up that ain't supposed to exist?'' he asked.

"Hey," I said, getting loose and punching him playfully in the stomach, "sometimes, believing is seeing."

I tripped him and he grabbed Cathy on the way down. We turned into a people pile right there in the meadow, rolling and laughing and tackling each other. Suddenly I sat up with my hands on my knees. "Hey," I said, "you ain't gonna tell nobody, are you, cowboy?"

"Not a chance," he answered. "I want to ride him too, you know. And if that darned G-man hadn't flashed his headlights on, I think Cath would've caught that old unicorn."

"If Wingate comes back," Cathy said, "and brings the sheriff, we can forget about riding anything but horses from now on. The way I see it, we've got to work fast. Otherwise we're through. Infinity might not ever come back if a crowd shows up out here."

"We come back tomorrow night, then," Bob said. "I'll stand watch on the road, and if I see anyone, I'll give a hoot like an owl. That way you can shoo him off before anyone gets a good look at him."

"If they haven't already," Cathy said. "All right, but Wingate is probably coming back with the whole darned army."

"We'll wait all night if we have to," I said, and everyone agreed. We did a three-way handshake, knowing that we might have only one more night before the whole thing blew sky-high. That is, if the army didn't get there first. I thought about the farm and I got worried.

"What about the harvest?" I asked. "If it's too hot to mow tomorrow, we'll have to do it tomorrow night with lanterns, unless Cathy gets the headlight hooked up."

"I'll tell you what," she said, "we'll cut wheat until it gets too hot. That ought to be around noon. Then when we break, you guys can gather and thresh it in the barn. I'll hook up the headlight so Dad can run the tractor tomorrow night if he wants to. That way it will be cool enough for him to ride. But the way it looks now, with all of us working, we'll have it finished in no time, even without the night shift. That silo's half full now, so it can't take more than a week and a half at the most."

"Yeah," Bob agreed, "your dad will give us tomorrow night off if we work all day. He ain't no slave driver, you know."

"Yeah," I said, "I guess you're right. There's probably nothing to worry about."

When we got up to leave, Bob couldn't find his hat. I heard chomping nearby. "Uh, oh," I said. Sure enough, Petula was having a midnight snack, and had taken a pretty good-sized chunk out of his hat. I wrestled it away from her and gave it back to him.

He just stared at me, and back at his hat. Then he looked at Petula. I thought he was going to hit me with his hat, but instead he put it on his head with the bite facing forward, then took a deep breath. "Well," he said, "I guess I'm officially a member of the Unicorn Huntin' Club. This is goin' to be our symbol." He pointed to the bite taken out of his brim.

"But what about Cathy?" I asked.

Bob reached over and swiped the hat right off her head. He put it in Petula's mouth and she took a big bite out of the brim. Then he handed Cathy back the hat. All the while she just stood there, astonished. "One for all, and all for one," he said, quoting the old Three Musketeers line. We put our hands together and made a big fist ball.

"The Unicorn Huntin' Club is now closed," Bob said. "No more members accepted."

"Except Mr. Tucker," Cathy said. "After all, it is his meadow."

"Yeah," I chimed in, "except Mr. Tucker. I vote that we make him head of the club."

"I second," Cathy said.

"Done," Bob said, nodding in agreement. "The first meetin' is now adjourned. Now let's go home and get some sleep. We got us a unicorn to catch tomorrow night."

Cathy and I rode Petula back to the truck. Bob ran alongside, trying to keep up. "Hey," he said at one point, "why did you name him Infinity, anyway?"

I pulled up on the reins and stopped Petula. " 'Cause you catch him by believing," I answered, looking at the hole in Bob's hat, "and believing is the way the heart expresses itself. The heart can stretch about as big as it wants to." I looked up at the sky, where the star-speckled heavens covered us like a warm blanket on a chilly night. "It can stretch as far as forever," I added, "and that's all the way to infinity."

"Well," he said, catching his breath, "don't make a whole lot of sense to me, but I reckon it's as good a name as any. But we don't got till forever to catch him; we got to do it tomorrow night. Unless he comes out durin' the day. Any chance of that happenin'?"

"Not much," Cathy answered, surprising me. I'd almost forgotten she was sitting behind me on Petula. "Mr Tucker told me he stays on the hills during the day," she explained, "and only comes down at night when the mist comes over the meadow. He likes to hide in the fog. That way he won't draw a crowd. He's really kind of shy, you know."

"How do you know so much?" I demanded, a little jealous that somebody else might know something about unicorns besides me and Mr. Tucker.

"Mr. Tucker called me," she said, "and told me all about it. He said that you might need some help tonight. I didn't believe him at first, but when he told me that the government man would probably be snooping around, I got worried he might take off with Petula when you went out on the meadow. He said that Wingate got kicked by a horse once, and that turned him against them for good. It seems he was beating his horse and the horse had enough, so it kicked him in the stomach. Mr. Tucker said Wingate shot the horse right there on the spot and has this thing against horses to this day. That's why I thought he might steal Petula when you weren't looking."

"That explains why Wingate hates Petula," I said. "He thought she killed the wolf by kicking it to death, and Wingate don't want that to happen to him, I reckon."

"Then it *was* you out on the road that night," Cathy said. "You're lucky you didn't get killed."

"Naw," I said, "there was nothing to worry about. It was Infinity that killed the wolf. Came right up behind him and . . ."

"How'd Tucker find all this out about Wingate?" Bob wanted to know.

"He's got connections in the army," Cathy said. "He called Washington and found out. He couldn't get them to commit to saving his land, though, or ours either. He tried to get both of our taxes postponed, but they said the taxes were not their department."

"Hey," I said, "we forgot to tell Mr. Tucker about Infinity."

"Let's tell him tomorrow," Bob said. "We've got to get on home. It must be past midnight by now."

We all agreed and went on home, me on Petula, and Bob and Cathy in the truck. I was glad to have more help with catching Infinity, even though part of me still wanted him to myself. I thought about that horn. Pure ivory, Cathy had said, and I remembered what the poachers did to the wild elephants in Africa for their tusks.

"Well," I said to Petula in the barn, "nobody's going to get that horn. Because that's where the magic is. Without that, all you got's another horse."

I patted her on the neck. "No offense, girl, but a unicorn without a horn is like a person without a dream. All the magic is gone. And when the magic's gone, life's just not as much fun."

32

A Bunch of Pups

The phone rang the next morning at breakfast and my mom answered. We didn't get a whole lot of phone calls, so I figured something must be up.

"He's what?" she asked with concern. "What for? Is he all right? No, I'll tell him myself." She hung up the phone and looked at me. "It's Mr. Tucker," she said. "He's in the hospital."

Before she could say any more, I dashed out of the kitchen door and ran to the barn. Mom yelled my name, but I could hear my dad say, "Let the boy go."

I was in such a hurry that I didn't even saddle Petula, just jumped on her back and grabbed her mane. We took off down the road towards town in a frightful gallop.

"Hey, son!" Mr. Greison yelled from his pasture, "the Kentucky Derby's already been run this year!" He cupped his hands and shouted, "You keep riding like that, and you may win anyway!"

I ran Petula as hard as I could, but I couldn't outrun the fear that was overtaking me.

The hospital was no more than a room attached to Doc Yeager's office. When I got there, I jumped off Petula and dashed for the door, jerked it open, and ran for the patient ward.

Sally Penhurst looked pretty startled, and tried to grab me as I ran past. She was built like she could carry a stretcher all by herself, and I think she could have tackled me if I had run straight at her. I got away by diving over her desk and tumbling towards the door. I barged through it and looked around.

There he was, lying in bed. It had to be him, because he was the only one in the room, but he looked different in that white gown, instead of his regular clothes. Tubes were stuck in his left arm and attached, on the other end, to bottles of clear liquid that hung upside down from a rack by the bed.

Suddenly, I didn't know what to do, so I stopped in my tracks. I couldn't hug him; I knew that much. I might disturb something. I'd never felt so helpless as I did staring at him. He looked halfway down the road to heaven.

Doc Yeager and Sally busted in behind me. When they saw that I could only stand and stare at Mr. Tucker, they didn't try to grab me. I felt Doc Yeager's hands gently on my shoulders.

"He's going to be alright, Thaddeus," he assured me. "He's just had a little too much excitement lately. You can sit next to the bed if you like." I didn't say anything, so he added, "He was asking for you."

For the first time it occurred to me that I had been selfish. I'd hardly thought about Mr. Tucker. I was all set to catch a unicorn and I'd barely remembered that he had made the whole thing possible. It had been his idea in the first place, and without him there would've been no unicorn. Now it just might be too late for his dream to come true.

I was upset at the way life had treated Mr. Tucker. Here was a person who believed in his dream, prepared for it by tearing out a walnut orchard and planting wheat he didn't harvest, and what did life do for him? It knocked the wind out of him. I knew everything wasn't fair in life, but I thought he deserved a better shake than he was getting.

I hung my head and listened to him sleep. He was breathing hard for a long time, and then he breathed easier, and fell into a deeper sleep.

Sometime in the early evening he came to. Sally had brought me a bowl of soup around noon, but it was still full, and now cold. She told me he had fallen in his cabin, but was only bruised and tired, and there was nothing to worry about. But doctors and nurses always said that, so I wasn't really sure I was getting the straight poop. Then I remembered how Doc had never lied to me, and I felt better.

"Mr. Tucker?" I said hopefully.

"Thaddy," he answered, "is that you?" He still sounded far away.

"Yes, sir," I said, relieved that he hadn't lapsed into a coma or something worse. "I'm right here."

I got up from my chair and stood by the bed, looking him over carefully. He seemed a little dazed and tired, but much better than when I had first come in. I breathed easier for the first time that day and was a little less mad at life.

"How do you feel?" I asked, just to be sure.

"Fine, Thaddy," he answered. "I feel just fine." He was starting to sound a lot closer to normal. I heaved a sigh of relief. His voice was clear and calm, and he looked almost as strong as usual.

"Now, tell me about the unicorn," he asked, looking me straight in the eyes.

"You mean you know?" I asked, surprised.

"Heard the hoofbeats around midnight," he said. "Sounded like a mighty big one. I was comin' out to see him, but I got excited and fell down on the way to the door. Couldn't seem to get up again to save my life."

"Are you hurt?" I asked, concerned. "They said you were bruised."

"Only my pride. I'm not used to havin' to call fer help just to get off the kitchen floor. But enough about me. Tell me about that critter. I want to see if it was the same one as before. Was he big?"

"Oh, he was big all right," I said, touching his right hand. He grabbed hold of me, as a signal for me to continue.

"How big?" he asked.

"Big. Bigger than Petula."

"Say, that is a big one," he admitted, his eyes opening wide. "Ain't too many critters in these parts bigger than that old mare of yers. Mighty big indeed." He paused to contemplate it, and then he asked. "And the horn?"

"Two feet," I answered with excitement. I measured it with my hands for him like I'd caught a big fish. "Maybe more. And . . . and as big around as my arm. It stuck straight out and spiraled to a point like one of those giant ice cream cones. Come to think of it, it was just about the same color as vanilla."

"What color was his coat?"

"Pure white, but kind of ghosty-looking, like he could vanish into thin air if he wanted to. He looks like a Kansas snowstorm when he moves, with a mane and tail as big and thick as winter blankets blowing on a clothesline. He had whiskers like you, only they were white, about as long as my hand, and not too curly. He had hairy hooves, too, and deep brown eyes. He was beautiful."

"That's him, all right. Same one as before. Did you ride 'im?"

"Naw," I said, shaking my head in disappointment. "Just when Cathy started to pet him, some headlights went on down the road—it was Wingate—and the unicorn ran away."

He'd been staring at the white ceiling all the while, perhaps imagining what Infinity looked like. He turned and looked at me. "Was Cathy's boyfriend there, too?" he asked.

"Yeah, we formed a club. The Unicorn Hunting Club. And made you president."

"To tell you the truth," he said, "I don't think it was the headlights that scared 'im off, since he could outrun a train if he wanted to. He may look like just a big horse with a horn, but he can run pretty fast, 'specially across those hills. Ain't nothin' can catch 'im on them hills. Not even a pack of wolves.''

"Then why *did* he run away?" I wanted to know.

He looked at me real serious. "Your sister must go alone," he said. "At least, the first time. There can be nobody else around till she rides 'im. Once she has ridden, others can ride too, but she must go by herself the first time."

"But . . ."

He squeezed my hand a little, and it felt like he was gaining strength. "This is one of them things only she can do," he said. "She *is* still a . . ."

"Yes, sir," I said seriously. "Checked her for teeth marks myself."

He gave me a funny look but didn't say anything, just thought for a moment. "Thaddy," he said at last, "I've got somethin' fer you. I wrote it down in that book on the night stand, just in case."

"In case what?"

"Sometimes when older folks fall down, they break some bones, and then get pneumonia or somethin' and can't recover. I wanted you to have it in case the end came and I had to cross over to the other side. No such luck, though. Doc says it's just a bruise. I'll be out in a couple of days, when he can get some crutches from Wichita. Seems the last person who used his set dropped them out of the back of his truck, and they got run over. So he sent away fer a couple of new pairs. He even gave me some newfangled medicine fer the cough. Darned if it didn't clear it right up. Guess I got my miracle anyway."

"No," I said, thinking how good it was not to hear him cough, although I had forgotten all about it until he brought it up. It reminded me of lying awake in the middle of the night and not being able to get back to sleep, and not knowing the reason why. I always knew something was keeping me awake, but I just couldn't put my finger on it, and then, without warning, the refrigerator or something would stop rumbling and its motor would shut off. I'd heave a big sigh of relief and drop right off to sleep.

I felt the same way about his cough. Now that it was shut off, peace and quiet filled the air to overflowing, and I could put my worry to sleep for awhile, at least about the cough. I was still a little worried about him falling down, though, despite Sally Penhurst's reassurance.

"Your miracle ain't up yet," I finally said. "You're going to ride Infinity, just wait and see."

"Well," he replied, "you've done pretty good without me so far. I see no need to butt in and spoil it now."

I pushed my hat back on my forehead, unaware until that moment I'd been looking at him through the bite out of the rim. "Nothing doing," I said. "If it wasn't for you, there wouldn't be any wheat field, and no unicorn, neither."

"I'll tell you what," he said. "Doc says I get out of here in a couple of days. I'll be ready to ride by then, crutches or no crutches. The unicorn don't care if I can hardly walk. I'll get up on 'im somehow." He leaned over and whispered, "Just don't tell Doc. He'd never let me out of here. Heck, I wouldn't have called 'im except I knocked the phone off the hook when I fell. Figgered I might as well make the call, what with the operator yellin' in my ear.

"Exhaustion, Doc says, aggravated by a cough. Plus a couple of bumps and bruises. But I know he's leavin' out the serious stuff. Doesn't want to worry me too much, I guess. Doesn't want me checkin' out of life 'til I'm ready." He paused and added, "Now, stop gabbin' and get the notebook on the nightstand there."

I reached over and picked up the notebook.

"Go on," he said. "You read it to me."

"Okay, here goes." I opened the cover. Inside, printed in bold letters, it said:

VERSE 3

Once upon a unicorn
A girl came riding by,
And I could see the secrets
Of the stars and of the sky.
She sang of love

> *Without a sound;*
> *Her heart reached out to me.*
> *"Yes," she smiled.*
> *"I see it now.*
> *I know you can believe."*

"Is that all of it?" I asked after a while.

"Not yet," he replied, patting my hand. "We still got three more verses left."

"I want to hear them all," I said with excitement.

"We'll get there," he replied. "Now run along home and eat. I can see from here that you let yer soup get cold."

"What are *you* gonna eat?" I asked.

He pointed to the bottles above his bed with his free hand, the one that didn't have any tubes in it. "That's my dinner right there," he said with a laugh.

"What is it?"

"It's sugar water. I guess they don't think I'm sweet enough." We both chuckled, and then I hugged him as best I could, leaning over the bed. He hugged me back with his free arm.

"Heck," I said, "you're as sweet as an old beehive full of honey." I pulled slowly away. "You going to be okay?" I asked.

"Only if you go home and eat dinner."

"Okay, see you later, then."

" 'Bye, Thaddy."

I started to leave, but first I had to ask, "What if you would've . . . you know . . . passed over to the other side? There are still some more verses that I haven't heard. So that means you can't go yet. Not until I've heard 'em all." I thought for a moment. "And you can take your time. I don't care if I don't hear the last verse for awhile. You just save it for me. I'll be ready in about fifty years."

"I promise, Thaddy. You'll hear them all 'fore I go."

I turned and started to walk out the door.

"Alone," he said, looking at me. "She must go alone."

As much as it hurt, I knew he was right. Cathy would have to go alone to the meadow. Bob and I would have to stay behind. Still, I thought, there must be something I could do. I just wasn't sure what.

"Oh, and there's one more thing," he said before I closed the door. "Cindy had a litter of pups last night. Doc's got them at his place."

"Pups!" I yelled. "Well, why didn't somebody say so?" I ran out the door and jumped on Petula, heading straight for Doc Yeager's. He had stuck his head in the hospital room a couple of hours earlier before he went on home, but he hadn't said anything about pups. Imagine, keeping quiet about such a major event!

On the way to Doc's I couldn't think of anything but pups, except once something else popped up like a target in a shooting gallery, and then popped down again. But I remembered it: it was something Mr. Tucker had said in the hospital bed. He had mentioned that Doc was keeping the serious stuff to himself. I would ask Doc about it when I got there, if I didn't forget. I didn't really want to forget, but I had visions of pups playing in my head, and that took priority over everything right then. Besides, Doc had told me that Mr. Tucker was going to be all right, and Doc had never lied to me, as far as I could tell.

33

Sir Lancelot Returns

Petula's hooves pounded the dirt road, kicking up a cloud of dust behind us like smoke belching from a locomotive. I loved to ride fast, and this was an excuse to run her full out.

There comes a point when you're riding fast when it seems like you're slowing down. You reach a certain speed where you cross into another world; you become one with the horse, and everything seems to move in slow motion. It's like watching the blades on a fan. They move faster and faster, until all of a sudden they look like they're slowing down, and when they reach a certain speed, they actually seem to be going backwards.

Riding is the same way, only the blades are in your mind. When you reach that speed where you become one with the horse, you stop being aware of the world around you. It falls away, and you're only aware of the motion. When this happens, your mind passes into a place all its own. The smallest thoughts become grand experiences, and you're gone.

If you speed up or slow down, the world comes back again. You feel faraway, like the first time I smoked one of my dad's pipes, except that you don't feel sick. You're like a visitor entering the world from another time and place. Everything seems strange and new for a moment, and then you're back in reality.

When I rode towards Doc's that night, Petula and I reached the exact speed to enter that place in my mind. Under normal conditions, she wouldn't have been able to get up enough speed to get there, but my excitement, exhaustion, and hunger lowered the speed, so that we passed into that special place halfway to Doc's.

The world faded away, and I became lost in my thoughts. I saw my old dog, Lancelot, running towards me across the field. He tumbled along like a small black bear, his big old ears flapping like flags in the wind. Those brown eyes shone like marbles in the sun, and that long pink tongue hung out of his mouth like a hot water bottle.

He came back to me in that moment, and I missed him as never before. Mom and Dad knew it had hit me pretty hard when I lost him, because I never got around to crying about it. I just held it in and swallowed hard. But seeing him running back to me that day brought it all up again, only this time I couldn't swallow. The feeling passed right on by my throat and found a way out through my eyes, turning to water as it spilled out into the world.

Lancelot ran past me, and out on the Flint Hills. I knew I couldn't go after him and it made me miss him more. I looked for his shadow out on the hills, but it was no use; he was gone. I turned away, water pouring out of my eyes and running down my face like a waterfall in spring.

I heard barking, and turning around. There he was, on top of the highest hill, trying to get my attention. He looked at me and his tongue flopped out of his mouth. His eyes were smiling, as if to say that he was fine and happy, and not to worry anymore about where he'd gone after that truck knocked him out of the world.

After a moment, he turned and ran away, looking back with one of those glances that said he'd found something up ahead, and he wanted me to follow. Then the vision of him began to fade, and I let go of him, knowing he was happy and that when the time came I could follow him, and we'd be together again.

The world around me slowly began to return. Petula had entered Doc's place, and I was back on my way to see the pups. I wiped my eyes a bunch of times with my sleeve, but water just kept coming out, until the feelings pumped the last of it from the bottom of my heart. My face dried up in the heat and wind, but my shirt was still soaking wet when I got to Doc's door.

No one was around, so I went out back. Doc was in his barn looking at his pregnant cow. He must've known I'd come racing over when I found out about the pups, because he wasn't all that surprised when I walked inside the barn.

"Looks like you fell in," he said with a smile, "at least from the waist up. I thought school was out, so you wouldn't be hiding out in the well anymore."

"Naw," I said, "I threw some water on me to cool off. I don't think anyone ever gets used to this heat."

"You sound like Sheriff Johnson," he said, looking back at his cow.

"Yeah," I admitted, "I stole that saying from him. About the only thing of his I've ever had any use for." I lifted my hat and scratched my head. "And don't go giving away any secrets about my hiding place," I said. "I may still need it next year."

"Ain't much of a secret," he said, feeling Daisy's belly. "Your mom's the one that told me."

"Mom! How did she find out?"

"Heck," he replied, "she's known all along. She just didn't want to spoil your sense of adventure. Said she knew you'd go to your dad out in the field anyway, and he'd find a way to send you off to school."

I couldn't believe it. "All this time I thought I had everybody fooled, and now you tell me they knew all along. What kind of a deal is that, anyway?"

"A good deal, I'd say," he laughed. "She knew you'd take to school better if she didn't force you. You catch more flies with honey than vinegar, so they say. But that isn't why you came. The pups are in the stall down at the end.''

I ran down there, and sure enough, Cinderella and her newborn family were snuggled up in the hay. There was a bunch of little black furry things attached to her belly, all about as big as my fist. I counted them a couple of times, and there were seven in all, as near as I could tell.

Doc came up while I was counting. "How many do you count?" he asked, placing his hand on my shoulder.

"Seven, I reckon," I said with confidence, "all black as Model Ts."

"Nope," he said. "That's what *I* thought at first. You missed one."

"Missed one?" I wrinkled my forehead. "Where?"

He pointed at Cindy's stomach. "Right there on the end."

"That's a white spot on her belly," I said, still not sure.

"Look closer."

I got a little closer, but not too close. I didn't want Cinderella to get upset. When I got about two feet away, she let me know with a low growl that I was just about close enough. I looked again, and then I saw it: a little black ball of fur with a white spot on its chest.

"It's him," I whispered. "Old Lancelot's come back to me."

"I don't know," Doc said, shaking his head behind me. "It's a girl."

"Well, he didn't promise he'd come back as a boy, but that's him, all right. I know it is."

"She's yours then, I reckon." Doc patted me on the shoulder. "As soon as she's ready to leave."

Something he said made me remember what else I had come for, and I brought it up before I forgot again. "Mr. Tucker says you're hiding something from him," I said, still looking at the pups, "something serious."

"Is that so? And what might that be?"

"Doc," I said, turning around to face him, "you've never lied to me before. So don't start now, okay?"

He stood up and looked out of the barn door, thinking about what I had said for a moment. "Yeah," he finally admitted, "I reckon you're right. But what's between a patient and his doctor is private, and can't be discussed with anyone without the patient's permission."

"But," I pleaded, "I have to know."

He turned and stared at me, a serious expression on his face. "What Mr. Tucker told you was his way of saying that people don't live forever. I can't tell you anymore, and I can't go back on my word. Sometimes that's all you've got that has any value: your word and what you believe in."

"Okay," I said at last, getting up and walking toward the barn door. "I guess I can understand that, though I don't like it none. A promise is a promise, I reckon." I pushed my hat back on my head. "But just tell me one thing. How long has he got?"

Doc didn't answer me. He walked back to Daisy and stroked her head. "Life comes and goes, Thaddy, even here in Flint Hills. Right now I got one cow. Next week I might have three, or I might not have any."

"Please, Doc," I begged. "I won't tell a soul."

He looked at me sternly. I could see that he wanted to tell me, but he couldn't.

"I promise," I said, pleading as best I could.

"I can't tell you. I wish I could, but it's strictly between doctor and patient. Those are the rules."

"Yes, sir, I guess I understand."

"You know," he said quietly, "that when he goes, he wants you to have his farm."

"Me?" I said, astonished.

"He says you're the only one who would take care of it. The only one who would plant wheat."

"How long, Doc?" I persisted, "How long has he got? Just give me a ballpark figure. A big ballpark if you like."

"Can't say for sure. Could be six months, could be a year, could be longer. That's all I can tell you. I've said too much already. Now get on home. Your parents called here once already looking for you. You'd better go now."

"I promise I won't tell a soul," I said on my way out the door. "I swear it."

"Tell what?" he said with a wink. "Who knows how long any of us got? That's the way life is."

I rode home trying to think of a way I could prolong Mr. Tucker's life. I still hadn't accepted him passing out of the world, and I didn't want the farm if he wasn't going to be around. It wouldn't seem like Tucker's Grove without him sitting on the back porch, rocking back and forth and spinning out stories. It just wouldn't be the same.

34

The Grandest Dream

By the time I arrived home, dinner was on the table. I told everyone the story about Mr. Tucker being worn out, and Doc sweetening him up with sugar water. I also told them about the cough being cured. Everyone was relieved. But I was extra careful not to mention the serious stuff. I wasn't about to break my promise to Doc and lose a friend.

"How'd Mr. Tucker get to town without us knowing?" Cathy asked. "The road's right out front. Unless he took the long way around—but that's five miles farther."

"That's what he did, all right," Mom said. "He made Doc take him around the other side, where the road loops back past the school." She scooped some peas onto her plate. "At least, that's what Sally Penhurst said when I called her back. He absolutely refused to go unless they took the loop. Said he didn't want to wake anyone at three in the morning by racing past the house. It couldn't have been any worse than that big truck the other night. Why, it almost turned the place into broad daylight."

"Mom," I said, looking at Cathy and Bob, "are you sure you don't believe in unicorns?"

Cathy and Bob both gave me a mean look, thinking I had forgotten our secret oath. Cathy even kicked me under the table.

"Well, I can't say I haven't heard all the talk lately," Mom said, passing the potatoes to Dad, "but to tell you the truth, the only corn I believe in is growing beside the house."

"That's what I thought," I said through a mouthful of peas. "Just checking."

"As I said before," Mom replied, "it seems to me that what Mr. Tucker saw wasn't a mythical beast, but some wild horse that came out of the hills. And with his poor eyesight . . ."

"But," I asked, "what if you *saw* one?"

"Well, that would be different," she answered. "After all, seeing . . ."

"Is believing," Cathy and Bob said together.

"Okay." Mom said seriously, "Now, I am well aware that you kids are riding out there at night and looking for this creature. But all I can say is . . ." She put down her fork and placed her hands in her lap, then leaned forward and nodded as she spoke. "First, try to get home by midnight. And second, be careful. Those wild stallions are dangerous. One even killed a wolf the other night." She put her hands back on the table and reached for her fork. "And that's another thing," she added. "Wolves."

"We'll be careful," Cathy assured her.

"Bob," Mom went on, "you got a rifle?"

"Yes, ma'am," he answered through a mouthful of potatoes, "but I broke the trigger on it awhile back. Ain't had time to fix it."

"Then you borrow one of Mr. Williams's."

"Might as well," Dad agreed. "I ain't had much call to use it except to point at peddlers. Unless, of course, you two are plannin' on havin' a shotgun weddin'."

Everyone laughed at this, but Cathy and Bob laughed more nervously than the rest of us.

"Really, Dad," Cathy complained, "you said you weren't going to say any more about it."

"Oh, I didn't mean nothin'," Dad answered, shoveling peas with his fork. "I just thought it'd be fun to throw rock salt instead of rice at the weddin'. When was that you were tyin' the knot anyway? I'm not forcin', mind you. Just askin'."

"We haven't said yet," Cathy replied with a little impatience. "We want to start college first, remember?"

"Be quiet, Ari," Mom ordered, "before you frighten the poor kid off. Now, you promised not to bring it up, and a promise is a promise."

"Yeah, Dad," I chimed in, "if you make a promise, you're supposed to keep it." Bob and Cathy gave me funny looks, but didn't say anything.

"Well, I reckon you're right," Dad said, looking at Mom out of the corner of his eye, "but in *my* day . . ."

"Your day is long gone," Mom said, and then she regretted it. An uncomfortable silence filled the room, and then Mom said, "I . . . I didn't mean . . ." Her face flushed red.

"Aw . . ." Dad said, "don't matter none. It ain't no secret anyhow. But if we don't get that wheat harvested by July, we'll be livin' in Wichita by the time the leaves turn. I hear it's real pretty on Main Street when the leaves turn red and fall," he went on, half kidding. "I wonder if they could use an old man on a tractor."

"Honestly, Ari," Mom said. "I swear that's all you ever talk about sometimes."

"Yeah," Dad replied, lighting his corncob pipe as though he hadn't heard a word. "Someday, when I can't farm this place no more, I'll trade the plow and cutter for a scoop. Then I can cruise up and down Main Street just scoopin' up leaves. Snow in the winter."

Mom thought it over more carefully. "Say, that's not a bad idea after all." She looked at us kids for encouragement. "Is it, Cathy?"

"No," Cathy answered, "I like it. Long as somebody else loads the snow."

Dad blew a circle of smoke in the air. "How about putting that headlight on old John Deere?" he suggested to Cathy.

"Right after dinner," she agreed. "The tractor's already cooling off in the barn. It shouldn't take more than half an hour to wire it up."

"Where'd you get the headlight?" I asked, cleaning the last of the potatoes off my plate.

"We borrowed one from Bob's truck," Cathy said.

"Yeah," Bob chimed in, "Don't need more than one light around here at night. I could drive the road blindfolded."

"Except when that fog rolls in," Mom said. "Now, you be careful. Some big truck gets turned around in that fog, and he's going to think you're just a motorcycle by the side of the road and run you right over. Just like . . ."

Dad grabbed her arm. He knew that it would remind me of Lancelot. "That's all right, Dad," I said with a smile. "Cinderella had eight pups last night, and one of them looks just like old Lancelot. Doc says she's mine if I want her, and Mr. Tucker already promised me one. She's got a white spot on her chest and everything. Why, I bet you it's old Lancelot come back to me. That's what I told Doc."

Everybody was happy for me, and we talked dogs for quite a while. That is, until Mom reminded Bob to be careful with his one-eyed truck at night, or put the headlight back on.

"Yes, ma'am," Bob said, hanging his head a little, "we'll be careful. My dad's goin' to pick up a headlight for me in Wichita next week. I told him I busted it out pitchin' rocks, since I didn't know if he'd let me use it on the tractor."

"But I thought your arm was no good anymore for throwing," I said, and everyone got a little embarrassed, since you weren't supposed to talk about such things, especially at the dinner table.

"That's my left arm," Bob said, not at all offended.

"I'm tryin' to learn to pitch with my other one. But I'm a little wild yet."

"Then you ain't givin' up on your pitchin' dream," Dad said with a smile. "Good, 'cause we don't like quitters around here. Do we, Thaddy?"

"Nope," I said proudly. "We sure don't. I guess farming and fighting go together."

Dad reached over and messed up my hair. "You're startin' to sound just like your old man," he laughed.

"I swear," Mom said all of a sudden, "the things you teach that boy. Oh, I know," she continued, raising her voice and her arms, "I've heard all of the speeches about fighting for what you believe in. And I think it's just fine. But there is going to come a time when we can't stay and fight anymore, when we've worked this farm out, and I just hope it's not the death of all of us."

"I thought we all agreed," Dad said, "that we were goin' to stay on and fight. Ain't that what we said?"

"I'm all for that," Mom replied, still a little upset, "but what about the rest of us? We have dreams too, you know."

Dad stood up and went to the window. "I *said* Cathy could go off to college this fall," he argued, "just like she planned."

"That's not the point, Ari," Mom said straight off. "I've kept pretty quiet about this. I've let you do what you want until now. But I can't keep quiet anymore. I get tired of pretending that this broken-down farm will last forever, and that you will too. Well, I have a dream too, and my dream is for all of us to survive. This family is more important than any old farm. And I aim to save us, even if we have to give this place up."

She looked at Dad with a stern expression. "And if you die out there on that darned tractor, you're going to ruin everything. Now, you can work during the day or you can work at night, but you're not going to do both. You're going to rest one time or the other, because if you die out there in that field, you'll ruin it for the rest of us and I swear I'll never forgive myself for letting you do it. There, that's my big speech, take it or leave it."

The silence that followed seemed as long as a summer sunset. I knew my mom had deep feelings about the whole thing, but this was the first time I ever heard her let them out in such a heated fashion. Dad and I both knew we had been selfish, pretending that Mom really didn't mind if we did what we wanted. The only trouble was that for us to realize our dreams to the fullest, it might mean the end of hers.

After much debate, Dad agreed to harvest at night, since it would be cooler, and the rest of us would help out with the wheat gathering, threshing, and filling the silo. I'd drive the tractor during the morning before it got too hot, since I won the coin toss over Bob and Cathy. They'd work at stacking and hauling the cut wheat. Dad would rest up in the shade of the porch all day, and ride John Deere from sunset until midnight, but no later. Mom would take care of everything else, including us, like she always did. I guess her point was that if she was going to take care of us, she wanted us to stick around. That was her reward for all of her work, which was really about twice as much as the rest of us ever did.

For the first time it really hit me that there was something just as good as insisting on living my own dream, that sometimes it felt better to give in a little in order to keep a lot more. And so I learned that compromise was a word that didn't mean defeat, but victory of a higher kind, the kind that kept families together. And although I didn't know it at the time, that may have been the greatest dream of all.

35

The Tip of the Horn

Later that night I met Cathy and Bob in the barn. Cathy was just putting the finishing touches on hooking up the headlight. She had even installed a knob on the dash so that when you pulled it out, the headlight went on, just like on the Chevy. We were not completely amazed, since there didn't seem to be anything she couldn't fix with some tools and time, but just the same we marveled a little at what she could do.

I repeated what Mr. Tucker had said about Cathy going alone to the meadow the first time. Bob was not very excited about it, but I pulled him aside for a powwow, and we made our own separate plans.

There was a cold wind blowing that night, and I had grabbed my leather jacket and brought it to the barn with me. I started to put it on when Cathy walked up and stared at me. "Going somewhere?" she asked.

"No . . . it's just . . . a little cold tonight so I thought I'd wear my jacket."

"Good idea," she said, giving me a funny look, "but I

don't think you'll need it. I'm going alone, remember?''

"Yeah," I said, looking at Bob standing behind her, "I remember. I . . . I'm going into town to see Mr. Tucker."

"Kind of late for that, isn't it?"

"Yeah, but he wants to tell me another story."

"Okay," she said, "just be sure Petula doesn't get the urge to circle back toward the meadow." She looked at Bob. "And that goes for both of you, understand?"

"Why . . . of course," Bob said, turning a little red. "We're just goin' into town to hear how the unicorn got his horn back, that's all, and check on Mr. Tucker."

Cathy knew we were up to something, but she couldn't figure out what. So she saddled up Petula and trotted off down the road, disappearing into the cool night air.

She could have walked down to Tucker's place, but it was five miles, and nobody wanted her walking alone at night out on the edge of our known world, especially with big trucks getting lost and taking the loop past the school. Not to mention the chance of wolves coming off the hills.

Of course, I knew it had been light shining from the tip of Infinity's horn that night when I'd seen him on the ridge, and not some big truck like I told Mom, but I figured everyone thought I was crazy enough without telling them my secret. I wanted Cathy to see the light for herself.

We watched Cathy saddle up Petula. As she rode out of the barn, Bob turned to me and winked. I looked at him and smiled nervously, hoping this would be the night Cathy would catch Infinity and knowing that if she did, she just might be in for the ride of her life.

It was all we could do to let her ride away without us. In fact, it was more than we could do. I don't have to tell you we didn't head towards town and Mr. Tucker in the hospital. We didn't even try. If Infinity was to be caught and ridden, we wanted to be there, legend or no legend, even if we had to watch from a safe distance.

With the moon looking like a headlight rising high in the black Kansas night, sharing space with a sky full of stars, it seemed like an awful good night to chase a critter with a horn on its head. This time we just might catch him.

36

Cathy and the Unicorn

Bob and I watched Cathy disappear down the dirt road. Then we fired up Bob's truck and followed quietly behind, far enough so she wouldn't catch us spying on her. When we got close to the meadow we parked the truck under the trees near the entrance to Tucker's cabin. That way, it would be kept out of sight and we could sneak up on the meadow without being seen.

The fog had lifted early that night, so we couldn't hide in the mist, which lay only in small patches on the meadow. We were forced to crawl on our hands and knees along the fence until we came to Petula. I tried to get her to act like no one was near, but she kept looking at us. For a moment there, I thought she was going to give us away, but luckily, Cathy wasn't paying any attention. She was out in the meadow waiting for Infinity to arrive.

Hours passed as slow as a snail crawling up a fence post. The moon moved halfway across the sky. I must have fallen asleep somewhere along the way, because the next thing I remember was Bob shaking my shoulder and calling my name.

"Okay, Petula," I said, thinking I had fallen asleep at another time and place and she had nuzzled me with her nose to wake me.

"Shhh!" Bob whispered. Petula stirred a little and shook her mane, her eyes fixed straight ahead on the meadow.

Cathy was sitting on a tree stump about fifty yards from the fence. We could see the top of her head as she turned to see what the noise had been, so we ducked down behind the wheat by the fence. It was normally about three feet high, but over the last couple of nights we had beaten it down, and had made a path into the field. Cathy was at the end of that path, and could almost see us through the flattened wheat, so we got as low as we could.

Suddenly the pounding of heavy hoofbeats echoed off the ground on the far side of the meadow, but we didn't dare look up. The hoofbeats grew closer and slowed to a walk. Cathy began to speak softly. "Yes," she said, "that's a good boy. Come closer now. Come on."

The hoofbeats grew softer, then stopped. The heavy sound of a horse breathing hit our ears. Bob grabbed my arm. "I'm goin' in for a look," he whispered, sitting up a little.

"No," I said, pulling him down by the jacket sleeve. "You'll spoil everything."

He took off his cowboy hat and got ready to crawl up the path. "I didn't come out here to sit on the bench," he said. "I'm goin' to ride that mustang." I grabbed his arm, forgetting it was the one with the war wound. "Come on," he insisted, holding his arm. "Let me show you how a soldier crawls so he don't get spotted. We were pretty reckless on the way over here, but this time we'll keep real low. Come on, or we'll miss him."

I stared at him, concerned. "But the myth says . . ."

"This ain't no myth," he said. "This is the dag-blamed real McCoy. So the myth rules don't apply. It ain't a matter of believin' anymore. It's time to take the horse by the mane. Now, you comin' or ain't you?"

I thought about it real hard for a second. "Aw . . . all right," I finally agreed, taking off my hat. "But no tricks. We get just close enough to get a good look. No closer, until she rides him. We've got to have *some* respect for the legend."

He messed up my hair. "You're a funny kid," he observed, "for a guy that don't like rules." He shook his head. "Okay, we'll just go lookin'. But once she's got him mounted, we ride too." He started to crawl up the path. Then he looked up at Petula. "We'd better stash the hats, just in case somebody gets hungry."

"Good idea," I agreed. We put them in the wheat, far enough away so a tied-up horse couldn't reach them.

"Now, watch close," he said, "and keep your head down."

We crawled on our bellies along the path for about a hundred feet, sliding across the straw. He looked back at me with a stern expression. "Keep that rear end down," he said in a loud whisper, "or you'll get it shot off, soldier."

I squished down as far as I could and we crawled on, a little more slowly this time. We must have looked like a couple of fat snakes slithering through the field, searching for mice.

A cold breeze rippled through the meadow. We instinctively looked back, and saw our hats fly over the fence. There was no going after them. They were gone, probably forever, but we had more important things to do than chase hats in the wind.

There was the whinny of a startled horse, and heavy hoofbeats galloped quickly away. We couldn't say a word, just looked at each other. We knew we were in trouble, so we turned around and crawled as fast as we could toward the road, hoping against the odds to sneak off without getting discovered.

When we got halfway back, I reached out and ran into a pair of cowboy boots. "Well," Cathy said, "you guys are a big help. Here we go and make an agreement and you dumbbells can't even stay home like you're supposed to. How, tell me exactly *how*, am I supposed to ride that critter with you two sneaking around and spoiling everything?''

We couldn't say anything, so she went on. "Look, I don't care if you don't have any respect for me, but can't you at least respect the legend?'' She stopped and shook her head. "How do you expect me to catch this beast if you keep breaking the rules?''

"But, Cath," Bob said, standing up, "we just wanted to get a good look, that's all.'' He threw up his hands, and then put them on his hips. I knew he felt the same way as me. We were both sorry we had broken our promise and scared Infinity off. And we were just as sorry that we got caught doing it.

"Yeah," I added, getting to my feet and dusting myself off. "We were going to let *you* ride him first.''

"Out!" she said, pointing to the road. "Out of here, both of you! And don't come back until I say so!'' There was fire in her eyes and thunder in her throat.

She was pretty mad, and the bad part was that she had a darned good right to be. That made it worse: We couldn't defend ourselves. As we headed for the road, we could hear her say, "I can't believe it, I just can't believe it.'' The words stung like bees on the nose of a bear trying to steal some honey.

When we got to the road, we noticed it was getting a little colder, and the wind had picked up again.

"Don't look good, Thaddy.'' Bob glanced up at some dark clouds moving in from the south. "Looks like twister weather to me.''

"Aw, it'll turn and head for Missouri or go north. That's what they usually do around here.'' I looked at his hatless head and his messed-up hair. "You and your dumb idea about stashing the hats," I said, shaking my head.

"Well, Einstein," he replied, "if it wasn't for you and your hat-eatin' horse, we might have gotten away with it.''

"Well, cowboy," I snapped back, "it wasn't her fault. It was the wind that gave us away.''

"Heck," he said, hands on his belt buckle, "I could've rode that mustang. Horn or no horn."

"Yeah, I bet," I said sarcastically. "But somebody has to catch him first."

"Why," he said proudly, "there ain't no critter alive I can't catch, with or without this bum arm. I should've brought my rope. Then I would've caught him, and rode him too."

"Without a saddle?" I asked, climbing up on the fence. "He's probably wild, you know. Why, we're even dumber than we look. We think he's going to walk over and let us jump right up on him, just like a horse you get your picture taken on at the fair." I shook my head in disbelief. "How dumb can we get? He's probably never been ridden, and we're just going to climb up and ride off. Cowboy, we haven't got the slightest idea what we're getting into."

Bob looked at me, a little confused. "But you said he'll let anyone ride him once he's caught. Don't you believe your own myth anymore?"

"Oh," I answered, turning to untie Petula, "I still believe, all right, just as much as ever. It's just . . . just like Mr. Tucker said. We think this is some kind of pony ride at the fair and it ain't, that's all. So that's it for me. I can see *I* don't have a clue as to what's really going on. I'm leaving before I make a bigger fool of myself than I already have. If my sister catches him, then come back and get me. Otherwise . . ."

I stopped. There were heavy hoofbeats on the meadow, and they were coming this way. The wind had died down a little, but it had cleared the rest of the mist. Our eyes were riveted on the wheat up ahead.

Infinity trotted up and stopped next to Cathy. He bent his head down and began to graze the wheat. We couldn't move. We just stood there frozen in time, like something out of a Norman Rockwell painting—Bob leaning back on the split rail fence, and me sitting on top of it, my boots resting on the lower rail.

Cathy slowly approached Infinity and held out her hand,

which held something round. By the way he took it and crunched it in his teeth, I figured it must be a walnut.

Cathy reached up and began to stroke his head. He didn't pull away this time, but stood motionless, letting her stroke his head and mane. She carefully moved her hand across his face and reached for the horn.

He got nervous and whinnied, pulling away a little. "No one's going to hurt you," Cathy said, stroking his mane. She stood back a few feet and looked him over. "My, you are a big fella, aren't you? You must be at least eighteen hands high."

She sat down on one of the tree stumps and looked up at him. Then she pulled another walnut from her pocket and held it in her hand. He cleared his nostrils and shook his big head, then drew close to her and bent to take the walnut. When he did, Cathy carefully reached up and touched his horn. He didn't pull away this time.

She slowly took her hand away so as not to startle him, and stood up alongside, trying to figure out how to climb aboard this huge dream horse.

She tried to climb up, but he pulled away. He didn't trot off, though, but stood as if waiting for her to find a way to get aboard. She tried again, but slid down his side and landed on the ground. Infinity was motionless, like a white marble statue in a park. She got up and dusted herself off, then took one more leap. Infinity steadied himself, as if waiting for her to land.

This time she sailed up and landed sideways over him, hanging like a pair of saddle bags. But then she straightened herself out and sat up, grabbing his flowing white mane. He stirred a little, and she patted his neck.

"Whoa, boy," she said, "everything's going to be all right. Easy now. Easy."

He seemed to calm down a little at the sound of her voice, but then he lifted his feet and stomped the ground anxiously, as if a race was beginning and they were in it.

Bob and I stared at each other in disbelief. We never expected he would let anyone up on his back, at least not that easy. But there she was, sitting upright as though she had ridden him before, outlined against the flickering stars above and the fireflies below. It looked like the fireflies had suddenly come out when the mist had left, and they buzzed around the meadow like a new galaxy giving birth to a thousand stars that spun in all directions.

She grabbed tighter on his mane, wrapping her hands around it like she was braiding a rope, and nudged his sides gently with her boots. She turned him around and trotted slowly away, at last disappearing through the trees.

I turned to Bob. "What exactly *is* your dream?" I asked, tapping him on the shoulder. "Besides baseball, that is."

He scratched his head and looked at me. "There ain't no other," he said. "Ever since I was your age I ain't had but one dream, and that's to pitch. The only reason I joined the Army was so I could pitch. The recruiter told me they had a team, and they were lookin' for pitchers. I believed him. Heck, the only thing I got to pitch was tents and hand grenades. Just wasn't what I had in mind."

He grabbed his injured arm. "Then I went and caught this chunk of metal in my pitchin' arm from a land mine, and . . . Well, I reckon you know the rest. I'd give just about anythin' to get my arm back. Pitchin' with my other arm just ain't the same. I can't hit the broad side of a barn with a watermelon."

"Is that why you're here?" I asked. "To see if Infinity can fix your arm?"

"What the heck"—he shrugged—"it's worth a try. I came here with nothin'. So what's the difference if I go home with nothin' but a pony ride. Ain't got nothin' to lose, I figger."

I didn't say anything, but I secretly hoped Infinity would fix Bob's arm so that he could pitch, because when I wasn't looking, Bob had snuck into my life and become my friend, and you always want the best for your friends.

So I just patted him on the shoulder and said, "I hope you get your wish. Almost as much as I hope I get mine."

"Why, what's yours? he asked.

"Nothing," I said.

"Aw, go on," he replied, "Tell me. I won't say nothin'. Besides, look how crazy mine is."

"Traveling to where the universe began," I told him.

"Well," he said, a little startled, "that might take awhile. So you'd better let me go next."

"Next?" I said. "Nothing doing. I saw him first."

"No, you didn't," he argued. "Why, I saw him when . . ."

He never finished his sentence. Infinity and Cathy came back into the meadow, galloping in full stride. I couldn't see light coming out of his horn, but it seemed to glow in the dark, like luminous ivory.

All the while Bob and I were frozen by the sight of them galloping smoothly across the meadow. Cathy's hat had come off and the way her blond hair flowed behind her, it seemed to blend with Infinity's waving white mane. They almost appeared to be one inseparable entity, moving gently back and forth. It looked like they had ridden together for years and were happy doing it.

At last the gallop turned into a trot and they approached us, stopping alongside the fence. Cathy's face was aglow, flushed with excitement. She looked straight at me, her eyes bright, clear, and intense.

"Want to ride?" she asked. "He's really quite tame. I'm sure he's been ridden before." She patted him on the neck. "He's really good, and really fast. So hold on tight."

I was absolutely speechless as I looked into the eyes of the unicorn. I was so choked up that I couldn't do anything.

"I'll go," Bob said. "That is . . ." He looked at me. "If Thaddy don't mind."

"No," I finally said, "you go ahead. I'll go last."

Bob helped Cathy climb down. She made a stirrup for him out of her hands, and he stepped into it. I was surprised that he didn't knock her over, but she pushed him up onto Infinity's back without much trouble.

After several nervous moments of turning in a circle, and getting a firm grip on the unicorn's mane, Bob finally got control of the animal and trotted off. When he got fifty yards away Infinity reared up, almost knocking Bob off his back.

But Bob held on, and soon they were level with the ground again.

"Steady," Bob said, "steady, old fella. Nobody's goin' to hurt you. We're just goin' to take a little ride around the meadow here, not run the Derby."

Infinity seemed to like Bob's reassuring voice, and he calmed down. Then they trotted off and disappeared behind the trees, taking a thousand fireflies with them.

37

Life Is a Ball Game

Bob vanished like a shadow into darkness. I turned to Cathy and asked, "What was it like?"

"Oh," she said, leaning on the fence next to me. "It was like . . . like nothing I've ever experienced."

"How is it different from everything else?" I asked, scratching my head.

"When you're aboard him, you feel things," she explained, looking out across the meadow. "It's hard to put your finger on, but you feel like you're looking into a mirror, only you look right past your reflection and into your thoughts and feelings. It's as if you really begin to see yourself clearly. Sort of like throwing a stone in a river—when the ripples die down you can see yourself."

"Well, what happened, exactly?"

"He took me beyond the trees," she answered in a far-away voice, "and we went out on the hills. It looked like a storm was coming from the south, but I wasn't frightened. I felt that nothing could touch us, that I belonged on his back, riding together with him. And it was the funniest thing."

"What?"

"Well . . ."

"Please, Cath, you have to tell me. I won't laugh, no matter what, I promise."

"When I was out on the hills, I felt like . . . like I was a part of the universe. Not just living here and occupying space, but actually a part of it. I felt that I belonged. And I knew my place in the world."

There was a long silence. Then she turned to me. "It sounds obvious," she laughed, "but the universe is some kind of big machine. And I have to figure out how it works. It was like a spinning wheel, spinning out the fabric of space. And the pattern was filled with all of the planets and stars."

She thought for a moment, and then got a funny look on her face. "*Listen* to me," she said to herself. "I'm starting to sound like Dad and Mr. Tucker. I can't believe I said that."

I wrinkled up my forehead. "Then," I asked, "you didn't mean what you said . . . Is the universe a spinning machine or not?"

"Just take my word for it." She shook her head. "Better yet, ride him for yourself and see. Things happen when you ride him. Things you never dreamed of, but it sure seemed real enough. I just don't know. I guess I'll have to ride again. Just to be sure, you understand."

"Yeah"—I nodded—"just to be sure."

Just then Bob came trotting across the meadow and pulled up to the fence. I could see the excitement on his face, and a warm glow in his eyes. "I could ride forever," he said with great satisfaction, "but it's your turn, Thad."

He got off and looked at me and Cathy. I supposed we should have known what he would experience on Infinity's back. It was the one thing he loved as much as life itself. "Ball game," he said, wide-eyed. "Life is a ball game, and I was born to pitch."

He worked his left arm. "Boy," he said, "this old arm

feels pretty good. I think the hole is healing up. I don't feel any pain at all now."

He picked up a rock the size of a baseball and threw it at the sign that said SCHOOL AHEAD. It must have been sixty feet away, but he hit it square in the middle, putting a pretty good-sized dent in it. Sure looked like a strike to me.

I looked back at Infinity, waiting for me by the fence. He had been standing there patiently all along. I jumped down and stood beside him. He was white as powdered sugar, and huge. There was no way I was going to climb up on him, not without some help.

With his hands, Bob made a stirrup for me. Then I got an idea. "No, wait," I said, "I can do it."

I climbed up on the fence post and Bob turned Infinity around. The unicorn snorted and pawed the dirt, kind of nervous-like. "Easy, boy," Bob said, holding onto his mane. "Just one more trip around the meadow. There's nothin' to get excited about."

Infinity got a wild look in his eyes and reared up, pushing Bob away. As he stood up full length on his hind legs, pawing the air fiercely, he looked twenty feet tall and as powerful as a cyclone. The unicorn's ear-piercing cry shattered the silence like a crystal vase crashing on a concrete floor.

The wind came up, colder and more intense than before. None of us had noticed that dark clouds had drifted in and smothered the moon. We looked towards the south in disbelief, and there it was, a swirling black cloud racing towards us from over the Flint Hills.

"Look!" I shouted, fear and surprise in my voice. "That's a twister!"

Suddenly headlights flashed on behind us, blasting Infinity with harsh yellow light. He bolted across the meadow and disappeared.

The headlights backed up and turned toward the road. We ran after them, but we were left in a cloud of dust as the car vanished into the night. We had a pretty good idea whose car it had been.

I looked down at the ground where the car had been

parked and saw a sticky puddle, so I bent down and sniffed
it. There was only one thing in the world that gave off that
kind of aroma: Kentucky chewing tobacco mixed with Kansas dirt.

"Come on!" Bob yelled at me. "That twister's comin'
fast, and it's lookin' for a spot to touch down."

Whatever feelings I had about riding Infinity were torn
away from me by that black whirlwind. It felt like somebody
had pulled the top off my heart and sucked out all of the
happiness. I vowed to search as long and as far as it took
to get Infinity back. It was the only thing that could fill me
up again and put the lid back on my heart.

I called Infinity's name as Bob and Cathy dragged me
away from the meadow. I turned for one last look, searching
the highest hill in the distance, but I couldn't see a thing
except black dust. He was gone, and my hopes and dreams
went with him.

38

Kansas Twister

The big twister darkened the night sky. A huge cloud, black as soot, was swirling in from the south. It couldn't have been more than ten miles away by the time we saw it.

It pushed a cold wet wind out in front of it as a warning to get out of the way, but it was like a spinning top on a hardwood floor. There was no way to tell where it would go. Sometimes twisters turned east and headed towards Missouri. Other times they just kept coming north. But once in a while they turned west and headed towards town.

The one we had been in the path of back in '40 took the roof clean off the courthouse. It picked up a couple of tractors and a truck along the way and deposited them five miles west of town. Nobody even bothered bringing them back, since they looked like they had been in a head-on collision with a train. About the only thing you could do when a twister came was to take shelter underground as soon as possible and wait for it to blow over.

We figured we had only three places to go that night: the school, Tucker's cabin, or my folks' farm. We decided we had enough time to get on home and tuck Petula in the barn. That way she'd have a fighting chance. That is, unless the darned twister picked up the whole barn. I knew my chances of finding Infinity were about as good as catching fish by hand, but this was no time for logic. After all, he had run off with my heart without so much as saying goodbye, and I didn't know if I was going to get it back.

I broke away from Bob and Cathy and ran out on the meadow. The wind was even more fierce than before, breaking small branches off walnut trees and flinging them clear across the road. Wheat waved in the meadow, thrashing wildly back and forth.

"Infinity!" I cried. "Infinity! Where are you?"

But it was no use. I couldn't see him anywhere. I walked back slowly. Then I heard him whinny, and I whirled around. He was out on the hills, on top of a ridge. I started to run towards him.

"Come back!" I shouted. "Please! Come back!"

Cathy and Bob caught up and dragged me away. I got loose once and Bob had to make an open field tackle on me.

"No," I argued, "let me go! He'll get killed out there. I have to find him."

"Thaddy," Bob said, his arms wrapped tightly around me, "you have to let him go. If he wants to, he'll come back. Otherwise, you gotta remember he wasn't ours in the first place, and me and Cath just stole a ride. I know you should've rode him first, but it didn't happen that way, and I'm real sorry. But you have to let him go now, or we'll all be swept up by that twister."

"But what if he gets killed?" I said, kicking and struggling with all of my strength. "I'll die. I'll just die!"

"Okay," he said at last, "I'm goin' to let go." He loosened his grip. "But if you don't believe he'll come back, then you've got no faith. And without faith, he'll never come back." I pulled away and ran for the hills. "It was your belief," Bob yelled after me, "that brought him here in the first place. So go on, run after him. But the only way you're goin' to catch him is to believe again. Otherwise, you can hang it up. 'Cause he ain't never comin' back. And you sure ain't gonna catch him on foot.''

I stopped running and looked up at the ridge. Infinity was gone. Beyond the hills the twister spun closer, choking off moonlight as it came. It must have been miles across at the top, and as big as a house at the end. It was searching for a place to touch down.

I turned and stared at Bob. I hadn't liked him much until lately. I thought he didn't know anything about life. But I was wrong and he was right. If I didn't have enough faith to wait for Infinity to return, I didn't deserve him. It was going to be the hardest thing I ever had to do, but the heart has no choice sometimes.

The wind howled fiercely at our backs. The twister was coming straight at us and moving fast. I ran past Bob and jumped on Petula. "Well," I yelled, almost getting blown off, "you gonna just stand here? We can't wait all night for some silly unicorn. Let's get a move on." Both Cathy and Bob could see I had no intention of being separated from Petula, and Cathy wasn't about to let me out of her sight, fearing I might ride out on the hills, so she got on behind me and we rode home tandem.

As we pulled out on the road there was water in my eyes, and it wasn't caused by the wind. I felt a lump in my throat as big and hard as a baseball. It took some time, but I was finally able to swallow my feelings. I wiped the water out of my eyes and held on.

I felt a little better knowing that I could touch someone who had actually ridden a unicorn, but it didn't make the hurt go away. I felt worse than if I'd never even seen Infinity, but there was nothing I could do except wait and hope, and take cover from that angry whirlwind.

We went back home as fast as we could, Cathy and me on Petula and Bob in his truck. The cold wind beat at our backs, pelting us with dust, twigs, water, and leaves.

Petula's hooves practically never touched the ground. When we got to the farm, the wind blew so hard we almost fell down trying to get off. We tucked Petula in the barn, next to Elmer and Becky, and headed for the house.

We were all shivering cold from the wind and water, but I still wanted to stay out in the barn with the animals. Nobody would let me, though, so we fought our way to the house and banged on the cellar door. It took both Bob and Dad working together against the wind to get the door open, but we finally managed to climb in and shut the doors.

"Sure glad to see you kids in one piece," Dad said, sliding the two-by-four in place. "That's a mighty big twister out there. And from the looks of things, it's comin' this way."

"Thank heavens you're all safe," Mom sighed, and gave hugs all around. "I thought you were gone.

"Here," she said, wiping her eyes, "take a warm blanket. Maybe it'll stop the shivering."

"Mom, could I stay with Petula?"

"Absolutely not," she replied, roughing me up with the blanket. "That tornado could take the whole barn, maybe even the house."

I didn't answer; I just bundled up to stop the shivering. We sat by the kerosene lamp and waited, listening to the wind whipping over our heads and the sound of boards creaking and cracking above. It whistled through the storm shutters on the basement window and rattled the cellar door. We knew we were in for a long night, since Mom was not going to let us out until after it was long gone.

"I've seen them double back," she said at one point, "and catch you looking the other way."

"Really?" I asked. "You're joshing."

"Why, it's true," Dad said with a grin. "One time a twister took the roof clean off my grandpa's cabin. And when he went out for a look, it put the roof back and took him in trade. They found him a week later floatin' down the Mississippi, sittin' in a bathtub and fishin'. He was usin' a picket fence for a fishin' pole and barbed wire for line. They say he caught sixteen catfish before the bathtub went under. Seems the fish swam into the tub and couldn't find their way out again. He said it was just like fishin' in a barrel in the middle of a river. Best fishin' he ever had."

"Aw, Dad, you're not following the rules. Only kids and

old folks get to make up stories." I paused and added, "I wonder if Mr. Tucker's all right."

"He's okay," Mom said. "Doc's got a cellar at the hospital. He keeps his medical supplies down there."

"And plenty of Kentucky whisky, from what I hear," Dad added. Mom gave him a stern look.

"You know, Mr. Williams," Bob said, "I heard about that speech of yours the other night, when you were talkin' to that army fellow about keepin' the farm. Ever since, I haven't been able to get it out of my head. It's like a light went on or somethin'. And it just kept forcin' me to look at my own dream. So I'm goin' to be a pitcher. I'm goin' to work this arm 'til it gets sharp. Heck . . ." He worked it back and forth. "Just the idea of pitchin' makes it feel a lot stronger already.

"I ain't goin' to let no little hole in the arm ruin my life," he went on. "I'm goin' to start pitchin' soon as this twister blows over. Maybe I'll make it and maybe I won't. But even if I only have a couple of seasons, so what. I've got to try. Shoot, I heard about a pitcher in Omaha had only one arm. If he can do it, I sure can. Just takes practice, that's all."

He looked at Cathy. "I figger I got six months before I can try out for the college team. Besides, there's more to life than milkin' cows."

Everyone looked at him funny. All the while we had thought he was going off to Wichita State to study the dairy business. We never even thought he'd try to pitch again. Frankly, I was just a little worried. I knew that riding Infinity had raised his dream up from where he had buried it, but now I felt maybe he had gone too far and was believing in something that couldn't come true. I felt like it was my doing, but before I could say anything, my sister spoke up.

"But I thought . . ." By the tone of her voice, Cathy was not disappointed, just a little surprised.

"I know," Bob replied. "I thought I gave up on pitchin', too. But to tell you the truth, I'm goin' to do both. If the pitchin' don't work out, I'm goin' to run the dairy just like I promised Dad. But I've got to try out my arm first. Otherwise, I'll spend the rest of my life wonderin' and regrettin' what might have been. Don't worry none about the dairy, I'll probably be goin' back to it soon enough." He listened to the wind whistling through the cracks in the shutters. "If there's one left after tonight, that is."

We were silent for a time, but after a while, Dad smiled and looked at him with an amused expression. "You might change your mind after this twister blows over," he said, "but I reckon you're doin' the right thing." He looked at Bob carefully. "You ain't been smokin' corn silk, have you?" he asked with a grin. "With all of that philosophy talk, you're startin' to sound like me. And that's dangerous in these parts."

"Dad," Cathy protested. "he doesn't even chew tobacco."

"So," Mom said, changing the subject, "caught any unicorns yet?"

We kids looked at each other. "Sure, Mom," I said sarcastically. "Some of us even rode him tonight." Bob and Cathy gave me a startled look, but they didn't say anything. They knew I was disappointed and couldn't keep it from coming out.

"What did you name this critter anyway?" Dad asked.

"Name?" Cathy said. "Well, we . . ."

"Yeah," Dad said, "critters got to have names. Even imaginary ones."

"Infinity," I told them. "His name's Infinity." Mom and Dad just looked at me. "Take my word for it," I said, "that's his name."

"That's quite a name," Mom said, watching the flame dance on the kerosene lamp.

"He's quite a horse," I replied.

"Horse?" Bob said.

"Yeah," I answered, "horse with a horn."

"Well," Mom said, "I hope he's still around tomorrow. After this tornado, there may not be much left of anything. It may all get sucked into the sky."

The wind suddenly picked up outside. The twister sounded like it was right overhead. We had to cover our ears to keep our eardrums from busting. There was a lot of creaking and groaning and a tremendous hissing sound, like bees buzzing about a hive. It went on for several seconds, and then it was gone. The tornado had moved on, but after it left there were tiny wheat kernels coming in through the cracks in the cellar doors.

"What happened?" I asked. "Where'd all this wheat come from?"

Dad took on a hard expression. "It either came from that field or somebody else's field," he said, "unless it came out of that silo."

We all stared at each other in fear and disbelief. If it had come out of the silo, our world had been carried off with the wind. There was not much else to say. We fell asleep hoping that our farm would still be there in the morning.

39

Opening Farewell

The next morning was calm and very quiet. We approached the cellar steps with great anxiety. Bob slid back the wooden bolt and pushed open the doors. Warm sunlight poured into the room like glowing molten ore into a mold.

The sun was so bright that we had to shield our eyes, but once we got outside we could see pretty clear. Our hats were pressed to the side of the house, held there gently by an early morning breeze. We picked them up and dusted them off. They looked pretty good—a little beat up, but all in one piece. We shook the wheat kernels out of them, and noticed that grain was scattered just about everywhere. Something else was wrong, but I couldn't figure out what. Then I looked up. The top of the windmill was gone—blades, tail, and all. It gave me a real uneasy feeling.

"Look," I said, pointing to the top of the tower. "The twister blew it clean off."

"Yeah," Bob said, shaking wheat out of his hat. "It don't look too good." We put our hats on and looked at each other, knowing what we had to do next.

We walked slowly over to the barn, expecting the worst, and praying we were wrong. The old red barn was still in one piece, and so was the house. Neither had been touched by the twister, but the thin layer of grain scattered all over told the tale.

When we rounded the corner of the barn, we saw what had happened to the wheat. It had blown away. The silo was still standing, but the roof had been torn off, and that hungry tornado had sucked all the grain out of it.

We walked inside the silo in despair. There wasn't enough grain to cover the toes of our boots, and what was scattered all over the yard wasn't enough to fill a watering trough.

We stared at each other as Mom and Dad came over from checking the house. Dad didn't even have to look inside the silo to know what had happened.

"Ain't you got some animals to be checkin' on, Thaddy?" he said, as if nothing had happened.

"Yeah," I yelled back, my voice echoing off the metal walls. The empty sound made me come to my senses and I raced to the barn. All of the animals were safe and sound, and that made me feel a little better.

I hugged each one of them real big, and they all looked at me sort of funny. But I didn't care, I was happy to see them, and I figured they were just as happy to see me. Becky and Petula did swish their tails and lick me a little, while Elmer just wiggled his little corkscrew tail as best he could. It was enough for me to see those tails swishing and wagging to know that they still loved me.

It was the one bright spot in the whole day, though I didn't know it at the time. Dad got out John Deere just like nothing had happened. But Mom made it clear it was just his opening farewell to the farm, and that over the course of the next week we would be saying our goodbyes. There wasn't near enough wheat left out in that field to amount to anything—fifty acres at best. It was pretty clear that Dad just wanted to get in his last week of farming before we moved to Wichita.

"We put up a good fight," Dad said at last, stopping by the fence as we watched him trim a row. "I can buck the

government," he added with a touch of pride, "and the
cattle ranchers, but nobody can fight Mother Nature. I
reckon it's as good a sign as any that it's time to move on
. . . Well," he said after a pause, "it's about time we joined
the twentieth century, anyway. Now, you kids go on out
and have some fun. Go fishin' or ridin', or . . ."

He looked at Cathy and Bob. "Go crush the hay in the
loft. But I want you all to do me a favor. Take some pictures
with your mind and stuff 'em away somewhere inside, and
when you get older and have a porch of your own to sit
and reminisce on, you take 'em out and dust 'em off. 'Cause
rememberin' is one of the greatest gifts life has to offer.

"Go on, now," Dad said, "get goin'. Don't you kids
got nothin' to do?"

The three of us walked away arm in arm, savoring his
homegrown wisdom as best we could. We weren't completely surprised, though, by my dad's acceptance of losing
the farm. He was a fighter, to be sure, but he was not a
fool. He knew how to accept defeat when he had to.

We figured he was right about something else, too. We'd
better get some fun in while we could, before the sun set
on our summer for good. Bob and Cathy went off together,
and I decided I'd go see if the twister did any damage to
Mr. Tucker's place.

Before I left, Cathy and Bob said they were real sorry
that I hadn't been able to ride Infinity. I said I understood,
but I wasn't giving up yet. I told them I was going back to
the meadow every night until we moved, if I had to, to wait
for Infinity's return. They agreed to go with me in case I
needed some help, and we set a date for that night.

So I saddled up Petula and rode off towards Tucker's.
When I got to the turnoff, I saw a yellow barricade across
the road. There were several brown sedans and trucks parked
nearby.

Wingate met me before I got there, and held out his hand
like he was stopping traffic. "Morning, Thaddeus," he said,
scratching his nose.

"Where'd you come from?" I asked, climbing down.
"We didn't hear any cars go by last night, or this morning,

neither. Except when you pulled off from the meadow last night.''

"Came in the other side of the loop,'' he said, ignoring my question and chewing on a big wad of tobacco. "You folks didn't sustain any damage I hope.''

"Nope,'' I said, "just blew the top off the windmill, that's all.'' I wasn't about to volunteer any information about our plight. I figured he'd find out soon enough, and I didn't want to give him the pleasure of finding out before we got a chance to say our proper goodbyes to the farm.

"Yeah,'' he said, "seems we found it with the school bell about five miles down the road. Didn't lose anything else, I trust.''

"Nope, not a lick,'' I said, straight-faced.

"You're lucky,'' he added, and spit in the dirt. "The schoolhouse lost the whole darned roof.'' He crossed his arms, as if to make another barricade. "That's why we can't let nobody in here. Sheriff called us in to assess the damage.''

I looked down the road towards Tucker's cabin. "But . . . I've got to check out Mr. Tucker's place. See if . . .''

"Already checked it out,'' he said, running his hand along the brim of his hat. "He's mighty lucky, though. Got no damage.''

"Well,'' I insisted, "you've got to let me in. Mr. Tucker sent me to pick up something for him.''

He plunged his hands in his pants pockets and rocked back on his heels, all the while chewing on that wad of tobacco like it was bubble gum.

"Well,'' he said, pushing the tobacco to one side of his mouth, "I'm afraid it'll have to wait. Nobody's allowed in there. Too close to the school. There's too many boards laying around with splinters and nails. You could get hurt.'' He stopped and smiled through his thin lips. Then he reached up and wiped tobacco juice from the corners of his mouth. "But if you tell me what he sent you for,'' he said, "we'll go fetch it for you.''

In a huff, I turned around and got back on Petula. I tried to ride around the barricade, but several army men surrounded us. Two of them grabbed Petula's reins. She kicked the air behind her, but the men held fast. I patted her neck to calm her.

"Mighty foolish of you, Thaddeus," Wingate said, turning around. "Now, unless you want us to take you in for trespassing, you'd better turn around and ride back home. 'Cause if somebody gives us any trouble, we might have no choice except to do something we wouldn't want to."

He lifted his hat and scratched his white forehead. "Boy," he said, "a horse as big as her would sure make a lot of dog food."

"Okay," I said to the men holding Petula, "let go, you're hurting her." They looked at Wingate, who nodded, then leaned over and spit the whole wad of brown tobacco on the ground. He wiped his mouth with his hand and pointed it at me.

"Oh," he added as I turned Petula around, "and don't be trying to sneak around back. We've got the whole place roped off."

I rode back home to tell Bob and Cathy what had happened. I didn't like Wingate much, and I didn't like him spitting on good Kansas dirt. It was like he was spitting on us and our way of life, and I sure didn't like what he'd said about Petula. It had sounded like a threat.

When I got home and told them the news, the Unicorn Hunting Club decided to hold an emergency closed-door session in the barn. We had to plan our strategy. I told Cathy and Bob we had to go back that night and sneak through the ropes. Otherwise we might not catch Infinity, and we sure didn't want him to run into Wingate's hands.

"But, Thaddy," Cathy said, "what if we get caught?"

"Then we get caught," Bob said. "If Infinity is still alive, we've got to get to him before *they* do. Otherwise, we're through. There's no telling what could happen if they catch him. Besides, Thaddy's got to ride him yet."

"Well," I said, "we have to go anyhow. We have to let him know we still believe. Because if we don't, we may lose him forever."

"If he's still alive after last night," Cathy said, and we

all looked at each other. After all we had been through, to lose him now would have been unbearable, especially for me. The farm would soon be only a memory. But I didn't even have a memory of riding a unicorn to take with me, and I wasn't going to Wichita without it. Not if I could help it.

40

Too Close for Comfort

That night we saddled up both horses and snuck around the back of Tucker's place. On the way over, we noticed Wingate's car and some trucks that looked like covered wagons parked along the roadway. One of the trucks even had a horse trailer attached to it. I wondered what it was for. There weren't any barricades set up behind Mr. Tucker's cabin, so it looked good for us to sneak in.

We hoped the trucks parked along the road were just decoys and that everyone else had gone back to town. We couldn't tell for sure, though, because a heavy mist was coming up on the meadow.

We waited for the mist to fill the meadow completely before we felt safe. Then we crawled in and waited in the wheat. It was very still, and some long, anxious hours passed, but we didn't see a thing. It was much too quiet for me. It felt like something was up. Usually, you could hear frog noises coming from the river in the distance, or the sound of crickets rubbing their spiny legs together, but not that night. There weren't even any fireflies out, and with the fog blocking out the moon, it was pretty dark and cool out there, too dark and cool for my taste. I began to get suspicious.

Finally, I couldn't wait any longer. "I'm going out by the school," I said at last, shattering the silence. "He may not come in this far with all those cars around."

"You can't do that," Bob said with concern. "You'll blow the whole thing. Just sit tight. He'll come."

"Look," I argued, "it's the only chance we've got. Unless Infinity knows we're here, he ain't coming under these circumstances. I've got to go out and bring him in. You guys stay here and watch the road."

"Thaddy," Cathy said, grabbing my shoulder, "be careful." Bob just shook his head. He didn't want to let me go, but he knew he had to. My need to ride a unicorn was greater than his and Cathy's, and they both knew they owed me one, so they didn't try to stop me.

It might have been just plain stupid to go chasing out after Infinity, especially in fog as thick as my stubborn skull and with the army parked nearby. But I was desperate. Even if I didn't get to ride him that night, I had to let him see me so he wouldn't think I'd given up on him. I just had to see that he was still there and still okay.

I snuck across the meadow, running from fog patch to fog patch to keep from being spotted by the army guards. When I got past the last row of walnut trees, I saw the schoolhouse outlined against the sky—roof, bell, and all. It was untouched. They had lied to me; the twister had missed the school completely. It had to be a trap.

The wild cry of a stallion pierced the air from out on the hills, sending shivers down my spine. The loud hoot of an owl followed right after it. I knew the voice of that owl, coming from the school bell tower.

He hooted again. Then he must have flown away with a powerful thrust of his claws, pushing the bell so hard it clanged several times. I took it as a warning to get out of there quick.

I ran back across the field as fast as I could, not bothering to duck into fog patches. I had to warn Cathy and Bob.

When I reached them I was out of breath. By the time I got the words out about how we had been tricked, it was too late. We could already hear heavy hoofbeats on the meadow. They were coming our way, pounding hard and fast on the firm ground.

We stood up and yelled, motioning with our hands. "No!" we shouted together, "Go back, Infinity! It's a trap! It's a trap!" We yelled at the top of our lungs, but it was no use. The hoofbeats stopped, just twenty yards away.

Engines started and headlights flashed on, surrounding the meadow. The drivers began to pull the trucks into a circle. The headlights made a crossing pattern, like spokes on a giant wheel of light, but it was more like shining swords of death.

Infinity reared up out of the mist. He had never looked so big, so proud, and so vulnerable. He gave me a piercing glance, and pawed the air with his powerful forelegs. He let out a menacing cry that echoed off the meadow like a scream in an empty canyon, then came down hard and bolted for the trees. Just before he reached them he saw a row of nets in front of him, strung between the branches of the walnut trees. He turned in another direction and ran, but again there were nets. Soon the whole meadow was a army of advancing headlights. Nets eight feet high shot up on three sides. They had him boxed in. Soldiers climbed out of the covered trucks and raced forward with ropes and guns, blocking the only exit.

"No!" I yelled. "No! Let him go!"

We tried to run for him, but a large thick net dropped over us. We struggled and strained against the ropes, but it was no use. They lifted us into the air, suspended from two trees. Though we floundered like fish, we couldn't escape— and we couldn't help Infinity. He was on his own.

He circled the meadow, looking frantically for a way out. But there was none. The men slowly closed in. They raised their rifles, pointing them at Infinity. We watched in fear, dangling hopelessly in the net.

"Run! Run!" we all yelled, but it was no use. One of the men threw a thick rope around Infinity's neck, but the unicorn pulled it right out of his hands. Three men jumped on the loose rope and tied it to a tree. Infinity charged against the rope, shaking the tree violently and fraying the rope in several places. He backed up and charged again, this time breaking the rope clean. One of the men cocked his rifle.

"Wait!" Wingate yelled. "I want him alive!"

Infinity spun in a circle. "Your light!" I yelled without thinking. "Turn on your light!" I knew I shouldn't have said anything, since I figured his light was only for special situations, but this looked like the end.

He reared and pawed the air, piercing the night with a powerful cry, then bolted for the school, galloping full speed towards the trees and the nets. I thought he was going to slam into the nets, but when he got six feet away he went airborne, clearing the net by a foot. He hit solid ground without breaking stride and galloped past the school. Soon he was out on the hills, running wild and free.

When he got to the highest ridge, he reared up full length, his silhouette etched in moonlight. He gave one last cry, and then he was gone.

Wingate ordered the men off the meadow. He didn't look at us as we hung in the net and cheered. The men were babbling to themselves about how high Infinity had jumped, and with such ease. One of them said he should have shot him, and that made me wince. The soldier who was guarding us started to lower the net to the ground, but Wingate yelled at him to stop.

"Leave that net until last! Get the rest of the nets in the trucks. We're pulling out of here. Now!"

The man yanked us back up to the top, about six feet from the ground, and helped the others pack the nets in the covered trucks. They lined up the trucks in single file on the road and waited for Wingate's command.

We kept waiting for someone to cut us down, but no one did. The trucks pulled off down the road, with us yelling at them. When they got about fifty yards away, Wingate's sedan stopped. He got out and walked slowly over to us, then pulled out a knife and flashed it at us in the moonlight. I thought he was going to stab us with it through the net, but he reached up to one of the ropes that held the net. He had a wicked smile on his face.

"Where's Petula?" I asked angrily, noticing she wasn't around anywhere.

"And Chester," Bob added in the same tone. "You'd better let us down, or Sheriff Johnson's gonna hear about this. And if you've harmed them horses in any way, I'll bust that nose of yours clean off your face." Bob was getting madder by the minute.

"You're an evil man," Cathy said, and it surprised me, coming from her. "You've got no right to catch our unicorn," she added. "You've got no right to go around crushing other people's dreams."

"Free country," Wingate said, without batting an eye.

"Yeah," I said sarcastically, "but this is Mr. Tucker's land. You're trespassing."

"Won't be much longer, I expect," he said with a sinister smile, still not cutting the rope. "Looks like we'll be taking that farm of yours too next week. Guess your dad lost out, kid. And if that creature of yours comes back, I reckon we'll get him too."

"He ain't never coming back!" I yelled. "And even if he does, you'll never catch him. Besides, what do you care? People like you don't believe in unicorns, anyway."

"It ain't unicorns we're interested in," he said, reaching up to cut the rope, "but we are interested in strange creatures."

"He ain't strange," Bob said, "he's beautiful."

I grabbed Bob's arm. I'd heard hooves on the meadow, and then there were two sets coming our way. Out of the mist came Petula and Chester, galloping happily towards us. I heaved a big sigh of relief, knowing that they hadn't been captured.

Wingate dropped the knife at the sight of them and walked quickly away. Just before he got to the road, he turned to us. "I've got plenty of time to wait for that thing to come back!" he shouted. "But you've only got a week. We'll catch him, and when we do, we'll find out what's inside that horn!"

I was going to yell something mean back at him, but Cathy grabbed me. "Let him go," she said calmly. "He'll never catch Infinity."

"Yeah," Bob chimed in, "not if we can help it." He reached down and tried to pick up the knife, but it was a little too far away from the net, and he came up a foot short. Chester and Petula came over and gave us curious looks. I was real happy to see them, especially Petula.

"Petula," I smiled, "I thought you were dog food for sure."

"Yeah," Cathy agreed. "Now come over here and pick up that knife."

"You too, Chester," Bob said. "Come on, boy. Pick up the knife."

Cathy and Bob coaxed and pleaded with the horses for a couple of minutes, then Bob turned to me in frustration.

"Come on, Thaddy. Aren't you going to help? How do you expect us to get out of this net?"

"Well," I grinned, digging into my pants pocket. "It sure was fun watching you guys beg for a change, but why don't we use this?" I flashed my pocket knife in their faces and they both gave me some funny looks. No one tried to slug me, though—afraid I'd drop the knife, I guess.

After I cut us down we rode home knowing we had failed, and that it almost cost us Infinity's freedom. I decided to go see Mr. Tucker in the hospital the next day and tell him about it, and see if he had any ideas about how we could get Infinity back.

Later in bed, I tried hard to fall asleep, but something kept bothering me. I was pretty sure Wingate and his men couldn't catch Infinity by themselves, but that night had been an awfully close call. And if Infinity came back and got caught, I would never forgive myself.

I couldn't go back and look for him. I just couldn't take the chance. I'd have to find another way to catch him. Anyhow, the meadow had been run over by the trucks, and the wheat had been crushed into the ground. I didn't figure Infinity would want to come back, even for a midnight snack, whether I came or not. So there seemed no point in going.

One other thing bothered me pretty bad. What did Wingate mean when he said he was going to see what was inside Infinity's horn? I didn't like the sound of that at all. When I thought about it, a great pain welled up in my chest. I didn't want to, but I knew I had to make Infinity go away.

Maybe I couldn't, but at least I had to try. I thought back on what Bob had said. If Infinity really wanted to see me, he'd still come back. I hoped he would, and if he did, I hoped it'd be somewhere Wingate couldn't find us, somewhere out of the reach of the world and all of its nonbelievers. I just didn't know where that place could be.

I finally fell off to sleep sometime later, and awoke the next morning to the crow of our rooster, cracking the dawn like a lightning bolt splitting a walnut tree.

41

Chasing the Dream

The next morning I rode to the hospital to see how Mr. Tucker was doing and to tell him about everything that had happened: Infinity's close call, the empty silo, and the bad news about us losing the farm.

I passed Doc Yeager on the way to town. He was heading towards my parents' place, and had our windmill tied on top of his ambulance. He said he'd found it halfway to town, and was returning it. I didn't tell him about our grain being gone, because I thought then he might change his mind about delivering the windmill.

The blades and tail were a little beat up and bent, but otherwise it looked in working order. He said the twister had jumped over the town, but had swiped the roof of the jail to let us know it had come by for a visit. I don't think it mattered much, since the jail didn't get much use anyhow.

When I got to the hospital, Mr. Tucker didn't have tubes in his arm anymore, and was looking pretty healthy. His black skin had its glow back, and his deep brown eyes sparkled again, like when he used to tell us stories on his back porch. He didn't seem the least bit concerned about the bulldozers coming to level his cabin next week. He wanted to talk about something else.

"Tell me about Infinity," he asked.

"He was like a Kansas snowstorm," I answered, my eyes opening wide, "big and white and wild. I thought they had him there for a minute, but he jumped right over the nets. I've never seen anything jump that high. You should have seen the looks on their faces when he sailed over their heads. Wingate was plenty mad at us when Infinity got away, but Petula scared him off."

I paused and thought. "What do you suppose makes Wingate so mean?" I asked. "I know he got kicked by a horse and all, but he don't limp or nothing, so it couldn't have been that bad."

"He's limpin' inside," Mr. Tucker answered soberly, "but don't you worry none about the likes of him." He scratched his beard and added, "They'll never catch Infinity unless he lets himself get caught."

"Why would he do that?" I wanted to know.

"He wouldn't on purpose. Except to save someone else from danger."

"That's why I ain't going out after him anymore," I said. "I can't risk his life. Why, I'd never forgive myself if he got caught on account of me."

"Nothin' you can do about it," Mr. Tucker said, looking seriously at me. "You can't change the way you feel about him, and so you just keep sendin' out signals, whether you want to or not. It's up to him to come to you now. All you can do is watch and wait."

"But I only got a week left," I said with a sigh, "and then I'm gone forever."

"I'm sure he knows, Thaddy." Mr. Tucker patted my hand. "He knows how long he's got."

We sat in silence for a long while, and then he said, "Don't you go worryin' none about losin' yer farm."

"What's there to worry about?" I said, with dejection all over my face. "The farm's already gone. The twister took care of that."

"That's all right," he said, and it caught me funny. How could it be okay if the farm was gone? "Let the farm go," he explained. "And if it's yers . . ."

"Yeah, I know," I said. "It'll come back to me. But how do you know when you're supposed to hold on to something and when you're supposed to let it go?"

"Beats me," he said with a wink, and we both laughed out loud. "You hold on to whatever you have to in life to keep from losin' yer sanity. But sometimes it's lettin' go that can *save* yer sanity. You have to figger out when to let go. Otherwise, holdin' on too long could drive you crazy."

"Where you gonna go when you get bulldozed off the farm?" I asked with concern.

"Don't rightly know," he replied, and looked up at the ceiling. "I hear I got some relatives in Tennessee."

"Tennessee?" I said. "Nothing doing." I grabbed his arm. "I'm gonna ask Dad if we can take you to Wichita with us. What do you say?"

"I ain't fixin' to be a burden to no one," he answered, looking back at me.

"Burden? Why, you ain't no burden. You and Dad could sit and talk for hours. I know you could."

"Well, I . . ."

"Promise me you'll think about it?"

"All right," he said at last, "I'll give it some thought. But let's not jump the gun. We still got a week, and anythin' could happen in a week."

"Like what?" I asked, frustrated by his blind belief, and a little jealous that mine wasn't as strong. "Everything's happened already that *can* happen, except for me—and you—getting to ride Infinity."

He gave me a stern look. "I thought I taught you better than that," he said, shaking his head. "You keep forgettin' that unicorns can bring dreams to life. And once you ride him, whatever yer dream is will most likely come to pass. That's the way it works."

"If I ever *get* to ride him," I said doubtfully. I still believed, but I was beginning to wonder how it could possibly happen under the circumstances.

"I hear you picked out a pup?" he asked, changing the subject.

"Yeah," I replied, suddenly excited, "a black one with a white spot on its chest."

"Got a name fer it yet?"

"Naw, ain't had time to think one up."

"Well, how's the mother and pups doin'?"

"I don't know. I only seen them once."

"Then I guess you'd better get over to Doc's and check up on 'em fer me, until I get out of here."

"When's that?" I wanted to know.

"A couple of days, at least that's what Doc says. And even if he don't let me, I'm goin' anyway. This place is too cooped up fer me. I need to get back to that farm of mine and say farewell."

I didn't say anymore. I just said goodbye and stopped to look at the pups on the way home. My little black Lab with the white spot was busy eating lunch, so I just looked and didn't touch.

Doc was home by then, and agreed that Mr. Tucker could get out in a couple of days. Since he'd seen what the twister had done to our silo, he knew we'd have to move to Wichita, and he agreed to take Becky and Elmer. He said he'd give my Dad a fair price for them, and I said as long as they went to a good home, I was happy. And could I visit them once in a while on weekends? He said yes, and the deal was closed.

The week that followed was even longer and more painful than the last week of school. My parents were kind enough to say Mr. Tucker could stay with us in Wichita, since Mom's relatives had room, but what I really wanted was to stay on the farm until I was good and ready to join the world. Naturally, they couldn't do anything about that.

I tried to enjoy myself as best I could, but I mostly moped around until I couldn't stand it anymore. I went fishing a couple of times, and once when I was skinny-dipping Billy Johnson came by with some other kids. It didn't hurt when he laughed at me for losing the farm, and called me an acorn-sucking chipmunk. But it did hurt when he started picking on my dream.

"I hear you found a stupid ol' horse with somethin' stickin' outa his head," he laughed. "My dad says yer makin' up stories about spaceships and stuff. Well, only little kids and idiots believe in that stuff, and you ain't no little kid no more, 'cept in the brain department. Looks like we're finally gettin' rid of you and that crazy ol' Mr. Tucker. Well, good riddance, farm boy. And take yer phony unicorns with you!"

I would have gotten out of the water and fought him, but some of the kids were girls, and I didn't want to show off my birthday suit to them.

He grabbed my clothes, but he didn't grab Petula or my hat, because Petula kicked the air behind her when he tried to lead her off. She didn't like being led off by strangers. He couldn't take my hat because I hung it on the branch with the beehive on it, and I knew he was too scared of bees to go out after it. Just to be mean, he had once hit an old beehive with his baseball bat, and got stung pretty bad. He swelled up like a hot air balloon and didn't come down for a week. So that pretty much kept him away from beehives.

I had been so cautious about hanging my straw hat out of Petula's reach that I forgot to hang my clothes out there too. I just never figured Billy Johnson would show up and steal my clothes again.

When I finally arrived home on Petula, my mom was starting to pack up the Chevy and had the hay wagon hitched up behind. She didn't say much about my birthday suit; she just pointed to the mailbox and smiled. I fished my clothes out of the box without getting off Petula, and put them on in the barn.

I knew it was going to be our last night on the farm, so I said goodbye to Becky and Elmer as best I could, feeling the pain come up in my chest where my heart was. We had just about the quietest dinner you can imagine, and then I went to my room to sulk in silence.

The sun still had a couple of hours left before sinking

out of sight and I got real restless. I was supposed to be packing up the things in my room, but I just couldn't get started. Instead I pulled out the mythology book and stared at the pictures of the unicorns inside.

I carried the open book to the window, looking out towards Mr. Tucker's place and the hills beyond. I remembered that if the dream truly belonged to me, it would come back and all, but when I glanced down and saw that unicorn on the page looking as big and bold as Infinity, I just couldn't take it anymore.

I snuck out to the barn, saddled up Petula and rode towards the school. Maybe I wasn't supposed to go out on the Flint Hills, but I just couldn't sit by and watch my dream blow away with that twister. Nothing and nobody was going to stop me, and I sure couldn't stop myself.

42

Last Night on the Farm

I rode out on the hills with the sun casting long shadows before me. My dream was about to go down with it, unless I could find Infinity that night, and ride him.

Petula and I galloped over hill after hill until the schoolhouse disappeared behind us. The wild grass waved in the wind, and the gentle hills seemed to roll on into eternity.

Finally we stopped on the highest ridge. The whole world had disappeared, except for the cloudless blue sky above and the deep green carpet of grass below. Then, strangely, the breeze that always blew out on the hills suddenly ceased, and the world got so still I thought it had stopped spinning on its axis. The only sounds were Petula's heavy breathing and the creaking of the saddle when I leaned over to pat her neck.

Her ears perked up and she stopped breathing for a second, listening to something in the distance. Then the angry howl of a wolf pierced the stillness. I whirled around in the saddle and saw him standing a few hills over, staring at us with hungry eyes. Even from the distance between us, I could tell he had spotted his prey. Another wolf appeared beside him, and another. Soon there were five.

I didn't wait for them to pounce; I turned Petula around and bolted for the school. It was a couple of miles away over rolling hills, but it was the only chance we had. As soon as we galloped away, the race was on.

Never looking back, I kicked Petula in the sides and headed for home. When I saw the school bell tower sticking up over the next rise, I knew it was going to be close. The wolves were only half a hill behind by the time we reached the last rise, and were gaining on us pretty quick.

"If you've got anything left," I told Petula, "you'd better use it now. Otherwise, it's all over."

It was no use; the wolves were right on our tail. The school was only over the top of the hill and down the other side, but we'd used up all our strength. Wild growls filled my ears and I could almost feel the breath of the wolves over my shoulder.

In the next moment, the lead wolf jumped. I could feel his breath curl the hair on my neck and his jaws snap at my back; but he missed his mark and rolled right off Petula's back before he could dig in. The rest of the pack kept coming fast and hard. Just as the next wolf was about to leap, I yelled for Infinity. I hadn't even thought about it, but it was the first thing that came to me in my desperation.

"Infinity!" I shouted. "Help! *Help!*"

The wolf never leapt. Maybe he was confused by my shouting, or maybe he heard something behind him, but he didn't take to the air. Me and Petula raced along the hill behind the school, the wolves right on our tail. When we entered Tucker's Grove, I couldn't believe what happened next.

The wolves slowed down and stopped. I turned around when I got past the trees to see if they were circling, but they were just standing there, perfectly still. Suddenly, their ears shot straight up and they turned their heads towards the hills. I heard the cry of a wild stallion in the distance. Hoofbeats were coming my way. The wolves didn't stick around to find out what was coming. They turned tail and headed for the hills, away from the hoofbeats.

I didn't move. If it was Infinity, I had nothing to fear; the wolves wouldn't be back. Looking for him, I'd gone where I shouldn't have, and Mr. Tucker's warning came back to me: "You can't go out into his world," he had said, "you must wait fer him to come to you."

It hurt more than anything to turn away from those hills, but I knew I had no choice. I nudged Petula gently in the sides and turned towards home.

When I got to the road, a wolf howled in the distance. It sounded like the one that had been crushed that night on the road. A thousand years seemed to have come and gone since then, yet it had only been a couple of weeks.

The sun was just going down when I got home. I put Petula in the barn and said one last goodbye to Elmer and Becky, since we were dropping them off at Doc's the next day on the way to Wichita.

Bob and Dad were nailing the top of the windmill back on. My dad wanted to leave the farm just like he found it, except for the silo roof, even though the government was planning to bulldoze it. That was the way he was. His philosophy was to leave the world as close to the way you found it, or even a little better if you could.

I looked up at them pounding the last nails in and then looked at the windmill blades. The wind off the hills suddenly picked up a little and spun them in my direction. The sun was almost down, but it found a way to shoot one last ray onto the blades, making a spinning wheel of light that shone towards Tucker's place for a few seconds. After that, the windmill turned and reflected the beams down the road towards town. Then the sun went beneath the horizon for good that day.

When I went to the house, Mom and Cathy were packing up the kitchen. The screen door slammed behind me, but no one said anything. They knew enough to leave me alone for the time being.

Once upstairs in my room, I began to pack. Everything fit in the boxes Bob had brought from town, so I took one last look out my window towards Tucker's Grove. Climbing into bed, I pulled up the covers.

For some reason I had finally given up trying to wait for a miracle and fell asleep so fast that I don't even remember dreaming. Here this was to be my last night on the farm and my eyes couldn't even stay open for it.

I awoke later to the glare of light pouring through my bedroom window. For a second I thought it must be morning, but though the moon was nearly full and as high in the sky as the sun at noon, it couldn't have been as bright as the light that woke me. What was going on, I wondered. Some dumb truck getting lost on the road again, or what?

Just then a bright beam of white light hit me in the face, and it wasn't coming from the road. It was coming from the fence by the barn.

I got dressed and snuck downstairs. It must have been pretty late, because everyone else was asleep. I closed the screen door carefully so as not to wake anyone, and ran to the fence.

For several minutes I looked around, but couldn't see anything in the field between our place and Tucker's. Finally, with great disappointment, I turned and walked away, convinced that my mind had played a cruel trick on me. But I had to say something, just in case.

"Infinity," I said to the field, "this is your last chance. I'm going away tomorrow. I know you're out there somewhere, so don't pretend you're not. I wanted you. I wanted you worse than anything in the world. Worse than anybody ever wanted anything. But I can't take anymore of this. I feel worse than if I'd never dreamed you up in the first place.

"I'll be back, though, you wait and see. You're not going to get away that easy. And if I have to ride out on those hills again, wolves or no wolves, I'm going to do it. And if I get eaten out there, I don't care. But if Petula gets eaten, then it's gonna be your fault. Because she doesn't know any better. She's just following me, and I'm chasing you. So I'll tell you what. When you're through fooling around and flashing your light at me, then come and see me. Because I ain't got time to stand out here all night and wait for no mythical beast.''

I turned and walked away, not really feeling much better, but glad I had gotten something off my chest. When I got to the well, a bright beam of white light covered me completely, and I turned around.

When I faced the light, all the troubles I had felt began to melt away. I stood there bathing in it like a bear cub in a stream: excited, soaked, and completely happy.

The light stopped, and it took a couple of seconds for me to see again, but I could hear heavy hoofbeats come up and stop by the fence. When I got my vision back, I walked over and put my foot on the bottom rail.

"Infinity," I said, looking into his deep brown eyes, "I knew it. I knew you'd come back. But why did you make me give that dumb speech? Just wanted to hear all my troubles, did you? Well, you got 'em. *Now* do you suppose we can we take that ride . . . please?"

Infinity looked as powerful as raging white water on a river, and yet as calm and beautiful as a snow drift after a winter storm. I was going to climb up on the fence to mount him, but much to my surprise, he bent his head down like a knight bowing before a king, and offered me his horn.

I reached out and grabbed hold of it. It felt as hard and smooth as ivory, and warm to the touch. It tingled in my hand, as if there was electricity flowing through it, and it glowed in the dark like it was filled with fireflies.

I took a seat on his head, right behind the horn. He stood up, lifting his head back with a mighty thrust that sent me sliding down his muscular neck to land on his back. The next thing I knew I was sitting straight up, holding on to his long, bushy mane. Power was running through him like water rushing down a rapids, and it made me tingle all over.

This was the moment I had waited for all my life, and at last it had come. There was nothing more to do but ride— across the field to Tucker's Grove, out on the Flint Hills and into the special place where only unicorns can go.

As fantastic as it seemed, I was at last aboard my wildest dream. I took one last look at the world as I knew it and then I nudged his sides. We trotted off across the field, and then we were gone.

43

Through the Fire

Infinity trotted off with his head held high. His spiraling horn pierced the night mist like a lance and his feet pranced lightly on the soft wet ground. He was sure-footed and strong, and I felt like a knight astride a powerful steed.

The mist hung low in the meadow, lying over the wheat like a white blanket on a bed of gold. Fireflies danced everywhere, following Infinity as if he was their source of light and they had come to recharge their tiny lanterns. I wrapped my hands tighter around his mane. It felt like the hair of a beautiful maiden and smelled of honeysuckle.

We moved over the meadow like the wind, scarcely touching the ground. When he was sure I had a firm grip on his flowing white mane, he slowly began to gallop towards Tucker's, avoiding the side of his meadow that butted up against the school. By the time we passed through the last row of walnut trees, he was in full stride. We raced beyond the schoolhouse and onto the hills.

He took the first hill in a full gallop, streaked down it and bounded up the next. I held on as my stomach leapt to my throat. I had never ridden so fast. It was wild, exciting, and a little bit scary, like a roller coaster ride at the fair.

The moon was full and bright yellow, the sky a deep shade of midnight blue. Stars blinked overhead in a stunning array, filling the sky like sparklers on the Fourth of July.

The grass swayed gently in the cool evening breeze and the mist had disappeared. We left the meadow and the fireflies far behind. They couldn't come where we were about to go.

The hills gathered in a long row, making a ridge like a runway to the stars. We bolted across the top of it where the grass was as short as a fresh-cut lawn.

I didn't think it was possible, but he began to race even faster, his hooves pounding like the roll of a war drum. I held on tighter and pulled his mane downward, trying to peek over his massive head. Even then I could barely see, but I could make out his horn piercing the sky and glowing like a lantern in front of me. I put my head alongside his strong neck. He was so big, and I was so small, that it must have looked like a riderless horse running wild across the ridge.

We reached that magical speed where the world seems to slow down and stop and begins to spin backwards like the blades of a windmill, and disappeared into the world of dreams.

I couldn't feel the ground beneath us anymore, or hear the pounding of hooves, but there was a great glow above me. Infinity's horn was pouring forth a single beam that flooded the sky in front of us.

It was true, I saw when I glanced back for a moment. We were pulling away from the earth. The school, Tucker's Grove, and our farm were growing smaller far below us.

Infinity beamed his light into a spot in the sky and it opened like a tear in a curtain. We rode through the hole to another world.

A deep blue sky appeared, like the inside of an enormous treasure chest lined in deep velvet, and overflowing with glowing jewels. There were dozens of immense spheres, spinning celestial bodies in a magical galaxy. They sparkled with the colors of the rainbow, and were suspended by pulsating strings of light. We traveled through them easily and quickly. Infinity attached his beam to the strings and we moved along at breathtaking speed.

We swooped in close to a sphere covered with precious metals, giving off shimmering rays of silver and gold light. There was the faint, familiar sound of soft music playing on its surface. I wanted to get a closer look, but Infinity just kept on flying.

Soon the treasure chest of spheres was behind us and we were racing through a sea of stars. It seemed impossible that we could be traveling so fast, yet I saw oceans of stars come and go, their light shining like sunlight on water.

We passed out of this immense sea of light into a bottomless blackness. The beam shining from Infinity's horn was the only source of light. I saw no way to cross the darkness, but Infinity seemed to know the way.

Eventually the sky ahead lit up in burnt orange colors. A hot wind felt like a bonfire on my face, and smoke rose a thousand feet into the sky. A thick cloud of black smoke set me coughing, and I had to put my sleeve over my mouth to breathe.

We raced on ahead. Suddenly, fireballs shot past us like flaming tumbleweeds. One came so close it brushed my leg. Flames licked my overalls, and I got scared.

"Infinity!" I shouted, "turn back before you burn us up!" He didn't listen. He just kept flying through the fireballs. The light from his horn kept most of them away. Every time one came directly at us, it veered off as soon as it came in contact with his beam. It made me feel a little better, but I was still scared. After all, one had gotten through and singed my pant leg.

A great barn appeared up ahead, engulfed in flames. It must have been the source of the fireballs.

Strangely, I flashed back ten years. I was being held in my mother's arms, and flames were dancing all around. My parents had told me that when I was a year old, the barn had burned down, but I'd been too young to remember. By

the time the townspeople had come to set up the bucket
brigade, it was too late: The barn had burned to the ground.

Now I was experiencing it as if for the first time. My
face felt as hot as a stove and my eyebrows began to burn.
I beat them out with my sleeve, and we raced forward into
the fire.

"No!" I shouted, "turn back!" But Infinity didn't listen.
We raced through the barn door and into the middle of the
fire, galloping across a burning bed of straw. Flaming boards
fell all around us, and I flashed back to that vision again.

I'd been lying on a hay bale in the barn, where my mom
had placed me while she milked the cow in the morning.
The phone had rung and she'd run to the house to answer
it when the cow accidentally knocked over the kerosene
lamp and started the fire. I saw Mom run through the flames
and scoop me up in her arms. Dad ran in and got the animals
out, but it was too late for the barn.

Now, for the first time, I knew why Mom never went
into the barn, even after the new one was built and we had
a new cow. That must have been one of the reasons why
she wanted to move to Wichita, so she wouldn't have to
look at the barn anymore and relive the memory.

A menacing roar blasted us from behind, pulling me out
of my memory and making the hair stand up on my neck.
My skin broke out in a heat rash and I felt the hair singe
on the back of my neck. I looked back and saw a prairie
wolf standing in the doorway to the barn. His blood-red
eyes were sizing us up with an evil look that pierced right
through me. He opened his mouth and growled, showing
razor-sharp teeth and a long tongue as red as an ember, and
split on the end in several places. Infinity turned to face
him.

The wolf roared and shot balls of fire out of his mouth
like flaming coals. He lifted his head and spit fire from his
nostrils, roaring like a beast from Hell. Flames shot ahead
of him for fifty feet, licking Infinity's legs.

I looked down. Infinity had burned his hooves on the
smoldering straw, but he didn't flinch. He lowered his head
and pointed his horn at the wolf. I grabbed his mane harder,

preparing for him to charge. The wolf roared again, shooting fireballs past my ears, so close that my hair almost caught on fire.

The roof of the barn was ablaze, and was going to fall any second, but the wolf didn't move from the door. He stood his ground, waiting for us to challenge him.

Infinity didn't charge. He began to vibrate all over, as though a surge of power was rising in him, and his horn began to glow again. A single white beam streamed out of it and focused on the wolf, bathing him in light.

The wolf screamed and vanished into thin air. He disappeared so fast that I wondered if he had ever been there at all.

The roof began to give out above us, groaning and dropping timbers to the floor. Infinity turned off his beam and transferred the energy to his legs. We dashed for the door, great burning beams crashing all around us. One of them landed in front of the doorway, angling towards the roof and blocking our escape. Infinity never broke stride. He leapt when we reached the beam, hitting it with his hooves on the way over, but he didn't falter. The whole barn collapsed as we passed through the door, barely missing us as we galloped by.

We rode into the black sky, and when I turned to look at the barn, it had dissolved into a pile of burning embers, flickering red and orange like a sunset on the plains. An enormous whirling cloud of black smoke rose a thousand feet into the dark sky above the ruins. Then a wind came up behind it, spinning it into a twister. It flew off across the blackness, blending with it so well that I couldn't see where it went.

Suddenly the wind cooled us like a bath in a mountain stream. I looked down to check Infinity's hooves. Steam rolled off them, making white clouds like a locomotive on the run. I hoped he was all right. I'd need him for the trip back, if there was going to be one.

44

Kansas in the Sky

Infinity galloped easily now, cruising across the black sky with power and speed. He was catching his breath and gaining strength with every stride. What puzzled me was that he wasn't overheated, even after the great speeds we had traveled. He only glowed, and gave off the sweet scent of honeysuckle.

He turned on his light and focused ahead on a spot in the darkness, lighting up the black sky. We seemed to be in some kind of cosmic wasteland, filled with old meteors and burned-out planets. I could make out the vague outline of volcanic rock and cosmic dust as we raced toward our destination. I could only imagine what lay up ahead, protected by this ocean of darkness.

Suddenly, out in this huge wasteland, my dream of seeing the place where everything had begun seemed to burn out like one of those volcanic planets. It was replaced by a new desire that began to take shape in front of me as we rode on through the endless night.

In my head I started to see visions of home: Dad on his

tractor, Mom on her pottery wheel, and Cathy underneath the car. I even saw Bob pitching rocks at the school sign. They all had big smiles on their faces, happy to be doing what they liked most.

Riding Infinity made me take a second look at my dream, and it had changed a little. Suddenly, I wasn't in such an all-fired hurry to see the center of the universe anymore. I still wanted to see it eventually, but it could wait. I couldn't make out all the features of my new desire, but as the pictures of everyone back on the farm faded away, I began to miss the folks something fierce.

I saw a flat planet up ahead, suspended in space. A bright yellow sun hovered overhead, casting a single beam like a spotlight that lit the place up as if it were broad daylight. As Infinity approached it I could see that it was a huge chunk of brown dirt, as if the entire state of Kansas had been pulled up out of the earth and was floating out here all by itself. A steady golden stream was pouring over its edges. When we got closer, the stream became a river of harvested wheat, its kernels falling endlessly into space.

We passed the edge and rode for hundreds of miles above grass-covered hills before setting down in the middle of this huge prairie and galloping across a ridge that reminded me of the Flint Hills. We trotted on for miles, watching as bronze-colored clouds gathered overhead. They fused together into one solid mass above us, blocking the sun. As far as the eye could see there were green fields, parted in the middle by a river of golden grain.

Infinity slowed to cross the wide river, crushing wheat kernels under his feet. It was like walking in deep sand, but he trudged across and continued onward.

The sky grew darker and the heavy clouds broke, sending showers of dusty-looking wheat down upon the land. It began to pile up like sand dunes in the desert and run down into the river. I couldn't believe it. Back home, all the wheat that was left wouldn't have filled a bathtub, and this place had enough to fill an entire county. Wheat fell like rain from the sky and ran in rivers off the edge of the world. Somehow it didn't seem fair.

Shortly after it started, the storm stopped and the clouds blew over. Once again the sun beat down hard and bright out of a clear blue sky, and it got pretty hot. Sweat beaded up on my forehead and streamed down my face. I shook wheat kernels out of my hat and wiped my face with my sleeve.

Infinity saw something in the distance and suddenly reared up. I almost slid off his back, but I grabbed harder on his mane and held on. An inch of grain came off us both. He came down and steadied himself, and then I saw what had excited him. The wind had picked up and was blowing grain over the land, directly in our faces. Great dunes of grain began to form around us, making a canyon for us to walk through, like a gateway to a desert kingdom. I got a little worried, wondering if the wind would shift and we would be buried completely in wheat.

I pushed my hat down on my head to block out the flying wheat kernels. It felt like being in the middle of a locust swarm. The wind must have been blowing forty miles an hour, but we kept going.

A few miles later, the wind stopped and I uncovered my eyes. The wheat had settled and I could see again. We stood on the edge of a great gorge, a thousand feet deep and a quarter of a mile across. On the other side was a farmhouse set back a ways from the cliff.

It reminded me of the farm back home. It had a big red barn and a silo standing next to it. The farmhouse looked like ours, only it was whitewashed and sparkled in the sun. There was a windmill turning slowly in a gentle breeze, but it wasn't all beat up like ours; it looked all shiny and new.

The wheat field behind it seemed to go on forever, only the wheat wasn't dusty-looking like the wheat that had fallen from the sky; it was shimmering in the sunlight like pure gold. In the distance I could see a green and yellow tractor moving across the wheat. I couldn't make out who was riding it, but he had on a straw hat and overalls.

That place drew me as nothing had ever drawn me before. If I hadn't been standing on the edge of a canyon, I would have gotten off Infinity and run to it.

I felt the rush of wind and water below, and looked down over the cliff. It was so deep that I couldn't see the bottom. The wind began to howl at the end of the canyon and then a huge black twister came spinning down the river like a top in a box. It banged hard against the canyon walls, sending huge showers of wheat spilling below. When it got in front of us it stopped, as if to block us from trying to cross. The top of it whirled just twenty feet below.

It howled and swirled fiercely, trying to pull us into its spinning center, but Infinity stood his ground. I grabbed my hat and held on tight, looking down into the twister's mouth. Trucks and tractors spun helplessly in its center. The top of a windmill tumbled out of control, along with a bunch of tin roofing that looked like the top of an old silo.

I heard a menacing howl; a black wolf with burning red eyes stuck his head out of the swirling mass. He roared so loud that it almost shattered my eardrums. He looked like the wolf in the burning barn, but I couldn't say for sure. The twister reached out and sucked him back into the middle of the whirlwind. He vanished with a scream that sent shivers down my back.

I looked over at the farm, sitting calmly on the other side. I wanted to cross that canyon more than ever, but I didn't want to take on that twister, even with Infinity's help.

He reared up and let out his wild stallion scream. He didn't care about the twister. He had come all this way, and wasn't going to turn back now. He backed up a hundred yards and got ready to charge.

"Are you sure?" I asked doubtfully. "Do you *really* want to do this? I mean, I appreciate all the trouble you went through to come all this way, but you don't have to do this on my account. I'm perfectly happy to . . ."

I never finished my sentence. He reared again, and when he came down he bolted for the edge of the canyon. He was galloping at full stride when we reached the edge. My heart leapt with his jump. We went out pretty far, but about halfway over we began to fall right into the twister. I looked up. The windmill sat motionless in the sky, but *we* were sinking, and it was getting farther away, so that I could only see the top of it.

Infinity moved his legs, straining with all of his might, but still we fell. He never lost his balance or stopped galloping, but it was no use. The swirling cloud below was sucking us in. Soon we were over the twister, falling into the jaws of death.

"Infinity!" I shouted in dismay, "turn on your light!"

He was tiring from the struggle, but I could feel him stir beneath me. He transferred the last of his energy to his horn, shooting a beam straight ahead, across the canyon. He focused on the top of the windmill. A gentle breeze spun the blades around, so that Infinity's light shone directly on them, and then bounced off and shot towards the sun. The sun shot forth its own beam, concentrating on the blades like light focused through a magnifying glass. White light reflected off the blades back to Infinity's horn, charging him with energy. He began to vibrate all over, filling with power.

Slowly we emerged from the whirlwind, pulled up by the light. We reached the edge of the canyon with the twister howling at our backs, still trying to suck us in. When I felt his front legs hit solid ground, I heaved a sigh of relief. Then his back legs hit, chipping off a piece of rock beneath us. It fell into the twister and shattered into pieces, but we had made it. Infinity turned off his light.

A menacing groan came out of the twister like the cry of a wild beast. It moved down the canyon and disappeared.

Infinity trotted forward and slowed down, stopping near the split rail fence that encircled the farm. The fence seemed different somehow. It looked like it didn't have any splinters on it. I dismounted and walked over to get a better look. It was clay brown, made of solid flint, and smooth as polished stone. I had never realized flint could be so beautiful.

45

The Crystal Farmhouse

I stared at the scene in front of me and couldn't believe my eyes. A glazed crystal farmhouse stood shimmering in sunlight like a beautifully cut vase. When I looked closer I could see unicorns etched on its surface, prancing and playing in misty meadows.

The barn was cut from a solid ruby, carved out to make a loft and stalls. The silo was like a crystal candy jar, with a top that set on it gently as a glass lid. But the windmill was the grandest of all. The tower was made of solid ivory beams running all the way to the top, where blades of sterling silver spun to a gentle breeze. A diamond as big as a sunflower sat in its center; it sparkled with blinding brilliance, shooting light in all directions.

I climbed over the fence. When I got halfway to the house, I remembered Infinity and looked back. He was feeding on the other side of the fence and seemed content to wait for me. I ran to the house and went through the kitchen door like I always did back home.

Everything was just as beautiful on the inside. The table

was set with Indian plates like those my mother made, only these were of fine china. The flatware was solid gold and heavy to the touch, and the glasses were pure leaded crystal.

I heard my mom on the side porch, singing a country song. I ran down the hall, almost falling down on the smooth glass floor, then stopped and looked through the window.

There she was, sitting at a silver pottery wheel, slowly spinning a ceramic vase.

"Mom!" I yelled. "Mom!" But she acted like I wasn't there. I went over and tapped her on the shoulder, but my hand passed right through her. I didn't know what to say at first and it frightened me a little, and then I said to myself, "Oh, I get it. You're a ghost, or an angel or something. Well, that's okay. I can handle it."

She stopped the wheel and got up to go to the kitchen. I reached over and touched the vase. It glowed with the warmth of my mother's presence, and I could feel her essence in it, and her love. It made me smile, and I got a little less worried about what was going on.

I glanced out the window and saw my dad harvesting a row of wheat. I couldn't resist running out to greet him, wanting to jump up on his lap as usual, but the closer I got, the more clear it became that he was a phantom rider, not really there. The wheat in the field was not wheat at all, but solid gold nuggets growing on stalks of silver. I couldn't resist stuffing a few nuggets in my jacket pocket.

Reaching the image of my dad sitting on the tractor, I watched him trim a row, bent down and picked up a handful of dark brown earth, and brought it to my nose. It smelled just as fragrant as a fresh cup of coffee, like it always did back home. It was good old Kansas dirt. "Well," I said to myself, "at least something's normal around here."

John Deere was made of solid emerald, with golden wheels that sparkled in the sunlight. "Heck of a tractor you got there," I said, but I knew Dad couldn't hear me. He got off and walked towards the house, hearing Mom call for dinner from the back porch.

I climbed up in the tractor seat and grabbed the steering wheel, put John Deere in gear, and rolled off over the golden field, pulling the silver mower behind. Mowing down the row I felt the presence of my dad sitting in the seat with me. It was a good comfortable feeling, like a phone call from a friend when you're new in town.

I stopped at the end of the row and got down, seeing a familiar figure on the back porch. Even before I got there, I knew by the rich black tone of his skin and the combat boots and the straw hat who it was. He had been telling stories to a bunch of kids, including Billy Johnson. Billy hadn't wanted to go home; he wanted to stay and listen some more to the fantastic tales spun out by the old black man; but Mr. Tucker said he'd best go before the sheriff got mad, so Billy scurried off down the road in front of the house.

When I got there, Mom, Dad, and Mr. Tucker were all sitting at the kitchen table, getting ready to dig in. A peach pie was cooling on the window sill. I knew Bob Greison couldn't be far away, and as soon as that peach pie hit his nose he'd be at the table before the knife hit the crust.

"Where are the kids?" Dad asked.

"Oh, out in the barn, I reckon," Mr. Tucker said. "They'll be joinin' us soon as the aroma of that pie reaches 'em."

I went upstairs, and when I passed Cathy's room, I noticed that Mr. Tucker's things were in it. I felt good knowing that he had moved in with us. I'd begun to consider him a part of the family, and was glad to see my parents had, too.

My room was the same as I'd left it; the only difference was that unicorns were etched in the frosted glass walls and the glazed glass floor. I looked out the window towards Tucker's Grove, but his place was too far away to see. Suddenly, there came laughter from the loft, and I knew Bob and Cathy were up there. I hoped they had some soft straw to lie on, instead of the gold and silver stuff that Dad was growing in his field.

Then, remembering the barn, I ran downstairs and out the kitchen door. The screen was made of tiny silver strands, and might not take too kindly to slamming. So I reached back just in time and caught it.

I ran to the barn and straight for the stalls. There was Becky, munching away, and on real hay too. A whinny came from the next stall. No one had to tell me whose it was. When I looked in, she was just the same as always, except she had an ivory horn growing right out of her forehead, just like a unicorn.

"I knew it," I told Petula. "I knew you were a special horse. It's just that we could never see your horn before. I'll bet you lost it when you came to Kansas, and now that you're up here, they found it and gave it back to you."

There was some pretty loud oinking going on behind me in the pigpen, and I ran from the barn to check it out. There he was, trying to wiggle under the fence. I looked at Elmer and laughed. "Well," I said, "I guess some critters never change. Here you are in the most wonderful place of all, and you're trying to get out. Well, I guess this ain't exactly hog heaven, especially without Doc's garbage, but I'll bet he's waiting for you right down the road."

I got thirsty all of a sudden, and walked over to the well. Lifting up the ivory lid to the water tub, I leaned it against the legs of the tower, took off my straw hat and reached down to scoop up a hatfull of water, drinking long and slow. It tasted just like back home. Some things just can't be improved on, even in the most beautiful place in the universe, and fresh well water was one of them. Kansas dirt was another, and so was peach pie.

The thought of that made me hungry, so I snuck over and stole a couple of pieces as the pie cooled on the window still, figuring a bunch of ghosts wouldn't miss it none.

I saw Mom look at the missing pieces when she took it from the sill, and she just smiled. Cathy and Bob had already run past me and joined them for dinner, so Mom knew they hadn't eaten the pie.

"Save Thaddy a piece of pie," Dad said as I watched through the kitchen window. "He should be joinin' us any time now."

"I'm afraid that won't be necessary," Mom said with a laugh. "He already took his two pieces."

"Then he'll be with us soon," Cathy said. "Good, I

want to show him that new light I got for the tractor. It captures sunlight during the day, and uses it to run the headlight at night.''

''What will that girl think of next?'' Dad said to Mr. Tucker. He reached over and messed up Cathy's hair like he always did with mine.

''Yeah,'' Bob said, ''I want to show Thaddy my fast ball.''

''And I got a story he won't believe,'' Mr. Tucker said with a big smile. ''It's about a unicorn that comes to Kansas, way back in '47.''

''You and your stories,'' Mom said. ''You and your wild, wonderful stories.'' She patted him on the arm.

I turned and walked slowly towards the fence, knowing that wherever this place was, it lay somewhere in the future and I couldn't be there yet. But I was grateful to have the visit just the same.

I didn't care much about the birthplace of the universe just then. This vision had made me realize that I wanted nothing more than to go back home and stay with my family.

Suddenly, a black Lab came running out of the wheat field, chasing a rabbit. I knew the look of him. I could never forget. ''Lancelot!'' I yelled, unable to stop myself, though I knew he couldn't hear me. ''Lancelot!''

Much to my surprise, his ears perked up and he looked my way. He stopped chasing the rabbit and ran over to me. I didn't expect him to, but he jumped up and knocked me down. He just about licked me to death. He was *real*.

''How come you're real?'' I asked, ''and nobody else is?''

Another black Lab came out of the field and chased after the rabbit. It was smaller and had a white spot on its chest, just like the puppy I had picked out back home. The rabbit ran past me, with the puppy chasing right behind. They both passed through my legs as if they weren't there.

Then it hit me. Lancelot was the only one that was really here. Everyone else was still back on the farm. So Lancelot really did exist in this world, but the others were just phantoms, due to arrive in the future.

He could lick me because for that moment I was real in his world, and not back on the farm. He was living here and he was waiting for me to show up.

It made me want to stay, but I knew I couldn't. It took me the longest time to get him calmed down, and I had a hard time explaining that I was only visiting and had to leave. I finally had to tie him up next to his crystal doghouse with a real rope I found in the barn. I gave him one last hug and walked away, knowing he'd break the rope when I left, just like he had done that night he got run over, but there were no big trucks out here to worry about.

It hurt pretty bad when I had to turn away from him, but he couldn't go back with me. I'd have to come back to him.

I decided I'd better go home before my heart broke. I stood and walked over to Infinity, still grazing contentedly in the wheat outside the fence. I put my arms around his neck. "You knew," I said with my head in his mane, "that it wasn't my time yet to be here." I pulled away and looked into his deep brown eyes. "But you brought me anyway, because I wanted to come."

He bent down on one leg. "Well," I said, and grabbed him firmly by the horn, "what are you waiting for? This isn't a train station, you know. We can leave anytime we want."

I climbed up behind his horn. He lifted his head and I slid down onto his back. He turned to give me one last look at the farm. I glanced one more time at the crystal farmhouse, sitting comfortably in its peaceful world. I looked up at the windmill, its shiny silver blades spinning out beams of light across the sky.

"I'll be back," I said to Lancelot, mist coming over my eyes. "I'll be coming back." He whined and barked a friendly bark, like he knew I had to go and that he couldn't come with me this time.

I nudged Infinity's sides and he trotted slowly away. I looked back once more. "Leave a light on for me, will you?" I said to the farmhouse.

As we rode away, the wind picked up a little and spun the blades of the windmill pretty fast. It turned our way and whirled out a circle of light, bathing us in its white warmth. The spinning of the blades began to make a sound like a country band playing softly. There were fiddles, slide guitars, and a honky-tonk piano, all playing in perfect harmony. The song was soothing, and alive with feeling. I could have listened forever, but it was time to go.

As we left, I bent over to whisper something in Infinity's ear. "Look," I said as gently as I could. "We don't have to take the scenic route back if you don't want to. The direct route's perfectly fine with me."

I made him go by Tucker's on the way out. There was a sign by the meadow, but it was so faded I couldn't make out any of the words except UNICORN. Mr. Tucker's cabin was made of solid polished flint rock, but he didn't live there anymore; he was with my parents. In the meadow by his house I picked a walnut off one of the trees and stuffed it in my pocket.

The golden wheat kernels I'd borrowed were not in my pocket; they were gone. I wasn't too surprised, though. After all, I wasn't supposed to be there yet.

I carried that walnut all the way home, hoping it would make the trip without disappearing. It was worth a try.

46

The Road Back

We went home another way, as if the crystal farmhouse had
been the schoolhouse and the road looped back towards
town. We passed millions of pulsating stars, vibrating with
the light of the universe. Infinity's beam shone bright and
strong. We soared across galaxies at an incredible speed.

Just before we came back into the Milky Way, we stopped
on a small planet. It was like earth, only the way it must
have been a long time ago. The sky was deep blue and the
clouds white as puffs of cotton. There were snow-capped
purple mountains rising miles above deep green valleys, and
rivers flowing with clean, fresh water. It was paradise.

This land was filled with lush tropical forests, meadows
full of flowers in bloom, and plains filled with wild wheat
waving in a warm breeze. The planet seemed to be waiting
to welcome people to its gardens.

There were animals like the ones on earth. Wild buffalo
roamed golden plains in great herds, powerful eagles soared
clear skies . . . and there were unicorns.

We arrived in a meadow full of yellow flowers, just after

a rain. A mother unicorn was watching her babies chase butterflies and play in the tall green grass.

I saw a sight I'll never forget, because it reminded me of a picture I'd seen in the mythology book. A rainbow arced its way from behind a hill, and the end fell in the center of the meadow. The baby unicorns went over to chase it, dancing in the colored light at its end. There was a pure black unicorn and a solid white one, and a third one was chestnut brown. As they played in the light at the end of the rainbow, their ivory horns turned golden in color.

I laughed at this and turned to Infinity, who was feeding nearby. "There isn't any gold at the end of the rainbow," I said. "It's just unicorns playing."

We rested near the edge of the meadow before making the final part of the journey. It made a good runway, since it dropped a thousand feet into a pure blue ocean below. We drank water from a fresh mountain stream and bathed under a waterfall nearby. The rushing water soothed my nerves. I lay down in a green pasture among the yellow flowers and fell asleep. Soon I began to dream.

I saw my dad in the field back home. He and Petula were plowing the earth to make it ready for planting. He was having a pretty tough time of it. He was pouring sweat and straining every muscle, even though Petula was pulling about as hard as a horse could pull. My Dad's eyes got all glassy, and he let go of the reins. He brought his hands up and clutched his chest, dropping to his knees.

"Thaddy," he said, strain in his voice, "you're gonna have to take over for me. Old Ari's not gonna make it. Here, son . . . take the reins. Take the . . ." And then he hit the ground. Mom came running out, and managed to get him in the car. That had been back in '42, and I felt like I was right there, though when it had happened I'd been sitting in school, daydreaming, as usual.

Something licked my face, and it woke me up. It was just before sunset, and Infinity was restless to ride again. He had nudged me out of my dream. I finally got my senses back, stood on a rock and jumped on his back. I didn't want to leave this beautiful place, but home was waiting for my return.

Infinity turned around to leave, stealing one last look at the unicorns playing in the meadow. Reaching forward, I patted his neck. He pawed the ground kind of nervous-like. "Yeah, I know," I said. "It's time to go."

I nudged his sides and we raced across the meadow. He didn't jump until we hit the edge of the cliff, then we flew away with incredible speed, like a star shooting across a summer sky. His body began to transform, and he became a beam of pure light. It took me in, and I merged with it completely. We were as one; there was nothing between us. We were shooting across the universe and heading for home. A million miles came and went; then, at last, we slowed to a gallop.

I felt myself separate from his beam, and we became beings with bodies again. "Look," I said, staring at the small, wet planet up ahead. "Isn't that Earth?"

Infinity focused his light on a spot in the sky, and it opened it front of us. We passed through the hole and circled the earth, gazing down on its clouds, water and continents. We flashed across the face of the moon and headed for eastern Kansas, setting down in the Flint Hills.

We galloped behind the school, and before I realized it, Infinity had turned and entered Tucker's Grove. I tried to stop him, but he wouldn't respond. He just kept heading straight for the wheat, unaware or unconcerned that there could be danger ahead. A bitter wind came up, and I shivered a little as we bounded through the mist.

"Whoa! Whoa, boy!" I shouted in desperation, but it was no use. Infinity galloped all the way to the wheat.

Suddenly, Cathy and Bob yelled at me to turn back. What were they doing here? They must have come out looking for me. By the time Infinity had stopped to munch on the wheat, it was already too late.

Headlights flashed on all over the meadow, and nets sprang up in a circle around us. I knew my only hope was to dismount and run for it, so that Infinity could leap the nets, but before I was able to jump down, a large, thick net dropped over us.

"Infinity!" I yelled, but he didn't struggle against the net. He just stood there, his powerful body poised as still as a statue. If he was to be captured, he would go with dignity.

"Okay!" Wingate shouted, appearing through the mist, "we've got him now. Careful with him." He turned and spit on the crushed wheat.

I refused to dismount, so they backed a horse trailer in next to us. "You'd best get down," Wingate said with a sneer. "We're going to take him dead or alive. It's up to you."

"I ain't moving," I said stubbornly. "You'll have to take us in together."

"All right, boys," Wingate said with a turn of his head. Soldiers with rifles crowded around. They clicked off the safety catches, raised their barrels, and aimed at us. "When I give the word," Wingate continued straight-faced, "shoot. Just make sure you hit the beast."

Cathy kicked the guard holding her and broke away to run up to the net. "Thaddy," she said with concern in her voice, "let them take him. They can't hold him. Nothing can hold him." She looked at the rifles. "But if they shoot him, it's over . . . for all of us."

"Yeah," Bob agreed. "And what about Mr. Tucker? Heck, he ain't even ridden yet."

Their words made me realize how selfish I'd been. Bob was right. If Mr. Tucker was to have any kind of a chance to ride Infinity, I had to get down, whether I wanted to or not. I didn't say a word. I reached over and hugged Infinity's neck.

"They can't hold you," I finally said. "People can't hold onto other people's dreams." I got down and crawled under the net. Infinity stood there while soldiers climbed under and strung ropes around his neck. When they got half a dozen heavy ropes around him, they lifted the net and led him into the trailer.

He went calmly, without a fight. When he got completely

into the back of the horse trailer, he turned and looked at me. He was still strong and proud, but there was a sadness in his eyes that I'd never seen before. I don't think he felt bad that he had been caught; he felt bad for us. I knew that if any harm came to him, I'd never be able to forgive myself. I couldn't go on as long as he was in captivity.

"Infinity," I cried, "what have I done?" I put my head in my hands. "It's all my fault."

Wingate approached the net. "Looks like we got him, thanks to Thaddeus here."

I tried to grab him, but Bob held me back. "Let him go, Thaddy. They'll never hold him. There's nothin' we can do. It was nobody's fault. We just got fooled."

No matter what anyone said about his capture, I felt it was my fault. I never should have let him turn into Tucker's. He could have gotten away if I would've managed to steer him around the danger, or jumped off before we entered the meadow. I was sure no rope or net could hold him, unless he let it. He had allowed it so I wouldn't get hurt; I knew that much. He had done it for me, and I felt ashamed, but I wouldn't give up. As soon as they let us go I would find a way, somehow, to set him free—or die trying.

They let us go after they pulled the horse trailer away. They had what they came for, and didn't need us anymore.

"Where are you taking him?" I asked, trying not to take a swing at Wingate.

"Not far," he said. "Just to town for some tests. Then we're going to let him go." He spit again on the crushed wheat. It left a nasty brown stain where it landed.

"Sure," I said sarcastically, "I'll bet you are."

"Then again," he added with a snide tone, "we might not. We've got to get a closer look at that horn."

"If you hurt him," I said, struggling as Bob held me back, "I'll get you. I'll get you bad."

He laughed at this, showing his tobacco-stained teeth. "You'd best get that old nag on home," he said, pointing to Petula tied up at the fence, "before she ends up like the white one here." He nodded towards Infinity. "But don't you worry none,'' he said with a wicked smile, ''We're going to take real good care of him.''

He turned and walked away. When he got halfway to his car, he looked back at me. ''Makes you kind of wonder,'' he said. ''What's inside that horn?''

I started to yell at him, but Bob put his hand over my mouth so I wouldn't get in any more trouble. When I finally got settled down, I vowed to find a way to free Infinity. Bob and Cathy said to count them in, regardless of the danger.

When I got home, the phone was ringing. Dad got up and took the call, while Mom stood by and listened. The sheriff was on the line. He said that no one was allowed to leave town until this whole thing was cleared up, just in case my parents were involved.

It might just have been the break we needed. It would keep us on the farm a little longer, and give us time to figure something out. Sometimes, just when things are at their worst, a small ray of hope pops through like a pinpoint of light at the far end of a tunnel. I just hoped it wasn't a train coming.

47

The Speed of Energy

My mom didn't wait until the next morning to bawl me out about riding on the hills. She hung up the telephone and started in on me. I explained a couple of times that there was nothing to worry about, since Infinity wasn't an ordinary horse. He could outrun any wolves that might come after us.

"Thaddy," she said at last, "the authorities don't think it's a unicorn. They think it's some kind of space probe. According to what Sheriff Johnson told me, the horn might be a kind of transmitting device to a spaceship or some faraway planet. I don't know what's going on; it all sounds just as crazy as one of your stories, and I don't know who to believe. Maybe you've all gone over the edge. You know, Thaddy, Infinity just might be some kind of strange horse living out on the hills that nobody ever discovered before. All I know is that they won't let us leave until this whole thing is cleared up. If this is some kind of prank, young man . . ."

"Aw, let the boy alone," Dad said, grabbing Mom gently

by the arm. "Whatever it is, we know he didn't just make it up. Not with the U.S. Army takin' such an interest in the matter. They don't have time to spend investigatin' fairy tales. Even if there ain't a war on."

Mom grew silent, thinking about what Dad had said. "I suppose," she finally agreed, "that's something to be thankful for; at least he didn't make the whole thing up." She got up from the living room sofa, where we all had been summoned to explain the strange events, and headed for the stairs. "Well," she said, turning back and looking at us, "this has been a long day. I'm going back to bed, and I suggest all of you do the same."

"In a minute," Dad answered. "I want to have a word with my kids here about chasin' after wild critters in the middle of the night."

After we heard Mom's feet hit the stairs, Dad leaned forward and gave Cathy and me a serious look. "Well," he asked, "what do you think, Cath? You're the level-headed one around here. The rest of us are seein' whatever we want, but I believe you know the truth. So, tell us, what is it? Space alien, unicorn, or what?"

A long anxious silence followed. "To tell you the truth," she finally said, "I don't really know. I always thought there were no such things as unicorns. And then along comes this creature riding right out of a myth and into our lives. If it's some kind of space probe, it's an unbelievable piece of engineering, and whoever made it could do just about whatever they want with us. Wingate and his little army don't stand a chance."

Dad stared at her. "I don't think it matters whether it's a unicorn or not," he said seriously. "The fact is that it exists, and can do what it does. It's like somethin' out of a fairy tale; but you've got to remember fairy tales were stories for things that couldn't be explained any other way.

"This creature may have found a spot in time somewhere, where the seam between the past and the future is as thin as a weddin' veil. And just suppose Infinity, as you call him, slipped through that seam and rode into our world from right out of the past, from a time when they say unicorns existed all over the world.''

"Dad," I said, scratching my head, "does this mean you believe us?''

He rubbed his brow and smiled. "Let's just say I'm willin' to give this story of yours a chance,'' he said. "I found that book on myths under your bed when we were startin' to pack up your room, and I did a little readin' up on the subject. Seems unicorns have been around a long time, a couple of thousand years at least. The fact that scientists have never found fossils of one don't mean much, since it's never been established exactly what the horns were made of.

"But once in a while, accordin' to the legend, a rare thing happens. A unicorn is born with a horn of pure ivory. It's this special creature that has all the powers everyone always attributes to unicorns.''

"Yeah," I said, "I remember reading that part. You mean like healing the sick and purifying water.'' I leaned forward on the couch, excited.

"And one more thing," Dad said, patting me on the shoulder, "that you would have learned if you'd read the whole book.''

I looked at my dad. "Darn, I knew I should've read the rest of the book, but I was too busy looking at the pictures.''

"Let him finish.'' Cathy bumped my arm from across the coffee table.

"If you'd have read the whole section on unicorns,'' Dad went on, "you'd have realized that those born with ivory horns are very rare, and they can use their horns to help them fly. They never die, so their fossils are never found. They live forever, sustained by light and sound from some far-off place.''

"Then the horn is like an antigravity device,'' Cathy said to herself, as if realizing a great secret.

"Let him talk,'' I said, and nudged her back.

"Not just fly,'' Dad informed us, his eyes getting bigger. "It seems they can travel at the speed of light and beyond.'' Cathy gave Dad a funny look, so he explained, "The first stage of interplanetary travel is the speed of light, but even at that, the first star is years away. But when light accelerates beyond its natural boundaries, it begins to travel at somethin' called the speed of energy. That makes it possible to go anywhere in the universe in no time at all, since time is shrunk down to almost nothin'.

"When the unicorn flies at the speed of light, he *becomes* light, and when he goes beyond that, he becomes pure energy. That happens when he reaches the speed of light times itself."

"Of course," Cathy said. "$E = MC^2$ like Einstein said."

"Einstein?" I said, rolling my eyes.

"Energy equals mass times the speed of light squared." she explained. "That means when the mass of the unicorn's body approaches the speed of light times itself, he becomes pure energy. That's the same equation they used to develop the atom bomb. The amazing part is that, instead of destroying himself, Infinity can transport himself across the universe at incredible speeds. Why, I'll bet he stores up energy in the horn, just like a battery, and when he needs it, there it is. When he wants to, he uses that energy to look inside us and pull out our wishes, and to fly us where they take us . . . Dad," she said at last, "do you suppose Wingate knows any of this?"

"Well," Dad said, and took a deep breath, "I did a little checkin' into him, too. Seems he's not with the Army Corps of Engineers after all. He's from some secret department in Washington that investigates flying saucers and such. Turns out our local phone operator overheard one of Mr. Tucker's conversations about something out-of-this-world in his meadow, and blabbed it to her sister in Washington. Next thing you know, Wingate's here doing a research project. If he gets wind of what that ivory horn means, Infinity's done for."

"But why would they hurt him if the horn's so valuable?" I asked.

"Well," he replied, getting up and going to the living room window, "what do you suppose they'd give to find out how unicorns can travel at the speed of light, simply by transformin' themselves into light beams? Not to mention the speed of energy? You can guess at the applications they'd have in mind."

"We can't let that happen." I stood up, excited. "If they take his horn, all the magic is gone. Then he'd just be another horse. That'd be like having your brain removed or something."

"Yeah," Dad agreed, turning around and looking at me, "but don't let Petula hear you say that . . . or your mother. At least not till I've convinced her that Infinity's a unicorn, and not some critter from another planet."

"Thanks, Dad," I said, walking up and hugging him. "I knew you'd come through. But how are we gonna free Infinity?"

"Don't know," he said right off. "I haven't figgered that out yet."

I looked at Cathy, and then I leaned over and whispered something in her ear. She nodded in agreement. "Dad," I said, "it's not official yet,'cause we have to clear it with Bob and Mr. Tucker, but as far as we're concerned, you can be a member of the Unicorn Hunting Club if you want to."

"That so?" he asked with a wink. "What are the qualifications? You can't have limited membership without qualifications."

I looked at him and smiled. "You just gotta believe."

"Well, then," he answered, "I reckon an old dreamer like me meets the qualifications."

The next thing that happened surprised even me. Cathy got up and started to walk towards the stairs like she was going to bed, but before she did, she reached out and grabbed Dad's straw hat right off the hat rack, pretty as you please. Before he could get to it, she ran out of the house. She came back a few minutes later, handed it to him and smiled. "That's our secret sign," she said. "All the members have bites out of their hats."

"Except Mr. Tucker," I said, and remembered that I hadn't seen him since Infinity's capture. He had an awful lot of catching up to do, and I was going to have to be the one to tell him. Besides, he might have some ideas about how we were going to free Infinity. Right then, it looked like we were going to need all the help we could get.

We all hugged each other and then went up to bed. "Work on Mom for us, will you?" I asked Dad, but he said it was always tough to convince a farmer's wife unless she saw it first. I decided I needed to get Mom over to see Infinity. Maybe then she would believe. Heck, Dad and Mr. Tucker needed to see him too, even though they already believed.

I went to bed and thought about how much things had changed lately. It was only a few days ago that we were laughing and chasing Elmer around the pigpen, and now we were fighting again. We knew the farm was lost, but at least we could still fight to save a unicorn from having his horn removed, or worse.

The odd part was that as long as they had Infinity and didn't figure out his secrets, we could stay on the farm, but it was not the kind of staying we had in mind. It was better to set Infinity free and lose the farm than prolong his captivity and keep the farm a few more days, at least from my point of view.

I almost told Cathy and Dad about my ride and the hole in the sky, which I figured to be the seam Dad was talking about, but decided I'd better keep it to myself. There are some things in life that nobody believes but you, and this figured to be one of them. In my opinion, everything my dad had read was gospel and not just some story told to pass the time and fire up the imagination. I didn't know how much Dad and Cathy believed about what was in the book, but I believed it all, and that was good enough for me.

I hoped and prayed Infinity could be saved before it was too late, and he lost his horn and became a horse. There was an apology to Petula in my prayers, just in case she had overheard the conversation about only being a horse. I threw in a prayer for Mom too, hoping she could see her way clear to believe.

I climbed into bed knowing my parents would start to unpack in the morning. That was a good sign. I just didn't know how long we had left, but hoping against hope had always been my strong point, so I left a little spot open in my heart in case another miracle wanted to split the seam and ride into my life.

Asking for a miracle was sure worth a try. The only other happy event I had to look forward to was the fireworks on the Fourth of July, but that was two days off yet. And in this unlucky summer, nobody was even talking about it.

48

The Medal of Honor

The next morning I rode into town to see Mr. Tucker. Bob and Cathy went along to help break the news.

"Well," I began, standing beside his bed, "I got some bad news." I hung my head.

"So tell me," he said, looking at a wheelchair in the corner. "What did they do, bulldoze yer farm?"

"Naw," I said, "worse."

"Okay," he chuckled. "What could be so terrible to make a boy hang his head like that?"

I raised my head and looked at Cathy and then at Bob. I decided to give him some good news first. I hoped it would soften the blow when he heard the rest. "I rode him," I said, "same as Cathy and Bob.

"And it was fantastic," I added.

"Well," Mr. Tucker said, and motioned for a pillow with his hand, "I'd better sit up fer this. I can't imagine any news bad enough to spoil good news like that."

I was about to put the pillow behind his head, but I stopped and looked him straight in the eyes. "Are you sure?" I asked, "that you don't want to take this lying down?"

He leaned his head forward. "Put that pillow right behind this old neck," he said, "and stop foolin' around. Are you goin' to tell a dyin' man the bad news or not?"

We all looked at each other and froze. He had gotten our attention. "Aw," he said, grabbing my arm, "I was just joshin' you. Doc's been sayin' fer years that I was dyin'. Besides, when you get to be my age, you almost welcome the opportunity to leave the body behind, before it leaves you behind."

He looked up at us. "I reckon I'm about due fer a new one anyway. Pity, though, a fella can't take his knowledge with him, and not have to learn crawlin' and calculus all over again. Sure would make my next life a lot easier to take."

"Calculus?" Bob said with surprise, "you know . . ."

"It ain't your next life we're worried about," I said, "it's this one."

There was an uncomfortable silence. Then Cathy said, "They've captured him. And taken him downtown for tests. At least, that's what they claim."

"Ah," Mr. Tucker said, waving his hand, "he only let himself be caught. Ain't nobody can hold a unicorn against his will."

"Six ropes," Bob said. "They had a big net, six ropes and a dozen men, so he gave himself up."

"He prob'ly just didn't want to hurt anybody," Mr. Tucker said with a wink, "or he'd have broken the ropes and got away. This ain't no ordinary creature. He had about as much strength as he has a mind to."

"Mr. Tucker," Cathy said, "the point is that they've captured him, and we want him back. They don't know anything about him, what riding him can do, and especially about the magic in the horn."

"I suppose that's true," he answered, "but if they don't believe in his power, ridin' him can't do nothin' fer 'em. The power is in believin'."

"Then you don't want to help us free him?" Cathy asked.

"Well," he replied with a shrug, "what's done is done. And if that's the way it has to be, then so be it." He glanced out the window, as if he had lost interest.

"But, Mr. Tucker," I said, "you haven't ridden him." I pointed to Bob. "Look, he already fixed Bob's arm. I know he can fix you up, too."

Bob flexed his arm. "Yeah," he said, "old pitchin' arm feels pretty good now. I don't know how he did it, but I felt some kind of energy pourin' into it when I was ridin' him. My arm got all warm and tingly, and then it began to get its old strength back. I feel almost as good as new. I know he could fix up whatever ails you."

"And *I* saw this incredible, perfect machine," Cathy said. "It ran as tight as a new gearbox. Believe me, there's a gear in there for fixing up people, and it's just waiting to be used."

"He travels at the speed of energy," I said, "and he can take you anywhere your heart desires. Heck, it was you that brought him to us. You can't let him stay in the hands of those that don't believe. It's like casting pearls before swine or something." Sorry, Elmer, I added to myself.

"We don't care," Cathy went on, "if we ever get to ride him again. We just want him set free. That's all."

"Well, that's almost true," Bob said. "We'd like to ride him again, but if we can't, and you're not goin' to, then we want him to go free. We feel responsible for his gettin' caught. If we hadn't been there, he wouldn't have come in the first place."

"I'm awful sorry," Mr. Tucker said, "but I just don't see what an ol' man in a hospital bed can do."

He paused and looked at us. "Yer all very lucky, you know. Only a few've even seen one, let alone ridden one. Be thankful fer that much."

"But . . ." I said. Cathy grabbed my arm.

"Okay," she said, "but we want at least to see him. They caught him on your land. And you can find out where they're holding him."

"You've got to help us," Bob added, "or we might not ever see him again."

Mr. Tucker didn't say anything. He just gazed out of the window as if looking into the past, seeing himself back on his farm, or perhaps in his youth.

"Aw, come on, Mr. Tucker," Bob said, "you were a kid once. You had dreams. If we don't fight for ours now, then when? Maybe you're willin' to let all of your hard work go to waste growin' walnut trees and plantin' your special wheat, but we're not. We're takin' over the payments on your dream. So it's up to you, but we can't wait around to see what's goin' to happen. Come on guys, let's go."

He got up and started for the door. Cathy and I were following slowly behind. I looked back at Mr. Tucker. There was sadness in his eyes. He felt our frustration and disappointment, and he couldn't look the other way; but still, for some reason I couldn't understand, he held back. I think he really believed that destiny couldn't be changed. But *we* didn't believe it, and destiny was going just a little too slow for us.

"Look," I said in desperation, "Wingate's starting to wonder what's inside Infinity's horn. And Dad says if they find out that's where all the power is, they just might take his horn away. If they do that, it's all over for us *and* Infinity, and it'll be our fault."

Mr. Tucker got a serious look on his face. He turned and stared at us, studying the pleas for help on our faces. "All right," he said at last, "call the sheriff. Tell Sally to get him on the line. And help me into that wheelchair. The phone's in the other room."

I ran back and grabbed the wheelchair. I took his feet and Bob his shoulders. We loaded him in and rolled him through the door. Sally Penhurst straightened her white nurse cap and gave us a mighty funny look.

"Get me the sheriff," Mr. Tucker said with authority. "I want to report a case of trespassin' and thievin'. Seems those army engineers took a critter off my land without askin' permission."

Doc came rushing out of his office. He must have heard the whole thing and could see we were quite serious about it. He crossed his arms over his smock, a stethoscope still in his ears. "Dial up Sheriff Johnson," he said to Sally, "before this old combat sergeant takes off with my bed."

"You were a combat ser . . ." Bob stopped himself and scratched his head. "But they're supposed to be mean."

"You want *mean*?" Mr. Tucker yelled, "I'll show you mean! Now dial up the sheriff!"

Sally got the sheriff on the phone, and Mr. Tucker shouted his orders into the receiver. It was a side of him none of us had ever seen before, but we sure needed it now.

"If I don't get permission to see that beast," he commanded, "I'll be filin' a formal complaint. Look, yer talkin' to Sergeant Washington Tucker, United States Army retired. One Hundred Twenty-Second Cavalry Division. And I'm not standin' by and lettin' a bunch of army engineers run off with my mount!"

"Cavalry?" Bob said. His jaw dropped, and he shook his head in disbelief.

"If I don't get satisfaction immediately," Mr. Tucker continued, "I'm gettin' on the phone to Congressman Fuller. He can take his Medal of Honor back unless I get some action. Now!

"Yep," he answered after listening to the reply, "that's right. I understand all that national security stuff. No. We just want to see him."

"Congressional Medal of Honor?" Bob asked in amazement, scratching his cheek and making a face.

"Yep," Mr. Tucker said into the phone, "I understand the importance of this to science and national security. No, we just want to make sure he's all right." He waited for the reply. Then he said, "Thaddeus, Bob and Cathy." He looked up at us. "No," he went on, "I can't come. You know I'm in the hospital. High blood pressure or somethin'. And if you don't let them in, I'll personally throw that Medal of Honor in Congressman Fuller's face. And I'll let him know whose fault it is."

"Yep," he finally said, "you can take that as a threat if you like. Goodbye." He handed the phone back to Sally, whose face had flushed the color of a redwood fence—on account of the phone conversation, I reckon. I thought her curly hair was going to go straight on us. Her pale complexion looked even whiter after the red subsided.

"Then it's true," she said to herself. "There *are* unicorns!"

"Of course," I said, "anyone can see that."

"He don't like it none," Mr. Tucker interrupted, "but he's agreed to let you kids see Infinity."

"Where is he?" Cathy asked.

"City garage," he answered, and motioned with his free arm towards the far side of town.

"Garage?" I said. "He don't belong in no garage. He's not a tractor, you know."

"Medal of Honor," Bob said, shaking his head, "you got the Medal of Honor?"

"I reckon so," Mr. Tucker said matter-of-factly, "but darned if I can find it. Lost it out in that dad-blamed meadow plantin' wheat a couple of years ago. Ain't seen it since."

"Well," Cathy said, grabbing me, "we'd better get going before the sheriff and Wingate change their minds and want to see that medal."

We were in such a hurry that we left Mr. Tucker sitting right in the middle of the reception room. We raced out the door, and then I ran back in. I could only think of one thing to say. "How'd you get the medal?" I asked. "In combat?"

"Naw"—he smiled—"snuck into enemy camp and stole their ammunition. They surrendered the next mornin'. Heck, you can't fight a war without ammo. "Hey," he added, "yer not very observant today."

"What?" I asked, not understanding the question.

"Didn't you see under my pillow? I have somethin' fer you."

"Oh, yeah," I replied, "I saw. I just thought it wasn't going to be very important. I mean, reading another verse, especially if there wasn't a unicorn left to ride."

I turned to leave and he said, "Thaddy, read it fer *me*. It may not seem important to you now, but someday it will be. Humor an ol' man, just once more, will you?"

He had a look of regret in his eyes that I had never seen before, as if life was a hotel and he was checking out for good and saying his last goodbye. I didn't dare bring the subject of death up again in front of him. I didn't want to think about it right then.

"Of course," I told him. "Of course I'll read it."

I went back to his bed, reached behind his pillow and took the papers that were there. I stuffed them in my pants and ran out the door. Behind me I could hear him shout, "Don't do anythin' foolish! Yer just lookin', remember?"

I heard all right, but telling an eleven-year-old not to do something foolish is like telling the wind which way to blow. It just don't work that way.

49

The City Garage

We went to Mr. Tucker's for some wheat, just in case we got to feed Infinity, and headed down the road towards town. When we arrived at the city garage, there were government vehicles parked all over the place. Doc's ambulance was parked there too. We wondered what he was doing there.

The military guard at the gate looked inside the pickup and signaled us through. He didn't look too happy about it, but guards always seem to look like they're carved out of stone, so we didn't think too much of it.

The garage itself was bigger than you might expect. It had expanded over the years to service trucks that broke down on the highway. There was plenty of room to house a critter, even a big one like Infinity.

Sheriff Johnson was waiting for us by the huge double doors. He held up his hands as if he was stopping traffic. "Okay," he said, looking through the window. "You can go in, but I don't want no one tryin' nothin'. This is a top secret 'vestigation and you shouldn't even be here, so watch it and don't touch nothin', is that clear?"

"Yes, sir," I said as we all climbed out of the truck. "We just came to see him." I noticed the sheriff was acting awful high and mighty. I guess it was because he wanted to impress Wingate. This was the same person who filled his face full of potatoes and pie down at the Flint Hills cafe, stole walnuts from Tucker's Grove, and laughed at his son stealing my clothes and stuffing them in the mailbox, and here he was playing big shot.

"Follow me," the sheriff said, wiping sweat and flies from his forehead. He led us inside through the service door next to the office. All three of the city cars had been parked outside in the yard, along with several U.S. Army vehicles. The garage was empty except for two armed guards with cement expressions and a makeshift corral of sandbags.

The sandbags were usually put to use when the river overflowed, but in this case they were arranged like a war zone bunker and stacked about four feet high in a thirty-foot-wide circle. Straw had been scattered about six inches deep on top of the concrete, and there were hay bales piled in the corner. They looked untouched.

I saw Infinity over the top of the sandbags. He had thick steel chains around his legs and neck. The ends were strung around a car lift about fifteen feet away. It was double padlocked. The worst part was how he looked. He reminded me of Mr. Tucker in the hospital. There were tubes taped to his legs, and one to the side of his neck. There was even one hooked around his horn.

When I came closer, I could see the tubes were really electrical wires, and were attached to some strange-looking machines sitting along the back wall. They were shaped like large refrigerators and had big glowing vacuum tubes in them like those standing radios people used to have. A chart recording device hooked up to them made squiggly lines back and forth. Paper piled up slowly on the floor in front of it.

"What are you doing to him?" I asked angrily, and started to run toward Infinity.

The sheriff grabbed me. "They're only runnin' a few

tests," he said, holding me back, "so cool off! Otherwise you'll have to leave right now."

I didn't listen; I had to get closer to make sure they weren't hurting him. I struggled and broke free. The guards quickly cocked their rifles and aimed at me.

Wingate came out of the shadows and waved them off. They stepped back and shouldered the rifles, looking more like machines than men. That bothered me, since machines might not care what happened to Infinity. I knew they were just taking orders and all that, but couldn't they act a little more human doing it? What was I going to do? Steal a unicorn from right under their noses? Come to think of it, that's exactly what I would've done if I could've figured out a way to do it, but it didn't look possible at the moment.

"We're not hurting him," Wingate said, chewing slowly on a big wad of tobacco. "He's going to be just fine. We're letting him go as soon as we finish these tests."

I looked at Bob and Cathy. None of us believed him.

"When's that going to be?" Cathy asked, her voice ringing sarcastically.

"In a couple of days," he said, looking at the sheriff, "that's all. Then we'll set him free on the hills."

"I want to pet him," I said, stepping forward. But the sheriff grabbed me and wouldn't let go.

"You can't right now." Wingate pushed his hat up on his forehead with his index finger, then wiped tobacco juice from the corners of his mouth. "You'll disturb the tests," he said, and spit on the floor.

I could see inside the office behind him. There was Doc Yeager, wearing a lab coat. What the heck was going on? I couldn't figure it out.

Doc was sitting at a desk, examining some papers. Then he looked up and saw us. Wingate signaled him to stay there, but he got up and came toward us anyway. When he opened the office door, Wingate said nastily, "Don't you have work to do?"

"What are you doing here?" I asked Doc from across the room.

"He's only fillin' in until the specialists get here from

St. Louis,'' Sheriff Johnson informed us, scratching his belly. "He's seein' that the unicorn's taken care of proper."

"St. Louis?'' I asked, scratching my head.

Doc just kept coming. When he got to us he said, "I don't see any harm in letting Thaddeus pet him, as long as he doesn't disturb the tests. Now, let him go, Sheriff. He isn't going to hurt anything."

"Yeah,'' I said. "I just want to pet him."

"You have quite a find here, Thaddeus,'' Doc said, his eyes on Wingate. "Unicorns were thought to be extinct centuries ago. If this one turns out to be genuine, you could be in for quite a reward."

"Reward?'' I said. "I don't want a reward. I just want him back.'' Even though I was a little perturbed by Doc's suggestion of a reward, I could see that he meant well. I think he was trying to influence Wingate in case he got any ideas about swiping Infinity's horn.

"What you've found here is of tremendous medical and scientific importance,'' he went on, "but something like this must be shared with everyone. You can't just keep him to yourselves."

"What do you mean?'' I asked, surprised by his statement. The sheriff let go of me, but I wasn't through arguing. "You mean we have to give him up so you can experiment? Nothing doing. We found him and we're keeping him, as soon as they're through with their lousy tests."

I ran over to Infinity, but when I got next to him, I couldn't say a word. I just stood there. He bent his head down a little and I reached up and hugged him as hard as I could. He still felt strong and looked as big as ever, but he seemed a little cold to the touch, a little pale, as if he were starting to fade away.

"Don't worry,'' Sheriff Johnson said, standing halfway between the sandbags and Infinity. "He's got plenty of food and water. He'll be all right."

"What are you doing to him?'' I asked. "These tests are killing him. He looks sick.'' I glanced at the pile of hay on the floor. "He doesn't look like he's eaten a thing. You've got to let him go, or he'll die in here. He has to be out on the hills!''

The sheriff scratched his double chin. ''Don't worry, he'll eat when he gets hungry enough. Besides, they're only keepin' 'im another week, ain't that right, Captain?'' Wingate didn't say anything, just nodded in agreement. ''Don't forget to tell them big shots in Washington that ol' Sheriff Johnson took real good care of him now, will you?'' Before Wingate got a chance to answer, Infinity tried to rear up, but was held fast by the chains.

''Steady.'' Doc said, concern in his voice, ''You'll hurt yourself if you're not careful, big fella. And we don't want you hurt.''

I turned and spoke to the guards. ''I don't think he likes your rifles. You'd better take them away.'' It was a nice try, but the guards didn't flinch. They just stood there like statues in the park.

The guard from the gate stuck his head through the open service door. He spoke to Doc. ''For you, sir. St. Louis Zoo on the line.''

''Zoo!'' I said, reaching up to grab Infinity.

''You're not goin' to let him go?'' Bob asked in anger.

''You're going to put him in a cage,'' Cathy added, dismay in her voice.

''Don't worry,'' I whispered to Infinity. ''I won't let them take you. I *won't*!''

Doc Yeager went straight for the office door, Bob and Cathy right after him. I stayed and held onto Infinity, knowing it might be my last time to hold him, and hoping they could talk some sense into Doc. It turned out they hadn't gone after Doc, but to the truck. They returned with a handful of Mr. Tucker's wheat. Bob approached Infinity, but the sheriff motioned him away.

''Wait.'' I said, ''This is the only food he'll eat. You've got to let us feed him, because if he don't eat, then he'll die. It doesn't matter what your zoo does, if he don't eat this wheat, he won't eat anything.''

''Is this that special wheat I've been hearing about?'' Wingate asked, his expression changing to one of interest.

"Yes, sir," I said, "finest wheat in all of Kansas."

"Well, then, Sheriff," he said, "I suggest you let him have it. This may be our only chance to get him to eat. We need him healthy."

"Okay," the sheriff said, looking at me. "But no tricks, understood?"

"Understood," I said. Bob took the wheat and walked towards Infinity. He held it out in front of him, but Infinity refused to eat. Then Cathy tried, but he still wouldn't eat. "Come on, boy," she urged, but Infinity just turned away. Finally, I tried to force some wheat into his mouth, but he wouldn't take it.

"Infinity," I said, "you've got to eat, or you'll die." Dejected, I plunged my hands into my jacket pockets. I felt something hard and round, shaped like an egg, but with creases in the surface like a riverbed. I pulled out the walnut shell and looked at it. It had survived the trip from the crystal farmhouse. I held it up to my ear and shook it. It rattled. There was a walnut inside.

I held it out to Infinity, slowly bringing it to his mouth, but he wouldn't take it. Finally he did, but when I hugged him one last time, he dropped it at his feet. "Come on, guys," I said, watching it hit the hay. "It's no use. He won't eat. Let's go. We'll try some other time."

"Well," Wingate said with a shrug, "you had your chance."

I didn't know he was going to refuse to let us see Infinity again. If I'd known that, I'd have tried to set the unicorn free, guards or not. I didn't find out until the next morning that nobody would be allowed to visit anymore. Seems Wingate didn't care much about Mr. Tucker's Medal of Honor. By the time Congressman Fuller found all the paperwork on the medal, it would probably be too late anyway. What they call bureaucratic red tape and all. Besides, Mr. Tucker had lost the darn thing out in his meadow, so he couldn't even present it as evidence to get an audience with the congressman.

I passed Doc on the way to the truck, and couldn't help saying what I felt. "You lied to us," I said straight out, "you're not setting him free. You're taking him to the zoo. And he'll probably die there, unless he dies here first. He's just not made to stay in a cage."

"But, Thaddeus," he said, trying to put his hand on my shoulder, "it may be his only chance. I'm trying to . . ."

"You lied to me," I said, not letting him finish, "and I thought you cared about him."

He started to say something, but I walked off with my hands over my ears, so as not to hear any excuses. I probably should have given him a chance to explain, but I just wasn't in the mood right then. All I could think about was Infinity fading away in that garage. When I got to the truck I took my hands off my ears, and I could hear Doc and Wingate arguing. It sounded like something about Infinity's horn, but I couldn't catch any of the details. I sure didn't like the sound of it, though.

Nobody said a word all the way home. There was nothing to say. We knew we were losing Infinity, and there was nothing anyone could do about it.

That night when I took off my clothes, I felt a lump in my back pocket. I had completely forgotten about the rest of the poem Mr. Tucker had given me in the hospital. I pulled it out and read by the moonlight coming in the window.

VERSE 4

Once upon a unicorn
A lovely girl came riding.
"Go on. Get up!" she smiled and said,
"And stop that silly hiding.

"The unicorn will bend his head
And lift you with his mane;
You'll split the sky and go inside
And then you'll surely gain.

"The secrets of the unicorn,
The source of light and sound—

For once upon a unicorn
Forever's where you're bound.

You'll land upon a silver cloud
And see the glowing sphere
The center of the universe—
And he can take you there!"

I folded the pages and thought about all that had happened. I didn't care anymore about the center of the universe the poem talked about, I just wanted to set Infinity free. I lay awake for hours working on plans, but none of them seemed to be good enough. Then I remembered those pups were still at Doc's and if he was going to be giving tests to Infinity all day, I'd better go the next day and check on them. I decided that I should've given him a chance to explain. The next day, after checking on the pups, I'd ride over to the garage and let him tell his story. After I decided this, I was finally able to go to sleep, but I can't say I slept very well. Time had almost run out, and I had to think of something fast.

50

The Wait

I did my chores the next morning and went over to Doc's. He wasn't around, so I looked in on Cinderella and the pups myself. They were squirming and wiggling around, all of them fighting for some milk from their mom. The one I had picked out—Guinevere, as I decided to call her—was having a little trouble getting a good spot on her mother's belly, so I reached down and moved her to the front. Cinderella didn't growl at me this time. I think she knew I was just trying to get the best seat in the house for my pup.

Afterwards, I rode to the city garage to find Doc, but I couldn't get past the gate. The guard said he had orders that there were to be absolutely no visitors under any circumstances. He wouldn't even go inside to look for Doc, but I saw the ambulance parked in the lot, so I figured Doc must be in there.

I went away, deciding that if I was going to get Doc's story, I'd have to ride over to his house after dinner and ask him to explain his actions. I waited until after dessert, but Doc still wasn't there. Mom and pups were fine, since

Doc had left Cinderella a mess of food and a big pail of water. I filled it to the top with fresh water and went home to wait. And wait I did.

A whole week came and went, but it seemed like a whole summer. The Fourth of July went with it. Nobody celebrated around our house; we just weren't in the mood. Doc never came home, or to the hospital either. I was going to ask Sally to have Doc call me, but I ended up deciding that he had his chance, and should have let me know what was going on with Infinity.

I saw Mr. Tucker every day, and he was getting stronger. He gave me another verse to the poem, but I just couldn't bring myself to read it. What I really wanted was a plan to free Infinity. It was too painful to read about something I might never see again, and I just wasn't strong enough to take it at the time.

I couldn't sleep and I lost my appetite. I began to feel more and more hopeless. My dream had become a nightmare, and I couldn't wake up to save myself. I began to feel it was a great mistake to have believed at all. Now Infinity was dying. Even though I couldn't see him, I could feel him getting weaker, and part of me was dying too. Nothing ever hurt so bad.

Then one day, while Mom was trying to get me to eat, the phone rang. It was Doc; he wanted to meet me at the city garage. Wingate had gone off for the day and was returning later that night. The experts from the St. Louis Zoo were coming the day after next, and they were going to take Infinity with them. He thought I might want to say goodbye.

I ran out of the house like someone who had stolen a hive full of honey and was being chased by a swarm of bees. Outside the barn I stopped, turned around, and looked towards the house. In my mind played the image of my dad on the porch, white smoke from his pipe swirling towards the sky. Mom sat in the swing, spinning out a sweater with her needles. I looked around the barn and thought about everything we had done there: threshing the wheat, stacking the barn to the rafters, filling the silo, feeding and milking Becky, daydreaming, and listening to hay crunching in the loft. Something was owed Mom and Dad for giving me a piece of paradise, and for holding on to it as long as they could.

"Mom," I said, bolting through the screen door and letting it bang shut, "you have to come with me. They're taking Infinity to the zoo day after tomorrow, and this could be your last chance to see him."

I turned to Dad, who was sitting at the dinner table finishing a piece of pie. "You too," I insisted. "You have to see him at least once."

Mom didn't say anything at first. She thought it over carefully, and then she asked with a smile, "Don't you think we should take Mr. Tucker?"

"Oh, darn," I said, getting mad at myself, "I almost forgot. Why, I'd never forgive myself if he didn't see him just once before he . . . just once, anyway."

"Well," Dad said with a wink, "standin' around here ain't goin' to do us no good. I reckon we'd better get goin' before that blasted Wingate gets back."

We piled into the Chevy, leaving Cathy and Bob, who were fixing something under the hood of his truck, and headed off to town to gather up Mr. Tucker. He looked well enough to travel, though we had to convince Sally Penhurst, and we all left for the city garage. We were coming to pay our last respects to Infinity, and nothing could have kept us away.

We pulled up to the gate, but the guard flat out refused to let us in without Wingate's permission. Doc came out to the gate and took me aside. He told me he had pleaded with Wingate to let Infinity go, that he should be released out on the hills, but it was no use. They had taken blood samples, hair samples, electrical readings and pictures, but Wingate still wouldn't let Infinity go free. Doc had finally talked him into letting Infinity be sent to the zoo, figuring that it was just about the only chance of survival for the unicorn. At least he would be cared for properly, or as properly as a horse with a horn could be cared for in captivity.

Doc said Infinity had become so startled by the camera flashes when they took his picture that a couple of times they thought he was going to break the chain, lock and all. Doc finally made the photographers stop, saying someone might get hurt if they kept on. He told me that Wingate was mainly interested in the horn, and kept asking if there was any way to take an X-ray of it to see exactly what was inside. Doc said it would be impossible unless Infinity was severely tranquilized, and then he might not come out of it like a regular horse would. Since his internal workings were still mostly unknown, it might damage his powers—or worse.

I felt bad that I had misjudged Doc, and apologized a bunch of times. We shook hands and made friends again. I should have known all along that he would try to do the right thing. Luckily, Doc let me off the hook, saying that he understood how much I cared about Infinity.

Doc reminded the guard at the gate that Wingate had left him in charge, and that we had Doc's permission to enter. But the guard wouldn't budge, since his orders were to let no one in under any circumstances unless Wingate cleared it first. So we were out of luck. We were not going to say our goodbyes after all.

Doc had a few more words with the guard, but it was no use. We went away disappointed, but when we got a little ways down the road, I made Dad stop the car and shut off the engine and headlights, while I climbed the chain link fence. It had barbed wire on top, but I made it over pretty easy. I managed to sneak up to the back of the garage without being spotted, and climbed through an open window by standing on some oil drums. I was in luck. The light was on in the office, and both of the guards were sitting at the table inside, playing cards and drinking. Doc was lying on some hay bales, on the other side of the garage, staring up at the stars through the open skylight.

He heard the noise when I climbed through the window, but he wasn't startled. He knew I was the only one crazy enough to try to sneak back, and he was waiting for me. He didn't get up, not wanting to alert the guards and give me away. He just kept lying there with his arms behind his head.

"I knew you'd come," he whispered, not looking at me, "so I left the window open for you."

"Thanks, Doc," I whispered back, "I knew I could count on you."

"Hurry," he said. "Wingate's due back any minute now."

I came around the hay bales and saw Infinity standing behind the sandbags. He was pale and thin, just like I figured. I knew he hadn't eaten since his capture. I ran over and hugged him; he felt cold, and he didn't respond. I was still hugging him when the service door opened. Wingate was back. I ducked down behind the sandbags.

"Evening, Captain," Doc said, trying to distract him, but Wingate didn't pay any attention. He walked straight for the office and bellowed at the guards. They were supposed to be on duty, and Wingate didn't like it at all that they were relaxing; it cost them their jobs. Wingate said that if they couldn't follow orders they could go guard the road to town with the others, who had been placed there to keep away any curious tourists who may have heard that a unicorn was being held in the city garage.

Wingate was fighting mad. So after dismissing the guards and threatening them with a court martial, he turned on Doc. "I've decided not to wait," he said, fuming. "That horn has got to be some kind of transmitter. I know it's sending out signals. It's even got the men acting crazy. I want you to sedate that . . . that thing, whatever it is. I'm cutting off that horn."

I shuddered when he said this, and it took all my will-power to keep from jumping up and hitting him. But I held on, knowing that it might hurt Infinity if I exposed my position.

"Look," Doc retorted, "I agreed to let them take him to St. Louis, but nobody's touching that horn. You so much as come near him, and I'll report this to Washington. I'd like to hear what your superiors will have to say about taking hostile actions towards a possible extraterrestrial."

"Then I see we agree on one thing," Wingate said slyly. "This thing is some kind of space probe, disguised as a mythical beast so we would welcome it into our midst like the Trojan horse. Well, I'm not fooled. If that thing so much as tries to break the chain again or send out any kind of signal, I'm going to shoot him and take that horn back to Washington."

He paused and sneered. "And I'll report that it was in the interest of national security. It'll be your word against mine, and do you think they're going to believe some *has-been* country doctor? I'm warning you, if you try anything, anything at all, I'll kill it!"

Doc didn't say a word. He knew that he had to be careful, with Wingate sounding like a crazy man, 'cause when someone gets in that state of mind they're liable to do just about anything. I knew I'd better not get caught, so when Wingate went back into the office, I climbed out of the window.

"I'll be back," I whispered to Infinity. "Don't worry. I'll think of something."

I snuck towards the fence on my stomach, not wanting to chance getting caught by the guard at the gate. The car was gone, but I was glad, knowing that Dad didn't want to get spotted with the Chevy parked by the fence.

I accidentally knocked against some oil drums along the fence, and the guard came out of his station. I squatted down between the drums and the fence, lying real still. He came over and shone his flashlight my way, waving it back and forth across the dirt lot, looking for whatever had made the noise. He came real close to me, and I knew it would be over as soon as he shone his light on me.

I crawled along the fence and snaked my way around the last drum, so that all of them were between me and that flashlight.

Suddenly an owl hooted. I looked up, and there he was, perched atop the city garage, his big eyes blinking and his head turning around towards me. He hooted again, louder, and the guard shone the flashlight on him. He flew away and the guard went back to the station house, satisfied that he had found the cause of the noise.

I snuck the rest of the way to the fence and climbed it as quietly as I could. It was almost quiet enough, but the guard flashed his light my way after I jumped down, so I ran as fast as I could towards home. When I got to the school, I decided it would be a good place to rest and try to think of a plan to save Infinity. The barn owl had stopped for a rest in the bell tower, and I was glad to see him. It made me feel like the place was safe. I always felt that way when he was around.

51

The Idea

I walked over to the schoolhouse, popped one of the windows open with my pocket knife, and crawled inside. I paced up and down the aisles trying to think of a plan to free Infinity, but I couldn't think of anything that made sense.

"It's not fair," I said to myself. "It's just not fair." I knew that if I didn't act soon, Infinity would be lost forever. He would be trapped for the rest of his life in the zoo, or Wingate might kill him, if he didn't starve to death first. He may have been special, but he still was living in an animal's body, and animals have to eat.

I sat down, pulled my hat over my eyes, and put my feet on the desk in front of me like I always wanted to do, but never could when school was in session. I put my head back and stared at the ceiling. A few minutes later I lowered my eyes and studied the blackboard. It looked too empty with nothing on it, so I went over, picked up a piece of chalk and began to draw as best I could. When I finished, a unicorn was prancing across the blackboard, head held high and proud. I filled in the body with chalk dust from the erasers.

I looked again at the white creature on the blackboard, galloping across the sky, feet above billowing clouds. And then it hit me. An idea flashed across my mind like a stallion streaking on the wind. It was wild and foolish, and it might not work at all, but it was just about the only chance I had.

I jumped up, dove out the window, and ran the five miles home. I was pretty much out of breath when I found Bob and Cathy. They were still working on Bob's truck. I was breathing so hard that it took me five minutes to get my plan out.

"It's crazy," Cathy said, wiping her hands on a grease rag.

"Yeah," Bob agreed, scratching his flame-red hair. "It's crazy, all right. I just hope it's crazy enough."

That night I was pretty easy to get along with, and I ate like a horse. Mom and Dad stayed at the table just to watch me eat. Both of them were relieved to see me eating again and wondered about the sudden change of appetite, but I was not going to reveal my plan until the smoke rose high on the porch. I just smiled and said that things were fine again, that I had accepted everything.

"I understand a little how you feel," Dad said. "I almost thought I was goin' to be givin' up ridin' that old tractor, but then I decided to take John Deere with me. Now, you can't take Infinity with you, but I promise you we can go visit him in St. Louis, even if we have to take the tractor to get there."

"Yeah," I said with a grin. "We can go visit him all right, but I think we'd better take the bus. Otherwise, the snow will be six feet high by the time the tractor gets there."

"Hey," Dad said, not blinking an eye, "snow's no problem. Cathy will have the scoop on John Deere pretty soon, if she can break away from that boyfriend long enough to hook it up. But," he added, looking at Mom, "that's kids nowadays."

"Aw," I said, "I guess I was just being selfish. I suppose

the whole world should be allowed a look at Infinity. Not just us.''

"You're taking a much better attitude about this, Thaddy,'' Mom said. "I'm proud of you.'' She reached over and roughed up my hair. Then she went to the hall closet and came back with a wrapped present. The paper had unicorns and rainbows on it.

"Here, this is for you.''

I tore open the wrapper. It was a new straw hat, and I put it on. "Thanks,'' I said. "Guess I was about due for a new one. Don't tell Petula, though. Maybe she won't notice.''

"We're just lucky,'' Mom said, "that the army agents haven't let the newspapers in to see that . . . unicorn. Fact is, they've barricaded the road to town from the main highway. No one who doesn't have business here can get in. I hear they're going to transport him to St. Louis in an armored truck day after tomorrow, so nobody can get any ideas about trying to steal him.''

I just stared at her, not saying a word.

After dinner I went to my room and waited for Mom and Dad to move to the porch for the evening. Pretty soon I could see smoke rising outside my bedroom window, and I knew it was a good time for presenting my plan to my folks.

I walked downstairs and out to the porch, where I sat on the swing with my mom. "Well,'' I began, "I've got a plan to set Infinity free.''

"But''—Mom stopped crocheting and looked at me—"I thought you had accepted it. Infinity's going to the zoo, remember? So that everyone can see him.''

"That was before dinner,'' I argued. "People will say anything when they're hungry.''

"Oh,'' she chuckled, "is *that* it? Well, then, what's this big plan of yours?''

"Well . . .'' I looked at Dad to get his attention, but he just kept puffing on his corncob pipe and gazing up at the sky. It was a bright, clear night, and a million stars studded the blackness like diamonds on a cowboy movie star's shirt.

"Well," I repeated, "what we do is catch us another unicorn, and use it to gain access to the city garage. Then, once we're inside, we unlock Infinity and set them both free."

"Mighty big plans," Dad finally said. I guess I got his attention all right, but his voice didn't sound as if he believed. "But where are you gonna get another unicorn and just how do you figger to get past the guards?" he asked.

"Wingate sent them to guard the road to town," I informed him. "There's only him and the guard at the gate. When he sees we've got another unicorn, he'll let us in for sure."

"Maybe so," Dad agreed, "but just how do you figger to catch another one by tomorrow night? That's about all the time you've got left, I reckon."

"You just leave that part to me," I said, and winked. "Now let me tell you what I need you and Mom to do. You *do* want to help with the escape, don't you?"

"Yes," Mom said seriously, "we both do, but you have to start talking some sense first. It took you a week to catch Infinity, and here you're planning on catching another in one night. I can't see how."

"Well," I replied impatiently, "let me explain."

After they heard the whole story, they both agreed my plan was nuts, but it just might work. Still, Mom was having a little trouble with it. I don't think she was fully convinced that Infinity *was* a unicorn, so she balked at her part of the plan. It must have sounded weird to a nonbeliever, and she didn't want me to look foolish. I finally had to bring out the ace I had been hiding up my sleeve.

"Mom," I told her, "it wasn't your fault about the fire in the barn. That old cow kicked over the lantern just as sure as Mrs. O'Leary's cow started the Great Chicago Fire."

She stared at me in shock for a second, and then doubt took over again. "You heard that from one of the kids at school," she accused.

"That might be," I said without flinching, "but I was there just the same."

When I saw that my ace wasn't going to turn the tide, I got desperate and blurted out something without even thinking. "Dad," I began, suddenly turning to him, "do you remember what you said in the field the day you had the heart attack?"

"Thaddy," Mom said, "that's not . . ."

"You said," I went on, ignoring her plea, " 'Here, Thaddy. Take the reins . . . Take the reins. I'm not going to make it.' "

My dad sat motionless in his rocking chair. When he heard what I said, his feet hit the porch and stopped the rocker cold. He turned slowly towards me, a look of shock and disbelief in his eyes.

"Nobody," he said, "nobody on God's green earth ever heard me say that. And I ain't never told a soul except . . ."

He looked at Mom. She had turned as pale as a white-washed fence. What I'd said had completely knocked the wind out of her. She couldn't speak for the longest time, and then, in a faint, faraway voice she said, "I didn't tell a soul. I never said a word about it to anyone, ever. How'd you learn these things?"

"Infinity," I answered. "I learned them from riding Infinity. He's full of magic, you know; he can show you anything—the past, present, and even the future."

In a minute she put down her crocheting, stood, and shuffled like a sleepwalker to the front door. "Well," she said slowly. Her hand rested on the door jamb, as if she was holding herself up. "I'd better get started. We've only got one more day to get us another unicorn."

"It just goes to show you," I told Dad when Mom had left.

"What's that, Thaddy?" he said, still in a daze.

"Sometimes," I said with assurance, "hearing is believing too."

I walked to my room and pulled the poem from under the mattress. For the first time in a week I felt like reading it, and for the first time I realized there were only two verses left. So I read the next verse real slow. It may not have been Shakespeare, but to a country boy from Kansas it was the most beautiful poetry ever written.

VERSE 5

Surrender all your cares to him,
And let him take you high—
And soon, I swear,
You shall be gone
Far off inside the sky.

You'll never be the same again
When you come back to land;
Yes, he is waiting just for you—
Go on, reach out your hand!

You'll ride and ride
Across the stars
To places and dreams so real
That finally, in a whispered thought,
Your self will be revealed—

And finally, in a silent thought,
All will be revealed!

52

The Plan

The next day I went to the hospital to tell Mr. Tucker my plan, but Sally Penhurst had taken him home. Doc had okayed him for release over the phone, even though the crutches never showed up. Doc said that he would be fine as long as he didn't get too much excitement and took his medicine. Unfortunately, excitement was exactly what all of us, including Mr. Tucker, were about to get.

Mr. Tucker said he was feeling much better. He had thought some more about what we kids had said, especially the part about Wingate being interested in Infinity's horn, and said he was about to bust Infinity out himself. He was going to drive down to the city garage and raise cain, but he liked my idea better. Besides, they were coming for Infinity the next day, so we had to try something pretty quick in order to bust him out, no matter what the risk.

My plan was crazy, all right, but it wasn't all that complicated. We'd show up at the city garage that night with another unicorn, saying it was mating season and that Infinity must mate or die. That was the reason he was dying, we'd tell Wingate, and our new unicorn had come out of the hills looking for him. We decided it would be better to have two live unicorns in captivity than one dead one. We were certain that Wingate would agree—at least that's what we were banking on. Besides, it would give him another horn to think about, and that was what he was really interested in anyway.

Once we got inside, we'd jump Wingate and tie him up in the office. Then we'd free Infinity and the new unicorn by loading them in horse trailers and trucking them out to Tucker's meadow. We knew we might have to run the gate if we couldn't get out with the unicorns. That's where Dad came in; he was going to run interference and ram the gate if he had to, using the scoop on John Deere. Cathy's job was to hook up the scoop on the tractor, and since it already had a headlight borrowed from Bob's truck, Dad would be able to see what he was doing.

Bob would help with the heavy part of hooking up the scoop. Then he and Cathy would go to the city garage, so we would have enough people to overpower Wingate and the guard. Our hope was that Wingate hadn't sent for reinforcements to help guard Infinity, but we had our doubts.

We were relying on Doc inside the garage to help us any way he could, though we didn't want to chance a phone call to him. Wingate or the guard might listen in, and then our plan would be foiled completely. We were also going to need Mom's artistic ability to help with the backup plan. She was to make a unicorn out of Petula by giving her an artificial horn and coloring her white, in case we didn't find another unicorn in time for the rescue.

I explained all of this to Mr. Tucker, and asked him if he thought we could pull it off, or whether he thought it was just too crazy.

"Crazy?" he said. "Why, it's downright insane. But it just might be wild enough to work." I stood by his bed and helped him sit up. He sat on the side of the bed and got dressed. "Hand me those ol' combat boots," he said.

"We've got a war to fight. But first"—he winked—"we've got a unicorn to catch."

He seemed strong enough to walk, but doing it took a little support from me. I held him under his arm, and we made our way to his garage and managed to climb into his truck. Our horse trailer was already hooked up behind it. Even though he had lost half his eyesight and all of his driver's license, he kept his old truck anyway. "Just in case," he told me, "somethin' comes up. Don't want to have to rely on some one else when I have to drive into town in case of some emergency." This, I reckon qualified as a state of emergency.

"Here," Mr. Tucker said, getting in the passenger's side. "Take the wheel. I ain't ready to drive yet."

"Are you sure?" I asked. "We might get in trouble."

"Not as much as we're fixin' to get into," he chuckled. "Now, get in."

I jumped in and sat behind the wheel. I was a little short, but I could see between the steering wheel and the dashboard. Mr. Tucker seemed to be getting stronger and there was a glow of fire in his eyes, but I had to ask him if he was going to be all right.

"Are you sure you're well enough to do this? I mean, I could catch the unicorn and pick you up later."

He tipped his straw hat back and gave me a stern look. "Heck," he said, "I ain't givin' you a chance to pull this off without me. I still got to see that critter, you know. If somethin' goes wrong, I wanna be there, just in case."

"Just checking," I said, trying to see over the dashboard. "Let me know if we're going to hit anything."

We got the old pickup started and lunged down the road. The rest of my plan included taking Petula to the meadow to use as bait to catch another unicorn, but in the event we didn't have much luck, Mom's artistic magic would be needed. That's why I had walked over to Mr. Tucker's and left Petula at home with Mom. Mr. Tucker and I had to pick up Petula and bring her over to his place. She was to ride inside the horse trailer so that nobody would see that Mom had transformed her into a unicorn.

Before we turned down the road to my folks' farm, Mr. Tucker put his hand on my shoulder. "Say," he said with a smile, "we got some time before Petula's ready. Let's go check on those pups. I haven't seen 'em yet."

"Yeah," I said, "good idea. I almost forgot that you haven't seen them."

We took the scenic route to Doc's, since I sort of ran off the road and ended up driving across the field. It was a little bumpy, but Mr. Tucker didn't say much, except he thought I had invented a pretty good shortcut, especially for when the river overflowed next spring.

"Nobody's goin' to have to wait fer the water to clear off the road next year," he said and smiled. "Sometimes you've got to make yer own road. I reckon this is one of them times."

The pups were all doing fine. Mr. Tucker liked the one I'd picked out, and he liked the name too. He said Guinevere was a suitable name for a pup born in the time of unicorns and fairy tales. He told me we were both lucky to be living in a time of magic, a time when miracles could still happen, and that I should hold onto this memory forever, no matter what happened. We both agreed that we needed just one more miracle to come running out of the hills. Otherwise we'd have to create our own, and it might not work as well.

When we drove over to my folks' farm, I couldn't quite get to the brake pedal, and I sort of knocked down Elmer's pen and the fence around the barn. Elmer ran out of the hole in the fence, and Becky followed along behind. I guess she was taking getting-lost lessons from the old pro. By the time we got Petula loaded up in the trailer, they were all the way to Tucker's Grove.

Elmer ran in front of the truck when we got there, and I accidently nudged him with the bumper. He tipped over and the truck stopped, without even using the brakes.

He wasn't hurt when I got out to look at him. "Thanks, Elmer," I said when he got up. "I was having a little trouble reaching the pedals anyway. Didn't know how I was going to stop this thing."

He just squealed a little, like he does when he's looking

for food, and took off for home. Funny, though, that was the last time he ran away. I guess he finally found something bigger than him that was just as low to the ground. He probably thought that old pickup truck was his pa come home to chase him down.

Becky was not the kind to go wandering off on her own, so she followed Elmer back home. Neither one of them left the pen again, even though the hole in the fence didn't get fixed for a week afterwards.

We parked the truck alongside the fence by the meadow and waited. The sun crept slowly across the cloudless blue sky until it was hanging just over the horizon, but there was no sign of a unicorn. I guess it was just too light out. Mr. Tucker wasn't about to let me out on those hills again; too many wolves out there, he said.

After the sun sank below the horizon and the burnt-orange sky turned to deep purple, the mist began to come up on the meadow. We knew this was our last chance. We waited for hours, watching mist fill the meadow like cotton candy, but still there was no unicorn.

"Well," Mr. Tucker said at last, "I guess we'd better go."

He was right: Petula had been our only chance. But the bait hadn't worked and now it was time to go. I got up and untied her from the fence, looking at the horn Mom had made for her out of glazed ceramic. We had fastened it with fishing line around her head and combed her hair over it so you could hardly tell. In the dim light of the moon, it looked just as if an ivory horn was growing right out of her forehead. She didn't really seem to mind too much. I think she liked the idea of looking like Infinity.

Mom had powdered her with bleached flour so Petula would look like a white unicorn. She was nowhere near as white as Infinity, but it would have to do. Besides, unicorns came in all colors, so it didn't matter as long as she didn't look like Petula with a fake horn.

One thing we hadn't planned on was what flour dust did to your nose. It caught me square in the nostrils when I went to untie Petula and put her in the trailer again, and I

sneezed. This startled Petula so much that she reared up
and ran straight across the meadow into the mist.

I yelled and yelled, but she was gone. A few minutes
later I saw her on the hills, standing on the highest ridge
like Infinity always did. She reared and gave a mighty
scream like a wild horse. Then she disappeared into the
hills. Mr. Tucker wouldn't let me go after her, and I knew
we were doomed.

We left the truck where it was and walked back to the
cabin. We waited on the porch for hours before we fell
asleep, and didn't wake until the sound of heavy hoofbeats
pounded across the meadow. A flash of white raced back
and forth, and then it slowed and stopped. It bent its head
and began to eat.

I slipped off the porch and walked slowly towards the
large white shape. Then I saw the horn, spiraling towards
heaven, thick as my wrist and as long as my arm. The
unicorn looked at me, just ten feet away. I knew those eyes.

"Petula," I said, "where have you been? We need you
to help us free Infinity. Where have you been, you bad
horse? And where is your halter? . . . Well, at least you've
still got your horn." I was relieved that she hadn't lost it
out on the hills.

I walked over and grabbed her neck, but when I hugged
her I noticed the horn had a soft white glow to it and that
it smelled faintly of honeysuckle. It was funny, but I thought
I heard the faraway sound of a country band playing. It
seemed to be coming from inside the horn. I reached up
slowly and touched it. It was warm, and vibrated with energy. It was not made of ceramic. Somehow, someway, it
had changed to pure ivory.

As I held onto it I began to fill up with a strange and
wonderful feeling, the same way I'd felt when Infinity had
shone his light on me. I held on for the longest time, and
then I pulled away and looked her over carefully. She was
Petula all right, down to the last detail. I recognized her
teeth and those sweet brown eyes. But she was no longer
covered with flour dust. Instead, her whole coat was pure
white.

"Where did you get that horn?" I asked, shaking my head in disbelief, "and this coat?"

I decided not to ask any more questions. After all, I had needed a miracle, I had asked for one, and now I had received one. There was nothing left to say.

I put her in the trailer and walked back to the cabin. I explained to Mr. Tucker what had happened and he just said, "There ain't no power on earth like the power of believin'. That's all there is to it."

Just then the phone rang. It was the city garage. "That so?" Mr. Tucker said. "Well, keep 'em there awhile. It might do 'em some good. Me and Thaddeus will be by in a little while to pick 'em up. Oh, and tell Wingate we got another unicorn." He hung up the phone.

"That was the sheriff," he said with a big grin. "Seems Bob and Cathy showed up at the city garage and got caught tryin' to pull the fire alarm. He called yer folks' place, but nobody was home, so he called here."

"That so?" I said, shaking my head. "Boy, these kids nowadays. You just can't trust 'em to stay out of trouble."

53

The Rescue

Mr. Tucker was feeling better, so he drove us to the city garage. I offered to drive, but for some reason he turned me down. I guess he figured we should take the direct route instead of the scenic one. Of course, he didn't have any depth perception on account of only having one good eye, so we worked out a plan. He drove, since he could reach the pedals a whole lot easier than I could, and I became his seeing-eye passenger. It worked out pretty good. I only had to grab the steering wheel a couple of times and get us back on the road. But we made it in one hour.

We pulled up to the gate with the horse trailer hooked behind. Our surprise was inside. We stopped at the entrance, and Mr. Tucker leaned his head out the window. The military guard glared at us and pointed his rifle in our direction. "We're here to pick up the kids that tried to set off the alarm," Mr. Tucker said, scratching his beard. The guard gave us a serious look. "Oh," Mr. Tucker added, "we got another one of them unicorns, too."

The guard looked at us sternly. Then he motioned with

his rifle for Mr. Tucker to get out of the truck. Mr. Tucker stepped out and walked slowly around to the back of the trailer. "Can't tell much from the rear end," he said.

The guard held his rifle in one hand and pulled a flashlight out of his belt with the other. He shone it into the trailer and looked around. Then he went back to the guard box and made a phone call.

"Let me speak to the captain," he said gravely. "Well," he said after listening, "just tell him they're bringing another one in. I need clearance for this." He listened again and hung up the phone. "Captain Wingate is busy right now," he barked. "You'll have to come back later."

Mr. Tucker looked at the guard with a severe expression. "Look," he began, "this here is the mate to the big fella in there. She's come a long way to be with 'im, and if she don't see 'im tonight, then he'll die. Didn't the captain tell you that unicorns only mate once in a lifetime? This is his last chance. If that unicorn doesn't mate tonight, he dies. Well, I don't know about you, but I sure don't want to be the one to tell the captain whose fault it was if that critter dies."

The guard's stony expression changed to a worried look, and he said, "All right. Roll 'em. But no funny stuff. You just take her in real slow and easy. If anything happens, I've got orders to shoot."

Mr. Tucker climbed back into the truck, but he had a difficult time and looked a little pale.

"You going to be okay?" I asked.

"Yep," he said, "just a little lightheaded, that's all. I'll be fine." He didn't look all that good to me. Maybe he shouldn't have come. Maybe he should've been in bed. I hoped seeing Infinity would help. If we got that far.

"Hey," I whispered, grabbing his arm, "do you think they'll believe all that stuff about Infinity? I mean only having one night to mate and all?"

He didn't look at me; he just stared straight out the windshield and said with a squint, "Beats me, but it sure got us in the gate." He paused and added, "And don't let the sheriff touch Petula's horn."

"Why not? It's real, as far as I can tell."

"No sense takin' any unnecessary risks," he answered. "Skeptics like the sheriff can ruin the magic. We don't know how long Petula's got before she turns back into a horse. Somebody like the sheriff touches it, and it might be over right then."

He started up the truck and drove to the double garage doors. I could see Bob's truck and trailer parked nearby. His and Cathy's part of the plan was to pull the alarm on the side of the guard gate and cause enough confusion to let the two of them make it inside. Bob figured that Wingate might not let the four of us in at once, especially with Doc already there and demanding that Infinity be let go.

It worked just fine, but what we didn't figure was that Wingate would call Sheriff Johnson to back him up. The bad news was that the sheriff's pickup was parked next to Bob's. The good news was that there weren't any other military cars around, except for Wingate's sedan. That meant he was relying solely on the sheriff as a backup, leaving his men to block off the entrance to town.

Actually, the guards were badly needed there. Since word got out that a unicorn was caught and being held in town, folks were already camping out by the road, hoping to catch a glimpse of the critter when they transported him to St. Louis the next day. It took all of Wingate's men to hold them back, the crowd, which was more anxious to get inside than folks at a supermarket opening.

The sheriff came outside and stood with his hands on his hips, staring at us. "Well," he said, "I understand you've got another one of them wild animals with you."

"Yes, sir," I said, leaning forward so he could see me.

"This wouldn't be some kinda trick, would it?" he asked with a sneer.

"No, sir," I said quickly, "this is on the level." I didn't feel too bad telling him a white lie, especially since Petula had turned into a unicorn.

"This one's a female," Mr. Tucker said. "If that male in there don't mate tonight, he's goin' to die. Especially since he ain't eaten in a week. We figured this was our only chance to save 'im.''

"Awright,'' the sheriff said, not quite believing us, "let's have a look-see.''

We both got out of the truck and walked around back. I got in the trailer and led Petula out. "My,'' the sheriff said, "she's a big 'un, ain't she? Not quite as white as the big fella, but it looks like a pretty good match.'' He paused and added, "That's a heck of a horn she's got there.''

"Oh,'' I agreed, "she's a beauty, all right.''

"Now,'' Mr. Tucker said, scratching his head, "you goin' to let us in, or do we take this filly back to the hills?''

The sheriff looked her over again from head to foot. "Mighty big girl there,'' he said, "must be seventeen hands high.'' He took off his hat and held it in his hand. "Let me have a feel of that horn,'' he said. "I didn't get to feel the one on the big fella. He gets too jumpy whenever you gets close to 'im.'' He reached out for the horn.

"Wait!'' I yelled, and he stopped. "The horn is a very sensitive spot on this critter.''

"You touch that while she's in matin' season,'' Mr. Tucker added, "and he won't come near her. Human scent ruins the whole thing.''

"That right?'' the sheriff asked, and gave us both funny looks.

"Absolutely,'' Mr. Tucker said. "You touch that horn and you've as good as killed 'em both. He won't even come near her. You might as well shoot 'em right on the spot.''

"Well,'' Sheriff Johnson said, "guess I'd better keep my hands to myself, at least fer the time bein'.''

"That's what I recommend,'' Mr. Tucker went on, "unless, of course, you want to explain who is responsible fer killin' these rare critters.'' The sheriff gave us both a stare, and scratched his head.

"Why don't you go check with Doc if you don't believe us?'' I suggested, bluffing.

"I wish I could,'' he said, "but he's still in there with Wingate. They're interrogatin' yer sister and that Greison boy about tryin' to pull the alarm. Said nobody should disturb 'em. No, sir, guess we don't want any more trouble. Especially with the U.S. Army." He put his hat back on and said, "Take her on in, I guess. But you'd better not be pullin' anythin'. Wingate says he'll shoot the big fella if he has to."

I looked at Mr. Tucker. Neither of us liked the sound of those words. We had to find a way to get the sheriff and Wingate tied up so we could free Infinity and his mate.

The sheriff went through the side door and slid the long two-by-four out of the latch. Then he swung open the double doors. We led Petula in, and he closed the doors behind us and lowered the two-by-four into place. My hunch was right about there being no guards on duty that night. They were all manning the barricades on Main Street. This could be the break we needed, but we had to think fast, before anyone got wise to the plan.

"Better get behind that lift there," Mr. Tucker said to the sheriff. "There's no tellin' how he's goin' to react when he sees her. He's liable to get mighty excited."

The sheriff nodded, but walked over and opened the office door instead. "Captain Wingate?" he asked.

"I said we're not to be disturbed!" Wingate shouted.

"But, sir. They've brought another one."

"I don't care if they've brought the missing link!" Wingate yelled. "These kids have got to be debriefed. Now shut that door!"

"But, sir," the sheriff insisted.

"Okay," Wingate finally said, "I'll be out in five minutes."

The sheriff closed the door and walked back toward us. It was just what we had hoped for. Wingate was too involved with debriefing procedures to come out of the office right away. Mr. Tucker stared at the sheriff and said in a whisper, "They need to be alone as much as possible on their weddin' night. Thaddy will lead her over. Let's you and I go outside and leave 'em be. Thaddy'll take care of it."

Sheriff Johnson gave Mr. Tucker a suspicious glance, but Mr. Tucker knew exactly what to say. "Look," He said, putting his arm on the sheriff's shoulder, "Wingate's got the key to the lock. I saw it on his belt when you opened the door. Heck, even a horse with a horn ain't strong enough to break that chain. Come on, let's take a walk. Yer goin' to be a part of history, you know.''

"Do you suppose," Sheriff Johnson asked like a kid at the fair, "that I could get my picture taken with 'em, just once?"

"Absolutely," Mr. Tucker said, "right after the big event here. Why, did I ever tell you about how the unicorn lost his horn . . . ?" I couldn't hear anymore. They had gone out the service door and walked away. Mr. Tucker was telling him all kinds of stories, I was sure of that much. I just wasn't sure what to do next.

I left Petula outside the sandbags. Infinity got a good look at her, but he didn't seem interested right then. I walked over and gave him a quick hug. I had work to do, and not much time to do it in.

Doc came out of the office. Boy, was I glad to see him, but there was no time for friendly reunions. "Here," I said, reaching out my hand, "help me with these chains."

We carefully unhooked Infinity from his wires. Then I slipped the chains off his legs, trying to be as quiet as possible. I had a hard time getting the neck chain over his horn; it wouldn't come off. There was just not enough slack to slip it over. "We're not going to make it," I said to Doc. "This thing won't come off over the horn. Come on," I pleaded, "think of something."

Infinity must have heard me, because he bent down on one knee. He shook his head and pulled, straining every muscle against the chain. It pulled taut and began to groan against the locks.

"Come on," I whispered, "you can do it. Nothing can hold you."

He backed up to the lift, and his eyes got big. Then he ran full force, snapping the chain like a whip. It strained but didn't break. He backed up again and lowered his head. He lunged against it, and again the chain snapped. It didn't break, but he had loosened it.

"I'll get something to cut this chain," Doc said, "or he'll hurt himself."

"No he won't," I said, "look at those eyes. Nothing can hold him now. Come on, Infinity. You can do it."

He bent down and searched the hay on the floor. "What are you doing?" I asked. "We gotta get going."

He came up with the walnut I had thrown there the week before, and crunched it in his teeth. "This ain't no time for dessert," I told him. "We gotta get out of here."

He backed up and crouched down by the lift. His horn grew the color of white-hot metal and began to vibrate with pure energy. He lunged forward with all of his strength and broke the chain right at the neck. It clanged on the concrete floor and the noise brought Wingate out of the office. He flung the door open and dashed out, chewing madly on his tobacco. He drew his gun and aimed it at Infinity, pulling the trigger back.

"Anyone moves," he said with fury, "and you've got one dead . . . *thing* on your hands." He turned his head and spit in the straw.

Bob and Cathy came running out of the office. Wingate whirled around, his gun pointed at them. Doc closed in behind him. I stood by Infinity, unable to move. I didn't want anyone to get shot.

"What are you going to do?" Doc asked. "Shoot all of us?"

Wingate turned again, facing us all. "I'll shoot if I have to," he snarled. "Now, everyone clear out." He kept backing up towards the office, keeping us in his sights. Suddenly he backed into a sharp object. It hit him right in the spine. He dropped the gun. Bob dove and got it. He pointed it at Wingate and said, "I think you might want to look behind you."

Wingate turned slowly around. Petula just stood there, her big old brown eyes staring innocently into space. It had been her horn that had poked him in the back and made him drop the gun. Bob opened the chamber and emptied the bullets into his hand, then put them in his pocket.

"Looks like I'd better hold onto this," he said, stuffing the gun through his belt.

"Good work, Petula," I said. "I knew we could count on you." But we had forgotten something.

Sheriff Johnson came running through the side door. Mr. Tucker couldn't hold him off any longer. He pulled his Colt .45 and pointed it around the room. "All right," he said with authority, "looks like the show's over."

Just when he got the words out, Mr. Tucker came through the door and plowed him over, knocking him to the floor. The gun went flying . . . There was a mad scramble, and Wingate came up with it. Before Bob could get his own gun reloaded, Wingate got up and aimed at Infinity. There wasn't anything anyone could do before Wingate started firing.

The gun just clicked. Sheriff Johnson had a sheepish look on his face when he explained to Wingate, "I don't normally keep it loaded." He flushed red. "It's too dangerous."

Wingate couldn't say a word. I guess he couldn't believe a sheriff would leave the bullets out of his gun, but this was Flint Hills, and the law officer didn't get much call to use his gun. So our dumb old sheriff never bothered to load it.

Mr. Tucker got up pretty slow. I think plowing into the sheriff had taken a lot out of him, but we managed to get him to his feet.

While Bob put the bullets back in the chamber of his pistol, we tied Wingate and the sheriff in the office and led our unicorns to the trailers. Infinity seemed suddenly to regain his strength. I think the fresh air and freedom helped—not to mention the walnut. He looked strong and powerful again, though he wasn't quite a hundred percent.

We loaded him in Bob's trailer, and Petula in the other. "Wait!" I said to Mr. Tucker, "I've got something to do first."

"Better make it snappy," he said, " 'cause I'm pullin' outa here."

"Go on," I said, running back to the garage. "I'll catch up to you."

I ran inside and killed the lights. Then I ran out of the

building, pulling the fire alarm on the way. I figured it would confuse the guard at the gate, and he might leave his post.

Mr. Tucker had already started to pull away. Bob and Cathy were right behind. I ran past them and jumped on the running board of Mr. Tucker's truck, grabbing onto the sideview mirror. I dove through the open window and got stuck halfway in between. My legs stuck out and I was kicking like a fish flopping on shore.

Instead of slowing down, Mr. Tucker stepped on the gas. He tried to pull me in with one hand while he steered with the other. He was going to run the gate. The guard wasn't fooled by the fire alarm. He stayed at his post, raising his rifle to aim at us. I think he might have shot, except he couldn't figure out what was flapping out the window of the truck. It just might have been Wingate, for all he knew.

We hit the wooden gate pretty fast, and it shattered to pieces. The guard stepped aside at the last second. I tried to get all the way in the truck, and made one last lunge. When I did, I accidentally kicked the guard square in the jaw. It knocked him out cold. That gave me enough of a push to fall into the truck. I sat up and looked back. The guard flat out on the ground, and looked like he wasn't getting up anytime soon.

"Where'd you learn to kick like that?" Mr. Tucker asked, still catching his breath.

"First time Dad took me for a haircut," I answered, "darn near broke the barber's leg."

We sped off as fast as his old truck could go, pulling the trailer behind us. It bounced down the road like a covered wagon. Bob and Cathy were right behind us, their one headlight dipping with the bumps in the road.

I wondered what had happened to Dad. He was supposed to run the gate with the tractor to help our getaway, but I guess he didn't get there soon enough.

Before the garage disappeared in the rearview mirror, we could see a set of headlights pulling out of the gate. They were moving pretty fast.

54

The Escape

The headlights were gaining on us. We looked at each other and then at the speedometer. We were going sixty miles an hour, and Mr. Tucker had the gas pedal on the floor. We knew we couldn't outrun the army sedan. We would have to think of something else.

Bob's truck pulled alongside. I grabbed the wheel and held it steady so we wouldn't collide while Bob rolled down the passenger window and shouted at Mr. Tucker, "We're goin' on ahead. No point both of us gettin' caught. They're comin' with guns. If I were you, I'd let that filly go. It's the only chance she's got."

Cathy put her foot to the floor and they sped away. A bushy white tail waved behind them in the trailer. "Got to get that girl to overhaul my engine," Mr. Tucker said with a frown. He looked in the rearview mirror. We had about enough time to stop and open the tailgate. We knew Bob was right. We were going to get caught, so our only chance to save Petula was to set her free, though I might not ever see her again.

We pulled over to the side of the road and jumped out of the truck. I opened the trailer and backed Petula out. I had to let go of her, but when a person loves a horse like I did, he just can't chase her off like some stranger.

I thought about all we had been through together, and saw her in my mind years back, pulling the plow and winning the contest at the fair. I saw her in the field when Dad had the heart attack, and when we rode to school and to the river to fish. She'd carried me home when I got my clothes stolen, and carried me away from the wolves. I had to tell myself she had already crossed over into eternity when she went out on the hills that night and got her real horn back. So she was already gone, and thinking that was about the only way I could make myself release her. She was already a spirit, come back to say her farewell to me and help me out of a jam.

Still, I had to say goodbye quick before I was completely overcome with memories. I reached up and hugged her as best I could. "Bye, old girl," I said, getting a little damp in the eyes, "I'll miss you. Save a place for me up there, will you? Come back and visit whenever you can. I'll be here, and I'll be waiting for you. And if you can't come back, wait for me at the farmhouse in the sky. I'll meet you there when it's my time to go."

"Thaddy," Mr. Tucker said softly, placing his hand on my shoulder. I knew what he meant, and slapped Petula on the rear with my straw hat. She hesitated for a moment, then bolted into the night.

"Good thing we took Petula," Mr. Tucker said. "I just hope she finds her way home."

"You must have forgot," I said, staring at him. "She's a unicorn now. She's got to make it to the hills."

He smiled and tipped his hat. "Like I said, hope she finds her way home . . . Kind of a shame, though, that you didn't have time fer a longer goodbye."

"Aw, that's okay," I said at last. "Now at least she's got a fighting chance."

The army sedan slammed on the brakes and skidded to a stop behind us. The sheriff and Wingate jumped out, aiming army pistols at us. We didn't realize that Wingate would have extra guns stashed in his office—and I knew that this time both guns were loaded. The men walked slowly up to the trailer. We stood in front of the tailgate, blocking their view, and stalling for time so Petula could get away. "Step aside," Sheriff Johnson ordered, "yer obstructin' justice."

"Over my dead body," I said, crossing my arms in front of me.

"Well, then," Wingate said, aiming his gun at me, "if that's the way it has to be." He wasn't chewing tobacco this time, and looked as mean as I'd ever seen him. His narrow eyes had the glare of a predator that had found its game.

"Wait," Mr. Tucker said, and held out his hands. "We're goin'." He grabbed my arm and we moved slowly out of the way.

The sheriff pulled a flashlight out of his belt and shone it in the trailer. "It's gone!" he cried.

We heard hoofbeats out on the field next to the road. The silhouette of a big horse appeared in the distance, running for the Flint Hills. It had a spiral horn on its forehead and a wild look in its eyes.

"Quick!" Wingate said. "We can still catch him."

"Which one is it?" Sheriff Johnson asked, confused.

"It doesn't matter," Wingate said, holstering his gun, "we'll get one or the other."

They jumped in the sedan and sped away. We got in the truck and followed behind. They were a good half mile ahead of us by the time we got near the Greisons' dairy. When we passed it, a set of taillights flashed on and off down the drive. Something was wrong. We slowed down and circled back. When we started down the drive, we met Cathy and Bob coming our way. They were on foot. "What happened?" I asked. "Where's Infinity?"

"We couldn't see too well with one headlight," Cathy said, throwing up her hands, "and we went off the side of the road."

"Yeah," Bob added, hanging his head. "And we picked

up an arrowhead. Front tire's flat, and I don't have a spare. Infinity's still in the trailer. We didn't want to let him go with Wingate right up the road.''

"Quick," Mr. Tucker said, "load 'im into our trailer before they circle back."

"I'm afraid it's too late," Cathy said, looking down the road. "They're coming back. You'll never outrun him in that old truck."

"Then let 'im go," Mr. Tucker said. "It's our only chance now. They'll never catch 'im. Nothin' can outrun a unicorn."

I ran to the trailer, opened the tailgate, and backed him out. Infinity didn't look strong anymore. He had lost weight, and breaking the chain had weakened him. He didn't look invincible; he looked tired and pale. I don't think riding in the trailer had helped either; he needed to run. I reached up and hugged his neck. "Come on, Infinity," I pleaded, "you can make it. It's your last chance."

I walked him around and he seemed to get stronger. But Wingate's headlights were coming closer fast. They were not more than a half mile away, and making a line straight for the turnoff. I slapped the unicorn on the rear, but he wouldn't budge. Then Cathy hit him. Still he wouldn't move. Bob slapped him so hard that he hurt his hand, but Infinity refused to go. He bent down his front leg and lowered his head.

"Look!" I said. "He wants to be ridden."

"Then you'd best be goin'," Mr. Tucker said, "before they get here."

"No," I argued, "it's your turn to ride."

"I . . . I can't ride 'im now," he answered. "I'm all banged up." He pointed at Infinity. "And who knows what shape *he's* in."

"Don't tell me you've lost your faith?"

Mr. Tucker didn't answer, just looked down the road. The headlights were only a quarter of a mile away now, and we could hear the engine race. A decision had to be made quick.

"I won't go," I said stubbornly, "without you."

"What do you mean?" he asked.

"Together," I explained. "We'll ride him together."

"Thaddeus," Cathy said, "you'll never make it."

"Yeah, Thaddy," Bob agreed, "be realistic for once."

"Realistic?" I scoffed. "With a dream? You guys got no faith. Why"—I pointed to Mr Tucker—"you even said yourself that he could outrun anything on earth. Well, we're going to prove it right now. One rider or two, what's the difference? I say he can do it, and anybody who doesn't believe it is in the wrong dream. 'Cause my dream says he can do it."

The car screeched coming around the corner and barreled up the drive, shining its headlights straight at us. They were getting bigger in a hurry.

"Come on!" I said, throwing up my hands, "It's now or never."

Mr. Tucker shrugged. "Well, guess we got nothin' to lose 'cept our faith."

Infinity held his position. I grabbed the horn and climbed aboard. Mr. Tucker got on behind me, with Bob and Cathy's help. He looked pretty tired and weak, but he put his arms around me and held on. Infinity stood up. He had a little trouble, but he made it.

The car slammed on the brakes and skidded to a stop sideways in the drive, not a hundred feet away. Wingate and the sheriff got out and pointed their guns at us.

"All right!" the sheriff shouted, "Stop right there! The game's over. Get down off that thing, whatever it is."

"Go ahead!" I yelled, "shoot if you want to, but we're not getting down."

Wingate cocked his gun. He was going to fire. If we were going to save Infinity's life, we were going to have to dismount. I didn't want to, but I put my arms around Infinity's neck and started to swing down.

Bob reached for the gun he had stuck in his belt. Just then a light came on about a hundred feet behind us, and approaching slowly. The chug of that engine sounded mighty familiar—I knew it so well I could have named it in my sleep.

Nobody said a word and nobody moved. A few seconds later John Deere pulled up alongside, Dad at the wheel. The scoop had been hooked up in front, and Dad pushed a button Cathy had installed on the steering column, raising the scoop to eye level.

He looked over the top of the scoop. "Anybody that tries to stop this critter," he said with authority, "is goin' to have to get by me first."

He put the tractor in gear and rolled toward the sheriff and Wingate. By the time Wingate opened fire, the scoop was fully raised. Bullets bounced off the scoop and ricocheted into the night, making an awful racket. The sheriff holstered his gun, realizing that he was outmanned, but Wingate emptied his. When he stopped to reload, Dad turned in the tractor seat and signaled for us to get going. Bob held his fire, not wanting to chance hitting us.

I leaned over and patted Infinity on the neck, whispering in his ear. He reared, and we almost slid off, but Mr. Tucker held onto me and I grabbed hold of Infinity's thick mane.

He came down on all fours and took off straight for John Deere. The sedan was just in front of it. We were about a hundred feet away, and closing fast. Wingate finished reloading and aimed at us. He was still aiming at us when Infinity took to the air, jumping clean over the tractor and car and landing without breaking stride. He galloped off down the drive, picking up speed as he went. Wingate never fired. I don't think he believed his eyes.

When we turned the corner, the sedan began the chase. Bob and Cathy followed behind in the truck. Dad poked along on John Deere, just in case we needed him again.

Infinity gained strength in every stride, stretching out long and pulling his legs back underneath. The headlights behind us were closing though, after about a mile. Soon the sedan was right beside us.

The sheriff stuck a megaphone out the window and yelled, "Give up and you can go free! We just want that beast! Give up before someone gets hurt!"

I leaned forward and pressed my head against Infinity's neck. Mr. Tucker curled up as best he could behind me. I whispered again in Infinity's ear, and he bolted away as if Wingate's car was standing still. We flew down the road, hooves barely touching the ground. I don't know how fast we were going, but as the car dropped behind us I could hear the sheriff say, "A horse can't run that fast."

Wingate, barely audible now, answered him. "*Nothing* can run that fast."

We began to pull farther and farther away. Infinity's hooves sounded like rolling thunder beneath us, and everything began to fade away. We reached that magic speed where the world slows down and disappears, and then we were gone.

55

The Release

I rode on the back of that powerful beast, unaware of anything except my head against his mane. Mr. Tucker held on tight around my waist, but I couldn't feel him anymore. I threw my arms around Infinity's strong neck and held on for life. This would be my last ride for awhile, perhaps my last ride on earth, and I wanted to hold him close.

I was aware only of him moving back and forth. My body felt at one with his. We were an invincible force, moving like the wind.

A glowing light appeared above me. I didn't have to look; I knew it came from Infinity's horn. Everything became white light, and there was nothing else except the distant, beautiful song of a country band playing softly.

The sky began to part and the universe opened up in front of us, but I wasn't ready to leave the earth. I had too much left to experience in life. I knew my time to go had not come yet, and that was enough to bring me back.

The world came slowly into view. Heavy hoofbeats pounded the ground below; we had entered the meadow.

Infinity stopped in the mist. He must have jumped the fence, but I don't remember, I'd been lost in the light and sound. We dismounted and stood beside him. He turned off his light and the music stopped.

I glanced at Mr. Tucker. He looked strong again, and had his glow back. "Go on," I said, coming out of my daze, "it's your turn to ride him . . . alone."

"Nope," he said, grinning with happiness. "I got my ride and it was just like bein' alone, only better, 'cause you were with me. Got my dream, too. You see, my dream was to have 'im come into the world so that others would believe, and he did just that.

"Sometimes we bury our dreams when we grow up, 'cause we ain't got time or energy to chase 'em anymore. And when the unicorn comes, it reminds us that we had dreams once, and they can still come true. The real magic is when he reaches inside you and dusts 'em off. He shows 'em to you so you can chase 'em again if you want to, but that's up to you. When he's done that, he's done all he can do, until it's time fer you to go back where you came from."

"And where's that?" I asked.

"The place where the universe began—but I thought you already knew that."

"Yeah," I said, "I guess I did. I just wanted to hear somebody else say it besides me and Dad. Someday, when I'm ready, he's going to take me there, but I ain't ready yet."

"Yeah," he agreed, "I sorta figgered that."

"Are you sure you don't want to ride again? I mean, just once more?"

"Oh," he said with a nod, "I'll get me another chance. When the time comes I'm sure he'll be here to take me away. But we got to let 'im go now, before the nonbelievers get here."

"Well, then this is goodbye," I said, reaching up and hugging Infinity's neck. "Please come back for us. We'll be waiting for you. And bring Petula with you."

"He will," Mr. Tucker said, "soon as it's time."

Infinity trotted slowly away. Just before he disappeared

into the mist, he turned and looked at me. I knew there could be no other feeling in my life to match what I felt for him. I knew also that I'd have to keep it to myself. I had loved Petula as much as you could love a horse, but I loved Infinity for bringing me my dream. That had its own special feel to it, like nothing else in the world.

He turned again and trotted off. I realized that I might not ever see him again, and my feelings began to overtake me. I chased after him, calling across the meadow, "No, don't go. *Don't go!*" But he was gone.

Everyone had arrived by then, and stood at the fence watching. Even Mom was there. Doc had gone and picked her up at his place, where she'd been checking on the pups for him, so she could catch a glimpse of Infinity. I was happy knowing she had seen a unicorn. I felt it might take away the last of her doubt when she saw how magnificent he looked prancing across the meadow. Finally I turned away, fighting the best I could to keep the feeling from spilling out of my eyes, but I couldn't.

"Kind of misty out tonight," I said, wiping my eyes. Mr. Tucker put his hand gently on my shoulder.

All of a sudden, we heard heavy hoofbeats on the meadow. My heart jumped. They were coming this way. I looked over by the fence and saw the sheriff and Wingate, who had just pulled up. They were picking up a net they had brought from the car.

"No!" I yelled into the meadow, "go back! *Go back!*" But it was too late. The white figure came out of the mist, and walked right up to us. Nobody said anything for a moment; we were frozen in place.

Mr. Tucker sneezed. Then the unicorn sneezed, and when she did, her horn came loose and hung down on her forehead. Then it fell to the ground. "Petula!" I yelled. "Boy, am I glad to see you!" She had come out of the hills and become a horse again. I figured it was Infinity's going-away present, to remind me of his magic. It didn't change the fact that he had left, but it helped to ease the pain a little.

I reached down and picked up the ceramic horn, and noticed something in the grass. It was metal and dull from weather and wear. I rubbed it and it got brighter. I showed it to Mr. Tucker.

"Well, I'll be," he said, wrinkling his brow, "my ol' Medal of Honor!"

I handed it to him. He turned it over and looked at his name inscribed on the back. Then he handed it over to me. "I want you to have it," he said.

"Oh, no," I answered, "I can't. It's yours. You're the one that . . ."

He unfastened the clip and pinned it on my jacket. "Fer service," he said, "above and beyond the call of duty. And fer showin' us that faith is more powerful than doubt."

"But . . ." I didn't know what to say.

"Fer me," he said, "wear it fer me. Till he comes back."

"Just till he comes back, then," I said. "Just till he returns." I rubbed it with my hand, and it got real shiny, almost like new.

He pulled a piece of paper from his hip pocket and stuffed it into mine. "Last verse," he said. "Read it when you have some time."

Wingate grabbed the sheriff and started for his car. "Quick," he said, "let's get some reinforcements out here before the big one gets away. We can probably still trap him in the meadow."

Much to my surprise, Mom took off after them. "Oh, no you don't," she said angrily. "You've caused just about enough trouble for one summer."

They had reached Wingate's car. The sheriff stared at my mom and said, "And who's gonna stop us?" None of us could say or do anything, not without getting arrested. Wingate reached in to grab the radio, but for some strange reason, the hand speaker, cord and all, had been pulled right out of the dash, and was gone.

"Come on," Wingate said to the sheriff as he got in the car. "Let's get out of here. We can still make it to town." He started the sedan and turned on the headlights.

Suddenly, John Deere came barreling up the road and smashed right into the back of Wingate's car, scoop and all. The trunk ended up in the back seat.

"Sorry, gentlemen," Dad said. "Got to get the brakes checked on this thing before somebody gets hurt. Darn thing kicks worse than an old mule when you try to slow him down. Guess he doesn't like stoppin'. He just wants to keep on plowin' and plantin'. It's the darndest thing."

"You're under arrest," Wingate barked, "for destroying government property, interfering with a federal investigation, and anything else I can think of."

Dad just laughed. "Fine," he said. "But it looks like we got a long ways back to town, so we'd better start walkin'."

"Oh, no, we're not," Wingate said, and commandeered Bob's truck instead. They sped off with my dad in the back. I was never so proud of him as when I watched the truck disappear down the road. He didn't look old anymore, even with the moon lighting up his face. He looked young again, and strong.

By the time reinforcements came, all the commotion had died down. There was nothing left to see.

Later that night as I lay in bed, I opened the paper and read:

VERSE 6

Once upon a unicorn
You'll never want to leave,
And all it takes
For you, my friend,
Is only to believe,

I leave you now
With one last thought
Etched deeply in your soul:
Just once upon a unicorn
And you will reach your goal—

And if you stay upon his back,
Your heart will find a friend,
And with his magic in your hands
Your life will never end!

For once upon a unicorn,
Your heart flies like the wind,
And if you let your feelings go
Infinity descends—
And if you let the magic flow
Eternity begins!

I folded the paper and put it under my pillow. The old owl was hooting in the oak tree, so I got up and went to the window. It was a clear night, and a million stars sparkled against the sky. I could see all the way past Tucker's Grove and the foothills beyond. There was a pain in my chest where my heart was, and it wouldn't go away.

Suddenly a star shot across the sky at an incredible speed and disappeared on the horizon. I looked again at the hills and thought I could see the outline of something along the ridge. It bounded up and down, but I couldn't tell whether it was just shadows dancing across my mind, or if my belief had called it up.

A brilliant white light came off the highest hill and spread out in all directions. A beam shone right in my window. I was happy in the light, and felt I would live forever. It was a wonderful feeling, one I will never forget. After a moment it stopped, and I turned from the window.

Cathy came out of her room and stood in my doorway. "What was that light?" she asked.

"Oh," I said with a grin, "just some big truck turning around on the road."

"Answer me something," she said, looking out the window. "What did you whisper in his ear to make him take off the way he did?"

"Oh," I said softly, "home. I just told him to take us home."

She didn't say anything. She turned quietly away and went back to bed. I climbed under the covers and immediately went to sleep. And began to dream . . .

I was riding Infinity, somewhere on the far side of the universe. It was dark except for his beam, but up ahead there was a great pulsating light. As we got closer, I could see it was a city resting on a silver cloud.

We approached a rainbow of colored light beams. Infinity set his feet on the cloud. His soft hoofbeats sounded as if he was running on a bed of pillows.

He slowed down and we stopped in front of a huge wall: a hundred feet high, it was, so long that both ends disappeared into the distance. It must have encircled the entire cloud and was many times bigger than any on earth.

It was made of immense precious gemstones, the size of pyramid blocks, stacked one on top of the other. They were so accurately cut that they fit together without a seam.

The wall must have been thirty feet thick. Each gem was large enough to span the entire thickness, and was about as high and wide as it was deep. Light reflected through the wall in all directions, creating a rainbow of lights that extended a thousand feet into the deep purple sky.

There were emeralds, rubies, the blinding light of diamonds, and precious gems of every color and hue. Each one was flawless, without holes or scratches, and polished until they dazzled in their radiance. Through the wall I could see a great city carved out of crystal, with towering spires that pierced the sky.

Shooting stars streamed overhead, lighting up the night like fireworks on the Fourth of July; I'd gotten my celebration of freedom, after all. One of them came close, and I could see it wasn't a star at all, but a unicorn.

It was pure black with a golden horn, and it carried a passenger in a white robe. The unicorn flew over the wall and descended upon the city. A dark brown unicorn with a crystal horn soared over the wall just over my head, but he was not carrying a rider. He headed away from the city and took off for the sky.

This place was like some vast universal station, with hundreds of arrivals and departures every minute. The unicorns were the ships that took passengers across.

White light came from a central light source behind the wall, and filtered through the gemstones in all directions. We flew over the wall, and then I saw where the light was coming from. There was a giant spinning wheel, and at its center lay a glowing sphere of pure white light. Smaller spheres came out of it, shooting off into space. They came to rest in their own special place in the sky. Some of them were racing back; their time to live in the sky must have been over, and they fell back into the glowing sphere.

We stayed for a long moment over the glowing sphere, bathing in its pure light, and then we turned to leave. In the distance, coming from the center of the sphere, I could hear the soft song of a symphony. I wanted to stay there forever, but somewhere inside I knew that I couldn't, not as long as I had dreams to live and a life back on earth.

Infinity turned on his beam and shone it into the center of the sphere. The sphere answered with its own powerful beam, aimed directly at Infinity's horn. He began to vibrate all over as light from the sphere poured into him. Slowly, he began to glow, filling up with pure white light. His body tingled beneath me, surging with new power. After a minute the light stopped, having filled him from his hooves to the tip of his horn. It was time for us to leave.

Infinity turned on his beam again, and aimed it into the sky. We pulled slowly away, over the crystal city and across the jeweled wall. He transferred his energy to his legs and began to pick up speed, until at last we reached the speed of pure energy. We shot across the universe, soaring past stars and celestial bodies of all shapes, sizes, and colors. We traveled so fast that I could no longer feel myself on his back. I became a part of his beam, completely absorbed in it and filled with happiness. We were one.

I woke to the light of the moon shining its way into my room. I lay there for the longest time, holding onto the dream. "Thanks," I finally said, thinking of Infinity, "for taking me where I wanted to go. Even if it was just a dream."

I fell off to sleep again and didn't awake until the sun replaced the stars in the sky.

56

Paradise Revisited

A week later I heard familiar sounds in the loft again. I was putting Petula in the barn and noticed that she still looked a little pale, even though I'd brushed the flour out of her hide. At least the sneezing had stopped.

I started up the ladder, but she reached up and grabbed my new straw hat off my head and wouldn't let go. "All right," I said, turning away from the laughter in the loft, "I can take a hint. Besides, we don't need her without teeth marks anymore."

Petula took off running and I chased her out of the barn into the corral. By the time I caught her, she had made a new spot for the sun to shine through on the brim, so that my hat had its usual look, bite mark and all.

I tried to pull it away from her, but she wanted to play tug of war. I might have gotten it, but she backed me up against the bathtub trough. I'd filled the tub just that morning, and when I got backed up against it, she let go. Me and the hat went for a little swim, all by ourselves. I stood up in the tub, dripping wet all over. I looked at Petula and then at my hat.

"Hey," I said, "I thought we were friends." She just looked at me with those big brown eyes. I shook my head and huffed. "Aw," I finally said, "here, you can have it."

I held out the hat. She took it in her mouth and began to chew. I watched as she started to make the hole bigger. "On second thought," I said, grabbing it back, "I've got a better idea."

I took my pocket knife out of my pants and cut two evenly spaced holes in the top. Just for the heck of it, I stuck one of the pieces in my mouth and chewed. A few seconds later I spat it out. "Phooey," I said, "I don't know what you see in this stuff."

I reached up and put the hat on her head, with her ears poking through the holes. "There," I said, "how's that?" She whinnied and nodded. "Well, old girl," I added, "you may not be a critter with a horn, but you'll do."

It seems that word had got out about the unicorn, and Tucker's Grove made the front page of the *Wichita News*. The government decided the place would have too much traffic if they decided to look for any more unicorns, what with people standing by the fence hoping for a sight of the critters. So the army pulled out of town a week later.

Charges were never brought against Mr. Tucker for blocking a government investigation, since Washington didn't want to go on record as having had anything to do with unicorns—as if they were space aliens or something. That must also have been the reason they dropped the case against Dad, even though the brakes on John Deere had been working just fine all along. They never pressed any charges against the rest of us, either.

Another funny thing happened. Somebody in the government decided our farm qualified for federal disaster relief because of the twister. So instead of moving to Wichita like we were supposed to, we got a loan to plant wheat and rebuild the silo, and a five-year extension on our taxes.

Before the IRS got around to taking Tucker's place, he

got a check because the army trampled his wheat crop with their trucks. Dad said it was the fastest he'd ever seen the government send a check. And even though Mr. Tucker didn't harvest it, it was still his wheat. So the army had to pay for destroying private property. Extra compensation was provided to pay all the taxes for the next ten years, since the court ruled that his privacy had been trampled as well, what with the tourists gawking at his meadow and all. I guess we got our miracle after all.

We heard that Miss Garcia had taken a job in Topeka teaching art. Mr. Thornton was our new teacher in the fall. He was all right, but I didn't like the bow ties and suits much, and I don't think he liked me coming to class late and barefoot and staring out the window towards the hills all the time, developing my theories on life and such.

One theory I developed further said that on the prairie it was the wind that decided our fate more than anything else. It blew the land away in '33. It blew the top off our silo and windmill in '47, and gave us back our farm when the government decided it had blown just a little too hard. And in the end, when it's my time to go, I asked for my ashes to be scattered in the wind, over the Flint Hills. It was the wind, I believed, that decided our fate on the farm, and maybe in all of life as well. Nobody tells the wind which way to blow. It's got a mind all its own. We can only turn in the right direction to catch it or take cover when it blows too strong.

It was six years later, in '53, when we finally took Dad and John Deere off the land, but he drove that tractor like a car all over Wichita. There was a John Deere dealership in town, and Dad spent hours down there talking with anyone who dropped in. The dealer was glad to have someone who knew so much about some of the older models, little things like adjusting the throttle and clutch.

Since they couldn't get rid of him, they eventually made Dad manager of used tractor sales. So he went from selling ideas to selling used tractors. Once a salesman . . . well, you know the rest. He was almost as happy as he had been back on the farm. Well, almost.

When he got restless for that old feeling of sitting on a tractor seat all day, he'd fire up that old yellow and green machine and take an extra long drive.

In the fall he scooped up leaves; in the winter, snow. In the end, they almost buried him with that tractor, but they parked it behind the house instead, in case future generations might find a use for it. He would have wanted it that way.

I think he'd be happy to know that where they buried him the grass comes up green in the spring, and Mom always puts yellow daisies by the headstone. And across the street, smoke rolls out of the courthouse chimney in the winter, just like it did from his pipe. He wouldn't have asked for more.

Mom started her job as curator of the Indian Arts Museum in '48, and she didn't have to move to Wichita to do it. There were so many people coming to Flint Hills to look for unicorns that Mrs. Simpson set up a souvenir shop and Indian arts museum downtown. Mom made pottery and sold it right out of that store. It was the best thing to happen to our finances in years, but we had to suffer through lots of picture-taking tourists for quite a while.

Mom sold quite a few of her own pieces over the years, but there was one I wouldn't let her sell. It was the plate with the white unicorn against the midnight-blue sky. It still sits on my mantle next to the picture of Cathy graduating from Wichita State, and, of course, the ceramic horn Petula had worn.

Cathy was at the top of her engineering class, and moved off to Detroit to design engines for one of the big car companies.

Bob Greison's arm was a mystery to Doc Yeager, but by the time Bob and Cathy got married, he had struck out a couple of hundred batters in college. He became a pitcher for the Kansas City Athletics for a couple of seasons, and then got a job as pitching coach for the Detroit Tigers, so he and Cathy could spend more time together.

Mr. Tucker got most of his eyesight back and kept on planting wheat. His health improved after that summer, and he lived on for fifteen more years before the cancer finally claimed him. Doc never could figure it out, since he was supposed to have only six months to live. I always thought it was on account of getting to ride Infinity, but nobody could say for sure.

I knew it was Mr. Tucker's faith, and not mine, that had brought Infinity to us. He just liked to pretend it was my idea. It didn't matter whether he had created Infinity by spinning a story, or whether Infinity came out of eternity on his own. While he was with us, he was real, as real as anything on earth, and that was all that mattered.

I couldn't say whether Infinity had saved the farm by sending the twister or whether it happened on its own, but I knew what I believed. The truth was that I got to ride my dream, and the farm was saved. That was good enough for me.

I went off to college when we moved to Wichita, but I didn't take Petula with me. She had died two years earlier and galloped off to horse heaven to wait for me. We sold Elmer at the county fair in '48, and Becky went to the big pasture in the sky in '49. We never did replace them. I guess Guinevere was enough to keep me busy as I got older. She made it all the way to '61, and now I have one of her great-great-grandpups keeping me company.

I finally got even with Billy Johnson by visiting his mailbox one dark night. When I left, it somehow had grown a beehive inside it. You should have seen him run when he opened the lid. I didn't know anyone his size could run so fast.

His dad stayed on as sheriff, since nobody else wanted the job, but we heard that Wingate ended up with a demotion that left him a corporal when it was over. Seems that he didn't do a very good job of confirming his space alien story.

I think the reason was that the blood samples they took of Infinity turned out to be no different from horse blood. The hair was horse hair and the pictures turned out okay, except the horn never showed up on the negative. So it didn't look too good for Wingate when it was all over. I figured it was just Infinity covering his tracks and not revealing himself to nonbelievers.

When I did get into college, I got my degree in philosophy and taught for twenty-five years at the University of Kansas. Dad would have been proud of that. I retired last year, and there was never any doubt where I would go. Mr. Tucker left me the land, and the old cabin still stands here by the wheat field. I fired up old John Deere and drove him over from Wichita, with my belongings in the back of a horse trailer.

I have a fresh row of walnut trees growing out by the schoolhouse—they sure look pretty blooming in the spring. The town doesn't use the building for a school anymore. Seems it's a state landmark on account of the walnut wood, the only one in Kansas.

There's a sign out front of the meadow by the fence, but it's so faded that I don't think anyone can read it anymore. They put it up when folks began to flock to Tucker's Grove wanting to see the spot where the unicorn had come into the world. The sign read:

UNICORN NATURAL PRESERVE

DON'T FEED THE ANIMALS

There was another sign, voted on during a closed door session of the Unicorn Hunting Club a week after Infinity's departure. I just put a fresh coat of paint on it last week, and straightened it up a little.

It had held up pretty well since the summer of '47, despite being right alongside the road between Greison's dairy and Tucker's Grove. We had decided to mark the spot where Infinity had made his last ride. So we knocked a couple of boards together and cut a piece of tin out of the old silo roof we found across town. We stuck it in the ground and nodded our approval. From then on that old strip of abandoned road would be known forever as Unicorn Highway—and nobody, not even Billy Johnson, messed with that sign. Time and the weather faded the paint, but not the memory.

No other unicorns ever appeared. They even had airplane rides over the hills, but nobody ever saw anything except wild horses and wolves. But still, people came and looked at the spot like a space ship had landed, or something. Except nowadays they're calling them UFOs. Most folks think that UFO stands for unidentified flying object, but when I look up on starry summer nights, it means something else to me. It stands for Unicorns Flying Over.

Things certainly have quieted down since that summer. The new road doesn't come out this way, and there aren't many cars on the old road; but once in a while, one of the big trucks gets turned around coming through town and ends up going by the school and down past our old farm. At night, their big, bright headlights light up the whole sky as they go by.

Except for the farmer who bought my folks' old place, I'm the only one left, but all I'm planting is special wheat. I see the other farmer giving me the once-over now and then. I guess he figures I'm up to something besides watching big trucks get lost on the old road. Every now and then, a cross wind catches the old windmill and turns it this way. The sun shines its beams on the spinning blades, making a tiny bright dot like sunlight captured on the head of a pin, and I think back to that summer in '47.

That farmer's got a daughter with a mighty inquisitive mind. Keeps asking me about the old days, and that faded sign out in front of the meadow. I reckon she's about ready to take over the payments on my dream, and I'm about ready to tell my secrets. She's got that faraway look in her eyes, and the seed of belief in her soul.

Other than that, I'm not up to much. It's just me and one of Guinevere's descendants sitting here on the back porch, watching the stars shoot across the night sky. I've got the Medal of Honor pinned to my old bomber jacket, and my straw hat on my head. Sure do miss not having holes in it, though—and I sure do miss that summer of '47.

A funny thing happened when I dug the medal out of the trunk. I found it pinned to my old jacket, right where Mr. Tucker had stuck it. The leather was still in pretty good

shape, but when I held it up the the light I could see the
thread marks on the back where my mother had fixed it.
They formed a pattern that had the habit of looking like a
horse with a horn in the middle of its forehead. The funny
part was that I had never noticed it before.

I discovered something lumpy in the lining that I had
never checked out before, figuring it was good old Kansas
dirt. The jacket had a tiny hole in one of the pockets, and
I opened it up with my pocket knife. There, shaped like
grains of wheat, was an ounce of pure gold. I must have
picked it up when I traveled to the crystal farmhouse, and
it had somehow got into the lining when I walked through
my dad's field of solid gold wheat.

Otherwise, things are pretty quiet around here, but on
certain nights the wind blows cold out on the hills. The
moon rises bigger than an old pumpkin, and a star shoots
across the midnight sky. Mist comes over the meadow as
thick and white as smoke from a pipe, and I hear something
rustle out in the wheat. I get a funny feeling deep inside,
and I can swear I hear heavy hoofbeats out on the meadow.
And I know, just know, he's come back for me.

He'll bend his pure white head and I'll climb aboard his
back. The sky will open like the wings of a dove and we'll
take that long journey across the sea of stars. We'll travel
as one, and we won't set down until we reach the land of
dreams. We'll stay in the crystal farmhouse until my dream
has passed into eternity. Then, when the time comes for us
to go, we'll soar across the universe and set down on the
silver cloud. We'll enter the sphere of light and sound and
stay on the far side of forever, until the end of time.

DAVID LEE JONES was born in 1948 in Nevada, Missouri, just east of the Flint Hills, but moved to California when he was five years old. He graduated from Golden Gate University with a degree in business management, and currently lives and works in Santa Barbara, California with his wife, their daughter, and their black Labrador retriever.

His love of storytelling began on his mother's knee, where he remembers not wanting to go to sleep until a story was finished. He started telling his own tales at a young age, entertaining classmates at school. He still tells stories to his wife and daughter, and, if no one's around, to his black Lab, Daisy.

Unicorn Highway is his first novel.

RETURN TO AMBER...

THE ONE *REAL* WORLD, OF WHICH ALL OTHERS, INCLUDING EARTH, ARE BUT SHADOWS

ROGER ZELAZNY

The New Amber Novel

KNIGHT OF SHADOWS   75501-7/$3.95 US/$4.95 Can
Merlin is forced to choose to ally himself with the Pattern of Amber or of Chaos. A child of both worlds, this crucial decision will decide his fate and the fate of the true world.

SIGN OF CHAOS   89637-0/$3.95 US/$4.95 Can
Merlin embarks on another marathon adventure, leading him back to the court of Amber and a final confrontation at the Keep of the Four Worlds.

The Classic Amber Series

NINE PRINCES IN AMBER	01430-0/$3.99 US/$4.99 Can
THE GUNS OF AVALON	00083-0/$3.95 US/$4.95 Can
SIGN OF THE UNICORN	00031-9/$3.95 US/$4.95 Can
THE HAND OF OBERON	01664-8/$3.95 US/$4.95 Can
THE COURTS OF CHAOS	47175-2/$3.50 US/$4.25 Can
BLOOD OF AMBER	89636-2/$3.95 US/$4.95 Can
TRUMPS OF DOOM	89635-4/$3.95 US/$4.95 Can